BERNICE RATHE

Bea Giovanni

MULTI-DELUSIONAL
MEDIA

Multi-Delusional Media
1900 NE 181st Ave #150, Portland, Oregon 97230
www.berniceraththebook.com

Library of Congress Control Number: 2013946067

ISBN 10: 0989756505 (Paperback)

ISBN 13: 978-0-9897565-0-1 (Paperback)

Publisher's Cataloging-in-Publication Data

Names: Giovanni, Bea.
Title: Bernice Rathe / Bea Giovanni.
Description: Portland, OR : Multi-Delusional Media, 2016.
Identifiers: LCCN 2013946067 | ISBN 978-0-9897565-0-1
(pbk.) | ISBN 978-0-9897565-3-2 (ebook)
Subjects: LCSH: Conspiracies--Fiction. | Women--Fiction. |
    Thrillers (Fiction) | Detective and mystery fiction. |
    BISAC: FICTION / Thrillers / Suspense. | FICTION /
    Mystery & Detective / General. | FICTION /
    Contemporary Women. | GSAFD: Suspense fiction. |
    Mystery fiction.
Classification: LCC PS3607.I466 B47 2016 (print) | LCC
PS3607.I466 (ebook) | DDC 813/.6--dc23.

This book is dedicated

To no one. I wrote this for fun.

Preface

To my readers, this book has definitely been a journey. This fictional novel is a first for me.

I started writing this book in 2013. But, I decided to scrap it. I was hesitant in writing a novel, since I have written scholarly articles which are far removed from the fictional genre. After encouragement from friends and family, however, I decided to revive this idea and write.

In writing this novel, it became a surprisingly fun process. I have found fictional writing is far more loose and open to deviating from the traditional grammatical conventions and scholarly voice. The process allowed a different point of view and voice and I absolutely loved it.

Admittedly, this process has also been extremely healing for me. I took this opportunity to write this novel for fun and as a narrative healing process. I hope that the themes, issues, events and characters in this novel help to draw attention to how real life issues and situations impact us all and how we can help make this world a better place.

BERNICE RATHE

Introduction: Early Life at a Glance

The scene opens on a sunny day, with a female with sun shades driving a futuristic sports vehicle with a personalized plate titled ABOSBTCH (short for a boss b!*ch), and music blasting (with Kelis 'Bossy' playing loudly). The female stops at a stop light to look over at the driver in the other vehicle and whispers 'like a boss' and nods away.

I could not believe how I got here, but I did. How did I get to be a boss and have such a fun and lavish life? I guess I need to go back in time to explain.

The year was 1978, gas was 65 cents a gallon, the first mobile phone system was introduced, and the average income was $10,000. Scratch that, I really did not need to provide that detail but I thought it would be cool and interesting to say the least. Anyway, I was born Bernice Giovana Rathe to a single, unwed mother in Macon, Georgia, my grandmother (or grandma, as I would like to say it) raised me until age 3 or 4.

Bea Giovanni

My mother (or mama, as some in the south say it) gave birth to me in her last year of college. Oddly, my mama wanted to be a nun but settled on being a social worker, as she could do more good in social work. If she became a nun, I probably wouldn't been born.

Later in life, I wished she would have become a nun. Let's say I hate my life and I do not know why anyone would bring a child into this messed up world.

I digress. As I was saying, my mama gave birth to me in her senior year in college. After my mama graduated, my grandma continued to care for me while my mama searched for a job all over the state.

My father was never around (actually, I didn't know him or of him). He actually denied I was his child. In fact, my birth certificate states "blank" for the father.

I did not grew up in the typical family. I did not come from a wealth of money, power or influence. While I would love to say I did, I did not grow up in that type of environment (you know like a "Let it to Beaver" type of family).

My upbringings, however, are humble; I can say with pride that I earned everything given to me.

BERNICE RATHE

My family composition is interesting. My grandma was part Native American and African American. My mother's father was part Caucasian and African American. I had five uncles; my mother was the only female out of her mother's children. (My mama had a different father than my five uncles.) My grandma sent all her children to Catholic school (while also attending Methodist, Baptist and Catholic Churches on a regular basis). A Catholic school education was the best education at that time (and still today).

I hung out with my five uncles a lot, as my mother had me in her last year in college and was still completing her degree. Plus, my grandma and grandpa (the father of my 5 uncles and the grandfather I knew all my life) worked during the day and my great-grandma (i.e., my grandma's mama) was old in age.

We didn't know the exact age of my great-grandmother due to the lack of birth records, impacted by war and slavery during her time. So our family estimated her age at that time to be 89. We do know that she was part Native American and her family like my great-grandfather's family were sharecroppers and former slaves.

Bea Giovanni

We do not know what Native American tribe my great-grandma belonged to, since she was not made aware of the registration during her time. They didn't want very many freed slaves, who were Native American, to claim land. So, there was a short window to claim Native American heritage via registering and get this, you had to read and write.

For the average freed slave, you most likely would not have heard about this registration and could not read or write to recognize the information. But, again, we didn't know really all that happened during that time.

[I would hear old folk tales growing up such as my great grandma had a "veil over her head" at birth, she had gifts and that my grandma had a "veil over her head" at birth too. I did not know what that meant, and my mama always discounted that stuff. My mama would say it was not true and not to believe in it.]

Despite neither having a lot nor having my father in my life, my childhood would become a happy one. My family did the best they could for all of us. I have fond memories as a child, i.e., fishing, traveling, holidays, toys, friends, family, etc.

BERNICE RATHE

My family ate together a lot, and my grandma cooked big meals. She perfected the art of big meals. She cooked foods that she could easily stretch.

For instance, spaghetti was one of them. My grandma cooked spaghetti so much I think my uncles got so tired of spaghetti, but I didn't. My grandma cooked the best spaghetti. She made chili spaghetti, chicken spaghetti, turkey spaghetti (I think you get the picture).

Because I came from a large family, if you blinked or forgot about your food, it was gone. You had to take your first and second portions at one time. If not, the food was gone with no seconds.

Mealtime was somewhat funny because I had one uncle who would say, "Look at that bird in the window" (or something like that). I would look and my meat would be missing from my plate. My uncle would be eating the piece of meat.

My grandma was really the sole breadwinner of the family, as my grandpa was an alcoholic who used his money for liquor. My grandpa would even steal my grandma's money to buy liquor. Regardless, we loved him, each in our own way; he was still a good person. Most of us were able to discern that certain things were unhealthy and not repeat those cycles (I couldn't say this about my father and his family as they never learned to identify and stop unhealthy cycles).

As I stated before, my grandma was the sole breadwinner; she was a very strong woman. She had to be with six children and an alcoholic husband. My grandma was popular and sociable and involved in local politics and other activities.

You could say my grandma was a trailblazer as well. She was the first of woman of color hired with the local court system. She was also frequently in the society pages of the newspaper.

I also recall sitting on the front porch with my great grandma eating ginger snaps. She loved gingersnaps and so did I. I snuck gingersnaps from her bag and she knew before I did it (it was funny at times). I also recall she gave me honey and milk to help me go to sleep at night. I loved honey and milk.

No one ever sat and talked with my great grandma because they thought she was senile. But, they were wrong. We would talk about everything. We even had a game we played. The game required you to guess the color and make of the car that passed by before it came.

My great grandma would be amazed that I guessed the right color and sometimes the make of the car. I got better each time. She told me I had a gift and to use it wisely. She also stated to me to make our family proud and that I will be a great person one day. I never understood what she meant until I became an adult. Sadly, when I was 4 years old, she died.

A strange thing would happen after that: I began having dreams of my great grandma. I also began having dreams similar to déjà vu. I had dreams where events would later happen and I caught on fast as to what the dream meant. As time went on, my dreams helped me better interpret the meanings and events in advance.

Sometimes, I did not have to be asleep to get these visions. It would appear to me like a TV (the receiver and broadcaster). I would tell my mama that these things would occur. My mama took me to a doctor and counselor and both results showed a normal and wild imaginative child.

Despite this, I would tell my mama the things I dreamed and these things came true like déjà vu. From there, my mama and her family told me to say nothing and to keep my mouth shut (to "turn it off" so to speak), as it was a chance it would come true. Oddly, I started to get personal mail on metaphysics, chakras and related stuff, which my mama would throw away.

My mama told me to imagine other things and it will go away. Well, for a long time, it did go away. My mama attributed this to being around my grandparents' arguments and my grandpa's alcoholism, and acting out and looking for attention. I did not understand any of it, but I did know that the dreams were not mere coincidence and I was not acting out looking for attention. I did not look at the dreams as a gift or something special but the direct opposite (like a curse).

But, I was the not the average child either. When I was about 5 years of age, I was somewhat popular, as I danced to Michael Jackson's Thriller and I was so good that I had local gigs where I was paid. It was exciting and fun, since I was on stage dancing in front of hundreds of people who paid me to entertain them.

My mama saved the money to pay for my school clothes and other things I needed. But, most times, I didn't want the money, as

BERNICE RATHE

I was a bit modest. But, at the time, I did not know anything about money.

Yet, I digress. I was a bit off track reminiscing about my early years. As mentioned before, my grandma's home was not a 'milk and cookies' home. But, you could tell my grandpa and grandma loved each other. My grandpa was a functional alcoholic (if you call it that).

My grandma and grandpa would argue a lot and fought each other. I recall my grandpa always sitting outside on the porch drinking with his neighborhood friends. My grandma would tell me to go to bed so that I would not see any of it, but I always heard my grandpa and his friends outside talking, drinking, and doing what people do when they drink and socialize. Despite my grandpa's shortcomings, he loved my grandma. It goes without saying that my grandma loved him too.

Getting back to my point, after my mama graduated with her bachelor's degree and found a job as a social worker, I moved with my mama at age four to Atlanta, Georgia. My mama had met my step dad (a fisherman), she later married him and gave birth to my little sister and later my little brother. I always believed my step dad was my father; no one told me different. It was not until my mama and step dad divorced that my family informed me he was not my father.

Boy, I took that hard. My mama had me go to counseling; it proved to be helpful because I had an avenue to vent where I could say the things I couldn't tell my mama and step dad; the counselor saw me as a normal child adjusting to divorce, which is not easy for any child. Later in life, I recalled this counseling helped develop and identify healthy relationships and people, i.e., how to navigate through life and form good relations with people. (My mama, being a social worker, taught me there is no stigma around counseling, as it was healthy to go, and you do not have to be diagnosed or have mental issues to go.)

The divorce appeared to be my step dad's fault. He cheated on my mama. I recalled someone calling my mama and telling her, they spotted my step dad and a woman in his truck at his friend's house. My mama got my siblings and me out of the bed (it had to be approximately 3 am in the morning). She drove to my step dad's friend's house, my step dad and some woman were sitting in his truck and my mama got out the car, pulled out a jack knife from the trunk and shattered his window. This was decades before Jazmine Sullivan's Bust Your Windows Out Your Car song.

Yes, women were busting windows back then too. People sat around and looked at what happened and walked away. They figured my step dad must have done something to make my mama mad. No cops were called, just pure emotion involved.

I digress. Back to my story: After my mama busted my step dad's truck windows, my sister and brother began crying and I began yelling to my mama, "mama stop, don't hurt my daddy!" I did not understand at the time all that went on between my mama and step dad.

Prior to that incident, I recalled my mama received numerous calls to our home with recordings on the answering machine with a female stating my step dad and her were together (appearing to taunt my mama). We would get recordings of the song, 'The Thrill is Gone." After growing up and experiencing life, I recalled the song and discovered it was a blues song. I guess the female tried sending it as a message to my mama. We later learned the name of this female after my mama got caller id. Her name was Betty.

Shortly after this busted window incident, my step dad moved out our home. He would come around every blue moon or so, and he would promise my sister a pony (a real pony). Guess what? The pony never came.

One day he came to the house and acted erratic. My mama told him to leave and stop making promises he can't keep, since he made lots of promises to me and my siblings and it disappointed us. My mama and step dad then fought in the bedroom. You couldn't mistake the sounds of stuff shattering and yelling. I took my brother and sister and we hid in the corner with the door locked.

My intuition kicked in. I feared my step dad would harm us because of his strange and erratic behavior. This feeling was deep down in your stomach. He later left and I checked on my mama to make sure he did not injure her. I called out for her and she said everything was fine. I asked her if she wanted me to call my grandma or someone. She said no.

Weeks went by, no one heard from my step dad. It was not until months later where he came to our home and he wanted to take us for a ride. My mama became suspicious and hesitant and made us stay in the house and not go outside with him.

Well, my step dad ripped the screen door away from my mama's hand causing her hand to bleed. Then, he pulled us out of the house into his truck and made us go with him.

I never saw my mama so scared. I did not understand the reason behind her fear until afterwards. She was thinking my step dad would kill us, since he had mentioned things like that in the past to her (as I was unaware of and rightfully so as a child I should not know these things).

Being the oldest and smart, I took account of the streets and businesses as we traveled with my father. I do not know why I was able to understand to do this, but I took account of these things while my step dad drove us around.

Once we approached his friend's home, I told his friend what my step dad did. An hour later, my step dad returned us to my mama. One of my mama's friends came to our home and started to report this incident to authorities.

Bea Giovanni

Later, I learned my step dad's friend contacted my mama and notified her of our whereabouts. Granted my mama and step dad were in a heated situation, my mama told me never let us go with my step dad again under any condition; her and her friend explained my step dad made threats in the past.

My mama did acknowledge I did the right thing in telling someone what happened. This may have saved my siblings and me from harm, since someone knew. My mama always told me to tell someone if you are in danger or if something is not right. I always kept that with me.

My siblings did not understand what happened at that time. Today, they don't even remember what happened but I did.

My mama, being a religious and traditional person raised us in the Catholic Church (because my mama went to Catholic School going up and continued into her adulthood), knew she needed to divorce my step dad but could not. Being a Catholic at that time, the church did not support the idea of divorce. However, it got so bad in her marriage to my step dad that my mama converted to the Baptist religion in order to get a divorce. So, we attended Baptist church and she raised us in the Baptist church as well.

So, in terms of my religious upbringing, diverse would be the word to describe it. Baptized at birth in the Methodist church yet raised Catholic, I then converted to Baptist because my mama converted to the Baptist religion, where I was then baptized at age 11. As a child in the summers, I would go to my grandma's AME Church (Methodist) when we visited my grandma for the entire summer.

So, I had a lot of religion in my life. I learned many things from religion, such as people are human and make mistakes. And no matter what God you worship, make sure the God and what you worship is a positive belief system that does not oppress or hinder spiritual growth and that you are contributing to the world. Most importantly, no one is greater than God, despite what people do and say.

As I mentioned earlier, my mama and step dad got a divorce (I just turned 11). What a bittersweet situation! However, my mama went on with her life and even obtained a Master's in Social Work. Years later, my step dad later regretted everything he did, yet a little too late. My step dad started to be a father to myself and my sister and brother, but, again, a little too late.

My family went through tough times when my step dad and mama divorced. You just don't imagine things like this happening when someone divorces, but it does happen, which is one of the many reasons why I later became an advocate for children, families and survivors of abuse and domestic violence. Plus, my mama, a social worker all of my life, was a significant influence in my life.

My mama was not too financial savvy and budgeting was not her thing. Ironically, my mama solicited my help in creating budgeting and helping her balance her funds each month to pay bills. (Yes, you heard right, my help at a very young age; I had to be 10 or 11).

Well, I become very effective and knowledgeable at budgeting and making financial sense out of something. My mama had very limited funds; she was a single parent raising three children on her own on a social worker's income. Enough said.

I am not sure if you know what a social worker's salary would be, but they do not make lots of money, especially in the 80s; my mother's first job was as a state CPS worker, she made approximately 19K a year until she changed jobs and made slightly more, i.e., 25K to 28K a year.

Despite helping others, my mama faced her own crisis (specifically, a financial crisis), but she got through her financial crisis. What my mama went through reminds me no one is immune from crisis. We all will have a crisis at some point in our lives. My mama handled it well.

Around my 12th birthday, my grandpa died. It would become a defining, unexpected event for my family. How he died would be just as traumatic for my family as well.

Every Thanksgiving or Christmas holiday, my grandma and grandpa would visit our home. We would have family talent nights (singing, performing comedy and anything funny).

Christmas 1990, my grandpa did not come. He wanted to stay in Macon with his twin sister. My grandpa came from a large family, being one of 14 children with a twin sister.

His twin sister received a devastating diagnosis that she had breast cancer. The doctor gave her approximately 6 months to live. So, he stayed in Macon to be with her.

Bea Giovanni

My grandma came alone to our home for the holidays and left after the New Year holiday.

Once she arrived back in Macon, my grandpa appeared to be deep in mourning. On a regular day, my grandpa would start my grandma's car in the morning and make her coffee. That morning, he did not.

As my grandma left for work, under the impression my grandpa worked long hours from the day before and was asleep, my uncle later found my grandpa dead. When the doctors performed an autopsy, they determined my grandfather died naturally in his sleep (and as old folks say, he died of a broken heart such as grieving for his twin sister).

Even more interesting is that my grandpa's twin sister died on the day of his funeral. On the day of my grandpa's funeral, I also saddened by his lost.

He loved him some Bernice. I was the first grandbaby. I loved my grandpa. He was a fun, loving individual, despite his alcoholism.

I recalled that my mama said that I locked myself in the bathroom and cried. I don't remember that, but, again, that is what my mama told me.

BERNICE RATHE

My uncle never got over the death.
Being my uncle found my grandpa, my
uncle began spiraling out of control (with
drugs, alcohol and never addressing those
issues).

[You see my family never liked
addressing issues, no matter if it was
through a counselor, pastor or doctor; it was
like the 'elephant in the room syndrome.'
No one wanted to say anything about the
elephant in the room, even though everyone
saw the elephant in the room.

I am one of few people who would
observe this and would address issues.
Essentially, I wouldn't ignore the elephant
in the room. My philosophy was in its due
time, you must comfort things via talking
and working through things in healthy ways
and holding one's self accountable and
others accountable, which is much healthier
than arguing and destroying your life.]

As I got older, I really missed my
grandpa. I saw other children with their
grandfathers and I knew I seemingly missed
out on time with my grandpa. I eventually
worked through my issues in missing my
grandpa.

As for my grandma, she worked through
the issues as well and even found herself

much healthier than before. She even completed her bachelor's degree, which is what my grandpa wanted her to do for many years.

As my high school years approached, I continued to mature and grow up. Not being the most popular student in the school, I considered myself a band nerd, an honor student and one of those people other students made fun of.

Also, commonplace for me involved being the victim of bullies, yet not by choice. However, my intelligence paid off years later, as I excelled in life, my career and had overall success later in life.

I got my first job at 16. I worked at a donut shop as counter help/donut maker. This job came as a result of DECA in high school. I loved DECA.

Also, I had another classmate, John, who got a job there. So, he put in a good word and I got the job. While this job may not be anything to anyone, it meant a lot to me.

The owner was nice and showed me how to make donuts and other pastries. The shop also sold food, so I learned to make food. This was a fun, first job experience.

Sometimes, I woke up 5 am on weekends to go to work and make donuts.

BERNICE RATHE

My mama drove me to work on the weekends. On weekdays after school, my mama worked, so I walked to work.

I later started riding my bike to work, as a creepy man in a car asked me if I wanted a ride when I walked to work. Every day, he did this, so I began taking different routes walking to work. I told my family and they gave me mace or pepper spray (I can't remember which one), and my mother would pick me up from work.

Despite this, I went to work. I loved the job. It was fun.

My mama did not like me working at the donut shop because John worked there. She stated that John and his family had serious issues. She would not explain what issues, but later I learned that John's father went to prison for killing someone.

Also, John's mother was not functional at that time and John and his siblings stayed with his grandparents who also did not properly care for John and his siblings. I did not care about that, since John was a good person. My mother came around to the idea that John was my friend, since she saw that he was trying to pull his life together and was nice.

Bea Giovanni

Anyhow, John and I would do silly stuff, on and off the job. Sometimes, he would walk with me to work since he heard about this creepy guy following me to work. Well, when he would walk with me, we would do juvenile stuff and we would have some interesting encounters with people and situations.

Like one time, we were walking to work and there was a person who ran to an outdoor gas station restroom. As we passed by the restroom, there was an interesting crowd of people. Apparently, the gas station attendants were cleaning up mess from that person who ran into the restroom.

Well, if you can't imagine what I am saying, let me paint a picture for you. In a matter of minutes (I mean about 5 to 10 minutes), John and I checked to see what happened in the restroom. When I walked into the restroom, it looked like a cow exploded. Human feces were on the walls, floors, and toilet. The sight was enough to make a person hurl. It was funny in a way but not. It was nasty!

Even though I had funny and interesting childhood experiences, I still endured a lot. My mama never treated me the same as my younger siblings, but I was no easy child for my mama, either. I was the oldest out of my mama's children. She was harder on me. I later figured out why.

When she received child support from my step dad, she would buy my sister and brother Reebok, Nike, Adidas or other name brand shoes or clothing. I got the Payless shoes. My mama stated it was because she received support for it and had to buy things for my sister and brother with my step dad's support money. To make up for this, my grandma and my uncles would buy me things that were name brand.

But, the bright side to things was that my mother allowed me to have my own room. She stated that I was more responsible and cared for my things better. When my sister and brother would not clean their room, my mother would make me clean it. Her reasoning: because I cleaned better than they did and I needed to show them how to do it right. I told her I show them all the time and they still don't get it.

Well, my mother stated to continue to do it for them, and they will get it. She was right. They did.

Later in life, my mama stated neither myself nor my sister and my brother were problems for her. She acknowledged that we were good children and each of us had our own personality.

When I got older, she stated that my little sister and brother looked up to me, and if I lead, they will follow. She stated she wanted me to be independent and strong, so the things she made me do was to make me stronger, since I did not have a father. I later (in my adult years) learned what she meant and why she stated it to me.

As for my biological father, as I stated before, I thought my step dad was my real dad. But, he was not. I guess no one wanted to break my heart to tell me otherwise. After my mama divorced my step dad and I realized he was not my father, I began asking about my real father. My mother and her college friends explained to me that my real father did not claim me as his child (he thought my mama cheated on him).

My mama and her friends even went to court to prove paternity, but back then there were no DNA tests available. So, the mother had to get at least two or more witnesses to attest there was a sexual relationship between her and the alleged father.

Like those old, outdated court processes, all my father had to do is cast doubt that he was not the sole person to be intimate with my mother. So, he lied and stated my mother cheated on him. I am not sure if he wanted to avoid paying support or something else.

I do not know much information on their relationship before me. All I knew was that my mama and my real father met on a local U.S. Air Force base, where my mama would work during the summer months. My real father was a first-degree black belt and taught karate at the college they attended too.

They dated for some time and both graduated from the same college. At that time, my father returned from the Vietnam War. Upon returning from war, many of their college friends stated he was a nutcase. People told my mama not to date him and that he was not a good person. She ignored the advice.

That's when my mama got pregnant with me. My father broke up with my mama before my birth. Again, I guess he was under the impression my mama cheated on him when she did not. At any rate, I don't really know.

As the story goes, my real father thought my mama cheated with one of her good friends, who later married one of her close friends. While I am sure my father has his own reasons and version of what occurred, my father never was in my life after that point. His name was not on my birth certificate, since he never acknowledged paternity and denied I was his child to others in Macon, Georgia.

To date, his name is not on my birth certificate; he has constantly failed to acknowledge me.

In my adult years, I will later appreciate that he was not in my life after discovering some dark secrets of my father's past that haunt him today and has affected my life and my daughter's life (While every family has its stuff, there is a "whole lot of crazy" in my father's family and I am glad I did not grow up around that.).

His family was so crazy that they even stated I was cursed, which later proved untrue, as the opposite was true. Besides, how do you prove someone is cursed with actual proof not based on folklore? Again, these people are some crazy somethings (I do not even have the words).

I could not tell you why they did not like me. But, they did. I figured they resented me for not being like them, not being a person who sucked up to others, and for being smart and having sense to be a good, well-rounded person. Many of them were not good people.

For instance, my father and his family would pretend to be a nice, wholesome, "do good" family. But, this would eventually be proven to be a front for something else and not truly who they were.

If you think I am crazy, crying wolf (or have cried wolf) or lying or that this is mere speculation or that I have a vendetta, resentment, jealousy, bitterness, envy or hate anyone, you are mistaken. This is about my truth, my journey and my healing of what everyone did to me.

In any case, I did not meet my father until age 12. I met him because my grandma said I asked about him a lot (after my mother and my step dad divorced) and one day she saw him on the way to the grocery store, so, my grandma told him to stop by her house.

As the story goes, he stopped by with his three younger children (from his marriage at that time). It was later in my teenage years I realized he had other children, in addition to these three children. He also had two older children (older than myself), each by a different woman. So, you can see "papa was a rolling stone" (both figuratively and literally). The next time I would see or hear from him would be when I was about 16 years old.

At age 12, my life moved on drastically, i.e., from mama's and step dad's divorce to meeting my biological father to becoming a musical child prodigy. How I became a musical child prodigy was quite interesting.

I always wanted to play basketball and volleyball and run track; however, my mother, out of fear, would not allow me to participate in sports. At birth, the doctor stated I had a sickle cell trait (I got the trait from my father; he was a carrier of the trait.).

At that time, there was not much research on it. What was known is that excessive exertion could be hazard to my health. Therefore, the doctor advised my mama to keep me away from strenuous physical activity like sports since my cells were sickle and oxygen may not flow to the brain or heart and I could go into cardiac arrest.

Obviously, as a child, I did not understand this. So, I was stuck playing in the band. That was the only choice for me in terms of extracurricular activity. This led me to focus my attention on music.

BERNICE RATHE

Because I couldn't play sports, I gave band my all. I played trombone, which was by accident, since I wanted to play the flute or clarinet like my friends. Most girls wanted to play woodwind instruments and I did too.

As I stated, playing the trombone was by accident, as the middle school band director told my mama that I had "big lips" and this would be perfect for playing a brass instrument. From that point, it was inevitable the trombone would be my principal instrument.

Later, I would go to my junior high band director yearning for other stuff to do. He saw my drive and, at first, he gave me a different instrument and a scale book to learn for the week (just to get me out of his face).

My junior high band director did not think I would learn the instrument and in a short period. But, I did. Coming back to my band director a week later, I learned a new instrument and all my scales and proper finger positions. Reading music in treble clef and bass clef became natural to me.

I continued to learn new instruments in each week. I found myself learning the entire brass family and then the percussion family. As time went on, I began writing and arranging music. The band director was so amazed that he wrote his dissertation on me.

He encouraged me to enter competitions. Most times, I did not enter them; he entered me and forced me to enter them. I became the only student from my school to win those competitions; I would later receive numerous invitations across the south to attend several honor bands.

My grandma was so proud of me. She would have the newspapers write articles on me in her city and the city where I lived with my mama. So, I was constantly giving interviews for the local newspapers. Media and society pages began featuring me.

My name became so popular that people offered me full college scholarships by the time I entered 10th grade. I had scholarships to top tier universities without even auditioning for the scholarships. They wanted me that bad.

I declined those offers, since I was unfamiliar with those areas of the country and would need support. My mother was my support system, who now at the time, was a divorced mother of three children (that included me and I was the oldest). So, she couldn't do everything for me and I didn't want to create worry that I was across the U.S. without help.

During that time, I excelled in music, academics and in having a high IQ. I was deemed a mild genius or a musical child prodigy by age 12, and I later tested as an INFJ (a rare type) in my adulthood. I graduated early at 17. By that time, my real father heard rumors of my success and he started asking me to come to his home for one weekend and even started sending greeting cards in the mail with $20 now and then. Why? I did not know.

Maybe guilt set in for him for not being in my life? Maybe he was an ice cream dad (the kind of father who feels guilty for not being in a child's life and buys them anything they want)? Or, was he just trying to get fame off my fame? Or, was he trying to show people he was always there for me, which was untrue? But, like most children, I did not reject the money.

My senior year (or I should say my junior/senior year since I graduated a year early) was interesting to say the least. I considered performing with a local Drum Corps group. My mama couldn't take me, since it was too far and she had to work. So, I asked my father, and he said yes. So, my father, his wife, his children, and I set off to the local Drum Corps International meeting.

I must say I was not impressed and very disappointed once I got there. My father and his family stayed in a local motel, while I stayed with the group sleeping on the floor of a local school. This was not a pretty sight. I later found that night we had to fundraise and make it to practice every weekend (even if I raised the required money, I pretty much would not have anyone to take me). So, I got up that night and left heading back to Georgia. I never looked back.

I realized the Drum Corps group was for people with strong support systems, money and other things. I did not have that. I came from a single parent home, with an absentee father (who denied me as his child all my life and later I found he never really cared about me).

While everyone has their story, many people told the same story of my father denying that I was his child. These people were his college friends and even his family members. So, my relationship with him was and is not the best and is non-existent.

Thinking about it, I felt my father was doing these things because he regretted how he treated me (i.e., denying I was his child).

BERNICE RATHE

Asking my father to take me to the local Drum Corps International meeting was like pulling teeth; he didn't want to do it at first.

In my final months of school, there was some school chaos (among outside groups) where police had to secure the school. At the same time at home, I wasn't giving my mama an easy time. I was the typical teenager (thinking I knew everything).

This teenage behavior gave my mama lots of stress. I wanted to forego college and enter the military. So, my mama had me speak to my real father, since he had prior military experience. After talking to him, he discouraged me with his scary, war stories and that the military was not the place for a female. He insisted that I needed to go to college and that the military was not for me.

Also, at that time, it did not help that my little sister had sex at age 12 in the junior high/high school gym. On the day of the ACT, I heard rumors about someone named Joann from junior high being caught having sex with a high school student from our church, the day before. But, I did not think nothing of it since my sister's name was Joey.

I rejected the notion that it was my sister, even though everyone stated it. I thought they have the wrong individual because of the name and my little sister would not do something like that. I was wrong.

On Monday, my mama came home from work because she stated she had a meeting at my sister's school. I told my mama that I had an idea why the school called her. I told her what others were saying. She said that is a lie and to stop lying.

Well, when my mama came back from the school meeting, she seemed to be furious with me for no reason. She acted out on me and we had a verbal argument.

My mama may have been frustrated with my sister and may have been taking it out on me. That is how it went when my little sister or brother did something wrong. So, my mama told me that I needed to stay with my real father in my final months of high school for safety (as my high school was experiencing safety issues) and because of family issues.

With less than 3 months before I graduated (at age 16), I stayed with my father, his wife and their 3 children in the countryside of Macon. It was an interesting experience to say the least. The area was one long, country road that consisted of many of his family members. In my short stay, I tried fitting into my father's family and connecting with him. All I wanted was to know him and spend time with him and have a father-daughter relationship.

My mama told me stories about him and I wanted to know if I had similar talents and acted like him and how he was as a child. I dreamed of having a father-daughter relationship with him. But, it never worked out.

Living with him, I felt like Cinderella. To this day, I regret ever living with my father. I have no good memories from living with him and his family.

Before living with my father, growing up, I was like the girl next door type. I wore things like a Michael Jackson t-shirt to baseball caps to a "Where's the Beef" t-shirt to tank tops. I usually played with the boys, no matter if it was rough play or competitive play. I hung with the boys. But, this all changed once I lived with my father and his family.

My stepmother didn't like me. She did very little for me. For example, I was not knowledgeable on styling my hair, since I had thick hair and my mama would take me to the salon. So, I would ask my stepmother to help me style my hair, but she wouldn't. Instead, she would comb and style her children's hair.

My stepmother was so rude to me about doing my hair that I had to go to my uncle to get my hair styled. He was a cosmetologist in the nearby area.

She also didn't like that my father would give me more allowance than her children. This was even though he stated I was older and needed additional money for teenage stuff (since I was a teenager and they were under the age of 12).

Other times, she did not like that my father was teaching me how to drive. So, he stopped teaching me how to drive since she objected to my father taking me out for rides in his truck and not with her children.

My father even tried taking me with him on his general contractor jobs where I would learn what he was doing on jobs, and I would be his helper. He had to stop that too. When I spoke up for myself against her, my father would either punish me, ignore me or use some other method in silencing me.

The only time I had freedom or felt like a human was going to my grandma's home (my mother's mother) or going to the next door neighbor's home (who were my father's cousins). I got close to his cousins.

They told me interesting things about my father and his family. For example, they stated my stepmother and my father were cousins. My father was also apparently 31 and my stepmother was 18 when they had their first child. Kissing cousins?

I guess people thought it was normal. But, I didn't.

They also stated my father was crazy, like a nutcase. I understood what they meant later in my adult life.

Like I said, I hated living with my family and don't have any good memories. I recalled one day coming from school (I believe on my 17th birthday) where the next-door neighbor's son, i.e., my father's cousin's son, wanted "help on homework." (I hope I did not confuse you). I helped him, as I was usually home first, since my stepmother worked at a paper mill factory, my father worked at his restaurant and was a general contractor, and his children got off school later in the day.

So, I helped my father's cousin's son with his homework, but he had something else in mind. He tried having sex with me, forcing himself on me. I had to fight him off me several times.

It was scary. I kicked him, and even tried kneeing him. But, he blocked my attempts. I continued to push him off me. Eventually, I was able to persuade him to get off me and leave.

From that day, I never answered the door. I simply played my music loudly and danced, trying to drown out the world and what happened.

I never told my father about it, since I didn't want to cause any more issues in his home. I avoided his cousin's son and played with his sisters. Shortly after, the son apologized to me in private and we made amends. I had no hard feelings since I looked at it as just a misunderstanding on his part (I was not making excuses for him but simply trying to be nice and move on with my life).

Later in life, I learned that what happened to me was a sexual assault. I did not know that at the time, since it was not something that occurred around me, when I lived with my mama. My mama, her family and my friends were very protective of me.

In any event, I forgave him, since it did not go any further after that incident.

BERNICE RATHE

[Interestingly enough, as he entered adulthood, he joined the military, an institution notoriously for high rates of sexual assault. Well, he later also married an older female. He would later keep in touch with me over the years.]

I graduated as planned from a Macon high school at age 17. Because I was in a rebellious mode before going to my father's home, I declined the top tier university scholarships, so I had to search for other opportunities. I did not regret it, though.

Weighing my options, I decided to attend college closer to home, as my father didn't want me to go to college out of the area. I was thinking 3-4 hours away from his home. But, he was thinking 30 minutes away from his home.

He even bribed me with buying me a used car to stay closer. I accepted the car, but I didn't guarantee I would stay closer to his home.

I started to apply to several colleges and universities in the 3-4 hour driving distance. I applied to one that sent a brochure to me. It had an interest card for its music program. So, I applied. I got a call back within 2 days (so quick I couldn't believe it).

Bea Giovanni

Well, I received "the call" and the band director introduced himself and asked was I interested in the music program and any scholarships. I stated "yes!" He stated, "Great, we need you. I see you play the trombone." I replied "Yes."

He stated he was familiar with my name, as he saw me at an honor band competition in earlier years. He stated he couldn't mistake me, since there were few female trombone players and few people of color in those competitions, particularly in the south, which was true.

He asked whether I could audition for entry into the music program and for a scholarship and he would set up a date and time for the audition. I stated to him that my transportation wasn't reliable and I didn't have anyone who could take the time to take me to the audition. So, he stated it was not a problem and asked me to perform a prepared piece over the phone.

I couldn't believe it (over the phone?). I went with it, despite my doubts. I pulled out my trombone and went to the phone that had a speakerphone option. My father asked what was I doing and I explained I was auditioning over the phone.

BERNICE RATHE

He and his family did not believe me. They even stated (in the background) that the audition was fake and I was being fooled, ridiculing me saying "ain't nobody gonna want me and nobody does auditions over the phone."

All of them laughed at me in the background as they watched me audition through the phone. I felt so hurt and was internally tearful. I felt as if "they don't care about me and how can they say something like this, they didn't understand I sent an interest card to apply for this program."

I continued (even in doubt) to audition. The band director later asked about the noise in the background and I explained it was my siblings playing around in the background. Moments after the phone audition, the director stated he would contact me later on a decision.

Well, the later meant 5 minutes (not days or weeks later). He called me back and stated I was awarded a full music scholarship. The director explained the scholarship conditions and I accepted. He stated the scholarship agreement would be in the mail for me to sign and return.

[My father stated to me that someone was 'fooling me' and no scholarship agreement will be in the mail. He said, "Just watch." Like clockwork and despite my father's words of discouragement, I received the agreement in a matter of days. I signed it and sent it back.]

Before I sent it back, I showed my father, his wife and his children thinking they would be happy for me. But, they were not. They were negative in attitude and behavior. What was interesting was that my father went around bragging to people that I got a scholarship by auditioning over the phone, even though he and his family discouraged me and laughed at me.

(My father would also pretend among his friends and family that he loved me so much and cared for me all my life, and people would believe him; when in fact, he never claimed me as his daughter, never was in my life, and he didn't give a "crap" about me. The mixed emotions I received from him and his family were crazy.).

Despite these mixed emotions and negative attitude from my father and his family, there were some people who were proud of me, which were my mama and her family.

One condition of the scholarship was to participate in the marching band. This meant band camp. This scholarship condition came quickly, since the band camp started in 2 weeks from the date of the scholarship agreement.

My mama and her family agreed to help me move my belongings to the upcoming band camp. They were very positive stating, "Whatever it takes to get you there." My father didn't help because he stated he had to run his restaurant and didn't want to leave his family, even though it was just 3-4 hours away.

The car my father bought me was a blessing and curse in disguise. I couldn't take it with me, since the university didn't allow freshman to have cars. Plus, my car had issues. It broke down and I needed money to get it fixed.

My friend was willing to fix it for $20 plus parts. It would have come to $50 in total with the parts. So, I asked my stepmother when my father was coming home for the day, so I can either ask him to help me fix it or to borrow money to get it fixed by a friend, who was a mechanic.

My stepmother reacted so negatively towards me when I asked about my father's whereabouts and helping to get the car fixed. She stated to me in a rude and aggressive tone, "What! You want your daddy to fix the car too, after he bought it! What else do you want? You want our family's money too!"

I was in shock and I was through with how she treated me. It was no secret that my stepmother didn't like me. My father's cousins, who lived next door, and others, who I told about how she treated me, understood she didn't like me.

I told her "What are you talking about? I don't want anything from your family. I just want to see if he could help fix my car. He bought it. I don't have a job or any money and it's been 2 weeks since I got this car. It should not be having these issues. Maybe he could take it back to the person who sold it to him? I don't want the car if this is what I have to go thru."

Walking away, I stated, "You never liked me. The only reason I am here is because my mama sent me here and not because I want to be here."

Well, she acted as if nothing ever happened and stated to me "I don't know where your daddy is. He'll be here when he gets here, stupid, little, bastard bitch!" As she stated this, I got so angry where I walked to the front door to pick up the plant standing next to the door and I approached her room attempting to hit her with it. But, this action never occurred.

As fate would have it, my father began walking through the door when he saw me in anger approaching her room. He took the plant out my hand and told me to leave his house.

With no place to go, I slept in my car in a church lot. I just felt safe there. The ordeal with my stepmother took a lot out of me; she was mean and evil towards me for no reason. My father and his children didn't ever see the things she did to me. It was my father's cousins next door and others who saw it.

[At times, I felt my stepmother wanted to kill me. Seriously! She acted so mean, jealous and hateful towards me. I didn't understand why. My father and his family would not know really what happened between my stepmother and me when I was 17. They didn't know my stepmother hated me.]

After my stepmother's confrontation with me, I went to my grandma's house (my mama's mama). She told me that my father brought my things over to her house and he stated that I never should come back to his house because I disrespected his wife.

Bea Giovanni

I explained to my grandma what happened and she stated, "It is fine, now, you see how his family is and that his wife does not like you. It is a lesson learned."

My grandma called my mama. My mama told me, "You understand now how they are and that you are a better person than they will be." Days later, my mama and my grandma helped me move for the band camp and scholarship.

Yet, it was in my adult life where I would realize that moment became a defining one. I would learn my father and his family were not who I thought they were (or at least claimed to be). They would also begin a campaign of hate and envy spanning many years that would later destroy their lives. The ironic twist was that my father, his family and those who helped them would later regret everything.

I didn't talk to him and his family for years; when I did, it was every 2 years or so for the holidays, he would call, not vice versa. I had about 3-4 hours of conversations with him in my life.

I later learned they were never really my family, though blood connected us. I was an orphan. I also learned I broke many vicious cycles my father and others could not.

BERNICE RATHE

So, why am I spilling my guts? To understand my story, you must understand how everyone since and before my birth played a part in this.

I couldn't stop the victimization against myself and my future child. I would find I was an unwilling victim before my birth and some in government helped these groups endanger my life, as many would believe in this hate propaganda.

I found these groups didn't believe in a loving and peaceful god and there was a clandestine group, watching me since birth and has watched as parts of government, my father, these groups and others stalked and harmed me and endangered my life; this unknown facet even had tons of evidence against these groups.

Most importantly, I uncover something else. Remember these things: my father's secret background, government, cult-like, hate and extremist groups, experiment and me (the victim) caught in the middle of all of this, not by choice.

Bea Giovanni

PART ONE

Chapter 1: The Journey Begins

So, summer 1995, I started band camp and it was an interesting experience (to say the least). I was the youngest of my peers, being 17. The first week of band camp was hell for me and for other freshmen students.

I initially was in shock because I did not know what hazing meant. After I figured it out, I thought people must be crazy to haze another human being. After going through it, I still did not get it.

Some people thought it was fun, and others did not. Wasn't there other ways to promote unity and strength among everyone? Like ancient practices no longer use or necessary, the same should be true for hazing, i.e., it is no longer needed; it does more damage than good.

I hated the hazing process so much, especially being one of the only female trombone players in the section. I wanted to leave camp and my scholarship. The band directors heard I was planning to leave and they did not want that, since they stated that they really needed me in the band.

I was serious about leaving. I called my uncles, my mama and my grandma to get me and bring me back to my grandma's house. No one would do it. My grandma told them not to get me, since this is something I had to experience and it was beneficial since I was getting my college education.

I was so determined and serious about leaving that I was planning to pawn my things to get a bus ticket back home. Don't ask me how I knew to pawn my things, but I did. I guess growing up with an uncle, who was on and off drugs, and who would pawn his stuff for money, I learned a thing or two.

The thought of pawning my stuff was a funny moment (now that I am older). But, at the time, it was not. I didn't care if anyone helped me. I wanted out.

The band director called my grandma. I changed my mind on leaving after hearing my grandma on the phone tell me the reality of the situation. Though the reality was harsh and my grandma told it like it was, the reality was it was true.

Bea Giovanni

My grandma was never a person to hold back (she told it like it was). She stated I could not quit and she would not let me quit.

On speakerphone in the band director's office, among the directors and myself, my grandma told me that I could leave the camp and scholarship behind and come back to her house, but there was nothing there for me. She stated my father and his family disowned me and my father never really claimed me as his child (so living with him was not an option). Also, she stated my mama was a single parent, and my mama did not have the room anymore at her house.

My grandma stated she had a room, but I would have to work at a fast food restaurant and pay her rent. So, the best deal for me was to stay at the camp and attend the university on a scholarship. Tearful as I was, I agreed and stayed at the camp.

Before I left the band directors' office, the directors stated to me that they wished they had more parents like my grandma. They also remarked that I had an opportunity to prove to my peers, this university system and others that females can make it. Apparently, they saw someone in me that I did not.

BERNICE RATHE

They were determined to keep me at the college and wanted me to succeed, especially after hearing what my grandma said afterwards. Apparently, my grandma told them about my background and accomplishments. That is when they knew I could outshine my naysayers. I left that office and never looked back.

Nonetheless, I made it through my band experience and very well. So well, I exceeded my peers in every area. I guess I just needed a little motivation.

After the first week, my peers understood that I was not the average person and I was very strong. I gained tremendous respect from everyone, especially since I really did have it harder than everyone. They never lowered the expectations for me but raised the expectations higher, because the directors knew I could do more.

My college years were interesting and amazing at the same time. I met many good people and interesting ones too. However, no matter how fun or bad my experiences, I kept my eyes on the prize.

Self-driven to excel, I wanted to graduate early from college and go onto graduate school. I wanted to excel and achieve even more.

Bea Giovanni

It appeared the more adversity I faced the more driven I became. You can say in many ways my "haters" made me successful. But, this is to say they don't get the credit, since they did not do the work (I did the work).

I entered the university as a Political Science major and with the hopes of being an attorney. Being 17 in college, I was one of the youngest students on campus. Because of this, I had a curfew (yes, a curfew in college.).

I discovered two sets of rules existed: one for me and another for everyone else. If band practice was not in session, I had to be in my room by 10:00 p.m. (on the dot). I had a dorm mother who monitored me and checked if I followed that rule.

I had strict rules placed on me, and the university and others had high expectations for me, which I later understood why. They wanted me to succeed because, again, they saw something in me that others did not.

Boy, if I did anything out of line, everyone knew. If I spit on the ground, someone knew about it. The same applied to my classes.

For example, as a freshman, my mama received my attendance and grade reports from the school. When my professors marked attendance, some were extra particular about me and some were not, i.e., whether I attended classes and stayed in them, which I did. I was a pretty decent student. I did not give the instructors issues and I followed the rules.

But, one day my mama called me and cursed me out because she thought I wasn't attending my History class. I only missed two classes that entire term (which were excused). My grades were very good, but the instructor didn't update the attendance reports to show my two absences were excused. I explained this to my mama.

My roommate laughed as she overheard my mama on the phone "going off" with my mama stating to me 'she did not work hard to bring me this far for me to mess up my life.' But, of course, I didn't think it was a funny situation because technically my absences were excused. Yet, my mama did not understand this.

The reason for the excused absences was my band performances. I played with the pep band on certain basketball game nights. One of the conditions of my scholarship required me to participate in music ensembles. One of those ensembles I chose was pep band.

I contacted the professor and informed her I stated this scholarship condition in the beginning of the class and the time conflict, which she approved the absences. She later apologized to me as she forgot to mark my absences excused and contacted my mama notifying her the absences would be marked excused. Let's just say I never skipped classes from that point on.

Also in my first year, I couldn't hang out in the student plaza after hours like other students. So, I found students who were homebodies (in the dorms) and formed friendships. After hours, I socialized in the dorm when not at practice and not studying.

People noticed I was not the average student and there was something to me. No one realized I was 17. If I had to describe myself, I was a shy, friendly, very young looking individual who sat in the back of the room wearing a baseball cap or something similar. Don't ask me why I worn the cap all the time, I guess it was easy to put on and not style my hair.

Others thought I was hiding myself from others, which was not the case. I never thought about it that way, but it is another way at looking at it. In any case, I was shy and I did not place myself in the limelight. Others forced me into the limelight.

Like in one of my Political Science classes, I had a professor who always gave me a hard time. He was my professor for several courses, so I couldn't avoid him. I couldn't understand it at that time. But, he would make me sit in the front row. I hated the front row.

When I was about to graduate, I decided to ask him why he always made me sit in the front row. The professor stated he heard about me and knew I was smart and could do better than sitting in the back, lounging as if I am stupid or something.

He said I was not stupid but very smart and my peers did not know this. In the simplest terms, he stated I had my peers fooled. The professor wanted my peers to know this, since I had so much more to offer everyone and I could be a potential leader.

It all made sense to me at that point. Since I started the university, people, who attended classes with me, would peep at my grades when we got the tests back, or when a professor acknowledged me, they knew I was very smart. I became so popular among

Bea Giovanni

the student body that people wanted me to tutor them or help them with papers.

I did not have money. My mama, being a single parent and a social worker, had limited funds. She sent $20 a month for washing my clothes, which is all she could send at that time. Plus, she figured my necessities were covered via my music scholarship, which covered my tuition and room and board.

My father never was present in my life and did not do anything for me. It was no support there. So, I made ends meet by typing papers and even performing research and writing tasks for many students, such as athletes.

The athletes loved me. Many of my friends were athletes, since I, again, was a tomboy or a girl next door type. Plus, I was in the band and we traveled with the teams.

I didn't rely on my research and writing skills alone. In fact, finding other ways to make money was a task. I would go home on different weekends and bring back my mama's gumbo that was frozen in a big bowl (the Texas Gold ice cream bowls) with a large side of rice.

Having a hotplate in my room, I warmed my mama's gumbo and rice and sell bowls for $1.50 to $2.00. It was enough to buy me CDs every month, since I loved music.

I avoided the pitfalls of clubbing and credit cards in college. How? Because of my age, I had limitations placed on me and this served to my advantage (as I would later find). For instance, I had a curfew, so I couldn't go to clubs. Also, because I was underage, I couldn't apply for credit cards.

Learning from my peers, I found that clubbing was overrated, as I saw one of my good friends get alcohol poisoned after a night of clubbing. It was so bad her parents took her out of the school and brought her back home.

When it came to credit, I saw my friends deep in debt, charging for any and everything. They were indebted to the point they had to get campus jobs, which interfered with classes and their social life. So, I learned that credit should be used wisely and not to borrow more than you can truly pay back.

When I turned 18, I didn't have those desires, as I, again, noticed the impact on my friends. So, my age limitations worked to my advantage, later in my college experience.

Bea Giovanni

I was also a so-called crab in the band (freshmen were called crabs). So, on top of the curfew and other restrictions of a freshman student, I also had obligations to the band. If you haven't picked up from the name, "crab" is a hazing term. Let's just say, I paid my dues and earned everything including respect, which is hard to do (being in a predominately male dominant band, with females in the trombone section being few and far).

I was young looking (I looked 12 or 13 but was 17) and one of few females in the brass section. I stood out like a sore thumb. Some upperclassmen in the band had names for me such as Brat (because I looked like a brat, but I wasn't). But, my line name or crab line given to me was "Predator."

People in the band knew the meaning behind my crab name, "Predator," but not many people outside the band knew the meaning. I later learned why after my crab year.

Do you want to know why? Not bragging, but other musicians saw me as a strong and forceful trombone player with technique. My embrasure was fierce. (Thanks to my middle school band director for being so observant of my "big lips." It would later help me get a full music scholarship. No one could touch my embrasure.). Not bragging, it's just the truth.

This explained why people who sat in front of me (in particular the trumpet players) moved their chairs away from my slide path. I thought it was because my slide might hit them, but it was actually because certain trumpet players who sat around me thought my sound was too much for their ears. They would even wear earplugs.

Predator was a good name for me, since I was seemingly like the predator in the movie, *Predator*, in many ways. Like a Predator who is unassuming and invisible to most people, some people viewed me as an ugly duckling, young and inexperienced, but this was not true. Also, I had braids like the Predator. Yet, as I started to play, my sound told another story of me in that I sat, observed, planned, and attacked (all while everyone mistaken me, underestimated me or did not see me).

Being a freshman and a typical ugly duckling, by the end of my first year, I did a 360. When I went home for a weekend, I changed my hairstyle.

When I came back to school, people did not know who I was. I began to become more sociable, since I was 18 and could do more and now I had no curfews.

But, it didn't stop my mama from laying the law down. My mama wouldn't let me go to summer school. I wanted to go to summer school to get ahead; plus, I was invited to join a Masonic group.

My mama and father (out of nowhere, since I hadn't talk or seen him since he kicked me out his home, and for some reason, he was furious) forbid me to join the group. They made sure I didn't join by making sure I didn't attend summer school. I had no way there, so I couldn't go.

[This interference in anything I wanted to do became a pattern with my father, as he appeared in my life in the most opportune times, to disrupt it and to prevent whatever he wanted, then leaving my life and continuing with his as if he did nothing and nothing happened.]

The next year, I was no longer a crab in the band. I socialized more and met more people than before. My popularity soared more than before.

As an upperclassman, but unlike my fellow upperclassmen, I did not participate in the hazing of freshmen in the band. I felt there was no need to do those things. My belief is to 'do unto others as you would have them do unto you.'

Hazing in my crab year was a required process, and in theory, I did not have any choice. I had to be in the marching band per my scholarship, and hazing is just an essential part of the band process. I know some people think it is stupid, but if you know the history of bands, it is not. We were like a family, and we had each other's backs. I was just one of the few who did not believe in hazing.

Nonetheless, my band experience proved to be a great one. Over my college and band experiences, from my first year to the last year in college, my mama and her friends were so proud of me. They would come to my marching band performances at the football games, whenever they got a chance. I always had someone cheering me on.

My father never really supported me, as expected. In fact, he went to only one of my band performances. I think my mama begged him to go and support me. So, there you have it, my father came to one game, out of all the years I was in college.

When he came to the one game, it was only him and his three young children. You can guess why my stepmother was not at the game. You guessed it: she did not like me (regardless of the reasons she or my father gave).

Once I saw my father, I was surprised to see him, yet excited. Like most band members, who family members or friends came to see them, I introduced (or at least tried to introduce) my father to the band directors and other band members. But, my father wasn't interested.

My father acted as if he didn't care, so I failed to introduce him to others in my life, who were important to me and supported me. I knew at that point (and later in my life) any efforts to bond with my father were out the question, as he really didn't care about my life or me. He was numb to the world.

[On a side note, if I had to describe my parents, they were like night and day. While my mama would tell me she loved me, my father never told me he ever loved me. My mama was a caring, compassionate and sometimes naïve individual. My father was a numb, deceitful and sometimes cold-hearted individual.

But, both were strong people. It was as if I came from both good and bad parents, my mama being good (like an angel) and my father being bad (like a devil). Both being strong in their own right. This is how I viewed them over the many years of my life.]

Nevertheless, my college life and my experiences were fun. I began dating in my second year in college. I didn't have sex with anyone because I didn't believe in having sex before getting into a serious relationship. I behaved like a lady.

I found many of my dating experiences were high quality, since males treated me with respect, for just that. But, it was until I met a guy named Milton.

I met him in the student union while checking my mail. At the time, his name sounded familiar; yet, I couldn't recall where I heard that name. He sparked an interesting conversation and asked me out. He later took me to a movie, one of my favorite things to do.

After the movie, he took me to a secluded area near an elementary school where we sat and talked. I am not sure where the talk led to Milton forcing himself on me, ripping my shirt, and attempting to rip off my pants. But, out of fear, I insisted he stop. I thought he was about to rape me.

Bea Giovanni

I fought, kicked and screamed, no one heard me. It was extremely scary. I was in a secluded area, away from anyone with Milton trying to force me to have sex with him.

In struggling with him, Milton got up and drove me to my dorm like nothing happened. Afterwards, I cut off all communications and left him alone. I could not believe it. I was sexually assaulted.

I told one of my friends, Susan, what happened. Then, she provided some interesting information about Milton. He was the boyfriend of our friend, Kat, who never really would appear with Milton in public, so no one knew Milton (but some people heard of Milton). I think this is why his name was familiar to me.

Shocked and surprised, I wanted to tell Kat, but Susan stated not to tell Kat, since Milton has cheated on Kat before and Kat does not want to believe anyone.

Milton, I guess, felt remorse for his behavior and waited for me at the band hall to apologize. He stated he wanted to apologize and did not want any band members roughing him up.

I stated to him I was over what happened and I uncovered he is Kat's boyfriend and that I was a friend of Kat's. I stated to Milton I wanted to tell Kat what he did to me, but I think it would hurt her more to know he was a dog.

He didn't know all Kat's friends, as he never hung with Kat and her friends. He hardly saw me around Kat as I did not always hang out with everyone, as I had band practice at night.

I told him no band members are coming after him, as I did not tell any band member and I am not that type of person to get someone to rough him up. I did state to him if I saw him doing it again to anyone else, I would make sure every female he womanizes knew what he did to me.

He promised he would stop womanizing. Well, let's just say this person changed his ways very quickly. Today, he is a preacher and he and Kat are married with three children. It is interesting how life works. Like the sexual assault on me by my father's cousin's son, I did not tell anyone. I lived with this for many years.

Bea Giovanni

Chapter 2: Chance Meetings and Endings

I continued to make strides in my education. I worked so hard I anticipated graduating early, with honors, which I later would do at age 20. But, before I graduated, I had a few things to accomplish.

My grandma was a great influence on me. She had been an active member of a sorority for many years and I saw the support and friendship she received from the sorority.

Growing up, I volunteered with her sorority (feeding the needy, painting houses, participating in health fairs and registering people to vote). So, naturally, I wanted to join the sorority on my campus.

Unfortunately, the campus didn't have an active chapter as it was on probation. Therefore, no intake could take place. Luckily, in my junior/senior year, the sorority's probation was lifted and it decided to have a line, so I decided to join.

I didn't have the funds to join the sorority. But, once my grandma heard, she paid for it. Out of nearly 500 applicants, the sorority only picked 103 people (or pledges). Everyone picked were fortunate to be one of the 103 selected. My number was 95 and my line name was "Epsilon's Excellence" because of my excellence in excelling in everything, including being a musical child prodigy.

I was what you called a legacy, since my grandma was in the sorority. So, I guess they gave preference to legacies. At the time, I didn't know about legacies or what it meant. I later found this out after making it into the sorority. There were many legacies on my line.

The initiation was interesting. The sorority initiation was not as difficult as it was for me in the band. I endured far worst being one of few women in the band than the basic hazing rituals in a sorority.

I loved my sorority. Outside my band experience, it was another great moment in my college experience. I felt a part of something important. I recalled my sorority was Christian-based but we had a sorority sister or two who were closeted lesbians.

Though it was a Christian-based sorority, they tolerated every female as long as you were a positive contributor to society (at least this is what I recalled). This was one of many things I liked.

I later met someone who was also in a fraternity named Jeffrey (most people called him Jeff). He was also a masonic member. So, I believed he had to be a good person, since I had older family members on my mama's side of the family (male and female) who were Masonic members and I always seen Masonic members serving and helping the public.

(On a side note, after graduating from college, this person later becomes my husband.) Many of my sorority sisters disliked Jeff. He transferred to the college after flunking out another state college. My male friends and sorority sisters told me they didn't trust him and that he wasn't good enough for me. Yet, I never listened, as I thought I was in love at that time.

Jeff showed interest and treated me right for the most part (at least in the beginning). He even introduced me to his family, specifically, his mother (Sheila). No other guy did that (ever). So, I looked at that as a plus and that this person was serious minded. But, who knows? He could have did this with every girl he met.

BERNICE RATHE

During the spring break holiday, we went on a trip to my hometown. En route to this destination, I stopped at my mama's house to introduce him to my mama and her family.

[At that time, my father and his family never met Jeff, since my father and his family never claimed me as his child and I did not know my father or his family that well or at all.]

Well, when I introduced Jeff to my mama, low and behold, my mama disliked him too. She stated also she did not trust him. To her, he seemed to be deceitful. I couldn't see what everyone else was seeing. I am not sure why, but I just couldn't see it.

In my junior year (or senior year in this instance, since I graduated early), weeks before graduation, I found that Jeff would not graduate in time. This is despite transferring the credits from his other school. After doing research on this issue for him, I found he needed two classes to graduate, which he took at his previous university.

I asked the department chair (who I knew well, as I volunteered at the department whenever they needed help) to review his transcript and to see if the classes at his previous school could be accepted. The department chair reviewed it and agreed to award credit for those classes. He was excited and appreciated I saved him another semester. So, he graduated with me.

After graduation, I had plans to attend law school at a top tier law school. Even though I have never been a person big on top tier schools, you can't deny there is a benefit in the marketplace. Plus, they had tons of alumni ready to help other alumni.

Besides, I always thought and heard it does not matter where you get your first degree. But, it does matter where you get your master's and graduate degrees.

The month after I graduated was a tough one for me. I wanted to go back to the university scenery to hang out with my friends (especially before I attended law school), since most of my friends were still in college completing their senior years. (Remember I graduated early from college too).

My mama did not want me to go back to the university. She wanted me to stay home and work a "normal job" and attend graduate school nearby.

My mama also promised me when I graduated I would get a new car. Well, this didn't work out. My mama and I had a very big argument because I wanted to get my car and go back to the university area. But, she wanted me to stay home. So, she refused to help me with getting a car.

My mama even called the dealership to stop them from selling a vehicle to me, just so I could not go back to the university area. I know this because I was at the dealership when she called. The salesperson and manager informed me.

They refused to listen to my mama; they stated I was grown and could make my own decision. Plus, they wanted the sale. Despite her efforts, I got a new car and left home.

I stayed with sorority sisters. Jeff was still at the university hanging with his frat brothers, and Jeff and I remained in an exclusive dating relationship. But, that summer, I got pregnant by Jeff (this turned my world in a different direction).

I was excited since I love children, yet scared because it wasn't like I was pregnant before. Not many of my friends were pregnant. Also, I was raised to believe you marry the individual and Jeff was taught so too. So, Jeff and I did.

Many of my friends thought Jeff got me pregnant on purpose. The reason they thought was Jeff was against me going to the top tier law school. He didn't have any plans to attend grad school or work at that time. Plus, he was just glad he graduated; he didn't want to do anything else.

For obvious reasons (i.e., pregnancy and marriage), I decided not to attend the law school. Instead, I became a high school teacher at age 20 and enrolled in grad school.

Teaching high school was interesting, as the principal, coworkers and students thought I was a student. I was one of the youngest teachers in the nation at that time.

Meanwhile, I encouraged Jeff to enroll in grad school with me, while staying at his mother's home one hour away.

I lost contact with friends and sorority sisters, despite attending the same college for grad school. I am not sure if it was intentional, but, Jeff didn't want me talking to anyone. I thought he wanted privacy during the pregnancy. At the time, I couldn't recognize this as a destructive, controlling, and potentially violent relationship.

The next months were interesting (to say the least). Let's say people are not who you think they are. I should have listened to my friends and my mama about Jeff. But, after

BERNICE RATHE

reflecting throughout my life, sometimes,
these events are the journey one must take to
understand one's purpose in life and
discover one's self in this big world.

Chapter 3: Lessons Learned and More

Where do I start? I really don't know where to start. The reason is that the person I married and had a child with (Jeff) was not the person who I thought he was.

When we dated, I thought he was a gentleman. But, after I got pregnant and married him, he changed and not for the better.

I later found that he had the problem (many issues) and not me. I am not a jealous person and I was neither jealous when I dated Jeff nor when I was married to Jeff. I was (and still am) an easygoing person who was very secure with herself and relationships.

The marriage was a mutual decision, since Jeff later revealed to me he had a child at 16, and wanted the next time he brought children into the world, to be married. (I guess that was something he regretted.)

Discovering he fathered a child named Victoria, when he was a teenager, was a total surprise to me. But, I never judged him.

BERNICE RATHE

I viewed the situation as fine as long as he was being a father to his child.

Anyway, at the last minute, we got married at his mother's home with his pastor holding the ceremony. There was no planning involved. It was a very small ceremony.

My family did not even come, since it was so last minute. His family did not come, other than Jeff's mother, his sister, and his grandparents.

Later, I realized he never really cared for Victoria. I saw Victoria possibly twice while married to Jeff. (This should have been another sign to me but, again, I did not see it as anything. I was young and in love).

Also, staying with Jeff's mother (Sheila) was quite the experience. She was a very big woman in size.

When she walked in the house, her footsteps sounded like a giant. You knew she was coming. I also learned via staying with her and Jeff that Jeff was a "mama's boy."

He always listened to his mother, even if she was wrong. He also always took her word over someone else's word. It was annoying at times, since Jeff would disrupt our family time to do things that his mother could have actually gotten his other (grown) siblings to do (who also lived in the same house).

His mother stayed in this small, old white house in the countryside of Georgia. (I guess their family had land or something and she stayed on this land with this house).

From looking at the home, you would think you were living in the slavery era. In any event, it was a place to stay, since I did not have to stay on campus attending grad school especially being pregnant. Plus, his mother insisted on this.

Jeff later quit grad school to work to pay for expenses for our child. His job was in another state and required that he live in corporate housing. So, I lived with his mother on a 24-hour basis, since I was still in grad school.

Living with Jeff's mother was the least desired thing in the world. Doing a basic task was an interesting situation.

Take cooking as an example. Because her oven didn't work, I couldn't cook any healthy items in the oven like baked chicken. Plus, she was territorial and did not allow me to cook in the kitchen alone.

It made me literally not want to cook in her home. I would be so hungry sometimes I would stop at a fast food restaurant every day. I would go to the fast food restaurants so much they knew me by name.

My blood pressure was sky high because I went to my doctor's appointment after eating a breakfast sandwich from a fast food restaurant.

Even so, I never really had any major issues in my pregnancy (with the exception of that high blood pressure, my doctor remarked I did very well and I did not have a difficult pregnancy).

Actually, my pregnancy was easy and any concerns were common.

At the time, I did not know what blood pressure was or meant. I just ate whatever my body craved. I craved orange juice, croissant sandwiches with sausage, egg and cheese, Chinese food, ice cream, oatmeal with brown sugar and cinnamon.

Oh, I craved pancakes with yogurt on top. After my pregnancy, I realized pancakes with yogurt was nasty but that's what I craved.

After having the baby, I lost the desire for those cravings.

I explained to the doctor and my midwife why I ate fast food. (Coincidentally my doctor was also my sorority sister, an older member, which I later found towards the end of my pregnancy via conversations with her). They helped me developed a birth plan where I could eat fast food but in a healthier way such as salads and grilled chicken options.

The plan helped solve that issue (for the moment).

My mother-in-law (Sheila) also thought I should have kept up my appearances better than what I was doing. While I had a happy pregnancy and enjoyed every moment of it, the pregnancy was not without issue (like most pregnancies).

She simply did not understand I was very tired, attending grad school (full-time) at night, and going through serious pains and worries. You would think another woman, especially who had three kids of her own, would understand the seriousness of a pregnancy.

Despite my mother-in-law's negative disposition, I still kept up my appearance, but it was never to her satisfaction.

She viewed me in the same manner as a celebrity or something and had a brand to maintain. It was annoying at times, and controlling at other times.

BERNICE RATHE

Also, besides being tired, our child was in a breech position twice throughout my pregnancy. If you don't know what breech means, it is when the child exit the body feet first. This is not a comfortable way in giving birth, and few women would tell you they want to have a breech birth. So, I was frequently at the doctor's office getting the baby turned out of the breech position into the right position.

Plus, I gained over 60 pounds and my body was not accustomed to this, especially being I was always a slim and tall person. In fact, as a child, my family, in particular my uncles, would make fun of me and tell me to go eat something because I was so skinny.

Before having my child, I have never had a weight issue. So, extra weight on my body took a toll on my daily functions like walking.

While Sheila's weight may have been heavy (for what appears to be most of her life and Jeff's family appeared to be very heavyset people), she adapted to that. But, I did not adapt to the extra weight very well.

Carrying extra weight on my body was not easy at all and I did not like the extra weight. I loved feeling and looking healthy and not fat or out of shape.

Bea Giovanni

In fact, after I had my first child, I made sure to lose the weight immediately and I did. I am not a vane person; I simply prefer to look healthy and be healthy, and good fitness is healthy to me.

I also had low iron levels due to my sickle cell trait and had to eat lots of greens and other foods with iron. Sheila did not understand this. No matter what I would do, she complained about something. I even tried explaining to her what the doctor and my midwife would tell me, but she simply did not get it.

I was close with my doctor and midwife, as I was a first time mother and wanted to make sure I was doing all I could to have a healthy pregnancy. I read the "When Expecting" book. I really was doing all I could to make sure our baby was healthy.

What really took the icing off the cake for me (relative to my mother-in-law) was the day I went into labor. I was about 1 ½ weeks overdue. I walked numerous times each day, as suggested by the doctor and midwife to see if I can dilate. Our child simply just did not want to come out into the world.

On the last office visit, which was 1 ½ weeks after the estimated due date, the doctor scheduled an inducement and a Caesarean section at the local hospital.

I called Jeff from work to tell him we were having our child that day. I also contacted my mama and her family who wanted to be there. My mother-in-law (Sheila) came to stay with me at the hospital until Jeff while my mama and her family were en route.

While induced (and under medications), my mother-in-law asked me whether Jeff was the father of our child. (I don't know what this woman was thinking). I, of course, stated yes and questioned why she would ask me that question (as if I slept around and the child was someone else's child and not Jeff's child).

Jeff arrived and my mama and her family arrived shortly thereafter. The doctor decided to perform a Caesarean section, since I did not dilate much after the inducement. So, I went into the surgery.

Once I came out the surgery, I asked Jeff's mother in front of everyone why she would ask me whether Jeff was the father of our child. Jeff's mother stated I don't know what I was talking about and that I was medicated and "making this up."

I looked startled and confused, since I know I heard her say this to me and I responded yes, Jeff was the father. I was amazed she would ask such a question.

The nurse in the room quickly explained to everyone in the room the inducement medication still maintains your normal functions as it only limits pain and its sensations. My mother-in-law's response that I was "making this up," was the icing on the cake for me (so to speak). I forever viewed my mother-in-law in a different light after that moment.

Putting that aside, Jeff and I had a healthy baby girl and I was also healthy. The nursing staff brought our child to me.

She was so beautiful. I picked our child's first name and Jeff picked her middle name. I decided I would choose a name that started with J (like Jeff's name).

I named her Jamie. Jeff gave her the same middle name as my middle name, as Jeff liked my middle name (which was given to me by my mama).

Before leaving the hospital, per my doctor and midwife's advice, I developed a care plan for Jaime and me, since Jeff was working out of state, and I would be recovering from the C-section. Also, having

BERNICE RATHE

a newborn and with one semester left in grad school, I needed support.

I asked my mother-in-law (with hesitation) to help care for Jaime on two week nights while I attended night classes. During the weekends and after completing grad school, the plan was I would move to my mama's house so she could help me with Jaime while Jeff worked.

The care plan worked out temporarily. I became suspicious of my mother-in-law. I later confirmed my suspicions. Every time, I came home from night classes Jaime would be very tired and sleepy (and sometimes deep in sleep).

Because I read about developing predictable schedules and habits for newborn and the doctor and midwife suggested it, I had Jaime on a schedule. So, I knew her habits including sleeping habits.

Well, I asked my mother-in-law why Jaime would be either sleepy, inattentive or playful when I get home. She would frequently state Jaime played all evening. But, I know this is not true, since she would be napping when I would leave for my night classes and my night classes were approximately 1 ½ hours long.

Bea Giovanni

I later learned from her own admission via a casual conversation about rearing children that she would be too tired to care for Jaime or play with her, so she would give her Tylenol to make her go to sleep. I was furious and upset.

I phoned my mama who told me that was crazy and dangerous of Jeff's mother to do that. There was no doctor's approval for this Tylenol to a newborn, and she was giving her this medicine for no reason other than to make her sleepy.

I checked with my mother-in-law to see what type of Tylenol she gave her. She stated it was the liquid adult Tylenol for cold and flu.

"What the $%^and?" is what I was thinking. (Excuse me, but this is the only effective way in clearly describing my reaction). I never told Jeff, since he was so close to his mother and always took her word as golden.

I immediately took Jaime to the doctor to see if anything was wrong with her. Fortunately, the doctor stated she was fine but to monitor her. The doctor agreed with me on the use of Tylenol or any medications without his approval was wrong, especially for a newborn.

BERNICE RATHE

He suggested not allowing my mother-in-law to care for Jaime. I took the advice and sought help from one of my sorority sisters who agreed to watch Jaime while I completed my remaining night classes.

I moved back to my mama's house earlier than expected (I am sure you can connect the dots as I wanted to get away from that craziness in my mother-in-law's house). I told Jeff I would be at my mama's house when he comes home for his vacation break from his job.

When I went to my mama's home, I felt Jaime and I were safe away from that madness at Jeff's mother's home. My mama was so helpful. She saved me from such grief and anger.

I told her what I experienced with Jeff's mother during my pregnancy and after and she was upset too. She was glad I had sense to get Jaime the right care and that my sorority sister helped me (despite losing touch with my sorority sister).

Chapter 4: Learning and Growing

J eff came home on his vacation break and decided to quit his job. So, he moved with me at my mama's house. Even though my mama did not like Jeff, my mama tolerated him since he was the one I married and the father of her granddaughter, Jaime. My mama welcomed him.

My mama's house was bigger and newer than Jeff's mother's home. So in my mama's house, we had our own area of the home. We decided to live there until we could save enough money to get our own apartment or house.

In the first few months, it was great, and then it went downhill. Jeff and I got jobs in Atlanta, Georgia and were doing well for a period. But, the jobs were not the jobs of choice for us, since we wanted to use our degree.

The economy sucked at that time for new grads. So, I worked at a fast food restaurant as an Assistant Manager. Jeff worked at a retail store as an Assistant

BERNICE RATHE

Manager, which was coincidentally located in the same area.

Our jobs were in close walking distance. We would frequently eat lunch together. I knew all his coworkers, as we ate lunch at his job, my job or other areas near the store.

However, I couldn't tell you what went wrong with Jeff and me. It appeared Jeff turned into a different person. This person was not the person I remembered from college.

I thought everything was great (i.e., sex, companionship, being a great wife and mother). I mean I really tried being that ideal person and wife for Jeff.

Here is where Jeff started to show himself. One day at my job, a male customer approached me. He stated to tell Jeff to leave his wife alone.

I was startled and confused. I couldn't talk to the individual in detail so I couldn't really get any other information than the message he gave me to give Jeff.

Later that day, I explained to Jeff the strange encounter. Jeff stated he did not know what that was about. I believed Jeff. We moved on from that situation and I never saw that male customer again.

Almost 2 weeks later, Jeff came home early stating his job laid him off. He began looking for a new job and thought he would get another one soon. Again, I believed him.

While I was shopping in a grocery store, I bumped into one of Jeff's former coworkers, his supervisor. He asked how I was doing and I stated great. I asked if they were planning to hire Jeff back, since he loved that job so much.

His former supervisor stated, "You don't know?" I stated "no." He stated, "Jeff was fired." I asked "why?" He stated someone caught Jeff and a female supervisor on camera having sexual intercourse in the stock room and management fired them.

At that moment, it all made sense why this male customer came into my job and stated to tell Jeff to leave his wife alone. I was very disappointed to hear what Jeff's former coworker/supervisor stated to me and thanked him for the information.

I went home in disbelief and told Jeff what I heard without revealing who told me. He stated he did not do it. Knowing Jeff, I did not believe his denial.

I never accused Jeff of cheating in the past and I was not a jealous person but very comfortable in our marriage. When this revelation occurred, it all made sense. So, I was astounded that he would do something like that.

I asked why would he do that and if there was anything wrong in our marriage or how I could change to prevent him cheating on me now or in the future (better yet, make our marriage stronger and better). I just couldn't understand it, as I treated Jeff so well (I treated everyone well in my life). I pampered Jeff.

Despite what was stated, Jeff again stated he did not do it. I even suggested we attend counseling with our pastor. Jeff refused and stated he did not do it.

Moving on from that experience, Jeff got a new job as an Assistant Manager in another retail store. For his trainings, he traveled out of state for training at other stores.

When traveling, Jeff would always call me from those stores' administrative offices and I spoke with other trainees and management personnel, who were excited to talk to me.

Almost one month later (after starting this new job), Jeff went to training on a Saturday in a nearby city. Jeff told me not to expect him to return until the next day. Later in that same day, I received a call from the district manager in Jeff's home store location asking to speak with Jeff.

Apparently, district manager explained he was doing spot checks at each store and Jeff switched days with an employee and wanted to speak with Jeff. They wanted to speak with him about a customer complaint from a previous day to find out how the issue was resolved, since Jeff was the individual who handled the complaint and he was currently not in the store. I stated Jeff is at a training session.

The district manager stated there was no training anywhere today for the company. I explained to the district manager this is what Jeff told me.

The district manager tried locating Jeff at the nearby stores, even stores out of state. No one heard of Jeff and everyone confirmed there was no training scheduled. When district management told me this, I was completely dumbfounded.

The district manager called back and stated he was firing Jeff and he did not have to worry about calling district management. District management informed me they did not know why Jeff lied to me, but he is not a training session and he switched days with an employee.

The other employee also stated Jeff said he had a personal vacation with his family and wanted to switch days. Of course, I was confused since Jaime and I were his family and I was not aware of any vacation.

At that time, cellphones were not popular, so neither Jeff nor I had a cellphone. Not even his job supplied cellphones. So, no one could contact him.

I called everywhere I could. I even contacted his mother. I was concerned. His mother and my mother were concerned too.

I thought the worst. Even his mother thought the worst (as something may have happened to him, since it was now late in the evening with no contact or call from him).

I decided to inquire with my bank to see if he used his credit or bankcards, as we had a joint account and access and we both used the same cards. They confirmed Jeff used his card at a local train station for the purchase of two tickets and at a Floridian hotel.

I called the hotel but Jeff did not register under his name but under the name of another individual (a female). The hotel connected me to the room, but no one answered.

I had no other avenue to contact Jeff. My only choice was to wait until he came home or called. His mother was also worried and wanted me to contact her immediately once I made contact with Jeff.

I was sick and deeply worried, I couldn't even care for Jaime at that time. My little sister cared for Jaime for the night. I cried all night. My mother comforted me and said it was irresponsible for him to do this.

I felt he was cheating on me again. I confided in my mother and his mother and told them he cheated on me months prior. They both were disappointed in Jeff.

Jeff finally came home at about 5 am on Sunday (the same time Jeff stated he would be back from the training). He appeared to be drunk.

Interestingly, I asked him about his training. He provided a lengthy story about the training and that he went out for drinks with the "fellows."

I stated to him that was interesting since his district manager called and wanted to speak with him. Jeff's face lit up like he had saw a ghost. I explained to Jeff what happened and that the district manager told me there were no trainings for the weekend and that the district manager fired him.

Jeff looked amazed and stated I did not know what I was talking about. He even tried telling me I was tricking him and lying.

Jeff got louder, so I told him not to wake Jaime. He then calmed down and explained he went to an Atlanta bar with his friend, Frank, from college. But, Jeff did not know I checked the bankcard activity.

I then explained our bankcard shows transactions for a train ride and a Floridian area hotel. He looked as if I caught him lying and cheating. What Jeff did not know was I packed his bags and his mother and I decided he would be better back at his mother's home.

Our marriage was officially on the rocks. We separated and I tried getting help for our marriage from our pastor and marital counselors. Despite trying to get help and reconcile, Jeff's behavior was one of bitterness, irresponsibleness and immaturity. He refused to seek marital counseling.

Jeff refused to talk to me or see Jaime. The last conversation I had with Jeff he stated, "He needed to find himself." My mama and my family were disappointed at

Jeff, especially being that he did not continue to be a father to Jaime.

From then, I never looked back and I fell out of love with Jeff. I would never see or hear from Jeff again.

[Years later, I was glad. Over the years, I developed a "hater radar" of sorts. It is easy to spot; haters hate.

So, when you spot hate like I did, my friends and I call it a "hater alert." We could have made a whole song about it, if we really wanted, playfully, of course.

Jeff was a part of that hater alert. I learned later he was a part of something more sinister than haterism. I would be glad I was not with him anymore.

I later learned meeting Jeff at college wasn't a coincidence or by chance. I would begin to recall I think I saw Jeff's mother and sister at a band performance, when our band traveled to their town years prior.

I also believe having Jaime wasn't a coincidence or by chance as suggested early on by my sorority sisters. Later in life (after thought-provoking coincidences), this makes an interesting connection between my estranged father and Jeff.

These connections come together later, which will shock you as to the extent of

BERNICE RATHE

these connections, my father's true identity
and role in this, the involvement and motive
of others, and subsequent cover-ups, as a
veil of secrecy would be miraculously lifted
and where a series of random events
seemingly would connect.]

꧁◆꧂

Chapter 5: He Said He Needed to Find Himself, But I Found Myself

Well, Jeff stated to me he needed to find himself and needed his space. Well, his space was several years, leading me to divorce him. But, it gave me time to also find myself.

After separating from Jeff, I finished grad school in one year at age 21 but never graduated, since I did not complete my thesis. At that time, I was so distraught over my marriage, I did not want to return to the grad school to complete my thesis. However, because I like to finish what I started, decades later, I returned to complete the thesis and graduated.

[Plus, after I separated from Jeff, his aunt, who worked at the university for many years, frequently harassed me and even made it difficult for me by tampering with my grad school records. I later had to get the Vice President of the university to lock my account unless approved by administration.]

In addition, at that time, our finances and everything Jeff and I had together were in disarray. Graduate school was the last thing on my mind.

I tried reconciling our bills and I discovered Jeff was hiding money from me. He established another bank account with the same bank.

He was taking my money and depositing into a separate account where he was gambling with these funds. This was extremely upsetting since he could have provided this money for Jaime's care and I was a stay at home mother.

I was seriously worried about our marriage. There was so much deception, and there was no hope for reconciliation. I grew farther away from Jeff.

I even had dreams about Jeff and these dreams were dark. I only had dreams like those when something bad was going to happen. From my interpretation of these dreams, it was clear I should not stay with Jeff.

I felt this void or betrayal in my life due to Jeff's behavior and feeling like it was my fault that our marriage did not work out. I would later learn he was the one with problems and not me.

After not getting anywhere with Jeff or our marriage, I decided to pursue my lifelong goal in going to law school and becoming an attorney, which I put off for Jeff and our marriage. I couldn't go to the top tier law school because I delayed my admissions to the top tier school and my LSAT scores were too low for other schools (primarily because I took the LSAT before I graduated from undergrad and I did not take any prep courses, and I did not have the funds to retake LSAT prep).

After other schools rejected me, I thought I couldn't get into any law school. But, for some reason, I found a law school in Texas where my scores did not really matter and were accredited; they had an admissions formula that was not contingent on the LSAT but factors such as GPA and future potential.

That same week in applying for law school and before I made the drastic direction to move on with my life, I sought guidance from other males. If you have not gotten it already, I did not have many good male role models in my life. (Possibly, still to this day, I don't have good male role models or mentors). Plus, my real father was an inadequate role model for a man.

Despite this and with hesitation, I contacted my father (out of sincerely seeking a male perspective) on what to do with my marriage. I told him everything that happened and my father actually stated "stuff happens and men will cheat, get over it. And spouses will have hidden accounts, so what! These are no reasons to separate or get a divorce." He was not a big help at all.

Shortly thereafter, I confided in my mama. She provided me with the sound advice. She stated I had a choice. She also stated not all relationships would be healthy.

My mama related her own experiences living in an environment with an alcoholic stepfather. She never understood why my grandma stayed with my grandpa. She thought maybe it was out of necessity or possibly the bond between her stepfather and her mama. But, my mama endured and came out of that situation.

My mama gave me the best advice: to pray on it and let God lead me to the right result. She also stated if the situation is abusive to you or your children, it is not a healthy one and to leave.

She was right on both aspects. After thinking about it, my marriage was an abusive one, and my child would experience adverse effects too.

Bea Giovanni

An interesting aspect to this story is that I prayed on it too. I prayed to God to send me a sign as to what I needed to do. Approximately one week after applying to law school and the night after praying on it (and less than two months after Jeff cheated and we separated), I received a miraculous turnaround response via a letter from the law school stating I was accepted.

I took that as a clear sign as to what to do. So, I moved to Texas to pursue my lifelong goal in becoming an attorney.

I was so excited. I instantly called Jeff. He was not happy for me at all. I said to Jeff "maybe we could move to Texas, start over and mend our marriage."

Jeff did not care. He stated "no" and that he was still finding himself.

I asked if he could care for Jaime while I attended law school. He stated "no." Years later after learning revelations about Jeff, I would be grateful he decided not to care for Jaime.

I was determined to go to law school, no matter the obstacles placed in my way. I knew going to law school would be a benefit in my life and for Jaime. So, no matter if Jeff did not want to care for Jaime, I planned to take Jaime with me.

BERNICE RATHE

My mama thought it would be too much for me (i.e., to go to law school and care for Jaime). So, my mama cared for Jaime, especially since Jeff did not want to have anything to do with Jaime and me. The plan was for me to attend law school, while my mama cared for Jaime in Atlanta, Georgia. My mama stated to send money wherever I could (if I wanted), but she did not need it.

Before I left for Texas, I received a call from a friend of Jeff's family, Mr. Birk. I knew Mr. Birk from my stay at my mother-in-law's home. After I moved from my mother-in-law's home, Mr. Birk always kept in contact with Jeff, our newborn child and myself.

He was really a sweet man. But, this call was strange but interesting at the same time. Mr. Birk told me my decision to leave Jeff was the best decision and to not look back. He stated Jeff has some issues that I may not be aware of.

I asked Mr. Birk what he meant by "issues." Mr. Birk stated Jeff was accused of molesting his first child when she was 4 or 5 years old (specifically, fondling the child while in the bathtub, when Jeff gave the child a bath). CPS was involved, but CPS could never prove the allegations.

Mr. Birk stated it was not the first time. When it happened again, CPS later placed restrictions upon him and he couldn't be around his child alone. His first child's mother, Linda, and her husband, Carl, were naturally, extremely mad at Jeff and did not like him.

Mr. Birk stated Jeff's mother was the only person the child could be around per the CPS order and per Linda and Carl's request. Jeff's mother was a teacher at that time, so she had validation as a so-called "responsible adult" and mandatory reporter under the law.

[This is even though she was not truly responsible from my experience with her. But, Linda and Carl had to put up with her for the sake of the child.]

Yet, what Mr. Birk told me made sense as to why Jeff did not always have Victoria around and alone. I only saw Victoria twice and it was when Jeff's mother (Sheila) would care for Victoria.

Mr. Birk was also stated Jeff's mother had issues too, as she would frequently cover up for Jeff. I gathered Jeff's mother had issues from my experience leaving with her. She was not fit to raise a child, as she drugged Jaime (as a newborn) to make her sleep.

At that time, I did not understand the full extent as to what Mr. Birk was telling me. However, I did heed his warnings and I stayed away from Jeff and allowed him to find himself (as Jeff put it). Interestingly enough, Jeff never really saw Jaime after our separation and never cared for Jaime or sent any support or funds for her care (at least not voluntary).

Jeff would later (for a number of years) refuse to pay support and he saw Jaime maybe four times in Jaime's lifetime, since the separation. Years later, I would discover the full extent of Jeff's issues.

Let's just say I was thankful for Mr. Birk calling me and for God in protecting my daughter and me from these issues. I later understood I did not have the problem in the marriage, Jeff had the problem (and his mama had issues).

My plans were in motion and I was set to attend law school. The only issue was that I needed a place to stay since the law school did not provide housing. I found a place in the school's housing ads prior to leaving for law school.

Bea Giovanni

The strangest thing and so coincidental is that, when I called the contact person listed in the ad, I discovered it was one of my line sisters (my sorority sister, Joy) from my undergrad college. We pledged together.

Joy went to law school directly from undergrad, while I attended grad school for a year after I graduated. The law school she attended was the same I would be attending. She explained that her previous roommate was also in law school and they did not get along (for whatever reason) and the roommate moved out.

Joy and I were both excited and she instantly thought having me, as a roommate was a great idea. On the surface, this was the perfect situation for both of us, since we knew each other.

So, we arranged the housing situation, as I would be sharing an apartment with someone I knew. Everything was coming together for me.

The only issue was that I had no money to move or do anything. Jeff had spent our money on gambling and other things and it did not provide any support after separating from him. Therefore, I had no funds.

Luckily for me, my mama made some calls to friends and I was able to work at a gas station for a short time before I went to law school.

I was able to make a couple hundred dollars. This went towards my move and basic needs in Texas. Obviously, a couple hundred dollars would not last long. I did not have a plan, other than to go to law school and find a part-time job.

My sorority sister told me to not worry about the books, since she just finished her first year and had the books. So, this was a relief for me. Now getting to Texas was a task.

My mama couldn't take me to Texas, since she had to work (and couldn't take time off work). Also, I had to bring my vehicle to get to and from school, so getting someone to drive my vehicle to Texas and getting that person back was a task.

She said to ask my father, since he has a truck and moving equipment and could easily move my vehicle to Texas. Well, I asked my father and he was not a big help.

He stated he couldn't help me, as he did not want to leave his family, and that it was the holidays and he needed to keep his restaurant open to make money. That really hurt me, since I thought my father would help me. But, he did not.

Bea Giovanni

Being that my stepfather and my mama had mended their friendship and both having moved on to different relationships, my stepfather would come around to help around the house on an infrequent basis. My stepfather heard I did not have anyone to help me, so he volunteered to help me drive from Georgia to Texas, since I never really traveled that far by myself (and I was unfamiliar with those areas).

Furthermore, my stepfather also did not want anything to happen to me on the road (being a single woman traveling alone). He took time off from his job as a day laborer (let's be mindful that he makes money by the day and would lose money for taking time off).

My stepfather's help meant a lot to me. Despite whatever happened in the past with my mama and my stepfather, I loved him. My mama and I thought it was a great idea, so my mama purchased a one-way ticket back to Georgia from Texas once my stepfather and I reached Texas.

This was one of many times I realized my real father really did not care about my life or me, as to take time out to help me in the simplest way. I felt as if he did not feel I was a part of his family too. He would easily do anything for his children within his marriage, but not for me, especially as my stepmother and I had a "falling out" in the past. Despite this, I continued to remain a strong, independent thinker and contributor in life and society (without his help).

Before I left for Texas, there were people in the community who heard I was leaving for law school, they were so proud of me. They thought someone from our community has made it, as there were not many opportunities in our community at that time. They thought I would be famous one day. They really thought that!

I didn't think so, but they did. Plus, they knew my mama and they knew me, so they had very high hopes and promise for me.

I really did not believe the support I got from my community. It was amazing! I did not feel so alone and I felt as if I could do this and give back to my community.

My mama was especially proud. Someone from a neighboring community held a garage sale in my honor and gave me the proceeds; it was not a lot (about $50). She let me take some clothes from the sale too, since I only had maternity clothes from my pregnancy.

Bea Giovanni

My grandma gave me a book on the most powerful women in the world and the Serenity Prayer. One of my uncles gave me a leather coat (he jokingly said I need style when I hit it big). All jokes aside, my uncle was very proud too.

During the drive from Georgia to Texas, I cried, as I had to leave my only child (nearly nine months old). I felt empty and less of a mother.

However, as my stepfather talked to me as we drove. We had a great father and daughter talk. He explained I was attending law school to make a better life for Jaime and myself and that I am strong like my mama and that he was proud of me.

He stated he had lots of regrets, including not being a good husband as to mess up his marriage with my mama. He stated my mama was a good woman and she deserved the best. He also stated he wished he could have been a better father to my younger siblings and myself.

As we talked, I had pictures of my daughter in the car as we drove. I stared at those pictures, as we got closer to Texas. I realized that my stepfather was right about how strong I actually was and that I could do this.

BERNICE RATHE

I left Atlanta setting off for law school in Texas with gifts and blessings from my community, less than $300 to my name, my vehicle, a leather coat, a book on the most powerful women in the world and the Serenity Prayer. At that moment, I would now know this moment would prove to be one of the truest moments in my life. These things got me through.

Chapter 6: Things Change

Finally, I arrived to law school. My hard work had played off. I thought I finally made it here. Well, the hard work only started.

During my first months in Texas, I would have nightmares and worries about leaving my daughter. My mama did not want to tell me, but later she told me that Jaime also did not want to eat or talk to anyone.

I would call and talk to Jaime sometime for her to understand and hear that I was not completely gone. She then would try to talk back in the phone. This helped both Jaime and me in the separation period.

The calls really helped Jaime and she got out of that phase within a matter of days. Within a matter of months, I made sure I either went home (back to my mama's home) or sent for Jaime to live with me during the breaks or holidays. This worked for both Jaime and I, for the most part.

When I started my first semester, Joy, my roommate (also my sister sorority) did not tell me she was on her last strike, in terms of passing her classes and being kicked out of law school. She had been at the school for at least one year before I entered the law school program. Joy did not do very well in her first year of law school.

She was to the point of flunking out of law school. I was not sure why she did not do as well. I thought it may have been the time she put into her studies, working and dating some guy named Ryder, a car salesman, who I only met twice. But, it was just too much going on for her at that time.

Joy was more concerned with her dating relationship than school. Joy was extremely concerned with dating Ryder, even though Ryder never came around often and stood her up for Valentine's Day. I recalled Ryder not returning her calls during that time. Later, he came around to see Joy two weeks later.

I told her that Ryder was not the person for her and she needed to move on and get serious about law school. She did not listen.

As for my law school performance, I perform sufficiently. I made it through and that is all I can say. Also, if you ask any law school student in the first year of law school, that is all that matters for many students.

Bea Giovanni

Things were looking up. I settled into law school quite well. I worked very hard to accomplish my goals. I even had my license plate personalized to the phrase "EPSEXCEL" This highlighted my sorority line name of Epsilon's Excellence.

After my first year, I decided to find a part-time job that accommodated my school schedule and provided benefits for part-time workers. I worked part-time as a package handler at night.

Later, I interned for a respected state representative, who was nice and helpful to me. Then, I later interned for a federal judge and gaining major recommendations from other state representatives and a state judge. Again, like I said, I worked very hard and people recognized this.

Joy became seemingly jealous of me (I feel), and others saw this as well. I guess she may have gotten that way because I passed my courses and she did not pass her courses and I guess she thought I had more success. Who knows?

But, everyone has a different law school experience. No one is the same. Yet, Joy's experience seemed to be very dramatic and one-sided.

BERNICE RATHE

My experiences with my law school buddies and study groups were amazing. I worked very hard and had study groups and formed friendships. My study groups and friends in law school all helped one another. We were determined and did not want to waste a minute of our law school experience.

In law school, this is where I saw the color lines or other prejudices seemingly removed from my experiences. It was no longer about color, but about knowledge and power. Though there were idiots who tended to push negative agendas like race, gender, religion, or sexuality, we did not let race, gender, nationality, religion or other classifications stop us from helping each other and being friends.

During my first semester, I met this female law student from Barbados named Deloris (or Dee). She instantly clung to me. I did not know why, since I was not popular in the school. Plus I really did not socialize with many people, other than our study group. However, we became great friends (for the time being).

I eventually decided that I was going to get Jaime so that I can alleviate responsibility from my mother. I had planned to attend classes in the mornings, while Jaime was in daycare. However, my mama told me there was no need as she could care for Jaime.

I insisted I wanted to care for Jaime as I did not like the idea of my mama taking on this responsibility, which was clearly my responsibility. Despite my insistence, my mama continued to care for Jaime.

I decided to work towards getting my own place eventually so that if Jaime moved with me or if Jaime and my family visit, I had an apartment. Plus, the apartment I shared with Joy was somewhat small.

Working at night as a package handler was a labor-intensive job, which I did not mind. I met some great people. I got exercise, it fit my scheduling needs, and I had some interesting coworkers.

There was a coworker named Bob, who was very nice to me. I couldn't understand why no one else talked to him as I did. I later realized he was a preacher. This is why I think most people avoided him.

Bob eventually invited me to bible study, which I accepted his invitation and attended on a regular basis. Bob was a very down to earth person and was not a pushy religious guy (you know the kind of religious fanatics who try to convert everyone and "bible bash" you). Well, Bob was not like that.

I had another coworker, Monica, who treated me very well. She was older than I was and she treated me like a little sister. I never had any older siblings in my life, so I welcomed it. She would invite me to shop with her. I would not have any money and neither did she, but she taught me how to window shop and shop on a discount.

She was a savvy shopper. She was one of those extreme coupon clippers (and this was before the reality TV shows on extreme coupon clippers). I mean she stocked her basement with coupon deals as if it was the Armageddon. Seriously!

Monica also had a Barbie collection that was worth millions of dollars. She started collecting and insuring Barbie dolls since she was 10 years old. I learn a lot about Monica and from her.

I learned she was a foster child for many years of her life because her mother couldn't care for her. Eventually, her father found her and he adopted her out of the foster care system.

My mama briefly worked in the CPS system and often handled foster care placements. So, Monica's story hit home for me.

Since Monica's experience, Monica became an informal foster mother to some of her friend's children. Because of how she cared for other children, she made me more aware and sensitive to the issues that foster children faced.

I met other people at my job. However, not everyone was sociable, and some were inappropriate. For example, there was a group of coworkers who were extreme in their thinking. Some people said they were members of a local militia group. I did not know how true that was. But, they were very suspect and anything was possible.

Nevertheless, there were other memorable moments at my job. There was one memorable occurrence at my job, which was a strange coincidence that later made me think that *only God* could have made this connection happen. This may have changed my friendship with my roommate, Joy, forever. How?

A coworker, Annette, and I sparked a good working relationship. Annette would be very open with me and others. She would share her marital woes with me and others at work.

BERNICE RATHE

[We had a lot of downtime between the plane arrivals and uploading planes, so we would sit, wait, and talk while waiting on the next plane to upload packages.]

Well, Annette expressed she thought her husband was cheating on her. Of course, I could relate, so we shared "war stories" (if that is the phrase you would use). Annette stated the female, who he was cheating with, attended the local law school and was from Kentucky.

I told Annette, "I hope you don't think it is me because I don't know your husband, and I am not seeing anyone. I have no time for anything." Annette replied, "No, I know you are not the female. My husband has been seeing this female for at least a year."

Annette asked if I knew anyone at her law school from Kentucky (or at least she believed the female was from Kentucky). Not really thinking about the question in detail, I stated, "No, I barely know anyone at the school, other than my study groups and friends in my classes and none of them are from Kentucky."

Days later, Annette would confide in me again about her marital woes and she revealed her husband's name, Ryder, and that he worked as a car salesman. I recalled meeting a guy named Ryder, because my roommate, Joy, was dating a guy named Ryder, also a car salesman.

However, it was not until days later I discovered Annette's husband, Ryder, was the same Ryder who was dating my roommate, Joy.

I couldn't come to tell Annette this out of fear of her disbelieving me. You know how some people think a person is lying when the person has told them something negative about their mate. However, somehow Annette figured it out on her own and even before I figured out Ryder was Joy's boyfriend.

How Annette found out was *nothing but God*. This is how it happened: I guess Joy had Ryder's home number and she called that number to talk to Ryder. Yet, somehow he was unavailable, and his children picked up the phone.

Joy never left a message. However, Ryder's children told Annette a woman called for Ryder. Ryder's home phone had caller ID, so Annette called the number back.

Joy's number was the same number as my number, since Joy and I both shared the same phone number (Annette did not know that it was my number, since we never talked via telephone and only at work.).

When Annette called Joy back, it was late at night (before I left for work), so I answered. Unaware of who was calling, since the caller ID showed it was a blocked number, after answering the phone, I said to the caller on the other end, "hey, your voice sounds familiar."

The caller (Annette) said, "Your voice does too." I said to the caller (Annette), "Is this Annette from work?"

The caller then said, "Bernice Rathe from work? Is this you, girl?" I stated, "Yes, this is me." We laughed together in amazement.

As I stated this, Joy picked up the phone and said to hang up, it was for her (Joy). I said goodbye to Annette and said I would see her at work.

[Little did I know that situation would be a very uncomfortable situation for me. I would feel like I was in an episode of a Tyler Perry's *The Haves and The Have Nots* or better yet *The Young and The Restless*. You pick. Whichever one, it was full of drama.]

I went to work as scheduled, not knowing what I would walk into.

Bea Giovanni

Surprisingly, Annette came to me with a disturbed look on her face. As I tried to avoid her, Annette walked near me and cried in my arms stating the female (Joy, also my roommate) told Annette she was pregnant by her husband, Ryder.

This was a shocker to me too, since Joy never told me she was pregnant. Apparently, Joy told Annette she was almost 2 months at that time. I didn't know what to do.

Was I supposed to go to Joy and explain how I knew Annette and what I knew? Was I to explain to Annette why I answered the phone and that my roommate shared the same number and my roommate's connection to Ryder? I didn't know what to do.

The first thing I did was I apologize to Annette, since I uncovered my roommate's connection to Ryder shortly after Annette discovered this. Annette never made the connection that Joy was my roommate until I told her that Joy was my roommate, which was why I answered the phone (because I stayed there and we shared the same phone).

Annette stated it was fine, since she knew Ryder was cheating and Annette thanked me for listening. I finished my work and left as scheduled.

BERNICE RATHE

When I arrived home, Joy was awake and on the phone. So, I decided I did not want to hide anything from Joy. I explained how I knew Annette.

Joy looked as if she was in shock and accused me of invading her privacy and locating Annette to ruin her life because I did not like Ryder. But, this was not true.

I actually thought Joy was seriously crazy to think I would locate someone who I don't know and ruin her life. Joy did not get that all of this was pure coincidence. In that, I coincidentally got a job at night at the airport as a package handler like many other law students, as it was the only job that fit my schedule and provided adequate benefits.

Again, it was mere coincidence. I don't know why I got a job at that location and met Annette and these things happened with Joy and Ryder. But, these things happened, and I was not looking for it.

After Joy and I talked about the situation, I thought everything was fine. I went to bed since it was late (or early in the morning to be exact). After sleeping for some hours, Joy was still awake.

Strangely, Joy began shutting doors and cabinets loudly and talking loudly on the phone. I came out my room and asked Joy politely to lower her tone and activities, since I was sleeping.

Joy was so angry (for whatever reason) that she threw a sharp object at me, then she threw pillows and pieces of furniture at me. I narrowly escaped her. I tried defending myself, as she got fierce with each throw and move.

I asked her to stop and even tried asking her why was she doing this. I later realized she was angry and upset at me about the Annette and Ryder situation. However, Joy never stopped. She was at the point of seriously injuring me.

I ran out of the apartment to the apartment manager's office, so that I could call the police (or to get someone to intervene). The manager asked what was going on and I explained Joy was physically attacking me and I felt threatened. The manager stated this has happened before with Joy's prior roommate.

The manager went to the apartment with me to wait for the police to arrive. However, the police was already at the apartment, Joy had beat me to it.

Joy called the police and alleged I assaulted her (when it was the other way around). She also alleged I assaulted her and that she was pregnant.

The apartment manager also provided information on Joy's prior roommate situation where something similar occurred. Despite what the manager stated relative to Joy's prior roommate experience, the officer explained because I was taller than Joy (and since Joy was a short and petite female), I looked like the aggressor and I was handcuffed.

So, the officer arrested me for Domestic Assault. After talking with the manager and me, the officer believed me and said she would put in a good word for me. However, the officer had no authority.

Because of Joy, my life would be changing, as I was facing a potential felony of Domestic Assault, homelessness as I could no longer live in the shared apartment, and a possible expulsion from law school (as Joy would later lie to the school about this incident).

[Later, I realized this was all because of Joy's anger, jealousy, regret and her frustration with flunking out of law school and also intentionally cheating with a married man and not wanting anyone to know about it. She created a plan to get rid of me and to ruin my life to cover up her insecurities and ill deeds.

She would later even spread lies among my sorority sisters and law school friends, to the point where I lost many friendships during that time.]

BERNICE RATHE

Chapter 7: Hard Work Pays Off and Even More

Immediately after the arrest for Domestic Assault, I had to stay in jail over the weekend, since it was a holiday weekend and no judge was available.

I called everyone I knew to get help. My mama was upset and wanted to know what happened. Of course, Joy told my mama all sorts of lies. My mama knew it didn't sound like me, since I am not a violent person.

After the lengthy holiday weekend, I finally got out of jail on a PR bond (i.e., a Personal Recognizance Bond). But, I had to pay to get out of jail. So, my law school friend, Deloris, from Barbados, bailed me out, along with my sorority sisters. They were helpful and supportive.

Before getting out, the judge ordered that I move out the apartment within a week's time and to stay away from Joy until the matter was resolved.

I didn't know where I was going to move or if I could get an apartment, since I had no credit history. Plus, I was working towards getting my own apartment, but this incident made it happen even sooner than expected; therefore, I had little funds and little time. But, God saw me through those moments.

I got immediately on trying to find housing. I stopped at the first apartment complex I passed, which was also near the law school. I stopped in and explained to the property manager why I needed an apartment.

She did not mind and even stated that she would charge me only $100 for the remaining days of the month and I could pay the security deposit and the first month's rental payment when I got my paycheck. It was a deal!

Because she rented to a host of law school students, she knew I would not be an issue and would pay my rent. Thank God for that apartment company!

In the mist of this situation, I tried very hard not to rely on anyone. However, I had no funds to pay the $100. My mama did not have any money to give me, since she was caring for my daughter, Jaime. So, she suggested calling my father.

I was hesitant in doing so, since my father and his family would think I wanted their money. I did not want anything from them.

Yet, I listened to my mama and I called my father to see if he could wire me $100 for the apartment. Unfortunately, he stated, "I can't help you with that. You are on your own. Figure it out."

After, he abruptly hung up. I felt so alone and abandoned. I thought he would rather me be on the street, homeless and in danger than to send me money for an apartment.

I even explained to him what happened. He acted as if I did this to myself, which I didn't. Luckily, my uncle (my mama's brother) wired me money, since he heard what had happened and had no reservations with helping me.

Though I did not need to pay my uncle back, I did. I pay my debts.

I would never forget his help. His $100 got me my first apartment on my own, though it was not under the best circumstances.

Deloris helped me move my items out my old apartment. I didn't want to go back to the apartment alone (in case Joy alleged something else).

Bea Giovanni

I had other law student friends and sorority sisters who heard about what I went through with Joy. They knew Joy lied and they were furious Joy did this to me.

After moving, Joy didn't stop with the allegations or harassment. She went to the law school dean the next day (after I got out of jail and moved out the apartment) to inform the dean I was arrested and convicted of Domestic Assault. She also produced a letter she received from the DA's office advising Joy of her rights with the case number and my name on it to convince the dean of this information.

The dean believed her. The next day the dean ordered me to her office.

I explained to the dean that the information supplied wasn't true, as an arrest and charge occurred, but a conviction did not occur (as the case was in the pretrial stage). The dean confirmed it via the court. The dean was furious with Joy for doing this.

Should I say more as to what happened to Joy? Well, because she was already on her last strike in law school and violated ethical codes with this false reporting, the dean kicked her out of school.

BERNICE RATHE

I thought that was the end of Joy's drama when the case ended; but, it was not. Even though the law school dismissed Joy, she still enrolled and attended one of my classes that she already took a year before.

I thought that maybe she restarted law school. I did not know how she was able to enroll in my class. I also did not know too much about her academic status and rightfully so, since there are privacy laws. So, I was in amazement and confused on the whole situation as to how she was able to enroll and attend law school again at the same school and attend my classes.

In the class, Deloris and I sat together all the time and Joy sat near us. I did not feel comfortable, since the court ordered me temporarily to stay away from Joy.

After seeing Joy in my class in the following week, I went to the dean's office to explain that Joy was in my class and that the court ordered me to stay away from her and I couldn't switch classes. The dean checked and I was correct, Joy registered for the class.

The dean was amazed that she was able to enroll and attend the class as she flunked out of school (and with the school eventually dismissing her). Interestingly to say the least!

The dean caught her in the class in the third week and ordered her out. The school blacklisted her for fraudulently enrolling into the school after her dismissal.

I continued my studies and I eventually resolved the Domestic Assault charge. One of my sorority sisters referred me to an attorney who handled the matter for me.

After learning of all that Joy did, the court dismissed the case. I was very thankful for this. I moved on and used that moment as an opportunity to work harder.

Deloris and I became good friends. We would study and socialize together. I viewed Deloris as a dear friend.

I even met Deloris' mother who appeared to be nice (and who would visit her from Barbados). I also met her brother, who eventually moved from Barbados to live with Deloris.

Things changed over time with Deloris, and I did not know why. One day, she just stopped talking to me. She stopped returning my calls, she stopped sitting near me in class as before and she even changed her class schedule all together. When I tried talking to her in public, she ignored me.

BERNICE RATHE

I think our friendship changed when another classmate, Sissie, hung with us. Sissie was a U.S. Army Commissioned Officer who flew from Kentucky weekly to attend school. Sissie (I heard) told Deloris things I allegedly said about Deloris, which, of course, was untrue.

Yet, Deloris never asked me whether I said these things. I guess Deloris believed this. As for myself, I don't believe everything that people tell me, so I really didn't know why Deloris stopped talking to me and began treating me like crap. It goes without saying that a potentially good friendship ended.

I continued to persevere. I admit it got lonely, since Deloris and I hung tight and we were no longer friends. But, I got over it and looked at it as the past, as the window of opportunity closed for her.

Since moving into my own apartment, I changed jobs because I needed more money and the situation with Annette made it uncomfortable. Plus, I switched jobs because there were some workers, who were extreme in their behaviors (racist and biased behavior), which made it uncomfortable for many workers.

Bea Giovanni

I got a new job working as a hotel night auditor. I got it because I was persistent calling every day. Seriously, I think I called everyday checking on whether the manager reviewed my resume and stated I needed a job at night due to law school. I think I even went up to the hotel to speak with the manager. Seriously, I was that persistent.

At any rate, I made a few dollars more than my previous job (but not much). If you haven't noticed, everything I did in life was due to my hard work (I didn't come from wealth). I had to be persistent, determined and hardworking.

With the extra funds, I traveled to and from my area to big cities and even took up new activities. One of the best things that happened was that the friendships that I lost in law school, I was able to find new friendships, outside school.

I took up activities like martial arts. I briefly learned Shorin Ryu, an ancient Japanese martial art. I was taught by the highest and oldest masters. I stopped the lessons due to my limited funds.

I later learned I had a natural talent for martial arts (though I would later learn I did not like judo but I liked other martial arts).

BERNICE RATHE

My curiosity for martial arts lead me to learn other forms years later.

I was never about belt tests. I was never one of those people who came to martial arts class with an attitude as if I have been doing this for years and I am the best. In fact, I just wanted to have fun and learn, which may be why I become good at martial arts.

I would later learn in 2009 that a strange coincidence, i.e., my sensei who trained me was my father's sensei's relative. They were from the same family, only my sensei was in a more ancient form of martial arts. Somehow, I want to believe I was led there by someone or something, but it was a weird but exciting chance where I learned some great skills.

Now the year is 2001, I eventually divorced from Jeff, and I was excited! It seemed like it took me forever since we had a child together, as the courts wanted to wait longer to see if we reconciled and to give him proper notice. He did not respond to the court's notices, so he was defaulted.

I think having a divorce on the docket for over a year, not having any contact with him, serving him in all lawful and legal modes and with him failing to respond, was sufficient to show cause why the divorce should be granted. What do you think? Well, the divorce marked a new beginning for me.

Yet, it seemed my new beginning was short lived. Ironically, his cousins would come to Texas and sometimes stay where I worked.

I recognized them from prior encounters with his family. I am guessing his family got my work information from the divorce decree. I really do not know how they knew where I worked.

His cousin (unaware I knew him) would come to the hotel acting friendly with me to solicit information asking if I was dating and who. Though at that time I was not dating, I never gave him any information. (Note: Around the same time, I would be ran off the road by strangers to and from places.)

Later, Jeff's cousin complained to my manager about me about miscellaneous things I had nothing to do with. I explained to my manager the connection and why this was occurring. She understood and prohibited this person from coming onto the property again.

[I forgot to mention my manager and her husband operated the hotel. Her husband was a retired police officer, so he had connections within law enforcement. So, not many people messed with our hotel.]

After the divorce, I started to date other people since I took the time during the year or so before the divorce to find myself and work on me (so to speak). I consider myself a nice person. I treated everyone very well (pampered may be a better word) and was a loyal individual to my mates.

Well, after divorcing Jeff in August 2001, I met someone, while walking from law school. His name was Sean.

Sean was a gentleman. He gave me his number. So, I called him.

Sean was a Golden Glove boxer and mentored youth in boxing (to keep them off the streets). He also was a church deacon. So, I thought he was the seemingly perfect person for me. But, I later would be wrong.

After one month of dating, Sean became possessive and jealous. He would say things like he saw me one day with another male following me. I was like "really!" (I did not have time for anything but school and work).

Other things he would do was wanting me to pick up the phone on the first ring when he called. I would do it to appease him. (I thought it was a minor request. Why not?)

One day, at my sorority sister's home, Sean called and she overheard his possessive nature. She stated to me it was an unhealthy relationship.

After listening to her concerns, I considered the dating situation with Sean. Seeing this for myself, I later told Sean that we needed take a break from dating.

I learned this is the wrong thing to say to a crazy person. Sean would later stalk and harass me.

He would leave written notes on food wrappers taped on my front car window about "wishing me well with whoever the guy is." Except "guy" would be replaced with an explicit word.

Sean's behavior was pure craziness! This was especially crazy, since there was no one else I was dating. I just needed space to consider the relationship.

Sean followed me to and from work, sometimes sitting outside my apartment or workplace. He would also appear at my job and ask my manager if I was working that day.

My manager asked him did I know him and if I was expecting him. Of course, my manager knew something was strange (and was alerted from a prior occurrence with my ex-husband's cousin) and asked him to leave.

My manager was supportive of me, since she was a survivor of domestic violence too and had five children. She later remarried a man (also my boss) who treated her and her children very well. Her husband was a retired police officer, and was a good guy, who also managed the hotel.

So, they made sure there were certain mechanisms and controls in place at night when I worked. This was to make sure Sean or anyone else who could do harm would be caught or prohibited from doing so.

Chapter 8: The Experimentation of Life

Not having many friends in law school due to Joy's actions and being isolated from the social scene being my law school was in a distant Texan city, I began looking for friends online. In 2002, I also began exploring my sexuality, as I now found myself frequently attracted to females. I met several people online chatting or just hanging out in the online social and gay chat rooms.

Ironically, I met someone who said she was psychic (her name was Umi). She offered free readings to everyone in the chat room. Well, I got a reading from Umi; she was able to pick up everything about me without providing vague information and without asking any questions. Initially, I thought she was in the chat rooms I frequented and she observed my chat information and that is how she picked up things about me.

But, Umi later began telling me things I never mentioned to anyone ever in life and that no one could ever know. No computer information could reveal private information like that.

She strangely stated in her reading that my real father was not who I thought he was and to not trust him. This comment came out of nowhere, as I never asked her anything about anyone in my readings, especially my absentee father.

Umi would then be a pivotal person in revelations she would reveal to me later in my life, which all strangely would happen.

Needless to say, Umi and I connected as friends and I looked up to her like a mother as she was about my mother's age. Despite looking up to her as a mother like figure, Umi would tell me all the time she was proud to be my friend and that she personally knew me. I confided in her for advice about relationships and my life in general.

We continued to IM (instant message) each other whenever we would see each other online. Our friendship grew and we would become virtually best friends. I learned more about her as our friendship went along (like, the fact she was gay).

Umi lived in New Mexico, but traveled all around the world before settling in New Mexico. The interesting thing is that we would become friends for nearly a decade without actually meeting one another.

So, after sometime in law school and feeling isolated and inadequate in my performance in law school (as it was not my best, since I had to work during law school), I decided to seek alternative solutions in my law school performance. I went to a hypnotist. There was an ad I saw posted somewhere that offered help in passing tests.

Don't get me wrong, I was not performing below standards, but for some reason, I never could move pass a certain level. Again, it was not my best. This was even though I had study groups, tutors, practiced on exams, etc.

[On a side note, I will later learn, there were haters against me, because they were jealous of my success. One of these haters was a professor, which explained why I had such a hard time in law school.

This person would cause blockage in my success. So, it was never my performance, as I was a highly intelligent individual and deemed virtually a genius. It was others with the issue and not me].

I am not sure if the hypnotism service worked. But, everything was going well in law school. I was about to graduate and I

BERNICE RATHE

received a job offer in another city. Of course, I immediately accepted the job offer; however, the start date was October 2002 (months before I graduated).

In the meantime, my mother continued to care for Jaime until I could establish myself, since my new job would not start immediately. My mother also thought I needed to get familiar with the new city and my surroundings once I settled into my job.

During this last year in law school, I also met my first girlfriend. Yes, you heard right, girlfriend. I began to test my sexuality.

Amy was her name. She was actually a twin (not identical). I (by chance) met her twin (Ally) online first in a gay chat room. Then, meeting up with Ally, I met Amy (Ally's twin sister). Ironically, both Amy and Ally were gay.

At the time, I was not claiming to be gay, but curious. I simply was looking for exploration. Ally and I were good friends (and nothing else); then, I met her sister, Amy, who came home from college.

Amy and I hit it off instantly. This is where I decided I wanted more than friendship with Amy. She wanted more too.

Well, after exploring my sexuality with a female, I realized I was lesbian. The chemistry was amazing. No, I did not think that I was a man or wanted to change my body sexual organs. I feel that if God gave them to me, it must be for a reason.

At times, I loved dressing tomboyish; then other times, I loved dressing sexy. Many times, when I dressed, no one could tell I was a female (and I was not trying to look like a man). Other times, I looked so young and attractive, people thought I was younger than I was and no one would ever think I was a lesbian.

I forgot to mention the obvious: the sex was off the chain! I felt this is what I was missing. I never had issues with sex (no matter if with a man or woman). I am very comfortable sexually and intimately as well as in relationships. In fact, I have a high sex drive.

Being from a large family, clearly, I have tendencies for a high sex drive. However, I am a lady in the public (and you know the rest; I will keep this PG). I was not and am not a person who kisses then tells. I love discretion, don't you?

I think if I was a man, I probably would have produced many (and I mean many) children. But, of course, by one woman!

BERNICE RATHE

In terms of my relationships, I was very nice to all my partners in any relationships I had (past or present). I pampered those in my intimate life. Some of my friends thought I was too nice and at times naive.

Throughout my relationships, no matter if with a male or female, besides love being the obvious answer, one of the keys to a good relationship is finding that person who will accept you as you are with all of your issues and tolerate your issues and be there for you and vice versa. No matter what someone says, everyone has issues and everyone comes with some type of baggage. No one is perfect.

I found that lesbian relationships were comfortable but complicated. Lesbians were even more controlling and possessive at times than some men. No, seriously!

There is this thing in the lesbian community called the U-Haul syndrome (if you want to call it that). When I first dated Amy, I did not identify this "syndrome" with Amy. But, it was alive and in effect. Amy met me and she wanted to move in.

Though this syndrome was in effect (with me being unaware of it), dating Amy was fun and adventurous. We traveled, partied and socialized together, and we knew how to give each other space. I even brought her home and introduced her to my mama and family in Georgia.

This is when I came out to my family. It was a shocker, but not really. One of my uncles was gay, so my family was already accustomed to the gay culture and "coming out." So, it was more of "an acceptance because we love you and want you to be happy" vibe.

As time went on, Amy became very controlling and possessive. For example, Amy and I went to the movies. After the movies ended, Amy asked if I knew a tall, slender female because she had been following us from the movies to our apartment and other places around the city days before. I told Amy she was imagining things and that I don't know anyone here, other than a few law students or work buddies, who Amy all knew.

Amy insisted that I was lying. I don't know what got into Amy, but she was out of control in her behavior. So, I told her to sleep on the sofa for that night, since we were in intense conflict. She, of course, refused.

Amy threw my fish tank on the floor. The tank had meaning for me, as it had expensive fish inside it and was given as a gift to me. Amy knew that it was a gift to me from a friend.

In all the chaos caused by Amy, the tank shattered and water was everywhere. I tried saving the fish. Meanwhile, Amy then proceeded to go to the kitchen.

Amy pulled out a knife and threatened me. I screamed and yelled trying to get away from her, as she was approaching me with the knife appearing to harm me.

Luckily, my downstairs neighbors saw water running from their ceiling, heard the arguments, and ran upstairs to my apartment. My door was open since Amy never locked the door. (I guess Amy was so upset she merely came into the apartment and began arguing with me.).

The police came immediately. My downstairs neighbor apparently already called the police prior to entering my apartment as they were concerned something happened to me.

Amy still tried harming me, even in front of my neighbors. So, my neighbors stood in front of me so that Amy wouldn't hurt me. My neighbors possibly saved my life that night.

Bea Giovanni

Because my neighbors heard the arguments and were present (for the most part) when Amy tried harming, the officer arrested Amy for Assault with a Deadly Weapon. She would later face Assault with a Deadly Weapon charge in court.

I need not tell you that I broke up with Amy from that point. I also stopped talking to Ally, since I would naturally have to bump into Amy or have some sort of contact with Amy via Ally. The court also made Amy permanently stay away from me. Plus, the court ordered Amy to undergo counseling for her anger and placed other probationary requirements on her.

I moved to another city, since I was about to graduate and start my new job in another city. Well, Amy moved back to her hometown, which was also the city of my new job. Ironically (and I guess life has a way at doing this), I discovered my job was a block away from Amy's mother's home. This was not by my design or doing.

I didn't know anything about the firm (remember this is the same job offer mentioned earlier). I actually applied for the job months before graduation per a legal newspaper ad I saw; there was no other information other than the ad information and fax number.

The firm's interview was in a downtown restaurant; in fact, they paid for lunch, and simply talked to me and never really interviewed me. The firm's partners had a different style in selecting candidates and I liked it. They liked me so much they held a second interview and paid for lunch again.

The firm was small yet a long-standing firm with three attorneys but I enjoyed my experience. So, there was not much online about the firm.

Having graduated from law school at age 24, I worked as a first year associate/paralegal. They did not pay me well, since it was a small firm. But, I gained some great experience.

The partners were old school and handled all sorts of matters. The firm's reputation was well known, representing the "street" (so to speak), having street cred. People viewed the partners as some of the best attorneys in the city. So, no one messed with them or me because I worked for the best.

The firm was small but not small-minded, with the exception of this older female secretary. She was jealous of me, and she was jealous of another female secretary. She was so jealous of us where the partners had to tell her to stop the silly antics with myself and the other female employee. Both I and the other secretary were close because she understood exactly what I was going through.

Despite that, I enjoyed my experience but I did not enjoy going to work. The reason (for me not enjoying going to work) had nothing to do with the firm, but more to do with the fact that Amy finished her probationary requirements and the court dropped the charge (since it was her first time in trouble). Therefore, with no restrictions placed on her, Amy knew I worked in the area (since I got the job during the time of our relationship).

Plus, Amy stayed with her mother, whose house was 2 blocks away from the law firm. Go figure! How convenient, right? To state the obvious, Amy would visit me at my job.

Amy knew gummy bears were my favorite candy, so she would come to my job and bring me gummy bears. I refused them and always told her to leave me alone. She would leave flowers on my car and she tried several times to apologize. But, I accepted neither the flowers nor the apology. I just wanted to move on with my life.

Eventually, Amy got the picture (at least I thought so). Well, I began dating another female (named Paula). I met Paula on a phone dating chat phone service. She lived in Arkansas, which was very close to my home and job in Texas.

Everything worked well between Paula and me. I met Paula's mother, who she cared for, and Paula's son. Paula was independent and had her own place and worked.

Paula was bisexual and had a son from a previous relationship. (Though I had a child and were divorced, once I came out, I maintained my status as a lesbian and did not claim I was bisexual; but, everyone has their own road in finding themselves too).

At that time, Jaime still was living with my mother, since I was still getting my feet wet and establishing myself, especially since my salary was very low. Paula and I dated for several months and our relationship got serious.

We stayed at each other's homes every other night. So, virtually, we were together every day and night.

I was in the process of bringing Jaime to Texas. I thought things couldn't get any better. Well, in August 2003, the firm's financial issues led them to lay me off and several other staff. So, this delayed Jaime's move to Texas, since obviously my money situation was not certain.

I tried finding work in Arkansas near Paula. While I was seeking work in Arkansas, guess who I see? Amy! Yes!

She moved to Arkansas (and in the same city as Paula). I thought this must be a coincidence. Amy stated she took a job in Arkansas and was dating. Amy gave me her number and address but I never contacted Amy. I just wanted to be done with her, as another chapter in my life.

This did not happen. I kept bumping into Amy around Arkansas and Texas. Again, I thought it was coincidence.

Then, I noticed (what I thought I saw) Amy sitting outside Paula's home. It was creepy. I told Paula about it and Paula said she remembered her face from somewhere too.

Paula brought up a dating site where one of Paula's friends remembered telling Paula that some girl on the dating site was stalking several females. Paula showed me the profile and it was my ex-girlfriend, Amy.

BERNICE RATHE

Someone had either created or changed Amy's profile to "IAMASTALKER."

If this was true that Amy was a stalker, she needed mental help. Hesitant in contacting Amy, I told Amy about these rumors of stalking females on a dating site; yet, Amy said she was dating someone.

But, I was not so sure as to what Amy was stating, considering the rumors of Amy stalking females, Amy moving to Arkansas (to the same city where Paula resides) and Amy and I previous dating history where she attempted to assault me. This is, in addition, to the fact that I thought I saw Amy sitting in front of Paula's home.

I just thought "why me?" At that point, I was tired of people stalking me.

Neither Amy nor Paula knew about my previous instances where male dating partners stalked me. I just couldn't understand what was going on with these people. Was it something I was doing to make them stalk me? If so, I wanted to find out what, so I can stop doing it. Seriously!

Paula ignored Amy's stalking and antics, but I did not. I asked Amy to stop it or I would report her to the police. After that time, Amy appeared to stop stalking me.

Amy eventually moved back to Texas months later then back to another city in Arkansas, which I learned from her sister, Ally, who frequently emailed me. Yet, I never responded to Ally.

(Remember I actually cut all contact with Ally and Amy because of Amy's threatening behavior in the past. But, Ally continued to email me, but she eventually stopped after seeing I was not responding.)

Meanwhile, Paula and I continued happily in our relationship for some time. I bought a used car for her, since she didn't have a reliable car. But I discovered she didn't have a license.

Apparently, she had been driving illegally for years. So, Paula and I agreed she couldn't get the car until she got a valid license within 6 months or else I would use the car.

In fall 2003, I met new friends. One was a male friend name Tommy. He was actually bisexual and the first bisexual male I met. (I always met gay guys but not bisexual. So, my friendship with Tommy was unique.)

Tommy was a cool dude and came from a good family. His mother was a doctor and his father was a retired teacher. Tommy's sister and I were close; his sister later became a reality TV star on a weight loss show.

After some time in being friends with Tommy, I later learned from his mother and his sister Tommy had issues. When I say Tommy had issues, he had issues. Tommy's mother and his sister informed me he had a compulsive disorder. But, at that time, these issues did not impact our friendship.

But, as our friendship progressed, Tommy displayed suspect, stalking behaviors. Later, my suspicions were correct.

Tommy was stalking one of his female acquaintances, as authorities caught him doing it. This resulted in several convictions of stalking and other crimes for Tommy. Because he had a diagnosed compulsive disorder (apparently his entire life) and didn't have any offenses on his record, the court gave him probation, ordering him to stay away from the victim and to attending extensive counseling.

I just couldn't seem to understand why I was attracting crazy people. Was it something I was doing? Was it because I was subconsciously thinking this is what I was worth or whether this is all I know (which is being stalked or destructive relationships)? I really did not know.

In the meantime, Paula became jealous of my friendship with Tommy. She started to venture out of the relationship. She cheated on me and I caught her in the act of doing it.

One day while Paula was in the shower, the phone rang and I answered as in any normal day. Well, the same phone dating service, we used to meet each other, called and stated Paula had a message in her mailbox.

I figured she closed the account, since we had been together for almost 2 years. However, I guessed wrong.

When you get one of these phone chat rings, the service provides the profile number in its message when it calls the recipient's number. So, I dialed the dating service and entered the profile number. Guess who I hear?

It was Paula's voice on the profile and she stated "Hey, this is P, I am looking for a girl I can hang out with, go to the club, and #$%k every now and again. Hit me up, if you like what you hear!"

After listening to the profile message, I was thinking "What da f%^k?"

BERNICE RATHE

I wanted to think the best in Paula, since we were together for some time. I again figured that it was her old profile and it was not deactivated.

Yet, interestingly, the service also can tell you when the last time the account holder logged into the account. So, I listened to the email to find out when was the last activity on this profile.

Apparently, Paula's last activity was the night before the service called. It was the same night we were together. Again, I was amazed and in disbelief Paula would do this to me.

I thought everything was going fine. Our sex life was amazing (at least I thought so). We were explorers in the bed and had sex on a regular basis with no reservations or hesitations. I later realized Paula was just plain promiscuous.

I never was that kind of person. If I date you or marry you, that is it, no one else. I treat my body like a temple and the only one to enter that temple would be my mate.

I approached Paula about it in a calm and non-assuming manner. I asked Paula if she still had a profile on the phone dating service and she paused, with a hesitant look on her face, and said "no."

With suspicion, I stated that is strange because the phone dating service just called and stated there was a message. Paula replied, "I don't have a profile on there."

Again, with suspicion, I stated that is strange because I called the phone dating service and entered the account number and your voice appears on the profile. I stated to her "You stated, "Hey, this is P, I am looking for a girl I can hang out with, go to the club, and #$%k every now and again. Hit me up, if you like what you hear!" and P is your nickname."

In serious disappointment, I told Paula it was over and I was packing my things going back to my apartment in Texas. Paula tried stopping me and said it wasn't over and I wasn't going anywhere. She hit me with a pool stick and I tried fighting back.

Paula's mother came into the room and pinned me down on the bed preventing me from defending myself while Paula beat me. Paula's son cried out for me then (and only then) Paula and her mother stopped. The beating lasted 3 to 4 minutes until her son came into room.

I immediately left and called 911, as I was bruised, beaten and bloodied. I also called Paula's friend, Rebecca, who stayed minutes from Paula's home. I also called Tommy.

I explained to Rebecca what happened. Rebecca was in disbelief and said "don't get back with Paula; she is no good for you." Rebecca came to Paula's home to be with me while the cops arrived.

Rebecca was so mad at Paula and her mother. Rebecca ended her friendship with them that day.

After telling Tommy what happened, he wanted to come to Arkansas and kick Paula and her mother's (should I say what he wanted to kick). I discouraged Tommy from doing it, since I knew Tommy would do it (Tommy was crazy like that, especially when it came to people messing with Jaime or me; we were like siblings).

I told Tommy I would be fine. I just needed someone to talk to. In short, I already decided it was over.

Tommy was supportive. He suggested as well as Rebecca to seek criminal charges against Paula and her mother. So, with Tommy as moral support and with visibly bruises on my face and body, Tommy and I went to the local Arkansas DA's office. I explained to the Assistant DA I wished to seek criminal charges against my ex-girlfriend and her mother for what they done to me a day earlier.

The Assistant DA was very hostile towards me and told me to "get out her office with that gay bullsh$t!" I was in tears, as I did not understand why she was not listening to me. I realized being a lesbian classified me as a minority, an undesirable, and not entitled to equal protection under the law.

The Assistant DA never considered the situation. I was not even in her office for 3 minutes. After I stated "ex-girlfriend," the DA did not want to hear anything else.

Days later, I took my car back from Paula to secure it, since she was an unlicensed driver and couldn't use the car until then. Plus, my name was on the car's registration.

To avoid any further conflict with Paula, Tommy and I waited until Paula fell asleep. Tommy drove the car back, while I drove my personal vehicle.

When Paula woke up in the morning, she called me and had some interesting words to tell me. After taking the vehicle back, I thought that was the end of my experience with Paula.

BERNICE RATHE

To say the least, I tried moving on the best way I could, as most break-ups are not easy in a person's life especially when you were the one wronged and, again, harmed. So, the best way (at that time) I knew how was to date.

PART TWO

Chapter 9: One Piece Comes Together

The dating scene seemed very good for me after leaving Paula. I began working in the capacity of an attorney with a local Texas City attorney's office, and I moved back to my apartment in Texas.

Even though not licensed as an attorney at that time, a state law allowed me to practice law without a license. My title was different, but I performed all functions of an assistant city attorney. I was one of the youngest in a prosecutorial role in the nation at that time at age 25.

I also got a part-time job as an adjunct at a private college. I made sure I had additional income as I was saving for Jaime to arrive.

However, just when I thought things were going great, in my adjunct role at the private college, I began experiencing some very uncomfortable situations with some students who disagreed with everything in the course. They didn't know effectively how to agree to disagree.

The students disagreed with the textbook, the course readings, and assignments (when I had no control over the syllabus and course offerings as the school dictated those things). There were also students who wanted an A without earning it and would complain until someone gave them an A, though rare for anyone to override the adjunct's grades.

But, uncomfortable situations I encountered for not these disagreements but the hostile ones. Some students were hostile and other students saw this. Apparently, unknown to me, there was a group of students in my class, who declared to other students they were a part of extremist and militia groups and were recruiting.

These same students, declaring their allegiance to these extremist and militia groups, stated to other students they would harm me because they just didn't like me. But the real motivation was the extremist and militia group's mission and bias towards certain individuals: minorities.

Well, some students blew the whistle on the students who claimed to be a part of these groups. There were a group of students who went to school administration to inform the school of this extremist activity and the threats made to my life.

Unaware of any of this, I noticed close security detail around me on several occasions. Yet, I never really took the security detail as anything but normal, since I was teaching at night and security detail would frequent the parking lots. But, apparently, the school took the students' concerns seriously, since the school wanted to maintain security and safety for everyone on campus and connected with the school.

I later left the school because of a lack of diversity and hostility of some students (where safety was just too uncertain for me and I would later learn much of the hostility came from the extremist activity on campus). In addition, I could no longer "moonlight" as the city attorney's office required me to be more active in the city affairs.

At that time, I still did not have Jaime with me. I needed to save for Jaime's move to Texas. So, I put an ad online seeking a short-term roommate.

In fall 2003, I accepted the only response, a lesbian from New Hampshire, named Heather. What a coincidence! (Keep this in back of your mind as it will relate later).

Heather was moving to Texas to be closer to her ex-girlfriend, a girls' high school basketball coach. Heather was a part-time sports tutor. She stated she had a job with a sports company that had positions in my area. I thought this was a good fit, since both of us were lesbian.

I did not charge very much rent for a room and utilities. Basically, she got a room with utilities paid for less than half the rent. It amounted to no more than $300. Most people thought I should have charged more but I was merely trying to save money.

Fall approached and Heather moved to Texas. It was an interesting experience living with Heather.

As the roommate situation progressed, I learned a lot about Heather. For instance, she had a communications degree. Heather also had family in Latin America and spoke fluent Spanish.

Things appeared to be looking up for me. I met a lesbian who was a few years older than myself, named Lori. Apparently, Lori was in the midst of a divorce from her husband. So, I was her "first" girlfriend.

Bea Giovanni

I did not know if Lori was experimenting with her sexuality or truly lesbian. So, I was cautious. I later found Lori was truly lesbian, but it took a long time to figure that out, since Lori always appeared to have bisexual tendencies (if this makes sense).

Lori was sexy yet interesting. For instance, Lori had a weird thing about cats. She gave her cats formal first, middle and last names and insured them. She thought one day cats would rule the world and needed formal names to enter the world. Interesting, right?

Needless to say, I overlooked her weirdness about cats. Lori and I enjoyed each other's company visiting some of the finest restaurants. I loved fine dining and she did too. The sex was not the best, since she was still new to the "gay thing" and exploring her sexuality. Plus, she was somewhat closed-minded.

However, I was there for her and really enjoyed her company.

When I met Lori, her husband moved out their home and began living with his girlfriend. Lori and her husband had a company together, so she was winding down the company. Lori also got a roommate to cut costs for herself.

However, something strange occurred after the roommate moved into the home. Lori stated while she was sleeping overnight at my apartment, her roommate allowed a government agent (or least that is what the roommate stated to Lori) into her home to "search and look around."

Lori was floored and rightfully so. The agent would not tell the roommate what it was about, but stated if the roommate did not allow the agent into the home "it would be trouble for the roommate." So, the roommate obeyed the agent's orders.

Lori and her roommate neither knew why the agent came around and into the home nor what the agent wanted or did. Lori thought it could be something connected to her husband's business dealings. But, she was still unable to locate the agent's identity, since the agent never left any information or identified himself to the roommate.

Moving forward with her life, Lori's divorce was later finalized and she moved out her home, since the home was sold. Lori found another place.

Months into dating Lori, guess who comes back into my life? Paula, my ex, from Arkansas! After I broke up with Paula, I stop taking her calls, since she was trying to get back with me (I never responded and never entertained Paula on those notions). In fact, I changed my number.

I had no problem with changing my numbers. It was a matter of giving my new number to my friends and family. So, she couldn't contact me via phone. Therefore, I thought I was done with Paula.

How she came back into my life was being persistent. Paula sat on my doorstep and waited for my arrival almost every day until I would talk to her. My roommate, Heather, let Paula in the apartment one day as well. However, my roommate did not know the history behind Paula and me.

After talking to Paula (I, being nice to Paula, and not offending her), she explained she wanted to be friends and see if we could work from there. I told her I didn't need any more friends. Of course, Paula explained she didn't want to end on a bad note with me.

So, I gave her a chance at friendship, but I told her there were no guarantees on anything else, especially as I was dating someone. (Paula looked as if I was lying to her about dating someone else.).

I never told Paula about Lori specifically by name. I only told Paula I was dating someone because I am a private person and I don't like sharing personal details with an ex-flame. Again, Paula never took that information seriously.

I told Lori that Paula re-entered my life (as a friend, of course). Surprisingly, Lori wasn't insecure at all. Lori had no issue with this. I really liked that about Lori, as she was a mature individual who knew how to handle conflict and trusted me.

Over a series of months, I found myself in a dilemma. This was because Paula didn't want to be a friend anymore. So, she forced me to choose as to who I wanted to be with.

Lori was secure with herself and our relationship. Lori knew I wouldn't stray or cheat on her, since this was not in my nature. But, I knew I had to choose in order to eliminate the dilemma, but which one?

I had a history with Paula and the sex was great; yet, none of my friends thought she was good enough for me. Lori was perfect, but I was her first (and likely wouldn't be her last). Plus, Lori was too passive and the sex was not great.

Bea Giovanni

I eventually chose Paula because of our history and I was able to forgive Paula for the past. How come? At the time, I was very forgiving. But, I really wanted Paula to be strictly a friend.

You see I typically would cut people off if our relationships end, whereas a friendship lasts forever with me (if you didn't cross me). So, for me, being friends with Paula was the best solution.

Don't ask me why I was like that; I just wanted to end that part of my life and move on. Basically, I wanted Paula as a friend forever. But, I did not really want to lose either person. Moreover, I knew I couldn't have both of them as girlfriends (if I could, trust me, I would). Despite this, Lori and I remain good friends.

Lori had no issue with being friends or with me moving on with Paula. Lori was mature and appreciated my friendship. Obviously, a relationship with Lori would have been better but that was the best I could do with the situation at that time to maintain my integrity and friendship with her, as I am not and was not a cheater.

From that point, I set clear expectations from the start of a friendship or relationship. Also, most of my friends enjoyed my friendship and did not want to ruin the friendship with an intimate relationship.

Heather and Tommy thought I was a 'mac,' but I wasn't. Though I am gay, they said they understood why both sexes liked me. They fashioned me as a good person who treated people well, humble, discreet when needed, fun, charismatic and was hot too when I wanted to be.

At one point, I thought Heather liked me. But, it could have been something else too, which I later connected.

Heather would frequently ask where I was heading, who will be with me, and what time I planned to return home. Heather insisted on me giving her this information. Sometimes, Heather would force her way into going with me wherever I was going and with my friends, including Lori or Paula.

I would sometimes made jokes to Heather about her following me and having police and helicopters follow me to make sure I am going to where I said I would be going (not knowing at the time, I was on to something with that line of jokes).

What was also strange about Heather was that she drove a 4-door vehicle with a Department of Defense (DoD) sticker on the front window and did not work for DoD (at least that is what she told me). (Note: the DoD is the world's largest employer, meaning there are thousands contracted or employed with the DoD).

Out of curiosity and being I never saw a DoD sticker like hers, I asked Heather did she work for the DoD or ever worked for the DoD. She hesitated and stated her brother worked for the DoD and that it was his vehicle and not hers. But, her story didn't add up because she had told me months earlier the vehicle was hers.

Heather was also very secretive about her belongings. She had a microwave like device in her room, but she seemed never to use it. It was near the wall to the adjoining wall of my bedroom.

Again, I never thought about it being suspect or weird. Though I had a microwave in the kitchen for our use, I thought her device was for warming food or had an extra microwave for her usage.

On some occasions, Heather would spark conversations about my father. It was always weird to me that she asked about my father, since no one, not even I, ever mentioned him. A conversation about my father was the farthest thing on my mind or as a conversation topic, since I didn't know him and he was not a part of my life.

She would ask about whether I knew him, why I don't know him, what was his name, does he call me, what he does for me, etc. I told her the same thing I told everyone else for years, which is he was never in my life and he always denied me as his child.

I also stated I didn't know my father other than the 3 months I stayed with him and I had no more than 3 to 4 total hours of conversation with him in my entire life. This was the truth about my relationship (or lack of a relationship) with my so-called "father" (if you want to call him that).

Again, I never connected any of Heather's questions about my father, the microwave like device and her persistence in knowing my whereabouts at all times, other than being a noisy person and having a microwave in her room.

Spring 2004, Heather went back to New Hampshire. I did not hear from her until a month later. Heather called me because she left a part to her juicing machine at my apartment. Then, she emailed her New Hampshire mailing address to mail the item.

This would be the last contact with Heather until 5 years later in summer 2009, where I would strangely see Heather in my hometown in Georgia, following me in a vehicle with a DoD decal. Coincidence? Who knows?

But, what I would learn is that my life denotes there are no coincidences. I would find Heather would be a key piece in proving my father's ties, these groups and their acts of terrorism against me and the government, corruption and certain parts of the government's ties, dating back since my birth and possibly before that time.

BERNICE RATHE

Chapter 10: And Another Piece

Things were going well in my city government job. I was ready to move Jaime to Texas. However, I had to wait until I got time off to do so, since Jaime couldn't travel by herself, being that she was a very young minor, and it made no financial sense to buy airline tickets for my mama to fly her to Texas and leave, while my mama missed valuable time at work.

Plus, I had to be more aggressive in my savings, as I was required to live closer to the city job. My original apartment was about 1 hour away from my city employment. This caused me to rent short-term housing to satisfy employment conditions.

I loved my city government job. Though not licensed, I received a decent pay rate for an entry-level city attorney position, though I was lowest paid in my department for my position because I had the least experience. But, there were expected pay increases in each year of service.

Bea Giovanni

One of the things I really did not get it was the assignment of offices. I also had the ugly office with no window. I guess this was a part of the hazing process of the new person on the block (so to speak).

I was amazed at the pay difference between my pay rate and a new attorney hired after me. His name was Chad and he was a former military JAG officer and used to work in the state's AG office. So, they played him 60K with benefits (starting salary, with pay raises after the probationary period).

Some attorneys who worked at the city attorney's office for many years did not get that amount. I would later connect many other aspects as to the presence of this person that was so timely after my hire date and why he was paid more than other attorneys.

The city attorney, Jill, assigned everyone specific caseloads, committee assignments, city requests and jury week rotation (since everyone had to do jury rotation and handle trials). Jill assigned me to a series of cases that no one wanted to take.

These cases appeared to be frivolous and insignificant (but, later, I learned they were not). Most people wanted the easy cases where it took less time and less work than other matters.

I took the cases and performed the necessary work (serving at the pleasure of the City Attorney). Well, these series of cases were complaints by minority city workers alleging that Caucasian city workers (in particular, police, fire, and street maintenance workers) were harassing, stalking, intimidating and threatening minority workers on and off the job.

The investigation was lengthy. The city attorney helped me with the investigation when she could, as I was interviewing entire departments and transcribing these interviews, while I drafted and generated a comprehensive 150-page internal investigative report. It took almost one year to complete the investigation (to do it right).

While the investigation continued, these alleged Caucasian workers were continuing to "rack up" complaints against them by minority workers. At the same time, minority workers were being threatened and intimidated on the job with use of racial slurs, Nazi and other hate-related symbols placed on city vehicles. It got so bad the media came, investigated and aired an exclusive report on it.

Bea Giovanni

Some examples include a Caucasian lesbian firefighter who complained about the tampering of her equipment and that someone tried killing her by intentionally trapping her in a burning building (after a fire investigation revealed so). African American and Latino workers complained certain Caucasian workers in personal and city vehicles (not performing their city duties) were following, stalking and harassing the minority workers during work hours and after hours in the community. They also complained qualified minority workers were receiving denials for mandated promotions.

The city didn't know how to effectively handle these complaints. Some Caucasian workers even admitted to doing some of these acts and they didn't care who knew. As they stated, "they were protected by the union."

There were even allegations of fraud, waste, and corruption in some departments. Workers alleged some workers were encouraged to harass and stalk workers and other community members, primarily of minority background (race, sexual orientation, gender, etc.). There were allegations workers were using city vehicles and equipment to do side jobs not connected to the city, and that some workers wouldn't even work but remain at home while clocking time and getting paid to do so.

Eventually, this forced the city to hire outside investigators to catch these offenders in the act. No one, other than myself, the city attorney, the mayor, and his staff, knew about the outside investigators.

Surprise, surprise! The city and investigators caught these workers in the act of committing harassment, stalking, intimidation, fraud and other things. What was also surprising was these workers were also stalking and intimidating public officials on local and state levels (and possibly on the federal level as well). Some of these public officials had no idea until the outside investigators were involved in this investigation.

These workers were very organized and they used electronic devices that provided location and private information into these people's and the officials' lives. The investigation led to uncovering more connections, which blew the case wide open.

These workers were connected to extremist, military, militia, radical, hate, and anti-government groups. Could you imagine these groups working in the public sector with access to sensitive systems and data and the ability to facilitate their group's agenda and the public trusting these individuals in uniform and with power and immunity to do whatever they wanted without question or accountability?

The city thought it was an isolated issue. So, the city settled quietly with the minority workers. However, later the city learned it was not an isolated issue. These groups were doing this stuff everywhere.

From this investigation, I performed so well on the investigation that there were rumors circulating someone was considering me for a judgeship or eventually a higher Assistant City Attorney position. I confided in a coworker named Holly about these rumors, since she used to be a judge prior to entering employment with the city.

Holly appeared to be bitter about her previous employment. She stated that politics forced her out of a judgeship, among other reasons. Holly discouraged me from taking any job with the city and encouraged to take stay in my position and be happy. Holly also began to get closer to me and began asking about my father and who he was.

BERNICE RATHE

I was not sure why she asked this, but I stated to her the same thing I have with everyone else. Other than the three months I stayed with my father and his family in high school, I don't really know my father and he have always denied I was his child.

At the time, I was preparing to take the bar exam. I purchased the prep courses and attended every session. I passed the prep course. I knew I was ready for the bar exam. So, I took the winter bar examination.

A week later, Holly suggested I get a detailed physical exam from her doctor, as her doctor, Dr. Sylvia Newton, was taking new clients (and I just got my benefits activated with the city). So, I did so.

Dr. Newton asked me how I knew Holly; I stated we work together in the city attorney's office. Dr. Newton stated I looked very young to be an attorney or even work at any attorney's office. I told Dr. Newton I get that all time, but I am employed with the city in the city attorney's office.

The doctor provided a comprehensive exam and suggested that I take certain medications. For what? I don't know.

I asked the doctor why and she stated that I was possibly working too hard and needed medications to ease the stress. This is even though I had no complaints on stress, sleep or anything else, and my tests did not indicate anything to the contrary.

I followed the doctor's orders and filled the prescriptions and took them. I later uncovered that these medications were for anxiety and depression and a sleep aid. I immediately stop taking those medications after learning about these medications.

I again asked the doctor why I needed to take these medications. Dr. Newton stated they were standard medications, which they were not. I never went back to Dr. Newton.

Years later, I think I learned why Dr. Newton did this. Dr. Newton had ulterior motives (that I later uncovered in 2009). I did not need any medications, as nothing was wrong with me.

In late spring 2004, I got my state bar results back and it stated I failed. I requested my scores, and it appeared that my essay scores were very low, even though my tutor checked and reviewed my answers and stated my answers were correct. I just chalked it up and decided to take it again. I thought many people fail the bar exam subsequent times so I was no exception.

My employment ended, along with everyone due to budget cuts, except Holly's employment. But, I would later find the stalking and harassment by government workers was not so isolated, as I became a target of similar harassment by other fire and police professionals.

After relocating back to my original apartment, which was an hour away from the Texas City Attorney's office, I began seeing Holly near my apartment building. I knew it was Holly, since, in the past, I rode with Holly in Holly's vehicle while working with her in the city attorney's office. Plus, she had a bumper sticker that stated something like "I am a proud parent of a military member."

Back to the point, I lived in a fairly closed-end apartment complex and everyone knew everyone and his or her guests. So, at first, I thought it was coincidence. Maybe Holly knew someone at my building?

But, then I would see Holly and a passenger in her car tailgating my car and laughing while driving off quickly. This occurred several times during the following months after my lay-off, with either Holly alone or with a passenger traveling an hour away from her home to my area. At the time, I never thought anything of these occurrences.

Also, en route to job interviews or looking for employment, I frequently noticed vehicles with firefighter or fire association stickers on the vehicles following me. Additionally, fire trucks, ambulance vehicles or police vehicles that would seemingly have an emergency, but there was either no emergency or shortly after would simply be going in the same direction and possibly to a business or side street where I was heading. These vehicles, not in an emergency, would sometimes cut me off. Sometimes, these vehicles caused dangerous situations and conditions for me and others on the road.

For instance, one day while driving, for no reason and out of nowhere, a vehicle with a firefighter sticker intentionally hit me causing significant damage on my vehicle's passenger side. The police officer that came to the scene of the accident asked for the other vehicle's registration and other information.

But, ironically, the person driving the vehicle was not the owner and did not have the information. So, the officer ordered the vehicle's owner to the scene to make sure the vehicle was properly registered and the driver had authorization to drive the vehicle.

BERNICE RATHE

Again, I never thought anything of these occurrences at all.

Shortly thereafter, Holly would become a judge, which was the same rumored position I was to fill. Read between the lines. Again, I never thought anything of these things. Keep this in mind as things get a bit more interesting.

My mama's health was getting worse and I could no longer allow my mama to forego her health to care for Jaime. So, I moved Jaime to Texas with me. However, in the meantime, I remained unemployed and unable to find suitable employment after working for the city. So, I collected unemployment benefits.

I even applied to retrain in a different profession. I tried attending medical assisting school, but I couldn't continue since I couldn't find suitable daycare services and I did not have sufficient funds to pay for daycare services.

But, never was beneath me, since I was just looking for work to pay bills and not necessarily status. I had friends who thought WTF! My friends thought I went to law school and ended up going to medical assisting school. They could not understand why I could not find a job.

But, I was not licensed and took the bar several times and failed. The economy was bad. These things prevented me from gainful employment. Well, at least that is what I thought.

Around that time, I left Paula because she seemed to be very negative and jealous. These things created a very uncomfortable and controlling relationship for me.

However, Lori and I always remained good friends, while she dated others. I encouraged her to date other people. Yet, I actually thought that Lori never really dated anyone (even though she said she was).

Lori was loyal to me, to our friendship and to past relationship. Lori was a nice person. She still had feelings for me.

A month or two later after leaving Paula, once I woke up in the morning, I realized that someone slashed all four tires on my car. A note was left on my apartment door in Paula's handwriting (admitting she did it). I also recalled receiving a phone call from Paula (the night before) threatening me.

I made a police report, but the police stated they couldn't arrest her because she lived in Arkansas and not Texas. Tommy heard about it and wanted to kick Paula's (I leave it up to your imagination). But, I told him not to do that. What I can say about Paula is that karma came around to her.

Years later, I discovered that Paula had some run-ins with the law and had turbulent relationships and horrible job situations after she damaged my property. I realized that Paula simply didn't want to move on from our relationship. She was a violent person, which I was not a violent person. I knew how to move on from relationships without violence and other negative acts.

For whatever reason, I never had an issue with moving on from situations. Cutting off situations, people, or things is natural to me. However, I guess it is not natural to everyone.

Meanwhile, life moved on and I was still unemployed. I was encouraged to apply to the federal government for a Special Agent and related positions with the FBI, DEA, and CIA. I immediately applied.

At that time, I thought this is right up my alley. I would perform well in those positions and I could give back via public service.

The government employment process typically takes a long time. However, the government got back to me in no time. They streamlined the employment process for me, since I applied for several positions with the federal government.

I completed all stages in the employment process in no time, including panel interviews, polygraphs, background investigations, medical examination, but not the mental examination. It was told to me the examination will be scheduled for another time.

I took initial examinations with the DEA field office for the DEA Special Agent position. The initial examination involved identifying as many details on a drug arrest from a video.

Apparently, one of the agents grading the examination stated I was one point shy of making the mark. Another agent disagreed and stated I actually got all details except one detail from the answer key and that I only needed to make a score of 80%. The agent stated I scored very well and it was one of the best the office had seen in a long time. Nevertheless, I did not pass go (the first agent who graded it said I failed).

Before I left the DEA office, I overheard the first agent, who graded my examination, state to the other agent that higher ups in D.C. did not like me. Interesting, right?

BERNICE RATHE

In my panel interviews for these positions, which were two separate interviews, the panel members asked non-related job questions. At the time, the panelists stated this relates to my employment application and is standard to ask. The questions were primarily about my father.

Again, as I explained to everyone else. Other than the three months in high school living with my father and his family, I did not know my father and he had denied me as his child.

The panel members would express gratitude and appreciation that I was pursuing government employment. They even stated I was the perfect candidate and wanted me. However, they had some lingering questions as to my father, as their initial investigation highlighted some issues there. I did not know what they were talking about. But, they assured me that there was no issue with me but with other people in my life.

The panel informed me of the next phase and that they will be investigating my background, including family members, friends, my employment history, etc. They also told me not to tell anyone I applied for any government position.

Months later, my father called me. I was shocked to hear from him, especially after not having contacting with me in many years, and because he expressed he did not care about me and I was not his child. He stated this to others and me in the past.

I asked him how he got my number. He stated my grandma provided the number.

My father asked me if I was applying for a government job. I asked him why and he stated, "Some man in a 4-door vehicle dog tailed him for miles." My father explained the man stated he was investigating my background, which included an investigation on any relevant person in my life (past or present) because I applied for a government job and needed to speak with my father. I stated, "Yes, I applied."

Weeks later, I had close friends contacting me about the government seeking to interview them relative to investigating my background for a government job. Then, my older half-brother (on my father's side), Travis, who I don't know, called me about the same thing.

I don't know how Travis got my number, but I think my father gave him my number. At the time, it seemed they were somewhat confused and scared at the same time, since they never went through something like that.

While the investigation commenced, I completed the polygraph examination and the examiner stated I passed all questions except one that related to drug usage. At that time, the government had a rule against any applicant who had drug usage in the last three years (recreational or not).

I stated I smoked marijuana once or twice in my life over 4 years before the polygraph exam. I explained it was months after I graduated from law school. During that time, I hung out with local hip-hop artists in the basement studio, rapping and arranging music.

I also explained I played a game with my friend, Ally, and her friends called "Shady Hearts." It was a game of truth or dare. The dare was to smoke marijuana. That was the only time I did so.

One FBI agent heard about the polygraph exam results and encouraged me to appeal the results to Quantico, VA. The FBI agent helped me appeal it to Quantico, but it did not change anything.

Bea Giovanni

So, despite going through all phases of the employment, the process appeared to have stopped because the one question on the polygraph examination. I received a nice rejection letter from the government (A "Sorry, we don't want you" letter.)

With hopes of federal employment shattered, I found legitimate work wherever I could find it: contractual and short-term. I was told to reapply for unemployment benefits in 3 months, since my benefits ran out (no extensions were granted at that time).

Because I took work wherever I could, I worked as a part-time online instructor, making approximately $500 a month, while trying to find full-time, permanent work. The part-time income (at that time) was virtually nothing and I got courses randomly and not every month but I made the best of it.

My law school classmates didn't understand my job. They believed online teaching was not going anywhere. They even laughed at it. But, later, they would ask me about how to obtain similar jobs since they hated theirs.

A month after the nice rejection letter from the federal government, I had a strange encounter with a man standing outside my apartment door. As I was leaving my home to pick up Jaime from school, this male stated he was a former FBI agent and he wanted to tell me something important.

This alleged former FBI agent stated: "You're okay; it's not your fault. It's your dad's fault." I was confused and asked was he speaking to me, as it was a very weird encounter and he was quick to mention this and walk away as he stated it. The male said, "Yes I am speaking to you, it's your father's fault." I never understood that encounter until years later.

Months later, there were more strange encounters with another male standing outside my apartment door. This male would stand outside my door around the time I planned to pick up Jaime from school. This male looked very mean and hostile. This male would be present at least twice a week or so for about one month.

I never made anything of it. I just thought he was visiting someone. However, he would follow me to the parking lot and drive off very abruptly when I would drive out the parking lot.

Three months came and I reapplied for unemployment. I received my unemployment benefits. However, this did not last long, because despite having a rightful claim to benefits, the state cut off my unemployment benefits.

The state explained that I was not entitled to unemployment since my quarterly period income was not sufficient, even though it showed sufficient on the printed quarterly benefits statement and letter they provided me in my second benefit claim.

They stated I was not entitled to the first unemployment claim because they stated I did not have sufficient income in my quarterly period from my city government job. It just did not make sense, since I worked for a very long time (even in law school and even on a contractual basis at HR recruiter firms after my city budget layoff).

I sought free legal aid and attorney advice and everyone stated the state was wrong. Well, you can't argue with the state.

No matter when or if I appealed, the state won. I owed all the unemployment back to them including my first claim. Could you believe this? The state said I was not entitled to unemployment at all (even though I worked for a long time and made sufficient income).

BERNICE RATHE

How was I going to pay it back? I didn't know, as I made only $500 a month (with the promise I would make more).

Because the labor industry dried up for me in Texas, I received no child support. I had no funds and was forced to pay the state back money I was rightfully entitled to. So, I paid the state and Jaime and I moved to the next state where I could find opportunities, which was Kansas.

So, in November 2005, I left my friends behind. I found a cheap apartment (with utilities included) in the burbs (45 minutes from Kansas City) where I could stretch my paycheck, since my part-time employer came through on their promise.

However, I barely made a sufficient income (not enough to have anything left at the end of the month). It was better than $500 and it paid the bills.

Despite this, I never called home for help. I did it on my own. Besides, my mama was ill and my father did not give a crap about me. So, I survived on my own, which I later was proud of, as I eventually made it out the financial slump far better than anyone else would expect.

Bea Giovanni

Chapter 11: Positive Outlook (At Least for
the Moment)

Moving to Kansas (near Kansas City), I found solitude and opportunity. I found friends, fun, and opportunities without much effort. This is to say I still worked hard and played hard. The fruits of my labor played off in big ways.

I worked my butt off, finding other jobs to supplement my income. I became a real estate broker (eventually becoming a managing broker) and even getting other professional licenses that could offer additional income opportunities. This was especially important because I couldn't afford to sit for any state bar (Kansas or Texas).

Most firms want attorneys licensed in the firm's state, unless it is a corporation and a bar license in any state is sufficient. Plus, I couldn't work under the limited court rule unless I got a job with a governmental entity or some non-profit entity. Moreover, I did not have enough experience and no one was hiring.

So, I found employment working at local colleges and universities teaching college courses. I became very popular among those colleges and universities, where they were requesting me to lecture on a more permanent basis than before and even lecture for special events and courses. Online universities were in demand and several online universities hired me too.

My income increased tenfold, making me one of the most successful online instructors (yielding over 100K annually by age 30 in 2008). My employers provided me with numerous awards and recognitions and a benefits package for part-time employees, so I was able to secure benefits for Jaime and I.

After finally achieving financial stability and seeing my friends complain about their jobs, office and company politics and mean coworkers and bosses, I realized I liked working from home.

In my spare time, I volunteered as a court-appointed special advocate. I found myself volunteering at my daughter's elementary school and serving on the parent board. In my community, especially in my daughter's school, they frequently would solicit me to run for a school board slot.

However, I declined, since I did not really know the community and political background. Plus, I wanted to give it some time, as I wanted to get to know the landscape and I was particular as to who I aligned myself with. Not everyone has the same interests and good intentions as I do.

Thank God, I didn't jump right into the school board position. I would learn from employees at the school and community members the school had a history of corruption and the same people sat on the school board (for over 20 years and then their family members would run and win to keep control of that power), which is why some people wanted to get fresh, new faces on the board (unconnected to the community).

During those times, I mainly focused on making more income, paying back the other state for unemployment benefits (though I was rightfully owed), finding a church home and maintaining my social life, which I all eventually accomplished in Kansas. I couldn't be happier than I was (at that time). I thought I finally made it out of the funky financial slump.

BERNICE RATHE

Yet, strange encounters began at my home in Kansas like in Texas. Again, an angry-looking male would often stand at my apartment door. I would ask if everyone in my duplex knew him and no one knew him. Eventually, a neighbor made a complaint to the police for suspicious activity since most people in the area had children and were very wary of such activity.

For whatever reason, I began to develop boils all around my body. I even developed a cyst in my head. I went to a doctor and the doctor removed the cyst via laser removal.

After the doctor removed and tested the cyst, the doctor explained to me she couldn't understand why the cyst was in one piece and appeared to be a foreign object. No lie!

While the doctor would not put it down onto my chart, she explained that this was not a cyst but something else (unknown to her) yet was documenting as a cyst as there was no other way in explaining it in my chart.

The doctor couldn't explain it. I am not sure what happened and as to why I got a cyst. I realized that something had to happen to me at some point and someone or something did it to me. This was not a common thing to occur for me, especially since I went through a battery of health tests just recently. I was in good health.

Fast forward a few months and surprise, surprise! In February 2006, I received an email from Georgia stating that they have arrested Jeff for child support evasion. Apparently, Jeff's refusal to pay support (also called child support evasion), amounted to over 20K, which makes it a crime in certain states.

Because it was an interstate child support action, they could enforce the judgment anywhere. They wanted me to know that either Jeff had to pay ¼ of the back support owed or remain in jail on a felony for child support evasion.

I learned through the child support action that Jeff fathered three additional children and he was married to his wife of his two children. This made it five children (and all were girls), as Jeff had his first child when he was 16, then Jaime, and subsequently 3 other children. Apparently, he was also evading support for his oldest daughter and the child after Jaime.

Boy, how time flew! I moved on with my life, and then I get this news. It appeared that Jeff's life really got out of hand.

BERNICE RATHE

Jeff's mother contacted my mother and sent a threatening message through my mama to me. Her mother basically wanted me to sign off that Jeff paid his support and that the amount owing should be discharged, so that he could get out of jail and care for "his family" (like Jaime was not his child).

I informed the state on the threats made by his mother. However, I don't think the state took my concerns seriously.

Jeff did and said everything he could to get out of jail. He told the Georgia's AG office that he was actually paying two different support orders on Jaime (1 in Georgia and 1 in Texas). This was untrue.

I got divorced from Jeff when I was in law school in Texas. In fact, Texas knew Jaime stayed with my mother for a long time in Georgia, while I attended law school (as the court placed this in the divorce decree). So, the state never enforced the support order, but instead allowed Georgia to enforce its order, since that was where Jaime resided.

Jeff even lied and stated Jaime didn't reside with me but with my mama and he should not owe support (though the Georgia AG's office stated it did not change his support obligation, as he had to pay support regardless where Jaime resided). Georgia's AG office believed his lies.

They contacted me to provide proof Jaime resided with me. The AG's office wanted a recent report card. I immediately faxed that information.

Interestingly enough, after I faxed this information to the AG's office, police officers followed and harassed me for miscellaneous things such as a taillight (that was functioning but the officer thought it was too dim), my plate not affixed properly, or my personal favorite is that my vehicle appeared to be swerving (even though it was not). I later made a connection to this harassment.

Eventually, Jeff got out of jail because Georgia made Jeff pay ¼ of the support owed. Then, he was required to make timely and complete payments otherwise he would be put back into jail, charged with a felony (evasion of child support to be exact), and ordered to complete his felony sentence.

The AG's office was more inclined to order him to pay the support because putting Jeff in jail for support evasion would defeat the purpose because he would be unable to pay the support. In addition, this was the goal of the support evasion law, which is to order support be paid for the child's wellbeing.

However, the AG's office and other law enforcement agencies would have wished Jeff were behind bars for a very long time, which they will find out later as to why.

I did not really worry about what Jeff was doing or not doing. I moved on and was a certified lesbian (and loving it!).

I never looked back at Jeff. After learning Jeff had five children and that he was married again and owed support to others, I think that was enough said! Don't you think?

My social, professional and home life were booming. I made sure I was a supportive parent, as I always been. I also made sure I found the best opportunities for Jaime to explore her interests and talents and grow into a mature and responsible adult.

My social sector and support system grew. I had friends galore. I would meet friends for girl talk, breakfast, lunch or dinner, especially as my schedule was flexible (I worked from home teaching online and sometimes lectured courses and events).

I even dated a model named Leslie. She was fine! The sex was awesome. Her mother liked me.

However, my friends didn't like her, as they thought again, like others, she was not good enough for me. While her beauty was great on the outside, she was very ugly on the inside. Her personality stunk and she did not know how to be a friend to me (or anyone for that matter)! Yet, I worked through Leslie's personality issues, as none of us are perfect and issue-free.

Sex was great. I had no issues with our sex life. In fact, Leslie satisfied me in so many ways and on a regular basis. I can recall a time when I was driving and it was like she read my mind. All of the sudden she began making love to me while I was driving. She pulled down my pants and went at it.

Other times, Leslie was so timely, again like she read my mind. It was no matter if I came home to her and she began making love to me. Or, if it was an ordinary day together enjoying our time, she would make love to me and vice versa.

In hindsight, I think we were in tune with one another, which would explain why she was satisfied me when I didn't have to say anything. But, like I said, she had some issues.

On one end, she did not want me wandering outside our relationship with anyone but her, which I didn't. Plus, it was simply not my personality to do so.

Despite this, our relationship was a rocky one. Leslie was bisexual and I always felt like she was lying to me as to whether she was faithful to me. However, I wanted to think better of her, so I continued to trust that Leslie was an honest person.

It was inevitable that I introduced Leslie to my family. So, I decided to bring Leslie with us to Georgia. Leslie and I traveled to Georgia for the summer with Jaime, as Jaime stayed with my mama during the summer months.

We initially was going to stay at a hotel, since my grandma's house was full with relatives staying there temporarily. However, surprisingly, my father (who I haven't heard from in a long time and relationship was strained and always nonexistent) invited us to his home.

I was hesitant and puzzled by his generosity, but Leslie felt it was for a short time period (the weekend) and free, so why not do it? However, she didn't know the history behind the non-existent father-daughter relationship.

Hesitantly, Leslie and I stayed at my father's home. We also figured we would not be there most of the time, since we were visiting areas elsewhere outside of Macon, Georgia.

While staying at my father's home, Leslie and I slept in different rooms. I slept downstairs, while Leslie slept upstairs (we were trying to be polite and not disrespectful, since my father really did not know I was lesbian).

Remember he never really was in my life, but for the 3 months in high school. So, he was sorely out of the loop on my life, friends, love life and anything important that a parent should know. In essence, my father did not know me then (and still does not and never really knew me).

During our stay at my father's home, Leslie eventually wanted me to sleep with her. So, of course, at night, I joined her.

I recall one night Leslie wanted something light to drink, and it was late at night. So, we left and drove until we found a store that sold wine coolers.

When we got back to my father's home, Leslie drunk two of the four wine coolers and she saved the rest for later. (I did not drink alcohol, so the other two wine coolers were Leslie's drinks. She eventually left the two coolers for my father as a kind gesture).

When we woke up the next morning, my father cooked breakfast for us. What a surprise for me since this was the same person to deny that I was his child!

What was also surprising was my father's behavior around Leslie. Recall Leslie was fine looking, curving and just the right size. (Remember she was a model.).

Well, I swore my father was looking at her body the whole time. I believe he was trying to make a move on Leslie.

I think this may have been why he wanted us to stay at his home, as he did not really care for me.

But, my father did not know Leslie was my girlfriend. I never told him. Plus, we were didn't have a father-daughter bond, so I really never shared things like that with him.

Besides, I was not offended by his flirting with her. Leslie and I had an understanding in our relationship that we were solely for one another and for the pleasure of each other and no one else, i.e., she was mine's and I was hers. So, basically, no one could come into that relationship.

Actually, both Leslie and I joked about it since most men would think Leslie is 100% straight, but she was not. Plus, men thought I was straight too, but I was straight lesbo.

Some men usually are disappointed when they realize a female is not hetero. The joke was on my father, as I never told him Leslie was my girlfriend.

We eventually left my father's home heading back to Kansas. En route to Kansas, my mama called my cellphone and wanted to make sure I was fine. I had my mama on speakerphone, so Leslie overheard the conversation.

My mama stated that she knew that this sounds like a lie but wanted to make sure. My mama stated she just got a call from my father saying that I was drinking and driving and that we (Leslie and myself) had a male traveling with us, and we had drugs with us.

I was shocked and even Leslie was in shock. Leslie and I both told my mama that was a lie and no one was traveling with us, we did not have drugs and did not do drugs, and we are not drunk. Leslie explained she had wine coolers the night before and left the package with two coolers in the fridge for my father.

I also stated that we were traveling back to Kansas alone and that it was no one but myself and Leslie. My mama told us to be safe and don't worry that she (my mama) did not believe my father anyway.

When we got back to Kansas, Leslie confided in me about my father. She said my father and his family didn't care about me. I asked her whether her concerns had anything to do with my father flirting with her. She said no.

Leslie stated my father and his family approached her when she was alone, before we left Georgia, about doing silly and hateful things towards me. They said she could get paid to do so. I thought Leslie was "pulling my leg."

I couldn't even believe something like that, especially of my father and his family or anyone for that matter. I didn't know my father and his family that well, but it simply didn't sound logically at first glance.

After the Georgia trip, things between Leslie and I became strained. She started to act strange with me. I planned a vacation trip for us, and she kept changing her mind and saying hurtful things to me.

Bea Giovanni

In the end, we went on our vacation trip and later I broke up with her. As my intuition led me to believe in the beginning, I learned she was lying to me. Leslie was seeing her ex on the side.

When I learned of this, I had to break up with Leslie. This is not the type of relationship I wanted and I simply did not want a relationship where I could not have my partner or mate in a committed and faithful relationship.

However, Leslie would not let me break it with her. She began displaying controlling behaviors and stating things like "we are never breaking up." I thought that was some craziness!

Eventually after several days of no contact with Leslie, she left me alone. Leslie's mother called me, since Leslie's mother liked me and asked why I broke up with Leslie. I had to tell Leslie's mother the truth.

After telling Leslie's mother that Leslie was cheating on me with her ex, she understood why I left Leslie. Leslie's mother would then tell me that Leslie has a history with the ex and they had been off and on for nearly 4 years. Leslie's mother would tell me that I made the right decision to leave Leslie.

Years later, I would learn that males were using Leslie for sex and whatever else they wanted. Leslie was very attractive. So, I could see why any person would want to be with her.

Yet, I always told Leslie that she should focus on her and get an education, so that she would not depend on a relationship to get her through life. Well, I guess Leslie didn't listen.

She married and had a child. But, it didn't seem like a good situation with her spouse. For whatever reason, Leslie's life ended up as I expected.

Leslie didn't focus on her wellbeing and getting an education to better herself. Instead, others used her for sexual pleasures and other whatever else they wanted from her, which was unlike when we were together. I treated her like a queen.

Things were okay for me (to say the least). I focused on me and I took a break from dating. I actually got into shape and was loving my new look. However, someone stole my identity and I had to pick up the pieces, securing my identity via making the required identity theft reports.

Bea Giovanni

I focused on my work, mastered it and excelled. I later learned I could master anything thrown at me, i.e., martial arts, education, career, etc. I was on the track in becoming a department chair and a tenured professor making substantial income.

Yet, this popularity changed over time rapidly. Just as I had many people who liked me, there were just as many people who hated me. Jealousy reared itself into my life.

I began getting students in my classes that would cause serious chaos and doubt on my teaching abilities. Here are a few examples.

For instance, I taught a 6-week Certificate course on Paralegal Skills. It was a course designed for people without a degree or background in the law. However, there were some students in my classes that should not have been in the classes. I got some students with Bachelor's degree who would take the course.

In one class, a male student, who possessed a Bachelor's degree in Criminal Justice and two Master's degrees in Criminal Justice related areas and consequently also a private investigator and apparently had been in the military for nearly 20 years prior to that, caused chaos in the class for other students. I was not sure if he had an issue with my sexuality, since most students often saw me supporting the gay student union.

During the first week, he would come into the class and complain that I did not teach him anything. The male student stated he couldn't understand how I was teaching (though I provided the class with a syllabus and an outline and the class would follow the outline of topics). He would stand up and debate with me and other students felt he was being very rude and disrespectful.

While he would rudely debate with me in class, it got to a point where other students told him in class that no one else had an issue and they all understood my lectures and teaching and to leave the class if he felt he was not getting anything out of the class. Well, this male student tried getting other class members to agree with him. However, they were not buying it.

Most people that took my classes were serious about the class, as it provided training and skills to become a paralegal. So, having this certificate would save some people time on an actual 2 to 4 year degree. No one was trying to ruin their future chances at a low cost way in getting skills and training into a career field.

The students felt so bad for me. They even complained to the school administration about this male student. Well, this student later removed himself from the class after much pressure from the students in the class and school administration. They gave the male student an ultimatum.

A year later, another student enrolled in my class and the class experience (as well as my experience) with this student was very interesting (to say the least). This student was a female student (widower of a former federal administrative judge) who wanted to retrain in the legal field. She would frequently call me for help on assignments, which was policy for the school to allow phone contact with the students.

Well, her phone contact became very frequent. She would call late at night about miscellaneous things. Yet, I would help her.

One day, I saw her in a neighborhood near my friend's home. The student instantly recognized me and asked me what I was doing in her area. I stated I was visiting a friend and we were apartment hunting, since I was moving to the city soon.

BERNICE RATHE

The female student stated she lived in the neighborhood, and her mother own a duplex and needed to rent the vacant unit. I told her that, after the class ends and if I did not find a place, I would consider her mother's unit (if it was still vacant).

She invited me to see the property, so I went immediately, since my friend was not ready to leave. I had my friend call me on my cellphone when she was ready.

The female student introduced me to her family. She also made dinner for me. I eventually left since my friend called and stated she was ready. You would think that this was a very good sign that the student was well-adjusted.

The class continued without issue from this student. The students would frequently eat off campus for lunch and I did as well.

The same female student invited me to join her at one of her favorite restaurants for lunch. So, I took the offer. I figured it was a cordial and friendly invitation.

Well, I later found out differently. The student would continue to call me late at night, despite not having any assignment questions. I entertained her calls in an effort as to not offend her.

Bea Giovanni

The student later called me in distress saying that her neighbor's teenage daughter went missing and they feared the worst, since the child got into an argument with the parents and ran away from home. The student stated everyone in the neighborhood was looking for the child.

I asked her did she need my help as I had friends in that area that could help too. My friends lived in that area all their lives and they knew many people and could get others to help. However, the female student hung up abruptly.

Before she hung up, there was commotion in the background and the student yelled and screamed like something happened to her or she discovered something. It was just unclear from the abrupt ending.

I kept calling the student three additional times and even left a message for her (since I was concerned and unsure if something happened to her). Well, I got a very rude message from someone who called from her phone. The voice over the phone was a male.

The male stated that I needed to stop calling his woman or he would hurt me and he called me some gay slurs. I was amazed and confused as to how he would know anything about my sexuality or me for that matter.

Besides, my sexuality at the school was not an issue, since the school encouraged diversity. I was one of few faculty members who supported the gay student union and other student organizations such as religious organizations. I guess this male figured I had some relationship with this female student, which I did not.

I explained to the male why I called and I was trying to make sure everything was fine, since there was an abrupt ending to my student's call. He stated I did not need to be worried about that and if I called again he knew where to find me (at the school) and would beat my (you know what!).

This male even provided me where he worked and told me if I wanted a "piece of him" to come down to the downtown federal building where he worked. Again, I was in amazement as to why he acted like that or what he was referring to. My friends also said it was strange for the male to call me like that.

I was scared (to say the least). I called my friends in that area where the female student resided. They told me there was no one reported missing in the area.

My friends suggested to make sure my surroundings at the school was secure, since this guy could be high on drugs or something (from what it sounded like to them) and to make a police report. I did not make a police report. I thought it would resolve itself, yet still taking precautions to secure my surroundings.

The next day, I went to class as scheduled. The female student came to the class and starting yelling profanities and screaming at me. She stated that I needed to stop calling her.

Of course, I was confused and wondered what she was talking about, since I only called her the night before out of concern from the last conversation with the student. Plus, she always called me for whatever reason and not vice versa.

Specifically, I explained to her that I called her back to make sure everything was fine, since the conversation ended abruptly. I also explained the student would call for assignment questions or other related reasons and not the other way around. I also explained a male caller contacted me from her phone.

BERNICE RATHE

The female student avoided anything I stated and kept saying loudly 'stop calling me' and things like 'I don't want you.' Again, I was very confused at why and what the student was doing.

The student stood in my personal space and seemingly was about to push me. However, the department chair heard everything (since the chairperson's office was nearby). So, the chairperson approached the student and ordered the student to leave the building.

I explained to the chairperson everything and the student's history in the class, including calling me for miscellaneous reasons and the lunch invitation. The chairperson stated that sometimes students may fall in "like" with instructors because of an "authority" complex and that has happened to the chairperson before as well.

This is similar to anyone in authority such as a police officer and citizen. The chairperson advised me the student may have been in that mode of thinking and to avoid the student at all costs; so, I took this advice.

Well, the student did not let the situation go. She immediately (after leaving the building) went to campus security and informed them I banned her from the class. This was untrue.

The chairperson vouched for me and informed security that she (the chairperson) ordered the student to leave considering the circumstances. However, it did not stop there.

The student, after not getting anywhere with campus security, alleged that I sexually harassed her. Again, this was untrue. I explained to them what happened the night before and the history of the student in my class and outside the class. Campus security instantly got it (and felt the complaint was frivolous and false) and they closed the case.

However, I faced shame and humiliation among my colleagues and students. The students heard about what the student did and some wrote letters to the chair asking the chairperson to remove the student and discipline the student. The term ended so I was unsure what happened with the female student's future at the school.

Surprisingly, I received a call from the student's mother. Apparently, the school called the student's mother, who suggested the mother talk to me. The student's mother informed me the student was bipolar and on medication and that the male who called my phone was the student's boyfriend.

The student's mother apologized to me. The mother stated the student was a habitual liar and was frequently trying to sue people for things they did not do. Of course, I was shocked to hear that information and that the student was mentally ill.

After such a confusing and crazy situation, I thought life moved on for everyone, especially the student. Well, it did not.

I never moved out the suburbs because the city's rental amount was sharply higher than the suburban rental rates. So, I remained in my suburban apartment.

Because my suburban area was small, I could see pretty much everything that was going on around you. To my surprise, I spotted this same female student (who now I knew was bipolar) in my area. Actually she was a block away from my home.

Initially, I thought this was a coincidence. However, it was not. Later, I spotted this former student near my daughter's school.

Because this female was bipolar and a habitual liar, I thought the worst. I informed my daughter's school that I had a disgruntled student (who was mentally ill) spotted near the school.

I tried describing the student's history of hostility with me (without breaching privacy). I asked the school to lookout for this student, and not allow her in the school and to contact police. The school kept this information in mind.

I also contacted the college to inform the college of the student's presence near my home and my daughter's school. I still did not know how the student was able to locate me, since I rented an apartment and I neither had a published address nor contact address with the school or other entities.

The college took this information seriously. Apparently, the college ordered the student to stay away from me and to complete the course online, as there were similar online courses. Apparently, she never completed the course as planned. The student eventually (well, at least from what it appeared to be) stopped these crazy behaviors and moved on.

I later resigned my name from the college's roster of adjunct instructors to protect myself from this student. Besides, this college was merely one of several colleges and universities I taught for. So, I figured one less college will not impact your income.

That summer, one of my friends and I traveled to a vacation spot in nearby Kansas City. While on vacation, I got word that my uncle (one of my mama's 5 brothers) died. It was sudden and no one knew his health worsened. Apparently, my uncle had a lung disease and was on a breathing machine.

From what was told to me, my uncle needed the breathing machine and he did not make it to the breathing machine in time. He instantly had a heart attack and died. My mama told me that he never went to the doctor to get the proper care, so the lack of care contributed to his failing health.

So, ending my vacation early, I went home (to Georgia) for the funeral. My mama's family is large. So, everyone came to my uncle's funeral.

I met several extended family members (cousins on my mama's side of the family) that stayed in Kansas. In particular, some extended family members (a husband and wife and their three children) were excited to hear that I lived in Kansas and that I went to law school, graduated and was a college professor.

These same extended family members were attorneys themselves (both the husband, Steven, and wife, Sharon). The husband worked in the U.S. Solicitor General's Office as an attorney and the wife worked in the private sector, but had previously worked in the public sector as a state and county prosecutor. When I got back to Kansas, I connected with Steven and Sharon, as they had invited me to their home for social gatherings.

At the time, I thought my extended family were average people (like myself) working hard and playing hard. But, I thought wrong. They were at the top of their careers and were something like heavy weights in their fields.

In fact, Steven and Sharon introduced me to their friends, who were also lawyers and heavy weights as well. Steven, Sharon and their friends were all eager to help me in my career. They stated I was a perfect candidate for lots of positions, as I was young and very intelligent; my background was solid, impressive and diverse, among other things.

They all wanted me to take the Kansas bar as soon as possible, as they had the perfect attorney positions for me. They were excited about the possibility of me joining them and connecting me with others with prestigious and affluent backgrounds.

One of their friends wanted me to work with them as assistant general counsel for a private corporation, while Steven and Sharon wanted me to work in the U.S. government as an attorney. However, first, I needed to get the law license, which would later prove to a difficult task (later you'll see why). An illegal immigrant could get a law license but not me and I am a citizen with a great background. Go figure!

Whatever the case may be, Steven and Sharon were good people (and still today). My mama and her family were proud of me and proud to hear that Steven, Sharon, and their friends were helping me. They had no issues with me being gay, either.

As I stated before, I thought Steven and Sharon were average, hardworking people. But, they were not. Steven and Sharon held fundraisers at their house on a frequent basis. They lived nicely in a plush, rich neighborhood (not for average people but affluent people).

Many fundraisers related to one of their friends (one of which would later be elected to his first presidential candidacy). I would later find out that my extended family were good friends with the U.S. President, as Sharon worked with his wife in the past. It was one year later, when I saw Steven and Sharon's friend's name on television for the presidential race, I knew that Steven, Sharon and their friends were preparing me for something bigger than them, as they were connected to power and influence.

They felt I would be a perfect candidate for high profile careers, as I was young, diverse and had several skillsets needed. Besides, who wouldn't want to be one of the key people involved in grooming a potential influential leader?

It goes without saying that my extended family on my mama's side are good people and not the average people, as they worked with and personally knew major public figures.

BERNICE RATHE

Chapter 12: Bad and Corrupt People

ate from others or to hate on others was not my forte. This is how I felt with those two students who gave me grief and the numerous instances of harassment in my classes. I never thought people would stoop that low. But, I guess there are people in life who are just bad and corrupt individuals.

Shortly after, I would learn this lesson hard and strong, as there were many bad and corrupt people around me in Kansas, including friends and even at my daughter's elementary school. The more successful I became, the hatred against me increased.

Well, as time passed, I started dating an older lesbian. I thought I had such bad luck dating people in my age group that maybe I should try dating older people. Well, that did not go so well, either.

I dated this older lesbian named Joanna (but she went by Jo). My friends again didn't like her. They thought she was conniving and not good enough for me.

Bea Giovanni

Jo ended up being more of a hassle than anyone I dated. When I first dated Jo, she was not dating anyone (or at least I thought). Jo told me she broke up with her last dating partner months before she met me, but she apparently did not tell me this partner re-entered her life.

Jo dated her previous partner and me at the same time. Jo was conniving. She called me a "dip." I guess she used me to "dip" out on her main dating partner.

I couldn't remain in that situation. It was simply not a healthy situation. So, I planned to leave Jo.

However, before I left her, I was involved in an accident where Jo was a passenger in my vehicle. The driver in the other vehicle hit us and admitted that he hit us. The other driver even admitted he was on his cellphone when he hit us.

The accident totaled my car, so I bought a used vehicle (a used Mercedes Benz). Jo got very jealous of me for buying the car, even though it was used and low cost.

Many people thought I paid a lot for it, but I did not. I 'wheeled and dealed' for the car via a used car inspection, car history and updates needed on the car.

BERNICE RATHE

But, boy, did Jo milk the situation with the driver! Jo pursued legal action against the other driver.

I would later find that Jo was a career lawsuit person. She sued people for real and fraudulent accidents and claims. As for myself, I did not really want to pursue an action against the driver.

I hated the entire situation. Because of the accident, Jo used the situation to stay in a relationship with me. Jo knew I was about to break up with her, so Jo used the car accident as a sympathy tool to keep me with her.

Well, it didn't last long after Jo's same conniving ways continued and I (without hesitation) left her and never looked back.

Life did not stop there. Later, I found there were bad and corrupt people located at my daughter's school and were the school itself. I know that sounds paranoid, like my other experiences. But, if anyone is a victim of stalking and harassment, then you know it is not paranoia. There are some people who can be simply bad people. Moreover, I am not stating every person is a bad person, just these particular incidences.

As I was explaining, my daughter's school (XJ #100 Elementary) was on the No

Bea Giovanni

Child Left Behind List. The school was a pre-K to 8th grade school (with less than 250 students) that serviced one small area of the suburb (while the other part of the suburb, serviced by another district, had numerous schools within it).

My daughter's school was the only school in our district. So, the community had no other choice but to attend XJ #100 Elementary because the other district on the other side of the suburb did not accept out of district applicants. The student had to live in the district's zone and not just in the same suburb. This is though the suburb was extremely small in population and geography.

The school was primarily a low-income school. Though the community's income should not dictate a school's performance, it sometimes explains why certain schools suffer (via the lack of funding and education or skillset of the community).

Due to its poor academic performance levels, the state considered closing XJ #100, as the school failed to make adequate progress. However, the school miraculously got off the list (even though the school never made the required adequate yearly progress ever in those years).

BERNICE RATHE

During Jaime's second year at XJ #100, the school hired a new assistant principal, Mr. Phinus. He was also placed in charge of student discipline. I am not sure what happened with the previous assistant principal (Ms. Nosom), but Ms. Nosom really cared for the students.

There was something about Mr. Phinus; I couldn't put my finger on it. Sometimes, my intuition goes off like a GPS radar. That radar would later go off so strong and hard it would open a can of worms for Mr. Phinus and a big secret that he and others placed in that school and in the community did not want out.

Mr. Phinus would discipline the students, but he was very inconsistent. Some students would complain Mr. Phinus had favorites and those favorites seem to be the school board members' family that attended the school.

During Jaime's years at XJ #100, there were lots of bullying incidents that occurred. Jaime did not adjust well to that type of environment, since I did not raise Jaime in those environments.

The students were violent and lived in poor and gang infested environments. This was indicated from how they were reacting to other students and in class. Some students demeaned smart students and the students whose parents supported them.

Yes, you guessed it, Jaime was one of those students who were smart and I supported her. Therefore, students, who were not so fortunate, teased and demeaned Jaime. Many students came from broken homes, parents were on drugs and gangs were present in their everyday life. Again, I did not raise Jaime in those environments.

At one time, some school members asked me and insisted that I run for school board membership. However, of course, I declined and continued to volunteer at the school via parent boards and the community partnership meetings.

In those meetings, I met area politicians, business people, and community partners. I would frequently voice my concerns that the school was not getting the same services as other schools in the area. For example, other schools had before and after school programs in conjunction with the Parks and Rec District and my daughter's school did not (even though it was the same suburb).

I also mentioned that I never received a Parks and Rec booklet for each season, despite ordering it via phone and online. It was as if they refused to mail booklets to my area of the suburb.

Everyone at that meeting who resided in my area agreed, stating he or she never received those booklets. I thought that those booklets would be helpful to parents in finding after school and extracurricular activities, since my daughter's school did not provide very much.

Many people on the committee didn't like my comments. It was no secret I was a lesbian. The community and school were traditional and hostile towards gays (despite having many blended families in the school district), which was one of many reasons why I was trying to move closer to Kansas City and didn't want to get involved in the local school board (in other words, there was a much more accepting attitude and inclusive value in the city).

In these meetings, as a parent who was asked to provide a voice for other families and the community, I even mentioned there was no music or art program at the school. I informed school officials and community partners I developed a wonderful idea years prior to this meeting for a creative arts program and would love to share it with them. Yet, they declined that offer.

Bea Giovanni

A community partner felt this was essential for the students. Outside of the meeting, the community partner verbally supported this creative arts idea and suggested I present it to Superintendent Sally Mitchum, as that was the first step before going to the school board with the idea. The partner even suggested to me grants were a great way in funding the idea.

I jumped on this idea and project and began working on it. The effort was easy for me as I developed a creative art program years prior and had an arts background.

The school year came and went. New teachers came and went. One new teacher was Ms. Kneipase. She became Jaime's 4th grade teacher.

I had an open door with Ms. Kneipase as well as any other of Jaime's teachers. Ms. Kneipase would frequently call me to come to the school when Jaime had issues with students bullying her and was not adjusting to the negative environment.

Ms. Kneipase also provided her cellphone number to call me relative to any school related issues or concerns with Jaime and we eventually worked together on a project. Therefore, we would frequently contact each other on that accord as well.

BERNICE RATHE

She encouraged me to volunteer in her class, since she needed help. I agreed to help whenever I could, despite my skepticism about volunteering in the classroom, since XJ #100 Elementary was a homophobic environment. Let's just say they treated gay families as if they were invisible or sexual deviants.

Despite my skepticism, I volunteered. My schedule was flexible as I primarily worked from home online, so I had the time.

When I volunteered, I noticed that many of the students were bored and sometimes students would get sick and sickness would spread to other students. Ms. Kneipase explained the school did not have funds for additional games or activities and disinfectant wipes.

Hearing this, I went and purchased some Mensa games that would help the students redirect themselves onto activities where they were learning and having fun at the same time. I also bought huge amounts of disinfectant wipes to make sure the classroom would be clean if needed, since it appeared that some students were passing colds and other illness back and forth to one another.

Bea Giovanni

Apparently, Ms. Kneipase and other teachers were overwhelmed as they were teaching more than one class of students. The school cut back on funding for the year not hiring many Teaching Assistants, instead used interns from local colleges. So, the interns were infrequent visitors at the school.

During my time volunteering in the classroom, I also learned a lot about Ms. Kneipase. After learning more about her, I really liked Ms. Kneipase. I thought she could be a good friend outside of the school, since she lived in the nearby area and I did not have many friends that lived in the suburban area.

I learned that she apparently was a former Olympic gymnast. Also, outside of the school teaching gig, she owned her own gym where she taught gymnastics and other things. I also learned she was very good friends with the Assistant Principal (Mr. Phinus).

I also learned other things about the school. Over time, there were also rumors floating around that there was school fraud occurring. School employees would frequently discuss this issue around me and other parents in school and community meetings.

From my research, things were not adding up with the school budget and grants. There were grants for technology, food and other things and the school never really used the money for those purposes.

For instance, the school received donated used and old computers fixed through a local store or computer repairperson, when there should have been all new computers in the computer lab. The school's website was outdated and had old info from the previous administration.

In terms of food service, the board hired one of the board member's family members to cook food, when there should have been fresh food from an outside company provided. The students would complain about eating sometimes raw and uncooked food.

There was nepotism rampant at the school. Many of the school board members' families were working there and were unqualified yet placed into those positions. In many instances, the school board members that participated in these fraudulent activities were the members that sat on the board for years.

Bea Giovanni

Later, after many people caught on to these activities, the school would tell the public and state officials "they were making changes" and even show something to show this progress or change. But, this was just something to quell the suspicion and rumors of unethical behavior, fraud and mismanagement. Nothing really changed.

What really took the cake was the rumor the school was "dumbing down" the students to get federal funds. I couldn't believe what I heard.

Apparently, the school struggled for years with school funding because it was such a small district. The only way to get federal funds was to offer specialized services. These specialized services included special education, free lunch and other aspects.

The scheme involved placing families on free lunch (even if neither wanted nor needed it). Also, the school encouraged families to bring the students to school on certain days in the beginning of the year for "head counts." The more students the more money provided by the federal government. They would include students who didn't live in the district or attend school.

BERNICE RATHE

The other scheme was keeping scores and learning low so there was a need for funding and specialized services. They would then hire school board member's relatives who would institute basic reading, writing, and math programs without hiring state credentialed professionals with degrees. Again, this was to cut cost and appear to be supporting the "community."

This explained why the school was frequently on the No Child Left Behind List. Yet, this isn't to say there were not students who legitimately couldn't learn effectively as other students. There were students who were intelligent and made the mark.

I frequently recommended to others in the school and the district that merging with the other district in the area would be more advantageous, which had several schools and was located in the same city.

Actually, I never really understood why there were two districts in a small suburban city (with less than 30,000 people), one of which was a district with one school (pre-K to 8th grade) and no high school, which was XJ #100 School District and the other district having several elementary schools and one high school.

Bea Giovanni

The one high school merged both districts' entering high school students into one high school. So, the high school serviced students from both.

Later community members and school employees informed me there was a history of racial tension, which was why XJ #100 Elementary was a separate district and why the other district rejected transfer students from XJ #100 Elementary into that district.

I don't know about them, but I think that sounds like discrimination and segregation. Or, I should say separatism, since no one likes the word "segregation" as it denotes some deep wounds for some communities and the nation. Truth be told, all of that madness is crazy. I simply cannot understand why anyone would discriminate or hold others back, when it only holds everyone back and it is just plain wrong. Yet, I digress.

What really was interesting was the school board members (especially the long-standing members) went along with the segregated practices (sorry, I mean separatism). Many people in the community believed the board was corrupt and going along with the separation because they made more money separated, since money went to two districts instead of one and XJ #100 district got funds that went into the pockets of (guess who?) the school board.

After learning this, everything started to make sense to others and me in the community.

It was no secret in the community. I just couldn't believe the school board did not care about the children and their education. They cared about money and keeping the corruptive practices going no matter the costs. I would later find that corruption ran deep in the XJ #100 school district (so deep, going beyond that corruption).

But, the irony is the district played a part in something bigger. I later uncovered why I was being targeted and the government's involvement and that the school district was a part of it.

You got it! My life turns out to be something bigger than I expected: a gift and a curse and I hated it.

Thinking about how the school treated me, it was clear they hated me and they were stalking and harassing me from the time I entered the school. But, they were merely one of several hateful and envious groups against me. But, why?

Bea Giovanni

You'll see, don't have a heart attack yet.
Wait. Am I crazy? You be the judge, with
evidence, someone else linked to this
complaining about similar issues, and
coincidences, what do you think?

BERNICE RATHE

Chapter 13: My Life Took a Drastic Turn and Other People Did It

I was overwhelmed and disappointed at how XJ #100 school district handled the education of its students (not to mention my child, since Jaime was a student in that district). I was in the process of trying to get my creative arts idea off the ground and use it for XJ #100 school district.

I thought (and many others thought) my creative arts idea would bring well needed elements to the school. However, the superintendent (speaking for the school board) would not see it that way (and there was a reason). But, I will come back to this shortly.

Spring hit and I received a surprising call from my father's oldest son, Travis (my older half-brother). I wasn't sure how he got my number, since I didn't talk to him. In fact, this may have been one of the only times I ever talked to him. Apparently, he got it from my father, who got my number from my grandma (my mama's mama).

Bea Giovanni

I initially thought Travis called to catch up on time. You see I really don't know him or any of my father's children.

However, the first question Travis asked was whether I worked for the government. I didn't understand the line of questioning, and I was a bit confused as to why Travis asked me this. I thought that maybe he was checking to see if I got the government job I originally applied for.

In any event, I stated that I was not working for the government but teaching college courses (both online and campus-based) for colleges and universities. Travis stated, "Good."

He later asked if I was experiencing any weird or harassing acts. I stated no and asked him why. Travis stated, "When you do, just remember, it's your daddy" and he repeated the same thing. Then, he stated "don't have any more kids, alright?" and asked him why. Travis stated laughing at me, "Just don't have any more."

Changing topics, he later abruptly stated "your daddy is not who you think he is." I, again, did not understand the line of questioning and was a bit confused. The conversation eventually ended but, before I got off the phone with Travis, he stated, "Remember what I said to you."

As time went on, I continued teaching and lecturing college courses. Interestingly, school board members' families enrolled in my campus-based classes. I recalled the family members' names and faces from school functions and meetings. I merely thought they went to the school and were taking classes like other students.

However, these family members would frequently cause lots of confusion in the class. It was to the point where students would come to me after class to inform me of what the students were saying and doing (i.e., being disruptive, talking and behavior during my lectures). The students were seriously concerned that other students were causing issues to their learning.

Some students couldn't focus. Luckily, the class was ending, and many students were able to bear through the class.

I continued working on the creative arts idea and even met with small business experts to get the right business plan and presentation together for a presentation before the XJ #100 school district.

In my efforts to secure the school grant funding and a creative arts program, I solicited the help of Jaime's teacher, Ms. Kneipase, since she had experience in cheerleading, gymnastics and other activities that could be helpful. Plus, she done this before (i.e., she has developed programs). We corroborated via email and telephone.

However, I never got that chance to present this idea to the district or the school. The superintendent at that time refused to entertain the idea. I couldn't think of any reason why she would refuse free help to create needed programs.

I offered to write grants for the school district. But, again, she refused. I later uncovered why she refused this help and why she and others in the district and school began harassing and stalking me.

I would be glad that I did not help them and did not present my creative arts plan. I would later go a different route with my creative idea that did not involve the district or school. The district and school would later regret what they did to me and Jaime.

[Two years later, in Fall 2009, a scandal revealed the superintendent was committing fraud in the district related to grants, which explained why the superintendent did not want me to write grants because she was allegedly writing grants. It would have taken away her additional income.

A local newspaper investigative reporter uncovered and reported the XJ #100 district superintendent was writing grants for the district and collecting 10% of the grant proceeds. The biggest injustice about this is the incompetent school board approved this in her contract, so she got away with it.

No one in the state had a contract like that, except this district's superintendent. So, you can imagine her pocketbook. She actually made more than some superintendents in major cities with more students and a bigger budget. Remember there was no more than 250 students serviced in the district.

As an example how she "jacked" the district for money is one of the technology grants. The superintendent received over 1.5 million dollars from the federal government to put technology in the classrooms, which never occurred (when I was there). As such, the superintendent received 10% of the $1.5 million dollars, amounting to $150K from one grant.

There were other grants. In addition, her pension, retirement options, stock and salary was not included in the amount. You can see the superintendent had a cash cow and did not want anyone to know about it. The district and community could have used that money.

A new superintendent would attempt to correct the wrongs. But, this superintendent was merely placed there to continue the corruption, while showing new technology equipment and other items, or ideas as a show of improvement or progress.

But, these things never took off as they should have. The superintendent's connection to all of this would also later connect back to the whole of the corruption. But, again, I digress.]

Meanwhile, in early fall 2008 while shopping for groceries with Jaime, strange activities began around Jaime and me. There was a group of Caucasian men and possibly one Caucasian women walking near us and would follow us down each aisle.

Eventually, they would stand near us and maybe pick up a can item or two. As they picked up a can, they would appear to speak to one another but did not really speak to one another (yet speaking louder) and say "you think you are better than somebody, don't cha!" I initially ignored it because I figured these people were actually talking among themselves.

Then, we went to the other side of the grocery store to get frozen foods. Again, these men and one woman were present in our area. Again, one of the men stated, "you think you are better than somebody," as he and the group laughed and walked off.

When we approached the checkout line, this group stood behind Jaime and me. They waited in line, while giggling, laughing, and talking about Jaime and me, i.e., mocking us. They described our appearance and how we didn't meet their standards. After we bought our items and left, they eventually bought their items.

While Jaime and I walked to our vehicle, their vehicle was conveniently located next to our vehicle. I noticed their vehicle had confederate flag stickers, military stickers, and a firefighter sticker on the vehicle. The individuals proceeded to drive out the parking lot as we drove out the parking lot. However, these individuals followed our vehicle and starting to tailgate and flash their lights.

At first glance, the situation would appear to be paranoia on my part. However, I later found it wasn't paranoia.

Bea Giovanni

I confided in a friend about this situation. She and I agreed that this was not paranoia. My friend suggested contacting the police. But, we figured the police would not take this suspicious activity seriously, since there was nothing unusual for the police to investigate and the people were not committing a crime (at first glance).

At the time, I had sufficient funds to hire an investigator and I did just that. The investigator asked if I had a copy of the store recipient, as he needed it to track the store location, time and date, activity, and store footage. The investigator located the exact footage and reviewed it before I arrived at the store and after I left the store.

The footage revealed this group followed us before arriving at the store. It also appeared others were working with them in the store and these individuals were either present before I arrived or after this group arrived. Whatever the case, the investigator later identified the group from the license plates on the store parking lot footage.

The investigator, having contacts in law enforcement, found these individuals were a part of a local extremist or militia group. The individual whose name appeared on the vehicle registration had prior convictions for menacing and public intimidation.

The investigator informed me on this discovery of information. He asked me whether I noticed similar activity around me. I stated to the investigator I didn't because I seriously didn't realize there was any cause for concern to look for such or thought people did things like this.

He asked if I could plan my daily and weekly schedule and provide it to him. He wanted to observe me from afar in my activities to identify and investigate the people and activities around me. So, I did so.

What the investigator later discovered would forever change my view of the world. I was not alone, as his view of the world would change too. [After realizing these activities around me, I would later recall similar activities occurring around me from my childhood, throughout my life, and to now. Interesting, right?]

Well, the investigator stated the activities appear like nothing criminal occurred yet these activities are criminal in nature, because these groups design them in this way. But, in actuality, these groups were committing acts of terrorism via networks of hate, criminals, extremists, rogue public employees with bias and extremist motivation (without committing noticeable acts of terrorism), as the acts were considered domestic terrorism and espionage under the law, if caught in the act.

These groups use CB radios, cellphones and signals in communicating with others as to the whereabouts of the victim. They also identify themselves as a part of these organized rings using police, fire, veteran and military stickers and attire (similar to gang identification).

Some observed financial transactions in stores and even used credit card skimming devices on cellphones or other devices to take the target's card info or other people's card info to commit identity theft and other crimes.

Those with connections or ties to law enforcement or government had access to information that others did not have. So, some tracked my credit transactions. Within moments after using my card, these groups would appear in or near the business (pretending to shop, etc.); or, they would appear at or near the business on various days if they noticed a pattern in my shopping at a particular store or business.

BERNICE RATHE

Some would apply and get jobs at any place I frequented, studied, worked, etc. or they recruited within. These groups functioned in a terroristic manner like terror cells and spy rings with limited or no information on the operations of the group.

After the investigator revealed this, it made more sense why I had other occurrences like this but never put it together. It was revealed these groups are following and harassing me everywhere.

He identified more vehicles and connected all these people to local vigilante groups, hate groups, extremist and anti-government activities and related activities; some had military training and affiliation as MPs, firefighters or EMTs. Many vehicles had either police, fire or military stickers.

Surprisingly, the investigator got information from some people willing to talk to him. They revealed some are hired while others simply join into it and solicit others to watch, follow, invade, listen and/or disrupt my life in any way possible and were doing so for years.

They did so in many forms, i.e., spreading lies, working in groups as informants, "lookouts" and "followers" on foot, in cars, bikes, or public transportation, monitoring and communicating my activities (while using this intel to later harass me). Others watched for good officers and others who know about these activities to alert others in these groups and even to discourage law enforcement and others in getting involved to help me or swaying them to join into the activities.

Some had news, radio and media accompanying these groups or to provide spontaneous, unscripted dialogue on air relating to the victim's personal life or a personal event.

Other information found was that my apartment and car were bugged with video and listening devices.

In addition, some people knew the reason behind the harassment revealing that it is "something my father did." So, the investigator began gathering data on my father. The investigator did not find very much information.

But, eventually, the investigator concluded it had to deal with state secrets about my life, my father and the government's involvement and some groups were unaware of this. The investigator told me not to trust my father as he wasn't a good person and may not be who I think he is (possibly a covert background) and that my ex-husband was involved too.

The investigator discovered these groups had the help of some agents (agency unknown). Initially, the investigator didn't believe these groups because of the strange reasons provided. These were hate groups and criminals, so their credibility was so-so; And some were stating things like I was special or anointed.

Strangely, the investigator found these explanations had validity, as some groups stated there was government involvement and if any group were caught, the government would deny its involvement or act as if it was not harassing me.

Nonetheless, the harassment intensified. There had been people from XJ #100 district and the community participating in these activities, stalking Jaime and me, vandalizing my vehicle and physically threatening us.

Strangers in the public, near me, would speak loudly, while replaying and creating similar private phone conversations or any activity I had with others. This even included these groups tapping my home phone and cellphone and even hacking into my email, which would later be true.

Bea Giovanni

Back to my point of all of this, my world would change from this point on. You see Jaime confided in me over something that occurred in summer 2006, while Jaime visited my mama for the summertime as usual. Jaime held a secret for years and did not tell me.

Well, while under my mama's care when Jaime visited my mama in the summertime (like most kids who go to their grandparents' home for the summer), Jaime told me (in a distressed look) that her and my niece were sexually assaulted by one of our distant cousins (he was about 16 or 17 years old at the time), while he was babysitting them. From Jaime's disclosure to me, I also believe he may have molested my niece. I was not sure.

Let me tell you, after Jaime told me this, I was upset, angry and wanted to drive down to Georgia and kill him. Words do not describe what I wanted to do to him.

Instead, I composed myself, called home and told my mama and my sister and brother what Jaime told me. I was so desperate to talk to someone, anyone, I even called my father and my siblings on his side. Because I was a mandatory reporter through my role as a CASA, I even went to the school to report it, since I did not know where to start since it happened years prior and clearly Jaime was having issues as to what happened, as she had guilt and was worried for my niece around him down in Georgia.

Well, after in an impromptu and confidential meeting with the school social worker and Jaime's teacher, I asked for assistance in finding resources to help Jaime and myself in helping Jaime and even how to report this. The school social worker was kind enough to refer us to a private counseling service, which we used and was a very big help.

On top of the trauma that Jaime and I faced from this incident, you know what happened after this confidential meeting with the teacher and school social worker. These people (if you can call them that) began to harass me and Jaime.

For instance, they would state that I had to wait in the office and follow a different visitor procedure than everyone else. They stated it was to protect their students, since they did not want any "molesters" to roam the halls of the school.

In the midst of this, school officials and staff were making interesting and strange comments about sexual molestation and even stated that I did not seem to be stable or have an education. This is though I volunteered in the community as a CASA and even had tons of education and had no issues with stability in life.

In the meantime, because I was a CASA, I frequently made visits to abused and neglected children at foster homes and even visited their parents on different occasions. These groups would frequently follow me everywhere including to my CASA visits.

In fact, these people made their way into the places and organizations where I visited (no matter if it was CASA related, business, or personal). These groups even compromised the security and integrity of those environments.

Because I became aware that I was being followed, stalked and harassed by hate groups and other dangerous groups, I did not want to endanger these children and their parents any more than what they have been through. Therefore, it was a strong possibility these groups would do the same at CASA (the volunteer organization) or the foster homes I visited. So, I had to make an abrupt withdrawal from my CASA role, which I really loved.

BERNICE RATHE

I did some great work in the community with my volunteer position. I tried explaining the situation to the local CASA organization, but they really did not understand the extremity of the issue.

In mid-December 2008, I went to my daughter's school to address concerns of bullying that my daughter experienced and to inform them of this recently discovered information and threats to our life. This did not help any, since the school later participated in the life-endangering acts against my daughter and me.

You would think that you could get help from your community such as your local school, but the opposite was true for us.

Anyway, in this December 2008 meeting, Jamie and I met with the head principal, Ms. Shmad, and the assistant principal, Mr. Phinus, in an impromptu meeting. I explained we were the subject of harassment and that I believed it was connected to my father's past. I also explained there were several community members involved in the harassment.

Tearful due to the acts committed against my daughter and me, I asked the school to keep my daughter safe while she is attending school, to take notice, document and report any occurrences at the school, especially being Jaime was subjected to bullying acts by others.

In the meeting, I had Jaime explain what she was experiencing. Jaime explained the bullying she experienced. Ms. Shmad didn't take us seriously on the harassment and stalking concerns, instead she stated she would revisit the bully policy.

If you rewind a bit, recall that several students severely bullied Jaime months prior to December 2008. A group of girls jumped Jaime.

On another day, the same girls pushed her on a sharp object, which almost punctured her chest near vital organs. These girls called Jaime names and gay slurs because of my sexuality.

There were numerous incidents like this and Jaime was not the only one they bullied. Other students experienced similar treatment. These bullying acts were primarily because Jaime was a top student, smart, participated in area scholar programs, and because I was gay.

I listened to Jaime. I knew she was frightened. It was motherly instinct.

Being that there was one week left before the holidays, I figured Jaime could take an early holiday break. But, after talking with Jaime that day of the private meeting with the principals, she did not want to attend that school again.

Jaime didn't feel as if the school took our concerns seriously and was fearful to go back to the school. I also did not feel as if the school took our concerns seriously.

So, I tried enrolling Jaime at the other school district in the same city, but they did not accept out of district students especially from XJ #100 district. So, with only less than 4 days remaining before the holiday break, I initially decided to homeschool Jaime.

I withdraw Jaime from the school the next day. That morning, Jaime and I delivered the withdrawal letter and asked for her school records. Also, Jaime and I said our goodbyes to her 4th grade teacher, Ms. Kneipase, as we had a holiday gift we picked out for Ms. Kneipase and another teacher at the school.

I also sent the withdrawal letter to the regional state education office and the school district. In the letter, I noted my concerns, grievances and why I was withdrawing Jaime. After contemplating whether to homeschool Jaime, I decided a school setting (and not homeschooling) was beneficial for her high academic progress. So, I enrolled Jaime in a private school, which she started after the holiday break.

In the meantime, Jaime and I were preparing for the private school start date, and she was excited. What would happen next would change our lives forever.

After the holidays and weeks after withdrawing my daughter from XJ #100 Elementary and having no contact with XJ #100 school district, XJ #100 district sent me a certified letter. I would like to call this letter the "XJ #100 letter".

The letter stated I was banned from the school premises because I made gun threats in my mid-December 2008 meeting with the principals, which was untrue.

In fact, this letter would be the first of many things to come from the school. In fact, I later found the school didn't help us because they too were a part of this sadistic harassment and cult-like activity in the area. Instead, they helped to cover up the harassment, hence the defamatory letter banning me from the school, which further endangered Jaime and I life.

I found school district members like the superintendent, the accountant and others appeared to be harassing me, along with vigilante/hate groups.

But, at the time of my disclosing this community harassment to the school, I did not realize that the school and district were a part of this harassment too.

The school district and others in the school would regret sending this letter and being a part of this harassment, as the community at large would turn against the school and the superintendent.

The school district thought I had something to do with what would happen to them, but apparently, the school district had some demons in its past and it crept back up on them.

Anyway, the letter specifically stated I had a gun in Texas and would come to the school with that gun. Another allegation stated I called a school employee's personal cellphone, frightened and threatened her, and that the school investigated my daughter's bullying concerns and concluded she was never a victim of bullying but seemingly was bullying other students.

Note: this letter was generated even though I withdrew my daughter from the district weeks earlier and had no other business with the district, so why would I come to the school. I wasn't a threat to anyone and didn't make any threats to anyone.

I was shocked and in disbelief as I never stated those things or done those things to a school employee and that my daughter was severely bullied, yet the school ignored our concerns. Thinking about the letter in detail, the only school employee I could think that could be the "frightened school employee" as mentioned in the letter was Ms. Kneipase, since I didn't communicate with any school employee and she was the only school employee whose number I had.

I instantly replied via email denying the allegations in the letter. I also initiated an email forward of the "XJ #100 letter" and my email reply with my concerns to the state regional education office and the state education department. Consequently, state officials investigated the "XJ #100 letter" and found the allegations in the letter against me were untrue and I was innocent.

Ironically, the board fired Ms. Shmad (as everyone, like me, thought Ms. Shmad wrote this defamatory letter). To my surprise, Mr. Phinus later becomes the head principal for the next two years replacing Ms. Shmad.

BERNICE RATHE

The state regional office encouraged me to return to the school, but they were unaware of the other acts committed against Jaime and I outside the school and the extent of the XJ #100 district's involvement. It goes without saying that Jaime and I didn't return to that district, as we were forcibly evicted from that area and denied an education by XJ #100 district and its community through harassment and threats to our life.

Oh I forget to mention a very important fact. Shortly after the defamatory letter was written, our home's door locks were broken and home ransacked. So, should I say more?

Anyway, I contacted the investigator who helped me in the past. He was shocked as well and advised me to leave the area, as it was clear that someone (or others, if not all) in the school was involved in this harassment. After hearing about the letter and our home being broken into and ransacked, the investigator took my concerns even more seriously than before and contacted federal authority.

So, the investigator instantly began investigating the identity of the letter's writer, which gravitated to Ms. Kneipase and the two principals. Ms. Kneipase was

Bea Giovanni

the only school employee I talked to via cellphone and the two principals, as the letter highlighted the private, unscheduled school meeting, what was stated in that meeting and the principals were only present.

In the meantime, the alleged writer of the "XJ #100 letter" also copied the letter to a local deputy and the superintendent of XJ #100 district, making police and district officials a part of the harassment. Later I found local law enforcement were a part of it far before 2008.

It would not be until later that the district and writer of this letter would realize their actions would not only open a can of worms for itself but would cut its hand off from help from others and me. Plus, this went beyond some funky $^& charter school program. The district and writer of the letter facilitated a very big lie that would endanger many people's lives. That included using local law enforcement resources to generate this letter of lies, which also endangered law enforcement as they were operating under false pretenses.

In addition to notifying the investigator, I notified my mama and others of the "XJ #100 letter." While on the phone with my

BERNICE RATHE

mama (as she was over my grandma's house), my father was apparently there too. I am not sure why he was over my grandma's house, since he really does not have a relationship with our family like that.

Yet, apparently, he was coincidentally present and he was asking questions to me via my mama while she talked to me. I heard his questions over the phone because he was basically yelling in the background, despite my mama was conveying information to me from him over the phone.

She stated my father asked me why I did not make a car payment this month. This was strange as I didn't talk to my father in years (or ever) and my mama never talks to him as he treated her the same as me (he denied us all my life). So, it was strange for my father (who I didn't talk to) to ask about my car payment.

Also, no one knew about my finances (not even my mama). I was financial savvy and responsible all my life and I paid my bills, so I didn't have money issues.

I realized my father knew more about my finances than he let onto. How and why were the questions that went through my mind.

Bea Giovanni

In terms of my financial savviness, because I made extra payments to pay my car off early, my lender stated not to make a payment for that month. Basically, they would be losing money on my loan, since I was 6 months ahead in making payments.

I also saved money in the bank. Yet, no one knew about this as like most people you keep your finances to yourself.

I told the investigator about the strange question my father asked. The investigator then told me to secure my bank account and transfer my savings over state lines in a different institution. The investigator was onto something.

The investigator stated my father's strange question further confirmed my father was a part of the harassment and that I shouldn't trust my father, as these individuals and groups were corrupt. He told stories of agents working with criminals and other groups to steal people's money and in committing other crimes.

At that point of learning my father was involved, anything was possible. I did as he suggested transferring my funds telling no one the specifics including him.

The harassment got stronger every day. I called my family informing them what was occurring. As the days went by and Jaime started the private school, we were getting death threats. Also, someone ripped out my vehicle's alarm, along with damaging my vehicle to the point of major repair bills several times in the same month. Other acts of vandalism occurred that are too numerous to list.

Like any sane and reasonable person, I made several police reports. But I later found some local authorities were not registering these reports in their police system, if so, it was not accurate. The investigator tried to help as much as he could. He reported information to local police contacts; yet, like many cases like mine, these contacts thought I was crazy.

I contacted the FBI, sent emails to friends notifying them of the dangerous acts against Jaime and me and kept as many people abreast as to my activities on a daily basis in case something happened to Jaime or me.

The investigator instructed me to record my surroundings and routes to and from places and save this information in a safe place and provide it to someone I trusted. He would later tell me to also save my recipients to all businesses I shopped, since business camera footage may be available, as these groups were following, stalking, harassing, and intimidating me in stores, on the road, in public and anywhere I went.

These individuals doing these acts would be as few as 10 or as many as 100 or more people participating on a daily basis. At the end of the month, one could easily log and record at least thousands of people involved in this harassment.

At the time, I thought my father's two daughters (both in the military at that time) could help and I thought they were helping, as they were calling me on a more frequent basis than ever. I kept them abreast. I even set up a separate email and an online storage account to upload and store videos of the activities I recorded for them to keep in case something happened to Jaime or me.

However, this evidence and videos were destroyed/deleted and accounts closed. I later found my father's daughter (the older daughter of the two, who is 7 years younger than I am) destroyed them and were not helping me. Apparently, she, her father and his children were involved in the harassment. But, why?

I had yet to figure this out. Years after, I discovered she stupidly tried using my business plan and logo as hers, stating she didn't use it as hers is different, which was untrue as she did. I later realized she was trying to steal my life and mimic me. As crazy as it sounds, she did. Ironically, she later worked for the DOJ/EPA with access to sensitive government systems. Apparently, the government did not do their homework on her.

To state the obvious, she would later regret everything she did against me as her life would be in danger. She and others were liars, evil, crazy, and impostors. She would be a part of this scheme of harassment and terrorism against me and the government the whole time.

My father, his family and these groups who helped him would later find there was others unknown to them always watching and listening for many decades and these unknown individuals knew the truth about everything. So, there was no escaping the truth or the wrath that will follow them.

Fast forward months later, I contacted my father's daughter, who destroyed this evidence, and asked her why she would do this. Interestingly, she arrogantly and stupidly stated "I did it to myself" and that it was something my mama did as if this harassment and life endangerment was my fault or my mama's fault.

I knew better, since my father's family had a history of this bu^%sh^t harassment.

My father's daughter didn't like me for many reasons: I was my father's oldest daughter, smart and apparently I disrespected her mother years prior. What she didn't know was her mother didn't like me and actually was a part of the harassment with her father.

She would later find (as I did) her father, her mother and her father's family were very bad and crazy people and she would be no different. She would find herself involved in ritual abuse, terrorism and espionage with her life in danger (among other things), along with her father and mother, their family and the groups that helped them, with no way out of it.

In fact, it would be too late to stop harassing me. She would also regret destroying my evidence as others will find she and others committed terrorism and aided in terrorism.

Needless to say, I quickly found I couldn't trust virtually anyone including family and even law enforcement. For instance, some cops were a part of it and others simply wouldn't help due to prejudice or jealousy because I drove a nice car and thought to have money. So, I was on my own without any police help or support from anyone. We were essentially left to our own devices.

I also later discovered some of my friends were harassing me too (yet acting like they were not). So, how would I know? Well, my friends would recreate or mention places I visited or private conversations with others, which I never mentioned to these friends the places or conversations. This indicated to me they too were a part of the life-endangering events on my life and Jaime's life.

I also noticed several friends and ex-girlfriends like Leslie and Jo in my area (though they lived in Kansas City, 45 minutes away). Then, I saw others from my area in other counties hours away as I traveled around the state and even out of the state.

I am sure you can come to a conclusion as to what they were doing in my area, which was stalking and harassing me.

Once I realized their involvement, I cut off my friendships with them. Some of them contacted police when I stopped talking to them, acting like they were concerned and to cover their tracks to document they were not a part of the harassment. But, this did not work, since I had recorded voicemails from them leaving harassing messages.

But the strangest encounter that occurred during that time was when I spotted my stepmother (my father's wife, now ex-wife) in the state of Missouri when Jaime and I were traveling to a friend's home. I noticed who appeared to be my stepmother at the same stop light as Jaime and I in the downtown Kansas City, Missouri area.

I actually thought I was hallucinating because my stepmother was driving with an infant in the backseat, when she only had three kids by my father.

I later discovered she had another child after she left my father, which, among other things, confirmed the driver was my stepmother and I was not hallucinating.

I told the investigator about this. He told me not to tell anyone about my stepmother's sighting. His advice was to not tell everyone everything that was occurring, as he was still uncovering all the people involved. The investigation lead back to my father, my ex-husband, hate, militia and extremist groups, my former employer and other connections.

BERNICE RATHE

Could you imagine the fear and life endangerment we faced? The same groups would sit and wait for us outside our home, to follow us, tailgate our vehicle, honk, flash their lights and run us off the road. Police would harass us as well.

As stated before, someone ransacked our home and broke the locks. Despite getting the locks fixed with high security locks, the best solution was to stay in local hotels, as we did not feel safe in our home.

Now, I remind you that this is approximately one month after the "XJ #100 letter" banning me from the XJ #100 school was written. So, at this point, local police and a number of other groups eventually joined into the harassment against Jaime and me.

During that same time, another incident happened when my daughter and I were in a store getting school supplies required for her private school classes. You see Jaime went to the restroom while I shopped. As she went to the restroom and came back, a creepy guy and a woman followed her.

They followed her down each aisle as she was looking for me. Jaime noticed what they were doing and ran. So they ran after Jaime.

Bea Giovanni

Jaime was so frightened she ran into the store manager's arms. The two individuals walked out the store before the manager could identify them. The manager located me near the checkout lane and explained to me what happened. Then, the manager called 911.

When the police officer came, he listened to both the manager and I. The manager confirmed Jaime was telling the truth and the manager had store footage to prove it. But, the officer didn't want it. Instead, the officer thought the incident was nothing.

But, what would happen next would be astounding to both myself and the store manager. The officer began asking me if I had a mental illness, since it appeared I was on psychotic medications.

This was untrue. I didn't look crazy, I wasn't on psychotic meds, and I wasn't acting crazy. Also, the manager and I were trying to figure how someone, who is not a medical professional, can make a determination on a person's mental stability, especially when there were no visible signs of mental illness or mental stability.

BERNICE RATHE

The manager and I both looked amazed and shocked at this officer's behavior and comments.

I stated to the officer, "Excuse me! No, I don't have a mental illness and I'm not on psychotic medications, why would you say that? My daughter was almost abducted and you're more concerned about my mental state and not my child's safety. Do I look crazy? How can you come to the conclusion I'm on psychotic medications from just looking at me?"

From the officer's demeanor and comments (or lack of concern), I figured he knew something about the harassment. This was because I wasn't on any psychotic medications; I had neither a mental health history nor a history of mental health hospitalization or anything that could trigger anyone to think I was crazy, which many of my lifelong friends could vouch for me.

After this incident, the officer walked us out the store and explained his background. He stated he resided in the same city we resided and that the area was a good one and he has never seen any hate group activity ever and the people are good people too.

Interestingly enough, he mentioned hate group activity without me asking or telling him anything. This was strange, as no officer would voluntarily give this information, especially when a member of the public (like myself) never mentioned anything of that nature.

It is interesting to note that weeks later, when I checked the area police department for the police call or report regarding this alleged abduction, there was no report found from the incident.

As I was saying about this particular incident, after the officer left the parking, Jaime and I were in the process of leaving the parking lot. In the dimly lit area of the lot, there was a minivan with an angry woman (resembling a soccer mom type) sitting in the lot with dim lights on the minivan.

The female driver abruptly pulled out her parking space and began driving into our space almost hitting my car. To avoid a collision, I maneuvered my vehicle to avoid this woman hitting us.

Coincidence, right? Where was the officer then? Right?

Despite this, I continued detailing these incidents of these groups and individuals and recording the activities around us. My documentation of these incidents revealed the same plates, people and links wherever I traveled (no matter my vehicle).

For example, if I drove in a rental car to another state, the same individuals in the same or different vehicles (some with the same license plates) would follow us to the new state. This is just one example.

My friends were keenly aware of what was going on, as I kept them abreast via email. One of my friends even began to suspect these groups were tapping her phone. So, she recorded a voice message to those calling her that "this line was not a secure and private line and you are being recorded." Thus, when anyone called her, they knew the line was not private.

I later suspected she knew more than what she was telling me. This would be true, as she was a part of the harassment too and she figured out that the harassment was bigger than she thought and she would be eventually injured by whoever was protecting us.

In the meantime, despite my pleas for help, no help came from law enforcement or friends. I felt so alone in Kansas and Jaime and I were scared. We were getting death threats, being followed and harassed, ran off the road, and blocked in parking lots, stores and other places, by Soprano type individuals to an average person to soccer moms. This is not to mention that I stated before we could not leave in our home, as it was ransacked and the locks broken.

We were being stalked everywhere, into stores and people with fire, police and military insignia, apparel or indicators were following us, waiting in cars, on foot inside or outside the businesses, eavesdropping on us, or posing with a cell next to his/her ear. This was in addition to the vehicles with military, fire, veteran and police stickers, plateholders and plates.

I called my mama and her family in Georgia to come and help us and to see what was going on. No one came because everyone was too busy. Plus, I think my mama's family didn't understand what was going on, as this never happened in my mama's family before. I recalled my father and his family always had things like this happen, as they were crazy.

At first glance, this would appear to be paranoia but I would uncover that it wasn't paranoia but Jaime and I were targets of several different groups.

My mama was scared for Jaime and me; she wanted us to come home. I told her we would be fine, as I moved out the XJ #100 district area into a nearby hotel until I got a new apartment in the city in two weeks and I already planned the move. I initially thought things were looking up since I found a potential law position in the city and just needed to pass the bar.

My mama told me to contact Steven, Sharon or their friends to see if they could help, as they were credible people and knew people in authority, outside Kansas.

I never contacted Steven, Sharon or their friends, as I didn't want to bother them at that time. They were busy, professional people who didn't need to deal with this madness. Plus, everyone thought I was crazy, so I knew Steven and Sharon might think so too.

I continued to study for the bar and stay at hotels to keep safe until we moved into the city. So, you can imagine the expenses I incurred: I was maintaining not only the unsecured suburban home but living in a hotel away from the area, due to the death threats, stalking, and our home being ransacked and locks broken.

Despite the odds against us, I was determined to maintain a safe, normal existence and life for us. As a parent, this was my first priority. I also placed Jaime in a private school about 45 minutes outside the XJ #100 area, so there was no need to reside in the XJ #100 area and we stayed away too.

Even though my mama's health was worsening (as she was suffering with kidney failure and diabetes), my mama wanted to help me with Jaime (getting her to and from school, cooking, cleaning, coordinating our move to the city or whatever was needed) while I studied for the bar that was approximately in 2 weeks. This was especially since I found a place in the city and had to move our belongings out of the suburbs in 2 weeks.

We had little time and no help. So, I planned to travel to Georgia to get my mother soon to take her up on her offer to help me.

Shortly after and unknowing that my father's other daughter was involved, I traveled to see my father's daughter (the youngest daughter), who was stationed at a U.S. Army base as a recruiter. I wanted to give her the videos of the activities, as she wanted to know what was going on.

She asked me to explain what happened to Jaime and me in Kansas. As I explained, she began recording me on a recording device, and she stated to continue and don't worry about the recording. She confided in me and told me things that would make sense to me later.

As she explained, she cried and stated that my father was crazy. She also stated her sister destroyed my evidence stored on the online storage site and deleted the email account and storage account.

She also explained that her sister and my father's oldest son, Travis, were crazy and were working together to harm Jaime and I because they were jealous and literally crazy, which made sense as Travis mentioned strange things months earlier about not having any more kids, i.e., reproductive coercion (coercing and intimidating me into not having any more kids).

She also tried telling me something our father did to her, but she stopped as she was choking from her excessive crying and tears. She later stated these groups and people were connected and my father was helping them harm us. (I was shocked in disbelief as to why my father and his family would harm us, when we were family at least that is what I thought.)

Bea Giovanni

She stated she saw something similar with her military friend, up for promotion. She explained he experienced similar harassment and stalking by police, fire, military, and some were Masonic members. He then requested a base transfer; the harassment and stalking stopped and he eventually got the promotion and learned these groups targeted him out of jealousy.

Crazy but true! These groups were hate and terrorist groups in every sense.

I put this new info in the back of my mind, as I couldn't really believe my father and his children were jealous and trying to harm us. Also, I could not trust anyone and what they stated, since it appeared they were trying to harm.

But, it all made sense as I noticed my stepmother was harassing me too. I never told anyone but the investigator. So, I knew my father's youngest daughter was telling the truth.

However, I didn't tell her that her mother was involved. I just couldn't, since she was already distraught over her father's and her siblings' behavior. Telling her that her support system (her mother) was also involved would be further traumatizing.

BERNICE RATHE

She would later find she couldn't trust her family and that I was the only one of her father's children she could trust, as I was sane, not evil and not a part of this network of madness and harassment.

Weeks went by, my car was vandalized again and numerous times after. I got it repaired weekly, requiring a rental car, as my car was inoperable.

Sadly, I realized my friends (now former) were involved too. They would call and play on my phone. However, I knew it was them.

You see I kept everyone's phone numbers (new and old) in my cellphone. So, they were so stupid to call from their old, deactivated numbers, as it would identify they were calling me.

I couldn't believe my friends were involved too. Months prior to all of this, I even gave one of them my second car. I even shared my financial success with my friends. It was a gift as her mother was a diabetic like my mother.

My friend's mother needed to get to the doctor and dialysis treatments, out of the area. So, I thought why not donate the car to them, since they needed it the most. I would do anything for them, including financially.

Bea Giovanni

I even treated my friends' children like my own. Anyone who knows me knows I love children. If I brought Jaime to an amusement park or outing, I took my friends and their children too. I bought them necessities, as some of my friends were unemployed and couldn't buy certain items for their children.

Sadly, I had to end those friendships. I didn't want to, as their children liked me and I liked their children too. But, it was clear my friends were involved and I couldn't place Jaime and me in those unhealthy, unsafe situations. So, I never looked back. I felt bad for their children, as they couldn't escape that madness.

My former friends didn't realize what they were participating in would endanger their lives, Jaime and I life (as I uncovered there were some groups protecting Jaime and I, while others were trying to harm us). But, it didn't matter what they knew but that they should have known what they were doing was wrong.

Regardless of this, I couldn't afford to expose Jaime and me to that danger, plus we were endangered due to the "XJ #100 letter" and the acts of others.

BERNICE RATHE

While it sounds paranoid, I didn't trust many businesses or people, as it appeared everyone was involved in this. People treated us badly as if we committed a crime.

Basic services became a hassle. For instance, a mechanic even purposely botched work on my car and would not fix the issue. So, I had to get it fix correctly by paying for the same service elsewhere, which meant I paid twice. Then, I had to contest the original charge, since it was botched work and was vouched for by the subsequent mechanic who repaired the first mechanic's work.

So, as you could imagine, when I shopped and gave others my money, I went to places that treated me well in the past. So, when I rented a car during the various repairs, I went to a familiar rental location.

After the repair, I returned the rental car. When I returned it, the rental agent drove me to repair shop. En route, the rental agent asked a weird question.

He stated, "Tell me what's going on with the harassment." I asked him, "What? How do you know I'm being harassed?" He stated, "Oh, I'm a DOJ agent."

I stated "I don't believe you, I've known you to be a rental agent for at least 2 years at the rental car company; you're no DOJ agent, you're a rental agent!"

Laughing, he stated to me, "Maybe you need to consider checking yourself into a mental hospital and getting on medication?"

I was upset at that point, as he was suggesting I was crazy and he was clearly a part of the harassment. I stated, "I'm not crazy, you're the one that's crazy, pretending to be something you're not."

He laughed again and stated, "no one will believe you that you're being harassed and you can't prove anything."

I stated "What? You're wrong, I got you on camera; there are at least two cameras near this gas station next to the repair shop. Plus, the businesses have cameras."

He looked surprised, startled and scared. I left his vehicle, as he looked at the cameras, pulling off very quickly.

Another strange occurrence happened directly after this one. Picking up my car, the mechanic wanted to show me something. He stated there was a GPS near the wheel well of the car. I told him I didn't put that device on my car and didn't know where it came from. I told him I had recent repairs on my car, i.e., engine, body, and wheelwork.

BERNICE RATHE

The device was a small (about 3 inches in length and width) black box with an antenna. The company's name engraved on the device. The mechanic and I looked up the company's name online. The company offered a GPS tracking for a monthly fee.

Little did I know, this was merely one tracking device by one group. I later found an entire conspiracy where my life was tracked, harassed, stalked, and privacy invaded via other means like hidden cams and listening devices in my car and home, using my cell device to listen to conversations, hacking into my internet, spyware on my laptop and phone, with some using government technology to do it.

The mechanic asked me if I knew anyone who would want to put this on my car. He asked if I had an ex who is crazy enough to do so, since in his experience, exes are the likely suspects. I told him I didn't.

After thinking about it, I quickly corrected that statement and stated it was possible my ex-husband could as he made threats in the past because of his child support arrest and is generally a bitter person.

Bea Giovanni

The mechanic suggested to go to the police (but the mechanic didn't know some local police were a part of the problem). I left his repair shop in shock and fear. I immediately contacted the investigator, who took the GPS info to research its origin and owner.

The investigator advised me to tell no one about the GPS, since we couldn't determine who put it there and he was still uncovering information on others involved in the harassment. He also thought it would be dangerous to remove it, since whoever placed it on my car could get angry and harm me, especially in cases of fatal attraction or exes.

The investigator suspected that my home was also compromised. Investigator and I later found there were snooping devices in my home, as the investigator helped me uncover this. I had to play music or whisper in my home for privacy.

The investigator also told me it was possible these hate/extremist groups and others involved were tracking me via GPS and other electronic means like credit card transactions, since some people would frequently enter the business I patronized, from the receipts and footage retrieved by the investigator.

Because I didn't have cash on hand all the time, credit was the only way to buy items or services. But, after hearing this, I was cautious from that point on. His suspicions on these groups' tracking activities were later proven correct.

Later, returning to the rental spot, I talked to the manager and told him what the rental agent said en route to the repair shop. The manager was confused and stated he doesn't know why his employee would state that he was a "DOJ agent" or anything out of the ordinary and about any harassment.

The manager called the employee into the lobby and directly asked the employee in front of me, "Did you tell this customer you are a DOJ agent?"

The employee stated, "No, the only thing I told her was I was a member of the local Moose Lodge."

The manager then stated, "Why would you tell her you are a member of a Moose Lodge, this does not sound right, I don't believe you. That explains why you insisted on driving her to the repair shop and not me. You were harassing this woman."

Bea Giovanni

The manager apologized to me and even offered to give me a free one-day rental, but I declined. I never went back to that location.

The same day I went to the Mercedes dealership for a separate unrelated repair service only the dealership could handle. I left my car and received another rental car from a different rental company.

Guess who was there at the Mercedes dealership? The rental agent who claimed to be a DOJ agent.

Well, he came to the dealership appearing to assist a customer renting a vehicle. Yet, it seemed staged as initially the rental agent was not doing anything but smiling and laughing at me.

When I noticed this, I wanted to make sure everyone knew he was stalking and harassing me. So, I talked loudly asking him why was he stalking and harassing me. The customer, he was assisting, spoke low, telling the rental agent to stay calm and don't reveal anything to her. I told the dealership to contact the police, so they did.

The police came to the scene. When they arrived, there was only one police officer at first. Then, two additional officers came later. But, these two officers drove to the dealership's back parking lot talking to one another in their vehicles. (This was apparent; anyone in the public could see the two officers discretely discussing something in the back.).

The first officer told me not to say too much to the officers (I think he knew something I didn't, i.e., the officers were corrupt.). Before the two officers approached us, the first officer took my statements regarding the stalking and harassment by the rental agent.

The two officers asked what was going on and I briefly explained. One of them took me aside, laughing at me, and asked if I had a history of mental illness or hospitalization, diagnosed with such or was on any psychotic meds. Of course, I stated, "No."

The officer then jokingly asked whether I would voluntarily commit myself. Going on with his "silly" line of questioning, I said yes, (as I was playing along with his jokes). Being sarcastic, I stated that I think I had an undiagnosed mental illness and I think the "government is after me." The officer laughed. This is what you would call a 'dirty cop.'

When the officer and I walked back where my daughter and the first officer were located, I explained what the officer told me about voluntarily committing myself to the hospital and that I felt he was harassing me, which later I would be correct. These officers would later try covering this up.

The first officer stated he would handle the situation stating he thought I was sane, my daughter was cared for, I had no family here, etc. The first officer then joked and asked for my number; but I didn't think this was funny. Shortly after this incident, Jaime and I left the scene, along with the officers (or at least I thought all of the officers left).

The episode with the dirty cop didn't stop there. The dirty cop waited in the gas station's parking lot, adjacent to the dealership.

Then he followed Jaime and I from the dealership and began flashing his mirror and bright lights at our car, laughing, and tailgating. I tried driving down a busy street, since the cop's tactics were dangerous and so others could see it.

Eventually, he stopped once we got on a busy street and I lost him (or least I thought). Jaime and I went to the hotel rested and ate. Then, we left to attend Jaime's extracurricular activity.

BERNICE RATHE

Recall we were not staying at our home in the XJ #100 district, since we received death threats, our home was ransacked and we were without adequate law enforcement and community support, especially since the defamatory "XJ #100 letter" was written.

The same day, near our hotel, a hotel guest knew me and stated a cop asked about me and my room number. Another hotel guest stated they wanted to admit me to the psych hospital.

I was thankful for this information. It later helped Jaime and I avoid abduction, rape, murder, or something else bad. The cop at the hotel was the dirty cop from earlier. I believed he possibly followed us from the dealership.

Later that day, the cop waited at our hotel with an EMS worker in an ambulance to admit me into the psych hospital. However, it didn't work as I left Kansas to get my mama to help me while I moved and studied for the bar exam.

When they figured out that it would not work, the dirty cop and EMS worker pretended to be doing something else.

You see the dirty cop and EMS worker looked suspicious to others in the area since nothing was occurring to warrant their presence. I believe they were going to take me without my permission and harm me. They tried covering this up later I found in a police report; who knows what they planned to do to Jaime and me?

Luckily, we were leaving for Georgia that night, so instead going to the hotel room, we left for Georgia in the rental car. Again, who knows what they would have done to us?

So, Jaime and I traveled to Georgia. Numerous vehicles with confederate flags, fire, anti-government, anti-religious, police, military, DoD, EMS and veteran stickers, plates and plateholders followed us to Georgia. Some people worn apparel with similar indications.

I later find some plates were improper, as the plates were expired, removed or switched. Some would not have any indicators on their vehicles or person but their backgrounds indicated police, fire and military affiliations, as I provided license plate information to the investigator en route to Georgia who uncovered this.

These groups ran us off the road several times. State police in each state stopped us for things like "I was swerving, I looked drunk or they wanted to see where I was heading and what relative I would be staying with."

I didn't drink or do drugs. So, I knew this was harassment so I never gave them information on where I was heading and who I would be staying with. Besides, what officer asks questions like that?

Yet, like the strange police stops and people running us off the road, there were signs directing us to safety, if it was a sign at a church or a billboard on the highways, which lead us to safer routes as we traveled home. These signs seem to know what we were experiencing.

I prayed to God to get us to Georgia safely. God never failed.

Chapter 14: Conspiracy

I thought that once we got to Georgia, we were safe and secure. Boy, was I wrong!

The harassment was only at its surface. It would later run deep (real deep).

Well to provide you with some time orientation. Remember the "XJ #100 letter" was written in late December 2008 and sent to me after the holidays, well when we arrived in Georgia, it was early February 2009 (at this point) when I arrived to Georgia.

Upon our arrival, one of my uncles (my mama's brother) was in the hospital and had days to live. His death was rather sudden and no one knew he was sick. So, our Georgia stay would be longer than one day.

Plus, my mama had to wait for her doctor to approve her dialysis transfer to the Kansas City area along with scheduling her air flight to coordinate with her health needs. This was necessary for my mama's health.

Jaime did not miss any school, since at that point we were in Georgia for about 2 days and there was a school holiday and the private school didn't count attendance (like public schools). The school basically allowed students to take off the required time needed for whatever purpose (i.e., family matters like funerals and grieving) and would work with the students in catching up on the materials on a one on one basis. This was because it was a private school and many families with wealthy backgrounds were paying full rate tuition.

Strangely enough, my father came to my grandma's house. I do not know why he came to her house. This is where my mama was staying and we were staying until we went back to Kansas with my mama.

I had not seen my father in years, and, as I stated before, I did not know him, we only had approximately 3 to 4 hours of conversation in my entire life, and he never claimed me as his child. In fact, my birth certificate states ****** for my father, which means unknown.

As I was stating, I did not trust my father, especially after he knew private information about my finances and other information learned via his own daughter and investigators.

Bea Giovanni

While conversing with my mama and grandma on the harassment Jamie and I experienced, my father interjected and asked me about my ex-husband and Jaime's 4th grade teacher. I asked him why he wanted to know about them. He would not explain, instead he would say things like "why the teacher?" and I asked him "what was he talking about?"

My father was talking strangely as if he was repeating information from someone. Then, when I turned to look at him, on his right part of his body, I noticed he had an earpiece attached to his ear with a wire going down his back.

Who wears an earpiece like that? No one, unless you are working in security or law enforcement.

Again, as I was stating, I asked him what was that and who was he talking to. I even drew my mama's attention to the strange wires from his right ear. But, he redirected everyone's attention on the fact that I was somehow lying and crazy and pretending. He continued ridiculing me and denying that Jaime and me were being stalked and harassed.

Again, I was not sure how or why he knew anything about the harassment when I did not tell him anything about it, other than the defamatory "XJ #100 letter." I merely thought maybe one of his two daughters told him.

As my father's strange conversation went on, he started to say things to me and my mama such as "he was never in a secret society, cult or some group, and that he worked for the Nixon Administration delivery packages."

Hearing these comments, I was confused and asked him why he was saying these things when no one is talking about anything like that. In fact, I was trying to explain what happened in Kansas with the school. He would not listen and stated I was crazy.

My father abruptly ended the conversation stating he had to leave. As he left I continued to discuss what happened to Jaime and me in Kansas, including the "XJ #100 letter" and the school area fraud and corruption. Thank God, my mama believed me because no one seemed to care about the life endangering acts that were occurring to Jaime and me.

Later that day en route to running my errands, my father called my cell. I had my speakerphone turned on, as I couldn't drive and talk without the hands free device on under the law. So, this meant that Jaime heard everything.

He asked about my current location. I stated vaguely and hesitantly that we were heading to a print shop. I was confused as to why he was asking and untrusting of him.

My father got irritated with me as I wouldn't tell him specifics and he began yelling at me stating I was not his daughter, I was dumb and stupid and would amount to nothing and that I was the only one of his children that was chemically imbalanced.

Jaime and I both asked him why he was saying these things. We were extremely hurt and confused by his comments.

After this disturbing phone call with my father, Jaime and I arrived at the local printing shop to print out my creative arts business plan and business cards, since I was shopping around for the right school district. I was determined to use the idea to benefit another school, as the idea was rejected by the XJ #100 district.

Remember I was also banned from the school. So, you could imagine I really did not want anything to do with the school after uncovering fraud and the life endangering letter and acts committed against Jaime and me by the school and community.

BERNICE RATHE

In the process of stepping out the rental car in the lot of the print shop, another car abruptly blocked our parked car. An unknown male angrily ran to our car and began screaming obscenities at us. Jaime and I jumped back into the car and locked the doors.

We were frightened because we thought this guy was going to harm us, especially being that we had experienced so many harassing situations in the past.

Jaime started crying out to me and said, "Mama, don't let him into our car, he is a bad man, I am scared and he will hurt us."

I said to her, "Jaime, I am not. I am scared too."

This unknown man damaged the driver's side window and continued to do it. He stated to get off the car or else.

I instantly began calling 911 to inform them that this unknown guy was attacking and assaulting us.

As I was on the phone with 911, there was a man sitting in his vehicle. This man, hearing the commotion, gets out his vehicle and walked towards our vehicle to help us, but this angry, unknown man flashed an ID and the man stepped back and watched from afar.

Bea Giovanni

Apparently, this angry, unknown man, who was attacking us, was a cop. I informed the 911 operator and I stated the angry, unknown man is in plain clothes and has a regular car.

I also stated to the operator that I don't know if his badge is real. It was not a badge but a paper ID not showing his official authority or any credible information.

I stated that I did not want to open this vehicle to this man, as he broke the window with his arm and he could harm us. Additionally, I stated I did not know why this individual was doing so, and wanted to wait until the police came.

After the 911 call, I called my mama. She stated she was on her way to the scene to get Jaime and me. Then, she stated my father just arrived at my grandma's house, and he would take my mama to get us.

I was not sure why my father was so friendly and helpful, as he never really in the past. He always denied my mama and me and treated us as scums of the earth, so to speak.

In the meantime, a female police officer arrived at the scene. She talked to the angry, unknown man first. Then the female officer approached our vehicle (since Jaime and I were afraid to get out) and asked what happened.

Jaime and I explained the man (unknown to us) blocked us, ran towards our car, and began screaming obscenities. I explained he asked us to get out the car, and when we didn't, he broke the window.

The female officer explained the angry, unknown man was an off duty officer from another jurisdiction and he said I sped through a school zone.

I was confused and stated "What? I didn't speed through a school zone, that's a lie."

She stated, "I believe you. It doesn't make sense. He is out of his normal area, and he blocked you and broke your window over a speeding violation. He also wanted me to ticket you for speeding and other violations. Don't worry, I'm not going to do that. He acted totally out of line, he shouldn't have done any of this. He should've called dispatch in this area."

I further explained to the female officer that I did not reside here, though I am originally from the area. I explained that I was here to get my mama to bring her back to my home state, and that several police officers, in virtually every state we traveled through, followed and harassed us.

I also stated that my parents were coming to the scene. The female officer stated she was going to get down to the bottom of this as to why the off duty officer really did this.

She further stated, "I want you to know this is not how police officers are, we are good people." She proceeded to walk back towards the off duty officer. The female officer sat with the off duty officer and talked to him. He eventually left the scene. Go figure, he doesn't stay on the scene.

Anyway, the female officer came back to our vehicle and waited for my parents to come to the scene. The officer explained to Jaime and myself that, while she was talking with the off duty officer, the off duty officer continued to insist the stop was a speeding violation and nothing else. But, the female officer did not believe him.

The female officer provided the off duty officer with her business card. Immediately thereafter, the female officer received a call on her cell from the off duty officer, while waiting with Jaime and I as we waited for my parents.

BERNICE RATHE

The off duty officer demanded the female officer ticket me. The female officer defied him and stated she was not. The female officer explained to us what the off duty officer asked her to do and she stated she refused to do so. From that point, the female officer started small talk to past time while waiting for my mama and my father.

My parents finally arrived. The female officer explained to my parents what I told her and what the female officer observed. I explained it too, then Jaime explained it.

While my mama asked questions and believed the female officer, my father was cynical and instantly stated all of us were crazy and delusional. He even strangely stated to the female officer that no one would believe her or us, there are no cameras around here and neither one of us has evidence.

Why would my father mention anything about cameras or evidence? Again, this was strange. I continued to doubt him. Plus, I did not to trust him after that comment and the prior conversations hours before, when he stated I dumb and stupid, I was chemically imbalanced and not his child.

The female officer left her business card with my mama and me. My father refused the female officer's card and acted as if he was superior to the officer. (I mean my father acted very male chauvinistic).

The female officer suggested for my mama or myself to make a complaint against the officer, since he was abusing his authority and broke my rental car window. The female officer said she would corroborate the complaint, since she also had some concerns with the off duty officer's behaviors.

The female officer left the scene. I drove our rental car back to my grandma's home, while following my mama and my father to my grandma's home.

So, we arrived at my grandma's home and we were there for about 5 minutes when a knock at the door occurred. I answered the door and it was a city police officer. The officer asked if I was Bernice Rathe and I stated yes.

I asked what this was about, my father interjected and sarcastically stated (while laughing at me), "It's about the traffic stop a few minutes ago, police like to follow up on things like that."

My mama and I were confused. My mama stated to the officers "what is this really about because the female officer told us what happened and my daughter didn't do anything wrong."

The officers replied, "We had an involuntary commitment order to admit Bernice Rathe into the psych hospital, her father made a complaint Bernice wanted to kill herself."

My father knew I didn't want to kill myself. Just look at the span of time that passed, I was running errands; what about the 911 call about the rogue officer, the female officer's version of events, then driving back to my grandma's house with my parents?

Plus, we were arguing over the phone about what I still do not know, since my father was the one talking crazy to me. So, you can clearly see my father intentionally did this to me. He was not helping me but harming me.

My family also realized this and my family cried. My mama and my grandma tried hitting my father, as the officers placed me in handcuffs, and my father, without hesitation and with much delight, signed the involuntary commitment papers. My grandma stated to my father, "You know she is not crazy. She needs our help. You know what is going on."

Bea Giovanni

I then realized my father may be a part of this and he essentially finished what the dirty cop and others tried doing days ago. His act would also discredit me.

Jaime yelled and screamed at my father stating, "Why are you doing this? My mama didn't want to kill herself. You said that she was not your child and that she was dumb and stupid and chemically imbalanced."

He told her to hush and stop telling lies. Jaime insisted to everyone in the room that I was not crazy and my father was lying.

Jaime stated to my father, "I overheard you on the phone with my mama a few hours ago. You even asked us where we were heading. You seemed upset and mad at us for something."

No one believed Jaime and through the anger and disappointment in seeing her mama in police handcuffs (and knowing that her mama may never be in her life again), Jaime fainted. One of the officers caught Jaime before she hit her head. She eventually woke up, but after they transported me to the mental health hospital.

[Meanwhile to the hospital, my father searched my belongings at my grandma's home. He also began asking about the people I communicated with in the last weeks, information about my banking information.

He even took information from my belongings, including my cell where it would be later inoperable and damaged, losing the investigator's contact information and other valuable photos and videos of the harassment activities by others.]

En route to the psych hospital and in tears, I explained to the officer he was making a mistake, and that I believed my father and my ex-husband were a part of this harassment. I also stated that this was a false report and false imprisonment.

The officer laughed and got on his cell talking to someone as he drove to the hospital. In his conversation, he stated things I was saying and laughing with the person on the phone.

Well the officer did not believe me (and may have been a part of the harassment in endangering my life and helping my father and others). Knowing this, I did not know if I would ever get out of that "crazy" hospital.

You see once someone places you in there and knowing the extent of the harassment, it is hard to get out (because doctors always assumed you are mentally ill no matter the situation).

Bea Giovanni

I explained to the officer to remember my name in case something happened to my family or me and that authorities need to investigate my father and my ex-husband, as they will have something to do with it. But, the officer ignored me.

We arrived at the psych hospital's admitting area. The officer went with me to the admitting doctor and stood outside the door as the doctor asked private questions such as menstrual cycles, sex, drugs, smoking, pregnancy (the long list of personal information and history).

The officer then texted someone via his cell after each response I gave to the doctor.

The admitting doctor remarked that I had good personal and health information, since I did not do drugs, alcohol, smoke and I had healthy habits. Yet, he did not notice I was not crazy or had suicidal issues, especially since I was talking to him, like in a regular convo (conversation for those of you who may not know that).

I guess he was not the evaluation doctor, just the "admitting doctor."

Transferring me into the general psychiatric patient population, I entered and registered with the hospital, having approximately $20 or so dollars in my pocket with my ID and credit cards in my wallet.

Because of this, I gave permission to my mama to enroll Jaime in public school while I was in the hospital. I was unsure when I would get out the hospital.

Also, at that time, my uncle died and I missed his funeral. This is something you can't get back. In fact, when he was still alive and able to talk to others, he was in the same state hospital as me but on a different floor. Despite the mitigating circumstances, the psychiatric doctors wouldn't allow me to see him before he died.

My state psych ward experience was interesting and scary at the same time. Staff told me the doctor would release me to go home within the 72-hour hold, as this was for evaluative purposes. They lied!

My first 24 hours, with no signs of suicidal or mental health issues, the hospital staff drug and medicated me. No assessments, no examinations, no nothing occurred before giving me psychotic medications.

Meanwhile, there was an unknown DoD female employee in my evaluation unit. Keep this in back of your mind, it's connected. (Oddly, for the first 72 hours, my grandma and my mama didn't know my whereabouts; the hospital kept me there and didn't notify anyone but my father, who signed the order. They said they called my mama, but they didn't.).

I tried contacting anyone that could vouch for my competency and what occurred in Kansas. I gave the doctors this contact info.

But, despite what my file stated or what the doctors stated, the doctors never contacted anyone as my references stated they were not contacted. My hope was that someone could inform the doctors that I was not crazy, and that I was a competent individual who was being harassed.

No hospital staff one believed me. I mean no one believed me.

I even informed the doctors they did not verify whether the person who committed was truly my father. He was not on my birth certificate and denied me as his child (all my life). (I even had doubts as to this man's validity being my father).

The doctors could have researched this information, since I was born in the same hospital. But, the doctors did not; they were working on the assumption that others verified this prior to placing me into the hospital. Basically, the doctors let a stranger involuntarily commit me into the hospital.

I stated to the doctors that this man (my father) was disgruntled. He lied stating I was about to kill myself and I didn't need to take medications.

Staff ignored whatever I said and they instructed me if I didn't take the medications the doctors would note in my chart I was non-cooperative and non-compliant and I would never get out the hospital. So, I had no choice but to comply.

The doctor placed me on three different medications, which later have adverse effects on me, like when I had violent seizures months later, and I never had a history of seizures before these meds.

The medications were Lithium (a powerful psychotic medication), Geodon, and Cogentin (for the side effects of the meds). Who in the hell takes stuff like that and have no adverse effects! These meds are not meant for anyone to take.

I gained weight, my skin turned colors, I developed boils all over my body, my muscles felt weak, my speech was slurred, my body shook uncontrollably, I drooled uncontrollably, I had a rash, I felt dehydrated a lot, I urinated frequently to the point of almost urinating on myself, and I had heart palpations. Despite this, the main doctor adjusted my Lithium levels.

Staff and even resident doctors who assisted in the daily medications, activities, assessments and CAT scans remarked that nothing seemed wrong with me. They stated in front of me (talking among themselves) "here's another that's not supposed to be here." They thought I should be released in 72 hours.

I even explained I had the bar exam in the next week or so and my uncle was dying and I wanted to see him before he died and I did not want to miss the bar exam. Yet, the chief doctor didn't see it that way. I stayed in the hospital for approximately 1 month.

My first week I shared a room with a schizophrenic patient, who hit herself on the head, screamed, and yelled to the top of her lungs. Days later, the doctor discharged her.

Anyway, I was glad as she had violent episodes and I slept in the same room with her. But, I was also confused: they discharged her though she didn't appear mentally well.

Go figure! She was still showing signs of this when she left. But, I guess I was crazier than she was that I stayed in the hospital for one month.

I finally got my own room. I figured I had to make the best of a bad situation; so, I met other patients, some were truly mentally ill, while others were not. Some people stated they were not mentally ill and just needed a place to sleep, food, or medical care and the psych hospital was the best option.

Meeting others, I realized how the mental hospital was a haven for those who did not have mental health issues. This was why the schizophrenic patient was released early.

In fact, the ones that needed mental health were not in the hospital and those who did not have mental issues were placed into the hospital. It appeared like a big experiment.

In fact, this may have been why it was so easy to admit me into the hospital based on the lie my father told. Actually, I believe I was followed by these hate and terrorist groups into the hospital, again, since it was easy to get into a hospital.

For instance, I even seen some pretending to do business at the hospital, i.e., dropping someone off, when I went on my outdoor excursion with my group, which was a perk if you were "good."

The question that lingered was: How would one know when or if I would be outside with my psych unit? It goes without saying that, during my time there, I felt like Nellie Bly, only falsely hospitalized. If you do not know who she is, research her.

As I was saying, nurses remarked that I was not like the other patients, as I was too alert, I took care of myself and was very smart. They started to think I wasn't mentally ill. Some nurses questioned how or why I got in the hospital.

Meanwhile, my apartment's rent was past due and I had to move out. This was because I was in the hospital and I had no contact with the outside world to contact anyone, other than my family and staff.

I didn't know what was going to happen with my online teaching jobs, as I was MIA, and my employers cared neither about me nor to search for me.

Psych hospitals only provide a bed and three meals (and maybe snacks). I couldn't call long distance and I had only email contacts of my online employers. Plus, I couldn't get onto a computer (what computers?).

BERNICE RATHE

Prisoners even have access to computers, but I digress.

I even tried having my mama research and contact my employers but she had no luck. The social workers at the hospital tried helping to locate my employer's information, but to no avail.

Staff suggested I contest the hospitalization via the judicial route, which many patients take. Yet, with my knowledge of the law, this would be ineffective. The court will not look at what led up to the hospitalization, only the hospital record which was falsely created by my father and those helping him.

Taking the judicial route was a gamble, as the court and my mental health attorney would not really consider the situation at hand but by limited rules under the law.

I also ran the risk of being permanently hospitalized. You see, if I lost the mental health hearing, the doctor could keep me in the hospital indefinitely and I would be declared incompetent by a court.

Basically, I was a sitting duck until I got out, which was when the doctor cleared me to leave. My doctor took his time. I was not a special case to elevate to the top of his list of patients to evaluate and release.

Bea Giovanni

Plus, the longer I stayed, I noticed a pattern and practice. State hospitals, especially psych hospitals, have a stake in long psychiatric stays because of research and government funds provided to each patient's care. So, you can see where this was leading for me.

Within one week, I had the psych unit down to a science. The nurses all rotated on different wings and floors. By the second week, I had a new nurse on my floor.

This new nurse on my floor recognized my name and face. Guess what? She realized I was her relative, i.e., her husband's side of the family.

She explained to me she knew I was not crazy, but she couldn't be on this floor. There was a rule against working in the same unit as a relative.

So, she requested a transfer to another floor. Before she transferred, she told me to tell my family to come and give the family history and information. Apparently, that was one of only a few ways the doctor would discharge me.

The hospital had a history in keeping patients for state money. This nurse and other staff knew it and wanted me to know once family history is established, then a care plan can be made. So, even though I was not crazy, I would have to go along with it if I wanted to get it since no one would ever take me seriously or care enough to investigate my concerns.

So, I did as I was directed. I called my grandma's home and instructed my mama to come and give family history.

After the family history was established, the doctor discharged me. But, it was not easy as I had to admit I was mentally ill (if not, I wouldn't be discharged). Plus, the doctor wanted to develop a care plan for me to continue taking those three medications, though I was having side effects.

It goes without saying that the doctor diagnosed me as mentally ill, despite not doing a true evaluation and investigation into my concerns. Specifically, I was diagnosed with bipolar-delusional disorder (even though I was not mentally ill but falsely hospitalized).

He thought I was smart but mentally ill. He was partly wrong. I was smart but I was not mentally ill.

Oh, I forgot to mention when I left the hospital a month later, my $20 or so mysteriously disappeared from my registered items. Ain't that a m$%^ad*!

Bea Giovanni

Before I left, I met one friend. She was schizophrenic and was truly mentally ill but appeared to be functional.

I also encountered many staff members before I left, who some of which provided me with advice and interesting information. In fact, a nurse on staff also gave me some advice. The nurse apparently knew the other nurse, who was my relative.

The advice was: "many people know what is going on with the threats to your life, don't worry those people will have a lot to answer to and will really regret everything done to you, and when the right people find out what has happened to you and when you gain great power, remember to use it wisely and help people as much as you can." It was interesting to say the least.

After hearing her advice, I thought maybe this nurse was crazy and she should be a patient in this unit. But, as my life shown me, I would later find she was definitely not crazy but on to something.

I returned to my grandma's home, as my home in Kansas was no longer available. I had no job; my jobs terminated me, as I was MIA and neglected my duties for nearly a month. Of course, this was due to the false hospitalization and not intentional on my part but my jobs didn't know this. So, I had no job, no income and had to move my belongings from Kansas.

I planned to go back to Kansas to get my belongings out the apartment and pay the two months' rent that was due, as my apartment manager charged me. This is because I could not move out in time as I was placed in the hospital, unknown to the manager.

If you recall, I gave my 30 day notice months earlier as I was moving around the time of the bar exam. Whatever the case, I was so lucky I saved money.

When I checked my voicemail messages from over the past month (since being in the hospital, I had no access to long distance), I got a call from my bank in Kansas that two people claimed to be my father and stepmother and wanted to get money out my account. The bank got suspicious of the two individuals and would not allow them to do so.

After everything I went through, I got seemingly suspicious (by the day) of my father.

Later on in the process of arranging for my belongings to be moved from Kansas, I was in the process of renting a truck.

Bea Giovanni

Strangely in this process, my father told my mama he was going to help me move my belongings. I did not ask my father, he volunteered.

Remember this is the same man who refused to help me move to law school, denied I was his child and called me dumb, stupid, and chemically imbalance.

Oh, did I mention he fraudulently put me in the hospital?

So, of course, I was skeptical and my mama was too, since he lied and placed me in the hospital. This man (my father) acted as if nothing ever happened. He was a very different person, but I did not fall for that.

I refused his offer, as I was upset with him and did not trust him (as anyone would be in my position). Yet, I had no other choice but to accept his offer. My mama told me he stated to her if I didn't allow him to help me, he would place me back in the hospital. So, I was forced. (I later found he was doing so to deceive authorities and others who might think he was involved in this harassment, which he was, or to otherwise deceive those on to him.

He didn't care about Jaime and me. I guess he figured helping me move showed he was helping me and not harassing me.

But, it didn't show anything but an opportunity for authorities and others to explore his motive, connection and involvement.

In the drive to Kansas, I did not want to fall asleep. The medications I was taking also made me drowsy so it was difficult to stay awake. Whatever I could do to stay awake, I did it.

I was afraid this man (my father) would harm me. In fact, my mama asked me to call her or text her every hour the mile marker location, since she was concerned that my father would harm me too.

Plus, my father strangely made conversation with me and indirectly threatened me and stated things like "I know what you are up to." I, again, felt confused by his line of questioning and never responded out of fear and he was driving, so he could have killed both of us by intentionally driving erratic. I seriously thought my father was crazy.

Once we got to Kansas, I had to get my vehicle, since I originally left Kansas with a rental car heading to Georgia (before the fraudulent act of my father placing me into the hospital). Upon picking up my vehicle, I realized someone again ripped out my car alarm. So, I went back to the car audio business for a repair service.

I arrived with my father at the car audio business. It took approximately 30 minutes for the repair to be completed. While I waited inside the business building, my father slept in the rental truck, which I rented it for the trip to Kansas.

I sat in the front lobby watching TV. I am glad I did so. I learned interesting stuff while in the lobby.

The manager made (or received) a call, I don't recall. However, he was loud and vocal in his office from the front lobby.

He stated to the person on the phone, "What's going on? This girl comes back to me with a ripped car alarm that I installed. You told me that you were just having some fun with this girl and nothing would happen. She brought her father with her too. This is not supposed to happen . . ."

Of course, I never told my father what I heard (or anything for that matter), since it was clear my father was a part of the harassment too. However, I had confirmation the harassment also spanned to businesses I patronized and that these groups somehow made their way into these places.

BERNICE RATHE

After leaving the car audio business, we quickly began moving my belongings out the apartment. While moving my belongings, my father took the liberty in taking my stuff. He never asked me for my things.

He took what he wanted and threw away the rest. I am sure he wanted to get the expensive items and any "dirt" he could find, which, again, was without my permission.

He also threw away everything including furniture, large items, and my file compartments that had the investigator's reports, documents and information. So, I no longer had the investigator's information or contact information to inform the investigator as to what occurred in Georgia.

I tried searching for him. I couldn't recall his name (the medications really took a toll on me). I think he was no longer in business (when I hired him but he had his license) and the investigator had a P.O. Box address, so I had no luck in locating him. But, I did not forget him for the help I received (as he was an angel in disguise).

My father and I headed back to Georgia. Back in Georgia, My grandma stated I could stay with her. My mama was staying with her since my mama's heath worsened. So, my grandma felt it was a great living situation, as I could help care for my mama.

Yet, it wasn't. Jaime and I were scared my father or others would hospitalize or harm her or me if we continued to talk about what happened to us.

So Jaime acted like nothing ever happened to her or me to keep others from deeming her mentally ill like they did me. Jaime would find pretending like nothing ever happened didn't stop any of this from happening or harm to come to us.

Whatever the case, Jaime and I stayed as long as we could. I used my savings to pay my bills and any bills for my grandma and my mama whenever I could, while caring for my mama.

I continued to take the psych medications as ordered by the state hospital. I had to go to the state hospital every month for new meds. During that time, my side effects worsened.

My family was scared for me and I was scared too. Not only did I have the same effects from the hospital, but also I started to sleepwalk, which I never had a history of doing so.

BERNICE RATHE

My family saw me sleepwalking one night. I did not know I was sleepwalking. It is not like sleepwalkers know they are sleepwalking.

For example, 4 am in the morning, my mama heard someone in the shower. It was me. I was seemingly taking shower in my sleepwear.

My mama asked me what I was doing and I apparently told her I was taking a shower to go out to the club. That's when my mama realized I was sleepwalking.

Another instance was when my mama saw a light outside her room window late one night. She spotted me in my car trying to start the car. My mama came to the car, asked what was I doing, and she realized I was sleepwalking again.

My mama apparently helped me out the car and placed me in her room. She didn't want me to sleepwalk and do something like that again. [Who knows what happened on other nights before she discovered I was sleepwalking?]

After this, especially almost starting my car when sleepwalking, my mama had my daughter and other family alternate sleeping near my room (on the floor at the door) so they could see if I began to sleepwalk again and somehow left the home so they could stop me.

But, my side effects got so bad that my mama had Jaime sleep on the floor at my room door, so I would trip over Jaime, if I would sleepwalk again. I continued to sleepwalk but this time I would trip over Jaime and wake up.

I hated those times and I was scared for myself. My mama said luckily I was not able to start the car or else I may have killed myself sleepwalking.

Once I was safe from sleepwalking out the house, I then started to have epileptic seizures. I never had a history of seizures (ever in life). This was a first.

The seizures were frequent, longer and violent. Whenever I took a nap during the day or slept at night, I got seizures. It felt like I wouldn't wake up and I would die.

Sometimes, I felt like I was swallowing my tongue or couldn't breathe, and my eyes were rolling to the back of head. I got so scared to sleep because of the seizures. (If you ever had a seizure, you know what I am talking about).

As usual, I had to get refills on my meds and monthly assessments by the doctors at the state psych ward. I told the doctor on my second visit about the side effects and that I did not believe I needed to be on medications and that I was not crazy.

I explained that my father lied to put me into hospital. The doctor stated if this is true, then the diagnosis was wrong and I should not be taking the meds. But, the doctor couldn't go above the doctor who diagnosed me, since the initial doctor was the highest doctor in the psych ward.

I was advised if the side effects persisted to inform the next doctor on my subsequent assessment. It seemed like the person simply passed the buck to the next person (so to speak).

After hearing this information and everything that occurred in Kansas, I consulted an attorney to see if I could get relief via legal means. The attorney initially agreed to take on the case.

In the meantime, I applied to sit for another state's bar exam. This also meant I needed to disclose the hospitalization to that state bar.

This proved to be a big obstacle for my admission to sit for the bar examination. The state bar wanted a copy of my patient file. I sent all the required forms given to me by the state bar to the state psych hospital.

Bea Giovanni

Meanwhile, I underwent a character and fitness interview. In the interview, the attorney said something strange. He stated to me "these men aren't going to allow you to get licensed." He was discouraging and sarcastic with me, then acted like he never said any of those things. So, of course, I was my "bipolar delusional" word against his.

After a month passed, the hospital never sent my patient file to the state bar. Strangely, the hospital stated there was no file in existence. The state bar association doctor contacted me and instructed that I would be required to undergo an evaluation, if I did not have the patient file. I had no issue with that, especially since I wanted to prove my sanity, but I would never get the opportunity.

Also in the process, the state bar wanted to meet with me. So, Jaime and I traveled to the other state for the meeting. However, it did not stop these groups from harassing us en route or there at the meeting. It was apparent that these groups were highly connected and had resources and the support of some in government.

Anyway, upon arriving to the state bar meeting, the state bar had approximately 15 members at the meeting. The state bar members asked me to explain the hospitalization. I explained the hospitalization, what led up to it and the side effects of the meds I was experiencing at that time.

After my explanation to the state bar, some members laughed and one of the members remarked, "These people are just trying to stop you from practicing law."

The state bar was insensitive to what was occurring. They acted as if they did not care. So, there was no help there, and I sensed becoming a licensed attorney in that state would be virtually impossible.

In the same meeting, I was told that I would not be able to sit for the bar examination without my patient file, even though I was previously told that I would be made to undergo an evaluation by their doctor.

I left in amazement and disbelief. Immediately after leaving the meeting, my attorney called me and informed me he was not comfortable taking this case and did not have time to take on the case anyway. So, that left me with no legal representation.

En route back to Georgia from the state bar meeting, Jaime and I were followed and harassed by vehicles with the same insignia and stickers as in Kansas, which included confederate flags, police, fire, military and veteran stickers, license plates and license plate holders and magnets placed sideways to resemble a confederate flag.

After noticing this activity, I stopped in a populated area to contact the state police in that state. The state trooper on the phone did not take me seriously when I told him hate and militia groups were presently stalking and harassing me. The state trooper acted as if these things don't happen anymore. Boy, was he wrong!

I also called a friend (at least I thought at that time was a friend) to make sure she knew what was occurring and provided the plates of some vehicles I noticed along the route. This was to secure if anything happened to Jaime and me, there was someone with real time information to provide law enforcement as to our whereabouts, the vehicles and people who may be involved.

With hesitation and fear, Jaime and I traveled back to Georgia. Luckily, we got back safely.

I made it to my psych medication and assessment visit. I explained the same things as in my prior visit and assessment. The doctor in this visit explained changing the initial doctor's diagnosis, being he worked in the same unit, would be tricky as it could create conflict, and no doctor in the same ward would do so. This was also due to malpractice issues.

Sadly, I was told that no one wants to admit someone messed up, as it is painful for another doctor, working with the same doctor who committed malpractice, to admit a colleague messed up.

Luckily, on my next psych med visit after I explained the same concerns and side effects, another doctor, who assessed me, wanted to phase me off the medications and reconsidered the diagnosis was wrong and that I was not mentally ill.

This doctor wasn't afraid to do the right thing, especially since she suspected I had been lithium poisoned. She tried locating my file; but, the hospital claimed it was either misplaced or destroyed.

But, this doctor was smart enough to search the computer database to retrieve the summary from the database. But, she could not properly change the diagnosis without the file.

Unfortunately, I couldn't wait until the doctor phased me off the meds. The side effects were worsening and my family and I were worried. It got where I wouldn't sleep because my family and I were too scared I would die because of sleepwalking out the home or a violent seizure.

Plus, I have a sickle cell trait that possibly complicated things. The lithium seemed to do more damage. So, out of necessity for my life, I stopped taking the meds "cold turkey."

I called the doctor and told her I was doing so. She didn't advise it, since people have died stopping their meds cold turkey.

My mama was scared for me too, since she was a lifelong social worker and saw the deadly consequences of people stopping the psych meds 'cold turkey.' But she knew I was suffering. So, I took my chances (I figured the meds and the side effects would very well lead to death if I didn't stop taking the meds.).

The doctor called my mama and me during the week to see if I was okay. My mama was a big help, since she made sure to note or observe anything unusual. After 2-3 weeks, the doctor was satisfied I was fine.

After talking with my mama, the doctor asked for my email and sent a copy of my hospital summary and advised me to get another evaluation elsewhere, since she was convinced I was not mentally ill and my father lied to place me into the hospital.

Now, off the meds and with things being no better than before, I continued to care for my mama, my grandma and Jaime. I still didn't have a job. After 2 months, one of my old jobs wanted me back, along with others. So, I went back (I had no other chance, I had no job). I was thankful, though.

I started teaching one class at a time, no longer making ample income, each year making less, since I lost seniority and my jobs (I held for years) lost confidence in my teaching ability. Who wouldn't?

Consider one day I was teaching very well to the point I was on the chairperson track, then the next day I disappeared, my cellphone was off, I did not answer my emails and I was nowhere to be found.

This was all because my father fraudulently and involuntarily committed me to the hospital. Yet, my employers didn't know this and didn't care to know this. You would think my jobs would be concerned and contact law enforcement, but they did not.

The harassment did not stop for Jaime or me (just because we were in Georgia living around family). In fact, one summer day in Georgia, Jaime attended her summer camp trip and saw Mr. Phinus (remember he was the assistant principal at XJ #100 Elementary in Kansas, when Jaime attended the school).

Well, Jaime came home startled and scared. She said to me, "Mama, I saw Mr. Phinus riding next my school bus when my camp group went to our field trip."

At first, I thought she was mistaken. However, she was not. Other children, on the bus, also stated Jaime said she saw him and they described him as wearing a XJ #100 Elementary t-shirt, wearing shades and driving a 4-door vehicle.

I recalled that there was a GPS tracker on my vehicle and the connection to the hate groups. It was possible Mr. Phinus was associated with these groups involved in the GPS tracking on my vehicle.

How else would he have known we were in Georgia and in these specific cities and locations, especially when the school did not have any of this information?

It began to make sense as to how Mr. Phinus located us. Thinking about the "XJ #100 letter" and the Kansas investigator focusing on the two principals and Jaime's

BERNICE RATHE

4th grade teacher, Ms. Kneipase, it made sense. It is possible Mr. Phinus was a part of the harassment too.

I promptly made a report to the FBI. However, the FBI agent stated this person's presence within the state was not a crime and it was a local issue. So, I made a police report with the local police.

No one at either the federal level or local level believed Jaime and me. I told my mama and her family and they did not know what to do.

As I was stating, the harassment did not stop. Another example was when I met with a friend (the same friend I met from the psych ward). Driving en route to meeting this friend, cars would attempt to run me off the road.

A stranger even physically threatened me with my life in the public while at the mall waiting for my friend. I would be followed home and to other places.

I frequently told my mother and her family, but what could they do? This has never happened in my mother's family.

My father participated in the harassment as well. Here's an example: my mama and I were holding an estate sale for my deceased uncle's estate (the same uncle who died during my false imprisonment in a mental health hospital).

Well, I placed online ads to sell my uncle's estate items. We sold everything and settled the house sale via my uncle's probate matter.

One day, one of the buyers called my phone and we met at my uncle's home. My father was over my grandma's home (for no reason at all, just being noisy; he had no business or reason to be at my grandma's house) and he overheard my conversation. He left when I left my grandma's home.

As I left and passed his truck, there was a young male in a 4-door vehicle parked adjacent to my father's truck in the street. My father, unaware I could hear him, stated to the male "follow her, she is going to her uncle's house. See what she's up to."

The young male followed me to my uncle's home, then he sat near the street entrance watching from afar.

I couldn't believe what I heard and saw. I told my mama and others. But, no one seemed to believe me. At that point, I knew my father was crazy and a part of this conspiracy and harassment.

BERNICE RATHE

Who was this man (my so-called father)? Why was he doing this? He was not helping me.

Putting me in the hospital and ruining my life was not helping me, and having this male follow me was not either. Telling the truth is helping someone. (I always wondered if he was my real father, as it just didn't seem like it. But, I digress.)

My father continued to stop by my grandma's home and taunt me. He would also mention hurtful things, especially when either anything good happens to me or when I begin to mention anything about the harassment. He would do this in front of others too.

My grandma and my mama would ask him to refrain from doing these things. One time my father said to me, "they believe you are crazy, not me. They don't think I am crazy."

He also stated to me "when you get the money they will give to you, give it to me, I deserve it, not you."

My father's behavior was strange and I never knew why he was saying these things and what money he was referring to.

I later learned what he meant by "the money." I was entitled to major (and I mean major) compensation and my father knew this. But, how he knew was the question.

I uncovered my father was partly responsible for the harm done and danger placed upon my life and the government and others owed me major compensation. I would also find my father cared neither for Jaime nor myself. He merely wanted the money I am apparently to receive, which I am still looking for.

In fact, after complaining to authority and the federal government in 2009-2010, I initially thought my compensation would be six-figures. But, in 2013 after learning what was done to me at birth, the involvement of others, my father and the government and getting advice from an economist, I am entitled to several million dollars.

Let's just say what they did to me constitutes a settlement like no other in history. Needless to say, all that I went through, I received zero compensation and no formal information on what happened to me.

I am not holding my breath. The government has neither substantially compensated nor admitted wrongdoing to anyone it has wronged.

BERNICE RATHE

Justice for victims like me is a fiction, which is why some in the world don't believe in god. Plus, few people want me to be happy, including having money and resources to improve my life after it was destroyed. After all the harm and suffering with these life-endangering acts and these groups, you would think money would be nice.

Despite this, my mama continued to entertain and believe my father. I think my mama still had "feelings" for my father. She would say things like I looked and acted like him, even though I wasn't raised around him and knew very little about him. She said it was just so ironic that my father and I could have the same mannerisms.

Then, in the brief conversations with him in my life, he would say things like I looked and acted like my mama, which I gotten most of my life because everyone stated I looked and acted like her. So, you could see how they may still had feelings for one another.

Back to the point, when my father would visit my grandma's house (which was rare), he would act nice and would bring food from his restaurant, and then he would start on his "crazy stuff." From this, I began to think my father was crazy. Anyone would think so.

Interestingly, my father was either unaware my life and Jaime's life was being threatened or he didn't care, as he was busy harassing me that he never asked and never realized all that was going on. Also, I never communicated with him like that, since we didn't have a father-daughter relationship.

In Georgia, I would find myself followed by similar people and vehicles. This was not the mental illness, paranoia or delusion at play. In some instances, while I shopped, there would be an individual in military police gear with the marking of MP (for military police) with a search dog in the parking lot directly standing at my vehicle.

He would order the dog to sniff around my vehicle. I was unsure if the dog was sniffing for drugs or a bomb. At that point, I was even more convinced that there was a conspiracy at play, as there was no need to sniff or search my property.

Some people even asked the MP the purpose of his presence in the parking lot. It goes without saying that many people were scared and afraid as I was. Again, this was not mental illness, paranoia or some delusion at play. And I know the MP was not helping me, especially from prior experiences with law enforcement and anyone connected.

With every incident or encounter with these groups, I continued to inform my mama and her family. After knowing this information, they noticed that these activities were real.

My grandma stated to leave home, as she wanted me to be safe and protected as it was becoming too dangerous for me here. My mama did not want me to go, but I respected my grandma's wishes and left.

Before I left, I wanted to make sure I documented what happened as I was involuntarily leaving my grandma's home. I called 911 and the police came out. They were familiar with me, not because I was crazy but because of my father's involvement in this matter.

One police officer asked was my father in the military and worked in the Nixon Administration.

I cautiously replied, "Yes." The officer then said, "I know what this is about and I will try to help you. Travel as you wish and get to a place where you feel safe."

Jaime and I traveled and settled in a place we felt safe, as we could not go back to Kansas due to the previous intimidation and threats against us. We traveled for a long time. My car was broken from previous vandalism, so we couldn't travel over 50 miles an hour (something was wrong with my powertrain). En route to our destination, Jaime and I stayed at hotels along the way.

Then, we traveled into Oklahoma. We stopped for fuel, paid and left traveling back onto the interstate. This is where we encountered a police officer (Officer Purvoc).

The officer was initially sitting near the on/off ramp area. He was far ahead of us, as we got off the ramp onto the interstate.

He slowed his car down very quickly and got behind our vehicle. This was strange for anyone to see. Imagine traveling as usual and you are far behind every vehicle on the interstate (as you got off the on/off ramp) and an officer slows his vehicle so slow as to maneuver his vehicle behind yours.

Well, should I say more? The officer stopped us and stated we were speeding (92 in a 70 mph zone), which was a lie. However, I didn't tell him I knew it was a lie; in fact, my car couldn't travel more than 50 mph, due to the vandalism on my vehicle that impacted my powertrain.

BERNICE RATHE

He asked what hotel we were staying at and if I paid with cash or credit at the hotel.

Who asks those questions on a traffic stop?

At that point, I knew this officer was dirty and harassing us. I explained I didn't feel the stop was legal.

How did I know it was a part of the harassment? Well, I had been paying with cash everywhere we traveled. In the past, the investigator in Kansas told me these groups could be tracking me electronically and via other methods. Credit transactions are electronic. So, Officer Purvoc's line of questioning indicated he was possibly a part of the harassment.

Officer Purvoc then ordered me out the car and handcuffed me. Jaime ran out the car in disbelief and anger and yelled, "Let my mama go, she didn't do anything." I asked Jaime to stay in the car and that it was going to be okay.

I was just as scared for Jaime as I was for myself. I didn't know if the officer was going to harm me and Jaime, since he handcuffed me and I couldn't do anything to assist my child if something happened to her.

Bea Giovanni

I simply did not know what this officer was going to do, since it was apparent that this officer was a part of the harassment. He could have raped or killed Jaime and me.

The officer searched me and took things out my pocket asking about the contents (even though I explained I had no weapons or anything dangerous on me). The officer's behavior and actions were grossly illegal and aggressive.

At this point, the officer committed an assault, battery, and I was falsely arrested, along with the illegal police profiling tactics, and I was about to be falsely imprisoned in the back of his police vehicle. Who knows what else he planned to do with Jaime and me?

Handcuffed, the officer ordered me into the backseat of his police vehicle and he questioned me. (Ironically, there appeared to be in-vehicle dash cams.). The officer, in a hostile and angry tone, asked me questions about my father, my father's older son, if I told anyone in the government about this harassment, why I was being harassed, why I was so special, and if anyone in the government knows or is helping me.

I would not give him very much information, since this officer could have done anything to me, possibly killed me as indicated from his hostile behavior. Moreover, I clearly couldn't trust him, as he was harassing me and endangering my life and my daughter was in the car alone. Plus, I really did not know anything, other than I was being harassed, stalked and threatened.

Jaime and I were in the middle of nowhere. There were no cars passing and no businesses. It was just the officer and us. I had every reason to fear this officer.

He would not let me go until I told him what he wanted to hear. But for the second officer coming to the scene moments later, Officer Purvoc possibly would have harmed me and Jaime.

The second officer came to Officer Purvoc's vehicle. Officer Purvoc stepped out the vehicle and met the second officer. They conversed for another 5 minutes.

Then the second officer approached Officer Purvoc's vehicle and asked if I was okay. I stated "no" and that I wanted to go to the car with my daughter. He instructed Officer Purvoc to let me go.

Shortly after, Officer Purvoc cited me and provided me with tickets for speeding and no proof of insurance, which were bogus. However, a month later, I paid the tickets, as I didn't want to go to Oklahoma after the incident with the officer.

I was fearful this officer would harass, stalk and harm me at the hearing or after. He was an officer and had access to sensitive databases. Plus, it was apparent that if I complained, this officer could track me down and harm me. Anyone in my position would feel the same way and the pay tickets as you had no other choice. This was not delusion or paranoia.

I finally settled in a new state: Idaho. Unknown to me, Native Americans called this area of Idaho "death valley." This would have some spiritual symbolism in itself as the prayer states.

I called my mama and told her Jaime and I was fine. She was unaware of the Oklahoma police stop. My mama's health was getting better, so I didn't want to worry her.

I instructed her not to communicate with my father or entertain him in any way. This included eating my father's food from his restaurant if he came by the house with food (as his usual peace offering). My father couldn't be trusted and could harm us. I believed this as the harassment intensified and he was involved.

BERNICE RATHE

My mama wouldn't heed my warning. A month later, after eating my father's food he brought to my grandma's home, my mama had a stroke and went into a coma. Instantly, I believed my father poisoned her. I couldn't prove it, but I knew he did it, attempting to cover up his role in this harassment.

Eventually, my mama got out of the coma and recovered. It was a slow recovery, but my mama was a fighter and she made it through the coma. Meanwhile, Jaime and I settled into Idaho.

Chapter 15: I Am Not A Terrorist

We settled Idaho but the stalking, harassment and hunting continued. Similar activities, indicators, individuals and backgrounds were present (like hate groups, extremist groups, police, fire, veterans, or military indicators). It seemed no matter where we settled or I worked these groups were there and continued to stalk, harass, and threaten our lives.

It was not enough they ruined my life (from the fraudulent acts of my father) and I did not have sufficient income or support from anyone. It was clear these groups did not like us, were jealous of us and wanted us dead.

Even in Idaho, I couldn't escape these groups' wrath. Someone stole my identity again. Despite making identity theft reports in the past, my efforts did nothing. I was a victim of these groups in nearly every way possible.

In public, these groups discretely replayed private conversations within our home like "staging" events and conversations between people via passing or while individuals were talking on a cell via passing and mimicked phrases we said to others.

It was clear to me not only they were tapping my phone (both landline and cellphone), but they bugged my home and car (with audio and video) and our communications weren't heard by the government alone but lots of others. They tracked my car, email and internet activity too. It was also possible they bugged the lines of the businesses or places I patronized or where I volunteered.

No one seemed to care my life and my daughter's life was constantly in danger. It sounds paranoid, but I was onto something that later proved to be true, as someone attempted to destroy my evidence on my laptop using a RAT. Also, my laptop had sophisticated keylogger software on it.

My home, car and other areas were confirmed bugged and under surveillance with suspicions there were people near my home prying in our private affairs. So-called agents and officers were directing businesses, my jobs and others to give them access to information or even spy, do or say certain things, which I later found was occurring since my birth. Some of these groups would later be caught running a secret police surveillance department.

What did I do to make people harm me since I was a baby? Yes, from my estimation and thinking back many years on these coincidences, I believe I have been targeted since I was a child.

It possibly never stopped and these groups do whatever they can to commit these acts. For instance, even when we traveled on vacation out the country, the stalking, mocking and harassment continued and never stopped. So, these acts are not limited by geography.

Over time, the tactics used by these groups changed like acting friendly, stating they were helping me, acting like they did nothing, or claiming they didn't tell others to do certain things. They changed tactics because they saw the tactics were obvious or it exposed them to good authorities and others who would help me.

Some individuals worn shades to disguise their faces, in case someone tipped off good and honest police officers and law enforcement agencies to the groups' activities and presence in certain areas. In fact, the shades never worked but it made them more obvious than before.

Others would drive vehicles with dealer license plates, use other people's vehicles (or rental vehicles), remove plates or bumper stickers, stand at bus stops and communicate to others my travel path, or even arrive at the places of businesses or locations before I arrived to appear as if they were there first or had nothing to do with the harassment.

Some people would even wear items that indicated our private and personal activities. They would even mentioned certain information in public via passing relating to our dealings or daily activities.

For example, pretend we took a trip to Zulu, Indiana. Weeks later, I would see people wearing Zulu, Indiana clothing, i.e., a cap, t-shirt, etc., a car plate, or people talking about the city or an email about the city.

These groups would also play ignorant or deny knowledge or involvement of any harassment if they were caught doing it, i.e., as if it was direct from a terrorist recipe book. Essentially, deniability was an automatic reaction for these groups, but over time, the denials didn't add up. The deniability only made it obvious, which ironically helps in bringing terrorism charges against the groups.

These groups even entered into my online environments, posing as students in my online classes, and entering my social media areas. Because my job required me to connect and accept my students on the social media professional networking sites, they harassed and tracked me.

But, this would actually give me evidence of this activity. In my classes, they mimicked my writing or personal communications style and inputted it into the class activities and discussions. For example, if I surfed the web, similar topics or words are included in the offender's discussion post.

Another example is when my family and I went to Disneyworld for the weekend (and no student knew this, as I didn't share such personal details with the class). Directly arriving from Disneyworld, students mentioned to me via email or in the class discussion boards they went to Disneyworld at the same location over the weekend. These emails or postings had no other purpose but to harass and intimidate me, showing they are watching me and knew my every move.

There were students who made threats via email and even created frivolous issues in the online class to complain about. One particular threat was clear and real.

As I graded the written assignments in my class, a student placed within his assignment that if I kept quiet, nothing would happen and if I did say something, they would kill me. This was a direct threat. I reported it to the federal government but the government never took me seriously and ignored it.

Another example was a student's assignment that had nothing to do with the class or the assignment. The class was a Basic Finance class and a student submitted a paper on her uncle who died of a lung disease.

She described how her uncle died, which was not only the same way as my uncle's death but the same lung disease. If you can recall, I mentioned one of my uncles (my mama's brother) died of a lung disease (he needed his breathing machine and was unable to get to it in time, went into cardiac arrest, and died). This is exactly what the student stated in her assignment.

Bea Giovanni

I wouldn't mention this to my employers, due to fear of losing my job. I was afraid the schools wouldn't believe me, as I was unsupported by the government and any credible and powerful entity.

Also, it was apparent my employers did not really care about me, since my hospitalization and no one inquiring about my whereabouts for a month, yet assuming I simply quit and stop working altogether. So, it goes without saying, I continued to treat these students respectful without alerting them I knew they were harassing me.

Plus, someone in my places of employment had to place these students in my classes, but who? Moreover, I made a complaint on a student and the school ignored it and stated the student did nothing wrong. So, you can see why I did not continue to report my harassment. What a great school and employer, right?

Also, my email accounts were hacked. I got an email from a vendor where I had an account for years when I lived in Texas. The email stated I registered for a marathon in Massachusetts, but I did not register for this event. The email also showed it was from a person named Slaven Sahtof.

BERNICE RATHE

The entry form provided all Slaven Sahtof's information. It showed that he was a firefighter in Massachusetts, his address, debit-credit card data and other information. He also changed from my username to "ILOVESLAVENTHEFIREFIGHTER."

When I contacted the vendor, they alerted me Slaven Sahtof hacked into my account, as the only way to get into my account was to hack into it or my email. Well, Slaven did both, since my security questions and answers were very solid. So, it was apparent he had to access my email in order to hack the vendor's site.

I immediately took action to change password and security information on my email account and vendor's site.

I alerted the federal government's cybercrime unit via its online cybercrime complaint. The site generated a report, but that was it.

Of course, the federal government never took it seriously.

Three months later, this same individual (Slaven Sahtof) did it again.

I received another email stating I registered for an event. I discovered that Slaven Sahtof, the firefighter, hacked into my email account.

Bea Giovanni

What this firefighter did brought up memories from my time working as a prosecutor. You see when I first uncovered similar unethical and illegal activity, it was while working at the city attorney's office.

I initially thought, "Does anyone have a brain, or is it just paper or fuzzy stuff in people's heads? Seriously! There were tons of people in government doing this stuff. But, how and why were the questions.

I felt like I was in Orson Welles' book, *The Time Machine*. Pretty much, everyone around me at that time, except for a few people, was mindless and soulless and doing this stupid and dangerous stuff against others.

I kept trying to make sense as to why firefighters, police and other government workers would harass anyone or me.

What benefit are they getting from this harassing behavior? What are they gaining from bullying another person?

How could these groups do these things without consequence?

Does this make them feel good about themselves to harass another individual?

Was there a lack of integrity, democracy or resources in certain governmental entities and agencies, especially when they are supposed to be a position of trust and integrity?

Yet, from my experience investigating similar claims by minority workers who alleged police and fire professionals harassed them, I saw a different side to public service. But, it was not merely minority workers who were the victims. There were minority workers doing it too.

Anyway, I digress. Back to what I was saying, the incidents never stopped with the firefighter. For instance, there was an incident that occurred when coming from dropping Jaime at her school.

A female in a SUV cut off me on the interstate highway and ran me off the road. The vehicle had a firefighter sticker on it. The female was sitting on the side of the road appearing to wait until I passed.

Once the driver saw me, she sped up behind me and continued to tailgate. Then, when I got over to the next lane to allow her through the lane, she proceeded to get into my lane in front of my vehicle while she ran me off the road and flipped me the middle finger.

She did not stop there. Once she ran me off the road, I got back onto the road and she proceeded to trap me via getting in front of my vehicle into every lane I traveled preventing me from moving forward. If slowed down, she slowed down.

Surprisingly, it was not until other cars saw this female driver's aggressive driving where the cars traveled between my car and the female's car to prevent her from harming me. I am very grateful to these other drivers on the road at that time, as they saved me from bodily harm or death.

The female, unable to do any additional aggressive driving, later left the interstate onto an exit area. Interestingly enough, months later, I seen this female in another city while I was taking my daughter to her music lessons. Specifically, this female in the same vehicle (same plates) drove by the place where my daughter was taking music lessons.

How did I know this? Well, I couldn't forget the female driver from the previous incident on the road. Plus, I kept a daily log on my activities, surroundings, people, places and things to document strange or coincidental events. Oddly enough, when I checked that log, the female driver's plate and make and model of the vehicle was on my daily log from months prior.

BERNICE RATHE

You know some people state geniuses have mental illness, but this is, at times, BS as some people are jealous of the success. As you can see, from these events, these are other people's issues and not mine's. Despite this, I do not let negativity hold me down. I was (and am) strong.

During that time, I sought resources and help from past mentors, employers, churches, advocacy groups to a U.S. territory's government entity, since it appeared the federal government was ignoring me or refusing to help me.

I never gave up on the good people in the U.S. government, despite uncovering the secret experimentation on me and targeting of me from birth. I continued seeking help from them, since I knew there were still good people left in the world.

I wrote, emailed, and faxed, whatever I could to get help. When it was clear the U.S. government would not help, I began crowdsourcing for help.

Because there were so many people involved in the harassment, my social life was limited to certain groups of people (i.e., those that understood my struggle and those who did not judge and immediately conclude I was crazy). That group was very small. It goes without saying but I also missed having companionship.

At that time, I had few friends, as most friends in Kansas failed me and eventually would be a part of the harassment. It was strange how I could go through a dark period in life and people around me are tested. These periods were not the product of a mental illness but manmade situations made to appear as such.

Most people would think that a person must have done something wrong or a person had to have some mental illness or issue when a person goes through things that are so unfortunate. However, this is not true.

How I look at it is that god (or the source, universe, karma, life or whatever you want to call it) tested my friends as well as me.

I passed, but my friends all failed their tests. What person in his or her right mind would continue to remain in friendships where people are using him or her or harassing him or her? No one would remain, since it would be sorely unhealthy. So, I had to start from scratch meeting new friends.

Surfing online on the gay social sites, I located an individual (a lesbian) who would become a great female friend and my life partner, named Natalie. At first when we met online, I was merely asking her about the best areas for fine dining, a good hairdresser and family fun places for Jaime and me to go.

Natalie gave me a list of places, but I was not familiar with the city, since we lived near Boise. So, she offered to drive us to those places.

Natalie and I would go places together and enjoyed each other's company. Eventually, we fell in love with each other. Jaime liked her too.

I had to tell Natalie about the harassment if I wanted to be honest with her and let her know what she was stepping into. Also, I wanted to make sure she knew I was not crazy if there were any issues of harassment that came up.

So, I told her. This included everything I could think of, including that I was a targeted individual, i.e., stalking and harassment by various groups including my father and his family, police, fire and military, many of which connected to extremist and hate groups. In essence, I explained there was a bull's eye on my chest and any and every body used me as their target to bully, stalk, or harass me or any other purpose.

Additionally explaining, the government allowed it to occur and participated in it, did not believe me and did not care. Some government workers were harassing me. Essentially, I sadly explained I found I've been targeted all of my life.

[In theory, I guess people involved in this harassment treated me as a slave or property. I didn't believe this and I knew that I was no one's slave or property.

While it sounded delusional or paranoid, Natalie, her friends and others later discovered my claims had validity. I was an easy target and, for whatever reason, no one liked me, despite having great friendships in the past, being a nice person and helping others. These groups were spreading lies, causing many people to dislike me and target me more than before.]

I also told Natalie everything that led up to us relocating to Boise, including the fraudulent act of my father placing me into the psych hospital. Natalie thought I was nuts! Ironically, she was a lesbian with a counseling degree and was a mental health therapist/counselor.

BERNICE RATHE

Surprisingly, she continued to date me. Natalie said I was a good person with a charismatic demeanor. She liked that. Plus, she was trained to identify "crazy" people and I was not one of them but very much sane and not crazy.

But, Natalie did not believe my "stories" as she called them. They were too unbelievable and out of a movie or something. Years later, Natalie would learn everything I told her had validity.

Back to my point, Natalie and I hung tight. We were best friends and loved each other. Jaime was adjusting well to our new home and social life.

Jaime and I did not go back to Georgia because of our bad experiences and wanted a fresh start. So, we continued to build our life.

Jaime had numerous friends and extracurricular activities including piano lessons. I enrolled her into a private elementary school. Later, Jaime transferred to a public charter middle school.

Summer 2010, Natalie, myself, and Jaime wanted to take a vacation. So, we traveled cross-country. Because I knew the harassment was still present and Jaime and I were fearful of the same things happening as they did when we came to Idaho, I solicited help from local law enforcement agencies, again, hoping that they could help.

So, I talked to investigators and some suggested to explain in writing what you are experiencing, where you are traveling and your schedule on the vacation, since this worked in the past with the investigator in Kansas. The investigator in Kansas was able to track my whereabouts as well as spot several people and groups in the act of doing these threatening, intimidating, harassing and life endangering acts.

I called this information Operation SOS. It was a combination of my investigative efforts and the data gathered from law enforcement and investigators in other states. The patterns I highlighted, connected to the harassment at hand and to domestic terrorist groups, were vehicles marked with plate indicators, bump stickers, insignia, or items in cars or windows, people in businesses, in the public, or in vehicles that worn indicators that were (or marked with) patriotic, or DoD, gun rights, fire, police, military, veteran, employees in veteran-owned cabs and other related aspects and themes.

BERNICE RATHE

I also suggested posing as these groups (by using similar stickers, plates or clothing items) to see who is doing what. I am not sure if it worked. This was one of many roadmaps I provided in combatting this, as there are other ways to catch these terrorists.

In any event, we continued our vacation. As Jaime and I expected, we were harassed. Despite this, God (or some higher power) had to be with us because we came back safely.

In the past, law enforcement suggested that I contact others in authority that either currently working or formerly worked high in government. That did not work out too well. Because I am not famous, don't come from a wealthy family or had privilege, everyone pretty much overlooked me or blew me off. So, it wasn't a surprise anyone I attempted to contact overlooked me or blew me off as well.

Far later, the government and everyone else wouldn't realize that I was a gifted individual who was actually predicting to them the events that would lead up to what I am talking about today.

No one got it and probably still hasn't; in fact, I didn't get it as well. It was like a TV receiving and broadcasting news but beforehand. The dates on the correspondence and things I wrote (every word) later came true. I don't know how or why, but they did.

Sometimes, when I was young and even today, I would know more about people than they knew about themselves. I am neither calling myself psychic nor claiming to have special abilities. But it is ironic everything I mentioned years earlier has happened and my words had meaning and validity.

Anyhow, I got over the numerous rejections by those in government and the government itself and I began to volunteer in the community and at Jaime's school.

Fast forward, I later volunteered at a domestic and sexual violence survivor organization. Because I was uniquely aware I was being harassed, stalked and targeted by these hate groups and others, I asked the organization to place me into a position where I wouldn't be working with victims or going to its confidential safe houses where women and children were staying.

I didn't want to jeopardize others' safety. These groups were seemingly making their way into every organization and entity I worked, volunteered, visited or patronized.

BERNICE RATHE

Also, in December 2010, I saw a volunteer opportunity for state elderly care ombudsmen assisting the elderly in long term care facilities. So, I volunteered.

Everything went well until March 2011. This was when my supervisor had some complaints about me.

My supervisor called me and stated I was too aggressive, and people, in particular staff, were afraid of me at the facility. I asked her who and why would say something like that. This is especially since I didn't really talk to anyone at the facility due to the busy and serious nature of the environment, and the staff seemed to be generally friendly.

Well, my supervisor could not articulate very well the concerns. Instead, she stated, "They are not going to tell you they are afraid of you and you are aggressive."

I asked my supervisor specifics on how I was aggressive. She couldn't tell me. So, I became skeptical, as I began to sense the supervisor wasn't being honest.

I invited the supervisor to help me on my visits to see what I was doing wrong and where I could improve. She accepted the invitation.

Bea Giovanni

On the visit, my supervisor admitted she didn't see anything I was doing wrong. I confided in her that I was a victim of harassment in the past and people would lie, intimidate, stalk and harass me.

The next day, my supervisor wanted to discuss the matter in detail, and wanted to meet in public, though we usually met in private. I didn't feel as if the meeting was legitimate and my intuition was right. I didn't feel supported so I resigned from the volunteer role.

I later discovered my supervisor was a part of this harassment, and she would later misuse her authority, along with a federal agent and others, assisting these terrorist groups.

After doing some research on the supervisor, she had a military connection or background. From my experience dealing with this harassment, there was a military connection related to certain groups involved in the harassment.

That same day, I arrived at Jaime's school to pick up Jaime at the scheduled time. I noticed there were several police cars in the school parking lot and a SWAT van at the corner and with other police vehicles blocking the entry and exit area.

BERNICE RATHE

I thought there must be a domestic disturbance in the nearby neighborhood. 15 minutes passed, everyone left the school's parking lot, I was the only person in a vehicle left, and the school was practically empty. Jaime never came out the school.

I got out my vehicle to go inside the school to get Jaime. Upon approaching the school, a male police officer stood outside the school door and asked if I was Bernice Rathe. I replied, "Yes."

The officer stated the authorities wanted me for questioning inside and ordered me inside the building. Confused and scared, I asked where my child was. He stated she was fine.

I asked what this was about. The officer replied he didn't know. Once I entered the room, I noticed a school staff member in the room. The staff member stated to be calm and that he was here per the caseworker's order.

I said, "Caseworker? What caseworker? What are you talking about?"

The same police officer entered the room. So, at that point, I was in the room with a staff member and the same officer. The officer (who stated I was wanted for questioning and he didn't know what the situation was about) stated there were some concerns with my mental stability.

Clearly, this officer lied to me when it wasn't necessary. Any fool could have noticed I was not going to react adversely if the officer would have stated the truth and that I was not a threat to anyone. Instead, the officer abused his authority and imprisoned me, as I had no other choice and I was deceived into the situation.

This also violated my right to obtain counsel immediately to advocate on my behalf and Jaime's behalf.

The officer mentioned the previous hospitalization and that my father had concerns I wanted to kill myself. I tried explaining my father lied and this information was old and from at least 2 years prior.

Then, the officer stated "we have emails you sent to the government and other people showing your mental instability" (though he or no one else can make a determination of anyone's mental instability from emails).

Also, the police officer stated, "I was told that you said you are "anointed" or the reincarnation of Jesus, is this correct?"

I tried explaining to the officer how I was being harassed, threatened and endangered. Basically, I tried explaining everything to the officer including how my father was involved in this harassment. But he would not listen. Instead, he stated, "well, there is no law against being crazy."

He also stated my mama agreed I was mentally ill, as they recently spoke with her.

I immediately called my mama on my cellphone to confirm this information and my mama stated some woman from a state CPS agency called her to confirm whether I was hospitalized and that's it. My mama stated to me she did not state I was mentally ill.

I explained to my mama what was going on. Being my mother was a social worker and having worked in CPS, she knew they were going to take Jaime. My mama stated she would be taking a flight to Idaho as soon as possible to avoid CPS placing Jaime into foster care.

In the meantime, I immediately called Natalie at work and told her what was going on. Natalie instantly came to the school.

Unknown to me, Jaime was in another room with a caseworker. Soon after, a female officer, took me into another room, where the CPS caseworker, Kami Dilnoh, and a second caseworker, and Natalie, who were waiting for the female officer and me. In the room, the caseworkers explained the situation, as they believed I was mentally ill.

Kami Dilnoh, the caseworker on the case, explained she received emails and other info from a federal agent alleging the following that: I was a terrorist, mentally ill, I wrote the U.S. President at the time, I was passing myself off as another Bernice Rathe licensed in another state, I never went to law school, I was armed and dangerous and that my daughter attended a homeless school.

My partner and I were shocked in disbelief. I knew then I couldn't tell anyone about the life-threatening acts and the involvement of others, as no one would believe me.

Despite this, I tried explaining to Ms. Dilnoh everything, but she didn't believe me. Instead, she actually laughed and was sarcastic.

Ms. Dilnoh did not hesitant in her response and action as she stated she was placing Jaime into the state's care, as she wasn't convinced I was not mentally ill (though she wasn't a licensed mental health professional and didn't evaluate me at that time and I wasn't a threat to myself or anyone else).

BERNICE RATHE

The female officer questioned Ms. Dilnoh's decision. The female officer may have been the only one with common sense among the CPS caseworkers. The officer stated "How could you come to a decision on this woman's mental health based on emails?" Ms. Dilnoh, with a cocky attitude (as if she had this case in the bag), explained she also received info from a federal agent.

The female officer said, "I still don't understand where or how these documents show any of these things you're saying. She doesn't look like or act like a terrorist to me. She doesn't look mentally ill and her daughter seems to be fine."

Despite this, Ms. Dilnoh took Jaime out my custody.

Ms. Dilnoh was sarcastic and unprofessional with virtually everyone. Her behavior was ridiculous!

She wanted to bypass placing Jaime into Natalie's care, despite state law mandating Natalie could care for Jaime.

What Ms. Dilnoh didn't know was Natalie was a therapist and counselor and knew the CPS laws. Once Natalie explained her background, Ms. Dilnoh changed her tune. Kami Dilnoh went from a "whistling Dixie" to as silent as a lamb.

Bea Giovanni

Kami Dilnoh agreed to allow Jaime to stay with Natalie instead of being in a third party's home (who we did not know).

Quite frankly, it appears to myself and others that Kami Dilnoh really did not know what she was doing and the extent of the harassment. She really thought I was crazy.

Ms. Dilnoh would later find out otherwise and try to cover up her negligence. She later finds herself involved in a very extensive conspiracy scheme, corruption and terrorism that would haunt her life and career forever.

That day, Natalie and I urgently called friends and family and sent emails to them to get letters of support to submit to the court, as there was a shelter hearing the next day.

The next day I appeared at the hearing with the letters of support. Yet, the judge didn't consider the letters of support and my background.

To the judge, my background meant nothing and the letters also meant nothing as they weren't experts, though, Natalie was a therapist, and Natalie's sister worked 20 years as a childcare specialist. The irony was the caseworker was not an expert either; yet the judge believed her. Go figure!

BERNICE RATHE

The judge set the case for the next hearing and ordered me to undergo a mental health exam. In fact, the judge made some very disparaging comments on the record, stating, "I read the documents and you need medical help! I hope you get medical help soon."

I thought to myself "this judge really is making a big judgment call and has not really heard my side."

Combined these biases and missteps with what Ms. Dilnoh would later do, all of these things would change the course of the case and Ms. Dilnoh and the court would miss an opportunity to catch these people in the act of harassing us and catching those committing acts of terrorism and human trafficking as well as an opportunity to prevent her subsequent unethical conduct.

So, what did Ms. Dilnoh actually do? Well, rumors generated Ms. Dilnoh was on her last strike with CPS, as she placed her in the investigative unit to see if she could show CPS she could cut it.

Apparently, in the past, Ms. Dilnoh committed some very negligent and illegal acts in another CPS unit. So, instead of firing her, the agency gave her a last good faith chance to show she can do the job.

Bea Giovanni

Well, Kami Dilnoh thought she had the perfect case to do so. She had information and documents provided by a "federal government agent" and a timely hotline call from the state elderly ombudsman supervisor allegedly stating I was mentally ill.

She also had a prior established history of my perceived mental illness via my father's act of fraudulently placing me into a psych hospital and the "XJ #100 letter" alleging I made terroristic threats. This was convenient to her in "making a case" against me. As you can see, you can see each act from my father, XJ #100 district and others played into this.

All Ms. Dilnoh had to do was get someone to corroborate this information, so she could present this information to the court, as an investigation was unnecessary (so she thought).

Ms. Dilnoh was eager to show her boss she could "cut it" that her biases got in the way. She began putting things into the CPS file that was untrue such as Jaime telling her certain things. Jaime and others, who were present during Jaime's questioning, also questioned the validity of Ms. Dilnoh's version of events and facts, as she violated several laws and our rights.

In fact, because Jaime was not alone with Ms. Dilnoh in Jaime's initial interview, the other person also stated Jaime never told Ms. Dilnoh anything. Many people believed Ms. Dilnoh used information from the documents given to her by the federal agent and inputted it into the CPS file as if Jaime or someone else stated this information, as to corroborate the information.

However, none of this information she tried corroborating was true. Kami Dilnoh would later find the information she received from the federal agent was false; yet, Ms. Dilnoh continued to pursue a CPS action against me and destroy my life and my daughter's life.

Ms. Dilnoh was so excited about the case she spread the news around the entire local CPS office. There were people within the office who knew mutual colleagues of mine who uncovered this.

She acted so unprofessional and idiotic, she began emailing people in the office mocking me and even "shopping around" for a mental health evaluator that would provide an adverse evaluation to support her mental health allegation against me.

Bea Giovanni

Some things Ms. Dilnoh said in her email were that I was like Russell Crowe in *A Beautiful Mind*. She even convinced a therapist to evaluate me indirectly, in my visits with Jaime. Ms. Dilnoh wanted other evaluators to observe me in public to support her claims I was mentally ill.

I am not sure how anyone could competently evaluate a person from afar or while in public, when an evaluator can't reasonably understand why or how a person is doing anything, as the individual could be waiting for someone, patronizing a business or talking on the cellphone or some other task where the evaluator is clearly not privy to and possibly knows very little about the individual's social life and happenings.

Ironically, Kami Dilnoh and others involved in the CPS case would find the information, provided to them and the court, was false. After learning that the information was false, Kami Dilnoh, CPS, the DA's office, the judge, and the attorneys involved in the CPS case would regret their actions. So much so, they diligently tried covering up their negligence and what they did to me and Jaime and said to me (on and off record).

BERNICE RATHE

However, it did not go without others noticing this because many acts were so unprofessional, negligent and careless any person could see they were wrong. They even placed some comments and actions on record while others were in the courtroom for every hearing.

None of the information reported and put onto the record were true. As an example and in fact, the XJ #100 district letter was used as a basis for the "terrorist" and "armed and dangerous" allegations. Again, none of this was true. That is merely one example out of many examples I could highlight.

For the CPS case, they assigned me a court-appointed attorney. My attorney thought the same thing as I thought, which was that the allegations were outrageous and had to be false. So, at the first hearing (the shelter hearing), my attorney asked Kami Dilnoh who made these allegations. Ms. Dilnoh refused to give the accuser's identity other than it was a federal government agent.

During the early stages of the case, Kami Dilnoh's first inclination was to begin placing Jaime into the home of her father, Jeff, as state CPS conveniently located him for the first hearing (the shelter hearing). The keyword I used here was conveniently.

Interestingly, Georgia had difficulties in locating Jeff, since he was frequently evading support but Idaho CPS had no issues and even had his cellphone number. How convenient, right?

How did they obtain it? I don't know. But, it would later be revealed the actions of the government agent and others were a part of a big conspiracy in human trafficking, sex trafficking, molestation and other crimes.

During the shelter hearing, Jeff stated via telephone on record he had never had any issues with the law and no allegations of abuse of any kind. Jeff acted as if he wanted Jaime to come to his home immediately and was the ideal parent and was concerned for her welfare. He expressed he would be willing to help state CPS in supporting my mental health determination that I was mentally ill.

Luckily, I did my research, in addition to my attorney performing her research. My attorney asked if I had anything supporting my case. I provided her tons of evidence and information. I even told her theories what I thought was occurring.

BERNICE RATHE

From my research, I learned two months prior to the state CPS case, the state of Georgia arrested and charged Jeff with Aggravated Sexual Molestation against a Minor and was still an active case when Idaho CPS took Jaime out my custody. Apparently, he allegedly molested a minor, like he was suspected of doing to his first child.

Remember at this point, he has two daughters from a second marriage and a stepdaughter in a third marriage. Yes, you heard right Jeff and his second wife divorced and he married his third wife.

Back to the original point, the court in Georgia ordered that Jeff stay away from the sexual assault and molestation victims and their families. If convicted, Jeff faced 25 years to life imprisonment on each act.

This information was timely and important to my CPS case, which this information was screaming out at me. I recalled a friend of Jeff's family told me years ago of Jeff's prior sexual molestation issues. Jeff was accused of fondling his first daughter and he couldn't be alone with her after that point. It all made sense. Jeff had a serious problem.

Bea Giovanni

I told my mama about Jeff's recent molestation charge and she was surprised to hear that information. But, at the same time, she was not. My mama told me she was so glad she cared for Jaime and that Jeff was not really around Jaime after she was born.

Jaime was my mama's first grandchild so my mama was very protective of her. My mama wouldn't let Jaime out her sight if I wasn't around. She only trusted me with Jaime. Her initial instincts about Jeff were correct. He was not to be trusted.

I also told others including my attorney in the CPS case of the discovery of Jeff's alleged crime of molestation and the previous information I knew. Despite learning of this information, my attorney did not want to fight the CPS allegations against me or to prove the CPS allegations were false.

Instead, my attorney had her investigator research my employment, my background and anything that was helpful to my case such as Jeff's recent molestation charge.

Then, my attorney stated that I needed to do a second evaluation that her firm would pay for. This would be secret (so my attorney instructed me not to tell anyone), as CPS, the DA, and court would not know about this evaluation. This would be similar to a double-blind study approach.

My attorney controlled legal strategy, so instead she just wanted to show I was fit. She would later regret not fighting the case as I suggested, i.e., head on.

It was a false case, so why not fight it as such and prove I am competent? Who knows, but it started to appear as if my attorney was not truly on my side.

A month passed and I did everything CPS required, I saw the state evaluator and he stated I was mentally ill. So, why wasn't I surprised?

Ironically, the state evaluator chosen by Ms. Dilnoh was a former military doctor who published articles about gang stalking victims, PTSD and related topics. Despite conveying to the state evaluating doctor the facts and that the allegations were false, he didn't believe me or possibly didn't want to (or he was a part of this too).

Instead he stated I was delusional and these things couldn't be true.

His results yielded I had a paranoid delusional-persecutory type disorder concluding I wasn't a threat or danger to anyone and I was fully functional, which the court entered onto the court record.

Bea Giovanni

Isn't it interesting I was pegged delusional despite the fact that the allegations were false? If I'm paranoid delusional, then everyone who has a car alarm, life insurance or washes their hands before cooking or eating is paranoid delusional. Right?

I complied with my attorney's requests and underwent a secret evaluation with a psychologist. I spent approximately 8 hours taking psychological and diagnostic tests. During my testing, the psychologist stepped away from his office as he received a call, i.e., his office was the basement of a home.

While the psychologist was on the phone, I overheard his conversation. Let's say the walls were thin. He eventually went upstairs when he noticed I heard him. But, in the process of overhearing the conversation, he was talking about me on the phone to someone else.

He made jokes and disparaging remarks about me. It goes without saying I didn't have faith in this evaluation, as it appeared (at that point) the psychologist was not only unprofessional but a part of the harassment. I never told my attorney or anyone else.

I was afraid they would think I was delusional. I also felt alone in the CPS ordeal. It would have not made a difference, as no one would believe me and my attorney was not really on my side. It seemed most people in the case were virtually not on my side but on my harassers' side, which would be later true.

My attorney was still no help in proving my competency. She initially resisted but performed a government background check. It revealed I was not on a terrorist or any suspect, criminal, or watch list (domestically or internationally). I did show I had a good record.

My attorney also contacted the other Bernice Rathe (licensed in another state) to confirm whether I used her identity or passed myself off as her. The other Bernice Rathe stated she never had an issue with her identity and that I never used her identity.

She also investigated my employment history and my employers all confirmed I worked there. My employers (past or current) also confirmed my dates, places of employment, and even provided good recommendations. I showed proof Jaime never attended a homeless school, but only public and private schools.

I never wrote our U.S. President, but CPS, the federal agent and their informers made allegations I wrote a U.S. President at the time, which if anyone wrote him would have been a free speech right. But, of course, I never wrote him. The allegation was merely that I wrote a U.S. President (which I never did) and nothing else, i.e., there were no allegations made that I made threats against the President.

Again, I never wrote this U.S. President in my entire life. In my opinion, the allegations were to prevent my success in society as others would think I was crazy and shouldn't be in any sector in society after knowing this and eventually kill me and take my child.

There was an allegation I was armed and dangerous. My government background showed that I was not armed and I was not dangerous. I did not and don't possess any gun or other weapons.

Additionally, I have never bought and have never been gifted a gun or any weapon. In fact, because of my father's fraudulent acts in placing me into a psych hospital, I doubt that I could even buy a gun.

Despite proving the allegations false, I was still pegged mentally ill per the mental evaluation and Jaime and I were still apart. The state made me undergo unorthodox (made up) requirements and continued to harass me.

Yet, once Kami Dilnoh heard of my ex-husband's charge she began backtracking and reconsidering sending Jaime to Jeff. Ms. Dilnoh even started investigating Jeff. But, interestingly, his contact numbers were disconnected and CPS couldn't locate him.

You see this was all too convenient. Jeff failed to cooperate with state CPS, though in the beginning he was very cooperative, which was before anyone uncovered his molestation charge. Interesting, right?

Again, despite cooperating and satisfying all CPS requirements and providing the allegations were false, Kami Dilnoh went onto the record stating she wasn't satisfied with the results. She wanted me to attend counseling and admit to Jaime and others I was mentally ill and to deny any harassment, stalking, police stops, the "XJ #100 letter," intimidation, or threats occurred or that I stated I was anointed and that others have stated I was anointed.

Basically, Ms. Dilnoh wanted me to admit nothing occurred, though they did (as there was independent, credible proof without my testimony).

Bea Giovanni

The court acted foolishly in not rejecting Ms. Dilnoh's requests. Additionally, the court ordered my attorney explain the results of the state evaluator's report to my partner, Natalie, and myself. So, the next day, my attorney met with Natalie, me, and her firm's investigator to explain the results.

Like others, the investigator doubted that my allegations of harassment and stalking by others were plausible. The investigator believed I was hypervigilant and the extent of my allegations and the numerous people involved were unrealistic.

My attorney then explained the results and the second evaluation (the secret evaluation). Natalie asked about this "second" evaluation, as she knew nothing about it since I didn't tell Natalie per my attorney's advice.

The attorney explained the secret evaluation results, which yielded the same results as the state's evaluation. Interestingly, she didn't allow Natalie or me to get a copy of that report.

The attorney stated the second evaluation report and any medical record from it was her work product, though it was my personal health information.

BERNICE RATHE

She also told me it was my best interests to accept the diagnosis and stop telling or emailing others these delusions and that my father and ex-husband were harassing me or CPS will take Jaime again.

She also stated there was no medication for this mental disorder and instructed me when I have a delusion or encounters like these to inform others I am delusional, explaining the extent of the delusions and possibly providing the evaluation report, if needed.

In the meantime during all of this CPS madness, I got word from my family the doctor notified them my mama was in a coma, non-responsive, and was dying.

Apparently, my mama had her leg amputated, but she did not tell many people about the surgery. She had an infection in her leg that spread after the surgery.

It was an extreme shocker for Jaime, Natalie and me. I had to immediately leave and go to Georgia, and I had to bring Jaime with me to see her grandma before she died.

However, CPS did not see it that way. The state would not even approve me to travel alone to Georgia or to travel with Jaime to go to Georgia out of fear I was crazy and would harm Jaime or myself.

How could they think this? Any reasonable person would have known otherwise. I always protected Jaime and me to the best of my ability. I would never hurt Jaime or myself.

In fact, I was the one who notified an investigator, law enforcement and others as to these illegal and terroristic activities.

It was not until 2009, I uncovered my father's suspect background. I have (and had) nothing to do with his family or these groups. I never grew up with them or knew them.

I was also a victim of these groups. I was not crazy, but others were creating these things on me to make it appear as if I was crazy.

It was bad enough I missed my uncle's funeral when my father falsely placed me in a psych hospital. Now, both Jaime and I were going to miss my mama's last days, especially as Jaime and I had a strong attachment to my mama.

After the state reconsidered my request, they allowed Jaime and me to travel with the condition Natalie went with us. I was glad the state allowed us to see my mama.

I felt very sad and upset CPS would create all this madness for Jaime and I and my mama was dying. This was on top of the fact, my mama had to see her daughter (me) fraudulently hospitalized, stalked, life threatened and endangered, and her granddaughter (Jaime) taken away from her mother (me).

No parent should have to experience or witness this when dying or ever in life.

Jaime's school donated funds for our trip, as we didn't have money for the unexpected expense. They were a big help to us. They really supported us at that time.

They couldn't believe what CPS was doing. The school was in shock how CPS handled the entire situation and the lies they spread.

Anyway, navigating through this CPS madness, we finally got to Georgia and immediately went to the hospital. My sister and brother left the hospital 15 minutes prior to our arrival and my mama was still in a coma and non-responsive.

But, once I entered the room, my mama miraculously woke up and began eating and talking as if nothing happened. The doctor came into the room, as he had heard the nurses speak of my mama's miraculous recovery.

Bea Giovanni

My mama was up and well. The doctor stated my presence was the right solution for her to get out of her coma. He knew my mama for years, since they worked together (i.e., my mama was a social worker in that hospital). He stated he never saw anything like this as a doctor.

My mama woke up, full of words. The doctor hesitantly informed my mama what happened. She was unaware she was moments away from dying. Upon knowing this, she was grateful for the doctor and our presence.

After the doctor and other staff left the room to attend to other matters, my mama met my partner, Natalie, for the first time. She instantly loved Natalie. She only knew Natalie via telephone conversations when she called for Jaime or myself in Idaho.

Because my mama was protective of Jaime and me, my mama did not trust many people with us. But, my mama trusted Natalie, once she saw Natalie really was a nice person and cared for us.

Plus, Natalie was a professional with a master's degree. Natalie was not like the previous girlfriends (i.e., uneducated, uncaring, shallow, street mentality and promiscuous).

BERNICE RATHE

Jaime, Natalie, and I sat with my mama laughing, reminiscing, and telling her about our journey to Idaho. My sister, brother and niece came back to the hospital after learning of my mama's recovery.

We had a wonderful time lifting my mama's spirits and health. My mama said to us she was blessed if she lived to see her birthday that year.

We stayed with my mama every day for about a week until we left to go to Idaho. While in Georgia, we also visited with other family members. En route to my other family members' homes, a state trooper stopped us (myself, Jaime and Natalie).

The state trooper stopped us for speeding. Guess what? He had a military insignia (an Air Force Veteran pin). At that point, I knew he was harassing me per similar encounters.

Also, the state trooper didn't know I had the cruise control activated. So, I definitely knew (Jaime and Natalie knew) I wasn't speeding. I tried explaining I wasn't speeding and that I felt the stop was illegal (and possibly connected to harassment). He didn't listen to me.

Instead, the officer intimidated me into silence with his threat of arrest. I don't know how you can go from exercising your free speech rights respectfully to the threat of arrest for alleging intimidating an officer, but this officer did so. I remained silent while this officer provided me with a bogus ticket.

What could I do? He has a big, shiny badge and appears to be credible as he is a police officer and a military veteran. I am just a 'nobody' who has been discredited and branded as crazy and delusional.

Nevertheless and despite this incident, we enjoyed our stay with my mama and other family members. In fact, my mama was encouraged and said she wanted to come to Idaho to see us, once she was better in her health.

When we returned to Idaho, I learned from staff at Jaime's school new details on what happened at the school the day CPS took Jaime out my custody. They told my partner, Natalie, my attorney, and I that Kami Dilnoh and several officers from various police agencies held a closed door, unscheduled, emergency school meeting with school officials.

In this closed door, unscheduled, emergency school meeting, Ms. Dilnoh and others explained I was a terrorist, mentally ill, I wrote a U.S. President at the time, I was passing myself off as another Bernice Rathe licensed in another state, I never went to law school, and that I was armed and dangerous and my daughter attended a homeless school. Ms. Dilnoh provided documents claiming to prove this, which was also used in her case.

After hearing these allegations at that time of the emergency meeting, school staff stated the school was in shock and didn't know what to do, as the emergency school meeting and subsequent procedures and actions of Kami Dilnoh and the officers were not per CPS protocol when handling CPS matters in the school.

The school didn't know who to believe, since Kami Dilnoh said a federal government agent provided this information, yet they never saw any indication I was mentally ill and only that I was a supportive parent participating and volunteering in the school.

My attorney learned of this too but really did not do anything with the information. Knowing this, everyone questioned Ms. Dilnoh's and this government agent's credibility. Everyone wanted to know the identities of the hotline caller and the agent. Ms. Dilnoh wouldn't give this information.

Despite this, CPS and my attorney forced me to settle and sign an agreement stating I was mentally ill, that the allegations against me were true, and that I was not being threatened, harassed or stalked, while signing over permission to access my daughter and I private counseling files from Kansas, upon which they dismissed my case, or my daughter would remain in foster care and adopted out.

After this so-called agreement, several parties who observed this case advised me to make complaints with the state and federal government, which I did. I also consulted with attorneys for the proper legal action.

Ironically, after the CPS ordeal, I would later see Kami Dilnoh in different places like an amusement park watching Jaime and I with a mean, angry look on her face. I took these occurrences as coincidental, I didn't want to believe Ms. Dilnoh was involved in hate and corruption.

Sadly, she appeared to be suspect after several coincidences like these. I later uncovered my CPS attorney became a part of the harassment and committed unethical and illegal acts in the case too.

BERNICE RATHE

Our lives went on but the stalking, hunting, intimidation, and harassment continued with our lives in danger and threatened. It goes without saying that Jaime and I had a different view of the world, government, and society. Our life was hacked and stripped away from us, with everyone having a 'free-for-all' to our lives and no consequence for their actions. Our next step was justice for what they did to us.

Chapter 16: Seeking Justice in the Proper Ways

Though the CPS case was over, I was determined to seek justice for Jaime and me. What everyone did to us was wrong, discriminatory, endangering and life threatening. We were embarrassed, shamed and ridiculed in communities wherever we went.

No one supported us. As years passed, we continued our counseling but we actually coped with the trauma by blocking it or we began blaming ourselves but not the perpetrators of this trauma. In time, we came to love ourselves more and even got closer becoming best friends.

I consulted with attorneys, many stated we had a case. While many attorneys may say this, we really did have a case. The only issue was damages as it was a matter of how much.

The problem was no attorney would take my case. They merely provided legal advice. The reasoning varied as to why they did not want to take my case. Believe it or not, many stated they were afraid.

Some attorneys have taken on the state and federal government in the past and lost big time. Either they were furthered harassed and lost business, malpractice premiums were high or their ethics were scrutinized, resulting in law licensing issues.

I didn't blame anyone. This was a fight no one wanted to take on. At the time, I realized this was Jaime and I fight and no one else's fight (though later I would realize this would be a fight the world will take on as it affects everyone).

Some of the advice given was to file administrative complaints to the state and federal agencies. However, the advice given was things I already knew. I figured it would be best that a licensed attorney do it for us.

The attorneys stated I could do it myself, since I was a law graduate, practiced briefly and knew the law. They had tons of confidence in me. Many were impressed I had a better grasp on the practice of law than other attorneys who were supposedly super lawyers.

So, I tapped into all resources. I even tried a female attorney who sued the federal and state governments on similar actions.

Bea Giovanni

This female attorney worked for the CIA in the past, sued them, and won.

Unfortunately, the female attorney stated she closed her practice. She said that fighting the government took too long to get compensation for her clients and for her law practice and the government did not play very well.

Other firms wanted lots of money that I didn't have. If I had lots of money, do you think I would have any issues in getting proper help from attorneys, the court systems or the government?

Despite life moving on, the stalking, mocking, hunting and harassment continued. Natalie, myself, and Jaime wanted to get away. We felt we deserved it.

So, we went on vacation to Disneyworld and loved it!

While we were on vacation, I discovered my email was hacked. When I researched it and my IP provider investigated, the hacker's IP address originated from the same city and area in Kansas where XJ #100 district resided. Interestingly, right?

After I discovered this, I started to gain more interest in XJ #100 district again. So, I located Ms. Shmad, the former principal, the same principal who allegedly wrote the "XJ

BERNICE RATHE

#100 letter" banning me from XJ #100 Elementary and its district. Well, I finally tracked her down. (Apparently, there were two people by the same name as Ms. Shmad and were both public educators).

Once I located the correct Ms. Shmad, I explained to her briefly what occurred to date, since Jaime and I left the XJ #100 district and Kansas. What Ms. Shmad would disclose to me would later surprise and shock me and forever change everything about this situation.

In my brief conversation, Ms. Shmad expressed anger against the XJ #100 district. She was very disgruntled.

Ms. Shmad stated she didn't write the "XJ #100 letter" banning me from the XJ #100 Elementary and its district and does not know who wrote it or why it was written. She also stated none of the information in the letter, except for my disclosure that people in the community were harassing Jaime and me, was true.

Ms. Shmad also stated the district fired her, and that she believed the school district was corrupt. Should I say more?

Well, Ms. Shmad and I concluded the letter was fake. I thanked her and even explained that she may need to get an attorney, as I planned to sue XJ #100 district and others.

I also told her that she may wish to sue whoever wrote the "XJ #100 letter" and the school district itself. But, Ms. Shmad needed to get an attorney or the government to find that out. I informed her I would be filing the lawsuit soon and she may be included in the lawsuit.

She wasn't happy about that. She didn't understand the extent of the harassment, why I was suing her, and that she had a duty to tell authorities of this harassment and that she did not write the letter. If Ms. Shmad had notified authorities, Jaime and I situation would be far different (and better) from what we went through as well as hers.

I warned her of the dangers others placed her in, and that there were possibly clandestine people watching and listening to her and these groups harassing me, who may harm her and these groups. Due to what was done to me by these groups, I told her I could not help her as others think I am crazy.

Unknown to her and these groups, the groups of militia and extremists (essentially terrorists) tried to make me crazy (or at least appear to be) and this backfired and worked against them, which her and others will see why much later.

These groups committed the perfect crime against themselves as they would become targets and not me. I think Ms. Shmad did not take me seriously. I also think she thought I was a part of that XJ #100 district madness. But, I was not.

I was a victim like her, trying to defend my daughter and me. In fact, I was under the impression she wrote the letter.

I instantly called my mama and told her the good news of what I found. She was so worried about us, so I thought good news would cheer her up about what happened to us in Texas, Oklahoma (which she was aware of), Kansas and now Idaho.

My mama was excited to hear the letter was a false letter. My mama knew it but she did not have confirmation of it. Now, she did.

It was good news because this proved that not only did I not make those alleged threats as stated in that false letter, but also there was a bigger conspiracy at hand.

It all began to make sense. Mr. Phinus was the only person in the meeting, besides Ms. Shmad, Jaime, and myself. He was the only one who could have written the letter, and also had access to the school and district letterhead. He also knew Ms. Kneipase (who is believed to be the alleged frightened/threatened school worker in the "XJ #100 letter," which was untrue since I didn't do so and she continued to contact me via email and phone after that letter was written).

It was very clear that Mr. Phinus' alleged activity of stalking Jaime and me in Georgia resembled the same activity as we had experienced before with stalking and harassment. There was no other way in knowing where we were located in Georgia during summer 2009, other than his involvement with these groups.

At the same time, I got an email from my old insurance company in Kansas. They were settling the auto case from 2007. I actually forgot about the case. This required our presence if a trial was pursued.

I was cautious about going to Kansas and explained to the attorney this was impractical, since hate groups forced Jaime and me out Kansas and threatened us if we returned; plus, we currently lived in another state.

I did not have any current intentions on pursuing the case. The only other person interested in the case was Jo. So, they continued with Jo as the sole party.

Knowing the possibility that I had to return to Kansas, coupled with the new evidence provided by Ms. Shmad, knowing that Mr. Phinus was involved in this and stalked us in Georgia after leaving Kansas, and the recent email hacking by someone from the same city and area as XJ #100 district in Kansas, I was fearful.

I consulted an attorney who advised to settle the matter, if I could without going to trial. In regards to the prior CPS matter, the attorney told me to go to my attorney in the CPS matter to inform her of the new evidence. This would be helpful in reopening the CPS matter and declaring the information supplied to CPS not only false but ruling that I was competent.

Well, I took the advice of the consulting attorney and went to my CPS attorney. But, my CPS attorney did not care. She stated since I was consulting with an attorney and the case was dismissed and her representation of me ended, she could no longer help me.

I told the consulting attorney. Not to his surprise or mine's, he found my CPS attorney committed a major professional error. My CPS attorney is a mandated reporter and is ethically and criminally liable. This was especially true if something happens to Jaime or myself and new evidence supports my allegations or if someone finds she is a part of the conspiracy, since there were suspect things she did or didn't do (unknown to me or others) or even disclose to me like my health records for the "secret evaluation."

In fact, I was made to sign a secret settlement with CPS in order to get my daughter back. During the time of the original CPS matter, my CPS attorney would not take the case to trial; she even told me I had to sign over access to my daughter and I private counseling records from Kansas, i.e., when we sought counseling after Jaime disclosed the sexual assault.

It was also during that time that my CPS attorney stated if I did not sign the secret settlement, Jaime would be forced into foster care forever. This essentially means she would be lost and possibly abused in the system.

As you can see, I had no choice per this threat. In this secret settlement, I had to admit I was paranoid delusional, go to counseling and admit this to others as well as Jaime, especially whenever I had "episodes" or encounters with these groups or police.

Little did I know, my CPS attorney would then disclose our counseling records to CPS, which then got into the hands of these terrorist groups. This is another reason why my CPS attorney failed in her ethical responsibility.

Oh, I also had to eliminate forks and knives from my home. Isn't that the stupidest sh&t?

How in the h*ll was I going to eat food? With my d@mn hands or with chopsticks? Was I supposed to sip soup?

Apparently, they thought I was a danger to myself and others, despite the state mental health evaluator's report that I was not.

It goes without saying that this left me with only spoons to eat with. So, not only was I forced to admit I was crazy but my human rights and Jaime's human rights were violated. But, no one seemed to question the reality of this secret settlement agreement, regardless how outrageous any of it seemed.

It was as if my attorney and others in the CPS matter, who were against me, were helping these groups and were committing acts of terrorism and violating my rights and Jaime's rights. Anyway, I digress.

Luckily, the auto case was settled, so no appearance was needed. Who knows what would have happened to me, since everyone thought I was crazy and I had no support from any government (state or federal)?

During that time, I also investigated the other state's CPS complaint against my ex-husband alleging he had molested a minor, which I learned during Idaho's CPS matter against me, alleging I was armed and dangerous, a terrorist, among other things.

Well, I uncovered the allegations against my ex-husband were true. I also found that Idaho CPS received this similar information on these allegations, yet ignored it.

You see after the CPS case against me, I inquired about the allegations against my ex-husband, I surprisingly learned that Kami Dilnoh also received confidential CPS information that my ex-husband's ex complained about similar harassment and stalking by police, fire and hate groups. She received this information from the other CPS agency that was investigating the allegations against Jeff.

Kami Dilnoh never provided this information to anyone, the court, or me. She intentionally withheld this information, as it supported that I was not crazy and that my ex-husband was involved in this harassment. This explained why Ms. Dilnoh instantly backtracked and didn't transfer Jaime into Jeff's custody in the CPS matter against me. Ms. Dilnoh was covering her butt (so to speak).

Needless to say, I made administrative complaints on all levels. No response occurred from the state. The federal government ignored my complaints too.

There was one federal complaint reviewed and determined that there was no illegal or unlawful acts (or actionable acts) committed against me and the agency was closing its file per its review and determination. The review stated I was free to file in any other forum available to me, which is the green light to file a lawsuit.

Before I filed the federal lawsuit, I again consulted with attorneys. Most attorneys told me I had one shot at this, since corruption will play a role. So, if I brought the action, to bring everyone, who were involved and harmed Jaime and I or at least contributed to the harm, into the lawsuit. This secured that everything was on record, regardless of the result.

Bea Giovanni

While the goal was to win, that result was less important than the goal to document and create a record to secure that if anything happened to Jaime, my family, or myself those involved and those responsible and anyone who helped them would be prosecuted to the fullest extent of the law.

Even if nothing happened to us, everything was on record for the world to see and authorities to investigate.

Some attorneys provided me with great guidance. I didn't know that so many attorneys have heard of these kinds of cases, i.e., crazy people-making cases (where plaintiffs are alleging abuse or other issues and the allegations seemed outrageous and untrue to believe). Most attorneys thought those kinds of cases were truly a product of the plaintiff's delusion and the plaintiff was crazy.

Well, these attorneys no longer thought I was crazy. As I stated before, there was someone else complaining and it connected my ex-husband to this.

After considering everything, the attorneys wanted me to nail these people. These attorneys saw how these groups destroyed, endangered and threatened my life and Jaime's life, when we are good people, and could do it to others including them.

The attorneys were astounded about the massive involvement of others and the domestic terrorism links of these groups harassing me. Some attorneys thought the federal government should have been "all over this case."

As others and I found, the ethics and suspect behavior of the attorneys in my federal lawsuit would prove my suspicions correct about this harassment.

After hearing my story, one attorney actually believed I was crazy, then the attorney began to research the case and found otherwise. The attorney even found a similarity I never thought about or found.

At first, I thought this attorney might be delusional. Apparently, the "other Bernice Rathe" who CPS alleged I passed myself off as (which was untrue), had a similar background as me. The difference was I graduated earlier than her (in high school and college) and even interned at the federal court before her, where she later worked in that same court.

Moreover, the attorney found me and the "other Bernice Rathe" was a part of the same sorority, but I pledged far before the other "Bernice Rathe."

Get this! The attorney also discovered the "other Bernice Rathe" was married to a firefighter. And, of course, the opposite was true for me: I was divorced and later became a lesbian.

After hearing this attorney's information and discoveries, I did not make any conclusions, since (to me) these things were just coincidences or similarities.

To the attorney, it was more than mere coincidence. The other "Bernice Rathe" was possibly using my name and background to gain favor and steal my life (so to speak). Basically, she was pretending to be me.

The attorney continued to research the case before I filed the federal lawsuit. This attorney and others found much of my arguments (if not all) were valid, real and true. This was especially the case after discovering my ex-husband's connection to this case, as his ex complained about similar harassment by police, fire, hate groups and others.

After knowing this connection and that someone else was complaining about similar harassment and this person alleged my ex-husband was a part of this harassment, let's just say this attorney and others didn't think I was crazy.

After getting votes of confidence from some highly respected attorneys, others and I felt it was time to bring the lawsuit.

Meanwhile, my mama's health worsened. Her second leg was amputated and an infection in her leg spread.

However, through her determination, my mama's health got better in no time. But, she was suffering in her own world, as she couldn't come to grips with losing her legs to diabetes and other health issues. Yet, my mama pushed through her recovery.

The next issue was to get her proper home care. This was a challenge and disappointment.

My mama was a public servant my entire life; she helped everyone. Yet, when she needed others, no one helped her. The systems failed when she needed the proper care.

I helped my mama in any way I could. I called disability advocacy groups, but no one could help. My mama's insurance didn't cover certain home care services she needed, even though she was totally disabled. So, she was stuck at home alone with no one to tend to her needs.

How would she get out the bed? Feed herself? Bathe?

To ease some worry and responsibility, I found a company online that shipped readymade meals for individuals on diabetic diets. The doctor thought the idea was great.

My mama did not have to prepare meals. She simply needed to put the meals into the microwave or oven.

So, I continued to order the meals and she loved them. My mama said the meals tasted delicious and not bland.

Sometimes, diabetic meals can be tasteless or bland because many elements are removed that most regular meals would have. But, these meals were not bland but enjoyable for her.

My mama's determination and health inspired me. Yet, I was not at my ideal weight, as the past psychotic meds caused significant weight gain. Despite not taking the meds anymore, they affected my body.

One day, I saw a documentary about healthy eating and fasting. It inspired me to hike, run, choose healthier options (sometimes) and just be active.

I told my mama about the documentary and that I wanted to do a 60-day juice fast. My mama said it was a great idea, since she would frequently talk about her regrets in not keeping her health in tiptop shape. She encouraged me to keep my health in check.

So, I embarked on a 60-day juice fast. I must admit it was difficult the first two weeks. But, after the first two weeks, I was really enjoying the fast. My body, my mind, and my spirit felt aligned and I thought only positive things. I lost all the weight I gained.

During that time, I continued to notify the federal government and those who expressed interest in what was occurring in the years of the harassment. My intent was to garner support and get someone to notify those high in authority who could help Jaime and me, as we were in danger on a daily basis and it did not matter where we lived.

During that time, I emailed a former mentor (keyword is former). I later learned this mentor (who I looked up to) became a part of the harassment. He contacted the U.S. Marshal's office and stated that I was harassing him.

When the U.S. Marshal contacted me, she suggested I stop emailing everyone and anyone on the harassment. She also stated my father wanted her to convey a message to me.

Bea Giovanni

Before ending the call with me, the U.S. Marshal said something strange and harassing. She said to me my father stated, "Are you taking your meds?" She laughed and hung up.

That's when I realized my father was again harassing me but this time through others. Everyone was helping him and even people in government. Why?

They didn't understand the danger placed upon Jaime and me but also the danger placed upon them. I later understood why my father, his family and those who helped them would be in trouble and danger, as there were others involved in the background who were protecting me and were powerful than any group or entity combined.

Need I say more? Is it not apparent I was being harassed and by who?

Fortunately, I had an attorney (also my friend and colleague) who contacted the U.S. Marshal and tried explaining to the U.S. Marshal what occurred in the past and now and that my father was not who the U.S. Marshal thought he was.

The Marshal didn't believe the attorney or me, thus ignoring the attorney intervention. The Marshal believed my father who stated various reasons to her as to why I accused him of harassment and other illegal activities.

My father told her I had a grudge or vendetta against him and others, I was jealous and mad at him, my ex-husband and others, I had "daddy issues" and that I was crazy and needed to be on my meds. Again, she believed him. Despite the fact I am a grown woman who don't have time for childish games or drama, this U.S. Marshal would forever regret what she did.

Little did this U.S. Marshal know is my father fraudulently hospitalized me and was using that hospitalization to discredit me.

Also little did she know she lost a valuable opportunity to catch my father and others (who helped him) in the act of terrorism and other crimes.

She didn't get the connection, my father's role and his identity in this situation and the lies you told her. (Truly, if she recognized this, she ignored it, didn't care and possibly was a part of all of this).

Moving forward, my mama's birthday came and she found herself back in the hospital. However, she was in good spirits.

In fact, I talked to my mama the night before and told her I had 2 days left on my

60-day juice fast. My mama was so proud of me.

She stated that I had proven to her that I was strong, which she said she always knew. I told her that in almost 60 days, I lost 50 lbs.

Days later, my mama called Jaime, myself, and Natalie and talked to us for a very long time. She said some great things to us.

Sadly, two days after my mama's birthday, I was notified my mama died. As she stated months ago, if she lived to see her next birthday, it was a blessing. Well, it was truly a blessing, as she lived to see her birthday

From prior nights' conversations with my mama, I realized my mama knew she was dying soon. Ironically, my mama died on the last day of my juice fast and she died naturally.

I had friends tell me my mama's passing on the last day of my juice fast was spiritually significant. During fasting periods, you are cleansing, detoxing, releasing, praying for others, and helping others, among other things.

My friends told my mama and I have a close spiritual connection and that my mama and I released our pains, worries and anything negative together. I never looked at it in that way.

Ever since, I remember my mama, her life, her strength and what she done for me through a yearly 60-day juice fast, after which reverting to my healthy eating lifestyle as much as I could. For myself, the fast also represented not only my mother's life but my spiritual journey and goal in maintaining a healthy lifestyle.

Over time, I would shorten the fast to 30 days or sometimes one week, due to medical advice directing me to not overdo the fasts. When I fast, I can fast. I mean I can really fast for a very long time, which is why the doctors did not want me to fast too often and not for too long.

This also meant I also found other ways to remember her life. For instance, my family and I participated in the Diabetes walk to raise awareness and funds for those who are suffering with the illness. We would also participated in other walks in remembering our loved ones, such as my two deceased uncles, in an effort to raise awareness of other illnesses and conditions affecting others.

Bea Giovanni

On the day of my mama's funeral, my father came to my grandma's home to attend the funeral. My mama's family did not want anything to do with him.

They remembered what he did to my mama and me including denying I was his child and that he had anything to do with my mama.

Oh, should I mention how he falsely placed me in the psych ward, and how he lied to everyone about everything? No one wanted him there.

He would later throw salt on my mama's funeral (so to speak). He came to the church and told everyone aloud, he wasn't here to support me but to support Jaime. Ironically, Jaime was not talking to him either and was mad at my father for what he done to us.

It wasn't like Jaime forgot what happened to us. She remembered everything that happened, what my father said and did by putting me in the hospital. She realized that my father was a bad man and was a part of the harassment.

My father didn't realize these things affected Jaime as she witnessed and experienced the same abuse and terrorism. Throughout our ordeal in each state and everywhere by virtually everyone, we were treated like prisoners or slaves without bars or chains.

Not the less, my mama's funeral was a wonderful send off. Many people spoke great things about my mama. My family and I really appreciated those kind words and stories.

There was a somewhat funny moment at the funeral as an elderly woman and a few others thought I was my mama. The elderly woman was convinced I was my mama. You could not convince her otherwise.

However, I was not my mama. My family and I chuckled and said to the elderly woman that I was my mama's daughter.

This occurred a lot in my childhood because many people thought I looked so much like my mama that they would mistake me for my mama.

However, despite the wonderful stories and time at the funeral remembering my mama's life, my father did not stop with unleashing his venom. He sent his two relatives to my mama's Repass.

His great aunts people diligently located me at the Repass asking others about me as if his aunts knew me, even though they did not know how I looked or who I was and had nothing to do with me..

Apparently, no one in his direct family, other than my father's children and my stepmother, knew about me. (At least, that's what they stated to me). His great aunts just heard about me because of my mama's death, as word spread "in the streets" of my mama's passing. So, they came to meet me.

I explained to them that I don't have a relationship with my father and his family. I also explained if my father sent them to get information or harass me to please leave. They stated no.

His great aunts sat there, while I ate, and caught up on time and life with me. They also stated that my father was crazy and explained to me their family history. There was some discussion between the two as to who my father was within the family (whether he was the brother or nephew of someone).

Apparently, they have some family secrets that were talking about. I was not privy to these things, so I disregarded whatever they were whispering among themselves.

In my conversations with his great aunts, I began to describe what I experienced with my father, his children, and my stepmother and the life threatening acts, fraudulent hospitalization, and the stalking and harassment by fire, police and hate groups. They looked at each other in amazement as if they had seen a ghost. They immediately told me they haven't seen this occur in a long time.

As far as the groups harassing, endangering and threatening me, they stated long ago when this occurred no one heard from those groups and individuals again. They were unsure what happened to those groups or who caught and stopped them, but they stated it was possibly something bad.

They stated these groups will not be a problem again. Not to my surprise, they omitted the part where their family were also a part of these harassing groups.

Hearing these tales, I didn't think anything of it, as it appeared to be old folk tales. Plus, I did not know them and did not trust them. So, trusting their "stories" was not even a thought.

Anyway, my father's great aunts asked for my address to write me to explain more about their family history and what I was experiencing with this harassment. They stressed my father, his children and my stepmother were crazy and would explain later.

Time passed, I never received this correspondence, as expected. Yet, it was irrelevant at that point as my life was endangered because of their family. Do you really think anyone wants to hear folk tales when his or her life is constantly in danger because of other people's bull87^t? Seriously.

Getting back to my point and my mama's death, there was a silver lining in it but it really wasn't. You see my siblings and I received life insurance proceeds. It was nominal, but my mama thought of us.

I wanted my mama back, not life insurance. I know that my mama's way in showing us that she loved us and wanted us to not worry about support was through life insurance. I recall that my mama always stated her children were good children and we each had our own personalities.

Yet, despite these things, my siblings and I faced the reality we were all we had. My mama was our support system, i.e., our mama, our daddy and everything. Without her, we were essentially orphans. Now that she was gone, we only had each other.

A year after my mama died, I married my partner in life, Natalie. As life moved on, I still grieved my mama's death. You really never get over losing your mama.

Despite all that I went through and were going through, these groups never stopped harassing me. I even learned a few of my neighbors were recruited to harass me, like in any area we lived. Some even moved to my area to continue the harassment and spy on me.

Actually, I stand corrected, the harassment did stop for one day or so. The harassment stopped during the government sequester and shutdown. I am sure you can read between the lines as to the connection and why.

But, I digress. Back to what I was saying, losing my mama was a major life event. During my grieving period, I had many emotions going thru me.

I recalled my mama stating I was a smart and gifted child. I was in honors courses in high school. I was good with numbers, languages, music, and the arts and now in my adult life was a college professor and an aspiring attorney, among other things.

Before she died, she said I made her proud, but she never saw me obtain my bar licensure. I always wanted her to see my swearing in and some higher position in society. However, that wouldn't be possible anymore.

I was also saddened at my mama's death and how people mistreated her like my father. I was angry and upset with him because he denied I was his child and that he ever had anything to do with my mama.

My father acted stupid with my mama. Then, he had the nerve to come to her funeral, like they were best friends or something.

At times, I wished my father was the one who died and my mama was the one to live a long, healthy life.

While she was not perfect, which none of us are, my mama did so much for others; she served the public well. My father was the direct opposite; he acted foolishly throughout his life.

Many times, I thought if I had a time machine to go back in time, I would make sure my mama never met my father. Yes, this would have meant that I wouldn't be born.

But, I didn't care. If it would have saved my mama, her family, me and Jaime grief, pain and fear (and possibly our lives), then it would have been worth it. Again, this was my grieving period.

BERNICE RATHE

I grieved my mama and Umi's death, as Umi died months after my mama's passing. I looked to Umi as my mother too.

Though Umi was a longtime friend and helped me years prior, towards the end Umi was suspect. But, I still grieved her, as our friendship was lost due to this madness of the harassment. I could not trust anyone including Umi.

Needless to say, God, my friends and my partner, Natalie, helped me through that grieving period. I attended grief support groups. I got back into my hobbies like music, fitness, learning foreign languages and mixed martial arts.

During that time, I realized I acquired great friends and a new family in Idaho, who were great, supportive and protective of Jaime and me. They were a direct contrast from former friends and the community in Kansas.

Everyone, who supported me and knew me, hoped that my father and his family, those groups and anyone that helped them to endanger Jaime and me, were caught by authorities and prosecuted to the fullest extent of the law. My friends and attorneys also encouraged me to sue the heck out of the people that done this to us. I went for it!

Bea Giovanni

With the guidance and consultation of attorneys, I filed a major federal lawsuit and brought everyone who committed these acts into civil court. While not perfect, as most attorneys have some grammatical and other technical errors in court documents, my pleadings and performance in the case met standards.

Having done all the work myself and had other attorneys oversee the process as I submitted documents to the court. The attorneys remarked that I provided work and responses similar to a seasoned, super lawyer. The attorneys were very impressed.

Some even mentioned that some seasoned and AV-rated attorneys couldn't do work in such a superb manner. [An AV-rated attorney firm ranks high in society. These are super lawyers and firms. So, I guess I did pretty well, considering there was a conspiracy to harm me, among other things like depriving me of my rights to practice law and just live my life.]

My federal court journey was interesting and a reality check for those, like me, seeking justice in a court of law. Attorneys, who I consulted and oversaw the process, were astounded by the lack of integrity and care and the dirty tricks played by the court staff, attorneys and even the judge.

I was shocked at the blatant disregard too, since I brought serious and real allegations before the court. Most judges would have acted with clear authority under the law to institute an immediate investigation into the matter, especially knowing another person was complaining about the same thing, which showed I wasn't crazy and I did state a claim, many claims. But, not in this situation.

Despite this, I followed the process and did everything I was to do per law. My original case was 300+ pages with exhibits. I properly served everyone, where defaults were likely against many.

The state and other parties didn't have good arguments. For example, the state argued I didn't meet jurisdictional requirements due to a lack of notice, and I didn't exhaust my remedies. They even argued I waived my rights to sue for anything done to me, since I paid the Oklahoma speeding ticket connected to the illegal stop, search, arrest and interrogation in the back of a police vehicle (on an interstate highway).

Bea Giovanni

All of these arguments were untrue and invalid. Simply put, the stop was illegal, as federal law trumps state law and allows for suing for civil rights violations. Plus, the citation and actions of the officers are intertwined into the entire case yet separate and distinct.

It also goes without saying that I was threatened. So, it was apparent that I had no choice but to pay the fine or risk my life.

Besides, would you go back to Oklahoma with the possibility that you will face the same officer who illegally profiled you (basically stalked you on interstate highways), then falsely imprisoned and detained you in the back of his police vehicle and could have possibly harmed or killed you or your child?

Under those circumstances, it is far safer to pay a ticket than contest it in that jurisdiction.

Also, as far as I know, no traffic court had jurisdiction over civil rights violations and conspiracy and terrorism claims. Whether I paid the ticket or not, the officer issued fraudulent traffic tickets and used illegal profiling and police tactics.

It goes without saying that before filing the federal case, I exhausted my remedies.

BERNICE RATHE

Do you recall the numerous correspondence and even the administrative complaints made, contacting state and federal police agencies (even local too) and virtually every agency ignored it? I wrote state and federal agencies and entities that could help or do anything about these life endangering and threatening acts against our life.

No matter how imperfect the writing or the situation, I gave notice far and above the legal requirements before filing the lawsuit.

Besides, who cares about grammar when your life is in danger? In fact, did any of you get my letters? I wrote many people and entities. So, this should count for something, right?

Anyway, it does not. This act of ignoring complaints is a pattern and practice in ignoring and dismissing these kinds of complaints and cases and even discrediting the complainant such as myself; but, why?

Oh, as I was stating, I included everyone. This included the firefighter, Slaven Sahtof, in the suit. In the lawsuit, he stupidly admitted to the hacking my email and third party vendor account via his letter (or what you can call an answer) to the court.

Bea Giovanni

XJ #100 District was included and the district hired an attorney. This attorney either did not know what the hell he was doing or he was doing suspect things in the case. Either way, the district's case was jacked the hell up.

After doing research, not much changed with the district, just the personnel yet the same corruption continued. I started to see why they hired this particular attorney as the attorney was not too ethical as well.

For example, for months during the lawsuit, XJ #100 district through its attorney only represented Ms. Shmad and the district. Later, after I filed for default against Mr. Phinus, the school district's attorney wanted to "pull the wool over" the court's eyes by saying he represented Mr. Phinus, though nothing on record showed so.

Further, before I filed the motion for default, the school district's attorney initially requested an extension to answer for the school district and Ms. Shmad only. Plus, Mr. Phinus later writes an incriminating letter to the court defaming and degrading myself, Jaime and Ms. Shmad. This was clear that the district's attorney did not represent Mr. Phinus, but the attorney goes ahead and says so.

BERNICE RATHE

This is not only unethical but creates a conflict of interest for the clients. This does not include the fact that the district's case was now compromised and jacked the hell up due to this unethical act on the part of the attorney and Mr. Phinus.

What the court and other parties didn't realize (or didn't want to realize) was Mr. Phinus was the true writer of the "XJ #100 letter."

If you recall, he was the only other person to have knowledge of the private school meeting with Ms. Shmad years ago, his memo was included with the letter and he was close friends with Ms. Kneipase, which meant she was a part of this too.

To state the obvious, he also became head principal after Ms. Shmad was fired, as everyone believed she wrote the "XJ #100 letter." These were all reasons why Mr. Phinus was the culprit in the letter, which also provides motive as to why he did it.

Do I need to remind you that Mr. Phinus was also spotted in Georgia months after we left Kansas?

Yet, he would deny this on record via his letter to the court, though it was clear he and others ruined Ms. Shmad's reputation and life, my reputation and life and Jaime's from his acts, these groups' acts, and connections to the hate groups.

Despite all of this incriminating evidence, Mr. Phinus continued to do so via his denial alleging Ms. Shmad, Jaime and I were liars.

Despite this, the court dismissed my case, allowing me to amend. How nice of the court, right? Well, time will tell how nice this court (or judge) would be to me or anyone else for that matter.

Well, taking this opportunity to amend and after looking at Slaven Sahtof's letter and the admission of guilt, I realized there was additional and new evidence supporting that Slaven Sahtof was lying to the court and he possessed private information about me and my family and it was not coincidental.

He hacked my email and third party vendor accounts and registered for marathons on two separate dates. Those dates were significant: they were the birthdates of my mama's other children (my sister and brother). This wasn't a coincidence, as Mr. Sahtof stated in his letter.

Before amending, I filed a motion for reconsideration and even provided statistics on the probability of Mr. Sahtof's so-called coincidence. As expected, the judge ignored it.

I, like most attorneys I consulted, expected the judge would ignore it. The reasons were clear: this was a case involving corruption, among other things (so cases like these are unpredictable since corruption can run deep).

For instance, few people want to touch these cases. In some instances, corrupt people don't want it on the docket or even entertained.

In other situations, courts view cases like mine as "crazy people-making cases." But the difference here was people really didn't know my case was a legitimate case.

However, all the court needed to do was investigate and research my allegations to find these things were true. Even if they didn't investigate or research the allegations, my complaint and all other pleadings and legal documents were clear, organized and legally sufficient and compliant on the level of a seasoned attorney. So it goes without saying that the court should have taken my case seriously.

Well, after the motion for reconsideration was denied, I later filed the amended complaint twice. Once, to fit the number of parties within a condensed 35 pages as ordered by the court. The second time was to enlarge the font, since the font was too small.

This also meant no one could sufficiently bring a suit within 35 pages with all the original defendants with standard font size. This is to say that the court made it difficult to bring the case in its original form.

So, this forced me to remove parties from the lawsuit. In the amended complaint, I had to remove my CPS attorney and others to meet to the 35-page limit.

You see I couldn't reasonably provide a short and plain statement naming all original parties and actions in 35 pages. I do not think anyone could have. So, I was forced to remove even more parties from the second amended complaint, otherwise it would be denied.

Despite the allegations and evidence, it didn't take the judge long to make a determination. This judgment call would forever change my matter and possibly his career (and the federal government's eventual investigation and prosecution against these individuals and groups).

BERNICE RATHE

The judge, without hesitation on his own motion, provided a dismissal with prejudice against all parties, based on 'a failure to state a claim' theory.

The judge didn't provide a pre-trial conference or any other tools that could help him understand the case. The judge also missed a chance to enter a restraining order or even provide declaratory relief, as I requested multiple forms of relief.

Sadly, it is too late to do any of those things. Plus, it is ineffective without complete relief. No new evidence or information can undo what this judge done, as a restraining order is too late and doesn't secure that these groups will stop.

His ruling in the simplest terms stated that I merely stated random, unconnected events of the injustices (sorry, indignities) I suffered and I failed to state "any" claim for relief.

The judge didn't really consider any of the information. If he did, he would have noticed my claims were valid as someone else (my ex-husband's ex) complained about similar stalking and harassment of police, fire and hate groups and she alleged my ex-husband was a part of the harassment.

Bea Giovanni

Dismissing my case with prejudice ruined the government's future case against these groups and gave these groups a green light to continue terrorism and espionage against the government, others and me.

Even though the complaints were sufficient, the judge didn't want to take the case; but, why? I am sure you can draw your own conclusions as to why. It was not merely because he thought I was crazy.

Interestingly enough, the dismissal with prejudice doesn't preclude another federal judge and higher or a specialized court from considering this case and reopening it in another forum, venue and in a specialized federal court, especially if there is new evidence and someone is caught in the act of committing these crimes.

It also doesn't stop a criminal prosecution against those responsible and others who furthered the conspiracy (or who would have seemingly overlooked evidence and tried to manipulate the legal matter) in this federal case. This included the judge in that criminal prosecution.

Ironically, the same day the judge dismissed my federal case, an officer stopped me for a traffic violation. I was taking Jaime to a summer camp activity,

BERNICE RATHE

Jaime and I were early for the camp, so there was no need to rush. In fact, we were having a good time driving to the camp.

One of my mama's favorite gospel songs came on the radio and Jaime and I were happy to hear the song. We sung and reminisced about my mama's life and our time with her.

We were shocked to see the officer stop us. This officer stated I was speeding in a work area, which was untrue. Jaime and I looked at each other in disbelief and in fear.

Understand we had bad experiences with officers. The last major incident involved a trooper who falsely arrested me and placed me into the backseat of his vehicle while angrily questioning me about my father.

Despite telling the officer of his mistaken belief that I was speeding, he wrote a ticket. Later, as suspected, he set me up. The ticket revealed the car's color traveling before me, which was light green; my car's color is far from any green color.

I recalled the vanity plate of the previous car because the car's driver was speeding and driving in and out of lanes. So, it was easy to recall that license plate. Plus, the automaker of my luxury car has never made any color like light green or green colored vehicle, except for Emerald Green (and my car, again, was not anyway near a green color).

I guess this is another coincidence, especially on the same day the federal judge dismissed my case with prejudice. Right?

Wanna hear another coincidence?

Well, I was rear-ended 2 months later in August 2013, guess by who? A military veteran.

The veteran rear-ended me as I was traveling in the downtown area (SW side of town). Immediately after the incident, he acted strangely with me. Later a van with government plates stopped next to my car and the van's driver, while on his phone, stared at me in an intimidating manner.

The veteran driver, who hit me, walked to the van and began talking to the van driver as if they knew each other. Of course, I thought this was not only surprising but not a coincidence.

I contacted the police who came to the scene to help exchange crash information. I informed the police about the accident and the van. The veteran driver admitted hitting my car to the officer but he denied the entire event with the van and the van's driver.

BERNICE RATHE

After leaving the scene, I went to vacation bible school, located on the NE side of town. Less than 2 hours after the accident, I spotted the same veteran driver blocks from the vacation bible school. Coincidence, I guess?

I digress. Or, do I? Back to the federal suit, the attorneys I consulted stated some judges throw out corruption type cases (and cases that could make waves and embarrass a governmental entity). It is usually done on a procedural move, no matter the evidence or if the events and facts in the case are real and shocking. The typical theory used is a failure to state a claim, since a judge can use subjectivity.

Attorneys told me in advance if dismissed on that account, then I would know what time of the day it was (i.e., corruption). They also stated there are groups and professionals who track dockets and will review and investigate certain claims like these, i.e., watchdog groups, investigators or the government itself.

When it is clear that a case had validity and satisfied the procedural requirements, then all eyes are focused on the judge and the adverse parties involved (i.e., the defendants and anyone mentioned in the lawsuit). But, I am not holding my breath for any of this.

But, the coincidences do not stop. The same judge who dismissed my case, guess what, became a secret FISA court judge shortly around the time the judge dismissed my case.

To put it simply, month 1 (suit filed), month 2 (suit dismissed with leave to amend), month 3 (suit refiled), month 4 (judge appointed to secret FISA court) and month 5 (suit dismissed with prejudice despite evidence and information supplied to court). Oh, there's even more interesting information.

If I am correct, then this judge is not on the right side of the law or government and the secret FISA court is compromised. But, there will be no ethics or criminal investigation into the judge, since who cares, right?

BERNICE RATHE

PART THREE

Chapter 17: Am I Anointed or Just Crazy?

I tried reconciling these events many times. I know some think I am nuts. But, I am not. I am not distorting my reality.

I don't have "mommy and daddy" issues. I don't hate men. I am not gay because of genetics, abuse, not having a father in my life, or whatever reasons people make up.

While my childhood wasn't perfect, as no one has a perfect one, it wasn't bad. I am a well-adjusted person who takes care of herself and others very well. I consider myself and my life lucky (or blessed).

Further, I neither hear voices nor have delusions. I am not stating it is the end of the world. I am neither on a corner with a sign trying to save people nor stating I am Jesus.

Also, I am not stating that all police, fire, veteran and military personnel are bad and corrupt and are a part of this madness, because they are not. Many of them put their lives on the line every day to protect us without regard to who we are.

I am also not stating I am anti-government or against government. In fact, I believe in government and that it has a role in society as we cannot reasonably police ourselves; for centuries, societies have tried self-regulation and sadly, most have failed.

Whatever the case I have been victimized by some evil people disguised in positions of authority and trust. They so happen to be associated with law enforcement and military, among others.

Some would call people like this haters, them, they or it. But, evil is the best description, since these groups and people do not always hate. Some befriend to gain information and access to you and your life to ruin anything they can. But, they do not want you to succeed or have anything.

They could be a friend, spouse, dating partner, family, in-law, coworker, neighbor, or a stranger. They disguise their purpose and themselves. Don't think they will change their ways, they will not. Evil is clever.

The activities I am describing are best illustrated. The best illustration is the movie, *Fallen*, with Denzel Washington, where people are walking pass Denzel and saying random comments or seemingly comments that seem a part of the conversation.

Well, this is what these activities entail and more. These activities seem to be demonic or evil, though the people doing it think it is just harassment. But, it is not. These activities are rooted in evil and sadistic rituals.

While I believe I am not crazy, those close believe I am not crazy and that I am a safe, responsible, goofy, down to earth, good person. I am not "stuck up" or into myself (far from that). The things I mentioned, experienced and witnessed have no rational reason than corruption, terrorism and evil.

What about the fact someone else (my ex-husband's ex) is also complaining about similar harassment of fire and police and threats against her life, who also alleges my ex-husband is a part of this harassment? We are unrelated and live states apart, and we don't know each other? No doctor can say this is a "shared delusional" situation.

After discussing this with others, it appeared to some of us that my ex-husband and others could be involved in a pedophilia ring and other serious criminal and covert activities (i.e., terrorism, as there are hate and extremist groups involved) and are getting the assistance of corrupt law enforcement (for whatever reason) in covering up these activities.

The evidence leads us to believe this per my ex-husband's history of suspected molestation, the recent molestation charge (and the mysterious removal from the court system, though it is still in the court and CPS systems) and the timeliness of a "government agent's" documents and information that I was a terrorist.

Plus, it became apparent to us my father helped these groups do it. He helped these groups endanger my life and Jaime's life.

This may have been an attempt to take my daughter out my custody and give my ex-husband custody, who was also allegedly caught molesting his first daughter and now another minor.

This attempt against my daughter and me was unsuccessful; whatever they were trying to do didn't work.

I and others also found my ex-husband had previous criminal charges, arrests, investigations and convictions like fleeing and eluding police, check fraud, evasion of child support (for another child) and other molestation allegations.

BERNICE RATHE

What was interesting about all of this was that a year later after finding this information, I would find all his charges and convictions were mysteriously removed from all court dockets.

This was especially interesting as Jeff was a teacher at that time and thereafter these things were taking place. I am not sure why the "bells and whistles" didn't go off for the education department in Jeff's state, but it should have.

I continued to reconcile why all of this was occurring and I knew I was not crazy. For instance, what about my father's family with a history of similar allegations of stalking and harassment by police and fire and ritual abuse by these groups and his family?

Many people, including my father's family, believed this was delusion of my father's family members, who experienced similar things, and it would occur so timely around the age of those with schizophrenia. Yet, later the harassment would be proven real and not a delusion. So, was it schizophrenia or manmade issues made to look like mental illness?

I researched my father's family history and found other interesting connections.

Bea Giovanni

Those in his family who alleged stalking and harassment by police and fire had one thing in common: a sickle cell trait.

I have the trait too. This isn't to be confused with the full-blown sickle cell anemia.

Nonetheless, my father has the trait, which is the only thing I have to prove I am his child, though he denies me as his child. So, he and I share a commonality: the sickle cell trait.

I began researching the trait's origin and other information. I found minorities mostly have the trait and it has certain reproductive and immunity benefits like immunity against malaria and possibly other diseases.

Was this connected? Who knows? But, this minority link explains one of many reasons why certain hate groups may have been involved, in addition, to bias and evil that may be present in those groups. Again, who knows?

Then again, this is another significant connection and pattern. I may have solved a mystery plaguing my father's family for years. But, they may never know the truth, since they have endangered my life in the process, which has also endangered their lives.

BERNICE RATHE

Why? Again, jealousy, corruption, and something my father done in his past (that has affected me). Interesting irony, isn't it?

Many people in my life, especially after these events started to happen, stated I am anointed. However, being spiritual, I didn't totally understand what they meant to the extent I should have. So, I searched and I even asked the church, pastors and other spiritual leaders about it.

They explained in many different terms, that god chose this person to do certain positive acts in the world and god and others protect the person. Others explained I had god within me and I was a manifestation of Jesus Christ himself.

That sounds crazy, right? They also told me to look to the scriptures, religious texts, or the bible and I will find the answer. I first didn't understand what to look for.

So, I just opened the bible. Go figure, when I opened the bible, it went to a page that described some similarities that I was experiencing or at least saw in others. How ironic, right?

For instance, the page fell on the story of Job. So, I read Job. Some things in Job were identical to my situation and I resembled his background and likeness, except I was a female.

Anyway, I thought I found the answer, but I only found one of the answers as there were different texts with varied versions of the same stories.

I then studied other stories and I couldn't believe that no one caught these similarities and symbolisms between the religious texts and my story.

What about when the CPS caseworker who wanted me to deny these acts occurred and deny I was anointed?

What about the people and government entities who denied knowledge of me or that I sent them notice of these acts of terrorism against me or the government or that they ever received notice at all of anything from me, even though I had proof (i.e., letters received from these same entities) showing they received them?

Then I realized these groups' behaviors and acts were similar to the evil talked about in the bible and that these groups were deeply in trouble and in danger. The texts showed harm came to those who harassed or harmed the anointed, no matter if these groups stopped harassing or harming the anointed person since going against an anointed person was going against god or even if they knew or not what they were doing and to who they were doing it to.

Then, I realized Joseph's story was similar here, i.e., age, Jacob's family, hate groups, oppressive systems and methods like systems of slavery in Joseph. The only difference was that I was a female.

Also, the year before the hospitalization, I saved 20K I later used for living purposes; that amount today is similar to what Jacob's family received for selling Joseph. Of course, I don't have this money anymore, since I used it for living expenses, as I lost all my jobs and income from the fraudulent hospitalization. But, you get the picture.

The similarities did not just stop at Joseph and his family but others in the story. For instance, what about the similarities between the cupbearer and Ms. Shmad and Ms. Kneipase and Potiphar's wife?

Like the cupbearer, Ms. Shmad failed to notify or disclose what happened, as the letter was false and Jaime and I were innocent.

Like Potiphar's wife, a former Olympic hopeful or beauty, Ms. Kneipase is a former Olympic hopeful and gymnast and not bad looking either.

Bea Giovanni

What about the XJ #100 school letter later proven false and full of lies? They used it as a vehicle to get the community, law enforcement and the government against me and to cover up the illegal activities of the district and these groups and their involvement? This was similar to Potiphar's wife's lie to get the slaves and others to act against Joseph to keep everyone from knowing she liked Joseph and to keep Potiphar and others secrets quiet.

Who hired and placed Mr. Phinus and Ms. Kneipase in the XJ #100 school district and why? Was it coincidental or something else?

Use your imagination for a second. I think you get the picture.

In Joseph's story, the truth came out about everything including Jacob and his family and others attempting to exterminate Joseph and steal his birthright. In the simplest terms, they jealous of Joseph and did not like him and sold him. Joseph wasn't supposed to be a slave, but his plight and fear awakened Joseph.

The truth also came out that Joseph didn't harm or threaten anyone and the real reasons would come out about Potiphar's wife. Potiphar, his wife, their families, the groups of slaves and communities were shamed and disgraced.

They would face torment, harassment and threats after the truth came out. The truth stunned everyone, i.e., the truth about Joseph's identity, gifts, skills and destiny.

Word of Joseph traveled quickly and the pharaoh heard about Joseph. The pharaoh couldn't let him slip away.

Joseph's destiny would be greater than ever, as the pharaoh, other lands and generations after would make Joseph one of the top in the land.

But, I got more out of the stories than mere similarities but I learned lessons. These stories teach us lessons, as many overlooked in Joseph's story the minor yet powerful details. While most thought Joseph's story was about forgiveness, it was also about justice; both coexisted.

Despite Joseph forgiving his haters, as I like to call them, this didn't mean consequence didn't result as God made sure of that. In fact, this would never happen to Joseph again and Joseph was elevated even higher than his original destiny.

This also didn't mean Joseph trusted his family as before. Time was another lesson, as the hate that led to Joseph's fate destroyed time and life for everyone. Time was lost with Joseph's mother, his family and his homeland.

Would Joseph's father and his family have done things differently if they could turn back the clock? Would Joseph's homeland have responded differently towards Joseph in helping him get out of slavery? Who knows?

What we do know is that time was lost for everyone, and that Joseph was a critical piece in Joseph's family and to his homeland. No one could match or duplicate his skills and abilities.

Joseph's unfortunate ordeal also destroyed many people. Once they sold him into slavery, both his nation and Jacob's family lost their destiny, prosperity and lifeline. Few people in his land knew Joseph was anointed and how harming him would change the fate of everyone.

It is important to note that religious texts vary but are clear: Joseph was beloved and loved by many, as he was Rachel's son. People loved Rachel and Joseph and were attracted to them.

Joseph was smart, charismatic and attractive. Despite what happened and being imperfect (like most people), Joseph had the best integrity of his siblings.

Another story that appeared in my turning of the bible pages was the story of Babel. With these groups (i.e., hate and extremist groups, rogue police, fire, and military) working together (no matter the purpose, intention, good or bad) and the pride that resonated among them, this effort resembles the same journey in Babel.

These groups' behavior indicated no one was greater than these groups, as no government and not even God was greater. Yet, we know this isn't true today, as no group or a collective would have more power than anyone or any entity.

I can go on and on with other stories. For example, David and Goliath was another relevant story. David slayed the giant, Goliath, but corruption prevailed.

The similarity here is that I sued a giant (i.e., several people in these groups and the government on all levels). In theory and on the face of the complaint, I won, but corruption prevailed.

Other things learned are that no one chooses to be anointed; you don't just wake up one day and say, "Oh, I want to be anointed."

Bea Giovanni

You don't choose it. No anointed person in any religious text has ever chose to be anointed.

Do you really think anyone would consciously choose to be anointed if s/he knew what it entailed beforehand?

When a person is truly anointed, he (or she) is so from birth and possibly before, as God only knows; there are neither substitutions, duplications nor replications of such.

Also learned is every action has a consequence to something or someone else's destiny and life. We are connected and these issues intersect. So, we must be keenly aware how we affect the world.

I also learned some in authority are no longer on the right side and may have never been.

I also learned my father and his family were never family to me. Essentially, God was my father.

Moreover, I learned the true meaning of family, and family don't do what Joseph's father and his family did or what my father and his family did.

My father and his family never realized their vicious cycles of trauma and abuse and they don't seem to want to stop these cycles, as it doesn't stop with me, no matter what someone tells you.

Again, why am I the only one of my father's children with sense? Am I anointed?

Speaking with religious leaders, they mentioned "touch not my anointed" stating anytime someone mocks or harasses the anointed or stands in the way, sabotages or manipulates the person's purpose or role in life, the bible has shown what happens to those people, who committed those acts as it's like they were playing a zero sum game with God; only they could never truly win.

They weren't spoken of or heard from again, since their fate and consequence was too awful.

These groups thought these things and act of choosing me was coincidental or a mistake. But, it was explained God doesn't make mistakes.

Picking me as their target was like picking a needle out a haystack, getting pricked hard and the bleeding never stopping, or like a diamond in the rough. Basically, these groups picked the wrong person yet the right one.

I can even go on with mythology and stories within it and the similarities. But, I will spare you going through the numerous stories there.

Again, if you have not gotten it by now, in each of these stories, there were happy endings and the anointed person ended up on top doing great things in the world. However, in my story, there hasn't been a happy ending, and I am definitely not at the top doing great things in the world.

For a second time, I am not stating I am Job, Joseph, David, Jesus or other religious characters. These are just analogies showing similarities among many situations.

Am I anointed? I don't know, but many people, including me, can prove these random events are not random, unconnected events and I know I am not crazy.

How do you reconcile any of this? Also, knowing what Jaime and I went through, how do you and your child learn to trust others again?

I now realize my entire life I had no privacy (phones, homes were tapped, possibly for several decades), my former friends, places, things and others have relevance and some intentionally placed in my life to discredit me, harass me, spy on me or recruited others to do it.

BERNICE RATHE

Pretty much, every former partner or friend, strangers in public and people in government and the military have stalked me. Why? What am I doing? Seriously!

If I knew what I was doing, trust me, I would stop doing it so the stalking and harassment would stop. While I am not perfect, I am a good person who believes in treating people as I want to be treated and I have done that.

So, why am I stalked and harassed? While some people find being a stalking victim is flattering or harmless, it is not. There are some crazy people that can actually harm others.

What about these people endangering my life? Is my father a part of a secret society, cult or covert group?

Why am I being punished for something my father did?

Did he do something to my mama while she was pregnant with me that affected me? Was he a part of a secret experimentation that affected me?

I don't know. But, there's evidence supporting this, as he and others did something to me. Every day new things are uncovered about him, my ex-husband and others, and everyone continues to ignore my pleas for help, despite the evidence to support my contentions and quest for justice.

Again, by no means am I stating I am Jesus Christ or have some direct line to God. Everyone has his or her own truth and beliefs.

I believe in God, the Lord, the Savior, and Jesus Christ. I also believe that God loves everyone and merely dislikes our ways or the acts we do. I strive to do right and live right.

To put simply and clearly, I have stood up for Jaime and I however, whenever and wherever injustice occurred against us and went unresolved, and I continue to stand up.

I sought help and opportunities all over; yet, no matter my issue or need, how I wrote, worn, said, did, how well I looked or education, no one helped me, but many did ridicule, reject, laugh, deny, harass, intimidate, stalk or failed to acknowledge me; some tried killing me and my daughter. But, why?

If I haven't stated it, I am neither a threat nor threatened anyone or entity. I am not trying to start a war (or whatever you call it), but these groups are. I don't condone violence. I am not mentally ill or paranoid delusional (though legally and clinically they say I am). I am not a part of a secret society or a cult; I am not a witch. I am not plotting against anyone or entity. I am not a spy.

I am a normal, sane person like anyone and deeply spiritual and good-hearted.

I am a person who treats friends like family. I am a giving, goofy, down to earth, loving person, despite what has happened in my life. I also like gummy bears, funny socks, MMA (training and as a spectator), food (I am a foodie), video games, puzzles, traveling, movies and normal activities.

I love music, art, plays and dance events. I like anything from classical, jazz, rap, blues, hip-hop, country, R and B, Christian, gospel, to rock. You might catch me doing the "Dougie," the Harlem shake, or the newest dance craze.

I am a tech geek. I love technology and the newest gadgets.

I will also dress, speak and act professionally in applicable settings and filter my speech, i.e., job or formal venues. I switch up my look and attire with unique styles outside those venues, i.e., Mohawk or other styles when not at work. I am a bit unconventional; yet, I know how to conform when needed.

Bea Giovanni

You wouldn't recognize me as I look young, have different looks and styles like a chameleon, this is who I am. On some days I purposely look like a bag lady.

You be the judge? Am I crazy because I do not conform?

People shouldn't judge, as they cut themselves from good things and good people. But they do judge and it is based on looks. Most judged me and didn't know me or who I was.

Look where it has gotten them. Nowhere. Despite what they may think, judging me only hurt them, not me.

To be clear, I am neither a feminist nor an activist; I identify as a human being. This doesn't mean I don't advocate or believe in human rights, as I do.

I also believe in justice that is proper and lawful, as this is not about salvation, absolution or saving people. I ain't a punk a$% b!@#h!, as I have a little gangsta in me.

We place boxes around ourselves not knowing what it means or looks like. I do know what a living human being is and looks like, and this is what I identify as. Placing boxes around ourselves and judging people from the outside is how evil has won.

BERNICE RATHE

Chapter 18: A New Journey Begins

I am a good parent and human being. No matter what people have done to me, this is a truth that stands. At the time of all of this and while waiting for a superhero to save me, I decided to return to school and reinvent my career. So, I got a LL.M. in Transnational Law (or what is better known as International Law).

This curiosity also lead me to get a M.B.A., which actually I remembered I originally wanted to get when I was considering law school. But, at that time, there were few dual degree programs, so I took the law school route. Getting my M.B.A would be the start of something new and great as a new journey begun.

In the meantime in waiting to be rescued from this madness, I got Jaime into a top private high school. Actually, it was an all girls' Catholic school.

The school was a great one and was very supportive of us and all of its families, since they believed in God. Whatever their formula or model in educating girls, they needed to bottle this up and package it to all schools in the world, since it worked. Jaime flourished.

The trauma we experienced became less important and Jaime was able to break out and be yourself without fear. Before, in her elementary and middle school experiences, she did not want to participate in any school activities. When she went to the all-girls high school, she instantly signed up for everything (and I mean everything). She danced, she sung, she led in organizations, she excelled in her academic performance.

I could not ask for more. I was extremely proud of her.

My marriage was going well. My partner, Natalie, and I would host private dinner parties where we had this rule to invite friends and new people each month so that we connect them to one another and we get to connect with our friends in the process.

Well, at one of the dinner parties, I was asked about my current career or what I planned to do with my LL.M. In response, I stated that I actually wanted to use it to work with the United Nations.

Guess what? Months after the dinner party, I received an email regarding a potential United Nations practicum or internship.

After hesitantly applying, since I just knew I would not be chosen, guess what? I was chosen and invited to join them, where I was a 2014 UN Delegate and invited back in 2015. Though it was an unpaid role since many UN roles and its affiliated organizational roles are unpaid, I was invited to present at world conferences and to speak on panel presentations with world leaders. It was one of the best highlight of my life and the people were awesome!

I worked hard achieving these things. So much so that I became a sensation in the advocacy community. People knew my name and some even knew my story.

I would be solicited for speaking engagements and consultations. So, whatever these groups told anyone to make them act against me were all lies and it did not work.

People began to see the truth from the lies and that I was a good, normal, healthy and sane person.

Despite my ordeal I grew stronger and wiser. I challenged myself in everything (no matter how uncomfortable): learning new things like computer coding, languages, new forms of martial arts, gaining extra skills, getting physically fit, placing myself in challenging environments and around others who challenged me.

In fact, the harassment did not stop there, as some instructors, students and staff harassed me. This is all while never revealing my notable and respected background. I wanted to be treated like everyone else.

I never went into any place with a sense of entitlement. I was like any other student. This also meant that whatever the case, these people who were harassing me were being used as pawns and were in danger.

But, how do you tell people who are harassing you that they have the issue and not you and that there are those in the background watching them harass me?

Also, how you do tell people that rogue elements in society are abusing and misusing their authority against you and against the government and that anyone who helps these rogue elements are assisting them in working against the government as well as working against me?

You don't. In fact, last time, I did, they said I was paranoid delusional. Oh, let me not forget when I sued, my case was dismissed with prejudice. So, it is best for people to figure it out for themselves.

Everyone thought I was crazy or believed the lies, friends and strangers talked about me, others slandered my name and lied about me, but I held my head high. I knew the truth and what we (Jaime and I) been through. Jaime knew the truth and what we been through.

She knew I was not crazy. My friends did as well. Actually, the ordeal drew Jaime and me closer to one another.

All of these things helped me or improved my knowledge and skills too, all while I developed new innovation.

Yes, you heard right. I created some innovative things in the process. I learned how to code (in my spare time, out of curiosity).

I believe it took me less than a month to learn how to code. Then, I immediately began developing apps.

I developed three apps, one of which was a free safety app that quickly drew thousands of users to download it. Not bad, right?

The safety app was popular for many reasons. One of the reasons was there was a need. I saw a need in the marketplace for a particular safety app for Android users and went for it.

In fact, there were options on the iPhone and iPad devices for this safety feature but not on the Android. So, I invented a safety app for Android users.

While I got great things from hard work doing it the right way, these groups stopped me from any notable or lucrative career. My efforts still were being undermined. No one who pays well or matters will hire me (few at best). Despite my knowledge, skills, talents, expertise and accomplishments, I cannot become an attorney, top executive, college president or any worthy job with lucrative pay and benefits as my potential suggests.

To be clear, these groups were not set up. They willingly committed these acts since my birth, having help to do so and used technology, while stalking, harassing and intimidating me.

I tried rationalizing why these groups would do something like this. For instance, maybe some couldn't question orders or authority? Even so, common sense tells you these acts against me were not right! It doesn't stop one from thinking and questioning logic, reason and the reality of the situation.

Then, I began to question how I was able to make it through this madness. Who helped me, watched over me and protected me then and now? If the government, others or family didn't, then who? How does one explain the coincidences?

My only logical explanation would be that help and protection basically came from above.

Also, trying to rationalize all of this, I tried searching online for information. Surprisingly, there were others experiencing this same madness. Lots of information came up on this. For example, if you search certain words stated here online, what do you get? Like police fire Masonic stalking. Interesting, right? That is if you can locate the information if the information isn't hidden; either way, you'll find it.

While you can't believe everything online, it is convincing and interesting information, especially if my ex-husband's ex is complaining about similar harassment and alleges he is a part of the harassment.

Or even the fact I investigated these kinds of activities when I was a prosecutor?

Bea Giovanni

What about the "government agent," who supplied information to CPS? Kami Dilnoh and CPS refused to provide the identity of the hotline caller and the agent, despite that the agent and others reported false information?

Would this constitute a possible espionage or terrorism charge against the agent(s) who provided false information to CPS and anyone working in the government, who helped my father and others do this, or those who accepted favors or bribes to place me in a hospital, make a CPS case or to dismiss a federal case or tampering with the federal evidence?

Some parts of government didn't help or protect me as it helped these groups. But, why?

I have a simple explanation. I believe that the government was scared and has little power (though it would seem like the government should, in theory, have lots of power, but it didn't). And, of course, the other reason is that the government benefits from these groups harming me. The government's connection and inaction wouldn't be uncovered and my claim to compensation would be denied.

BERNICE RATHE

This inaction or discrediting emphasized there is an unwritten practice ignoring situations like mine that denies me of human rights, life and dignity.

While activities target minorities, they really target anyone including law enforcement and can be used everywhere. It is like you cannot tell good from evil.

The activities are also similar to the Gestapo. Or if this was a movie, it would be like Hydra v. Shield. In essence, anyone could be a part of this and you do not know it. This is a Pandora's Box that cannot be closed, similar to a confluence of evil.

If you are wondering how people can become so evil or even a part of this harassment, well, it is quite simple. Evil needs consent. These groups all gave consent agreeing that they will protect and serve regardless of authority or reason behind it.

Or, some even took oaths of so-called "brotherhood" or "fellowship." Again, with the understanding, no questions asked or no reasons matter, just that a 'brother' needs help.

For others and individuals who do these things, they are just evil or otherwise seeking acceptance or power or control.

Bea Giovanni

If you think these activities, individuals and groups are only in one nation, you are right. This spans across the world, as there are individuals, groups and activities furthering evil, while in disguise. History shows this to be true as well.

Whatever the situation, this is how evil worked into the government, individuals and these groups.

BERNICE RATHE

Chapter 19: Justice Not Served

Let's recap: Several wrongs have been committed against me, and I didn't received justice.

I gathered tons of evidence and information but the government or anyone in authority didn't cared to consider this evidence or even investigate this.

Let's not talk about the numbers of people who knew the truth, that I was a victim and targeted. Yet, they said nothing.

No one blew the whistle on what was occurring with Jaime and me. This journey to justice has been discouraging (to say the least).

In theory, we are to follow the proper process to receive justice. Or, that if we see something, say something. Or, that we are to help our fellow human being, when in need. But, what I highlighted shows something different.

Growing up watching my mother work as a public servant, I wanted to work seeking justice for others. So, I decided at an early age to become an attorney and fight for justice; yet, oppressive and discriminating people and systems derailed this dream.

My journey shows I navigated via various systems seeking justice. Yet, justice never occurred for Jaime and me.

Looking at the U.S. Constitution and Homeland Security's byline, "If you see something, say something," by the time my journey reached this level, these terrorists made this byline look to me and other victims alike: "If you see something, don't say anything, especially if you are a minority, or you'll be threatened, harassed, and endangered" or "Who do you think you are?"

I reported and disclosed valuable information on terrorism and corruption, along with uncovered deep secrets people were trying to hide to save themselves via harming me.

Authorities treated me neither as a human being nor a victim. Instead, they supported the terrorists and pegged me as a perpetrator, a criminal, a terrorist, a fraud, an unfit parent, and incompetent, among other things to discredit and destroy me.

They effectively got scores of individuals to believe these lies and deception and to act on these lies and deceptions. Others joined into the melee to endanger my life, just because, while others looked away.

What was clear was that everyone was desperate to conceal the truth and discredit me. This is to say that they knew the systems and those within these entities wouldn't do anything to help, wouldn't believe me or do their jobs.

I even was harassed in my volunteer activities. In some instances, I was the only person of color and I was trying to help them diversify and bring and bridge other communities into their community. Despite trying to help nonprofits with my expertise and unique abilities, they harassed me out of the nonprofit boards.

I was not even protected when doing UN work. For example, I was harassed by another colleague when I was working on an UN initiative. She began 'gas lightning' me (for lack of a better word) and even stalking me. Yet, no one would believe me. Guess why? Everyone thought I was crazy. She was deemed credible in everyone's mind and I was not.

Because of what I been through, I felt like I wanted to choke her out for the crap she was doing. But, like in other instances where people harassed me, the defamation and slander she spread about me eventually backfired on her. So, my thoughts or feelings on choking her the hell out dissipated.

This harassment showed not only these individuals and groups' ignorance but their racism. In fact, this became a trend as I uncovered every place (even when I was not aware of the harassment) including places decades ago that mistreated me or harassed me never flourished again.

What did this mean for the government? Who knows, but what is known for sure is that the government will face an enemy it has never faced before and an enemy it was not prepared to face, though everyone thought they were prepared.

These cases mark dark histories for the government. We pretend like things changed. But, with secrecy and acts to conceal the truth, this shows times didn't changed, just remixed and hidden away.

Things like these (that happened to me) can neither be fixed, corrected, resolved nor healed if no one is aware of these things and if no one really wants to address them.

It is like a wound that appears to be healed, but isn't and a person doesn't want to reopen it to properly fix, correct, resolve or heal it.

Everyone and every system failed me, i.e., the mental health, legal, justice or the public educational system. But, why?

The easy answer is corruption, money, power, influence, and a lack of integrity and leadership of those who count and matter.

Other questions are why and how were these groups doing it. They needed government cooperation, as no one without specialized technology or governmental systems can easily do this.

Is espionage involved? Why would anyone do this to me or anyone else, i.e., these groups were like fools doing the "bidding" of others, allowing others to dictate how they feel and act? Are these groups the so-called slaves like in religious texts (if viewed in that way)?

From the acts of these groups, my father, others, governmental inactions and those in authority to intervene or stop this terrorism and protect me, many people didn't realize the consequences these acts or inactions had on others and me.

No one is immune or exempt from reporting possible terroristic activities against a citizen or group such as minorities.

Bea Giovanni

I kept disclosing to the courts I am a victim
of domestic violence and terrorism and there
was another person complaining about
similar acts alleging my ex-husband was a
part of this.

By the time these groups realize what's
occurring, that everything I said was true
and that I am not crazy and these lies they
spread were not true, these groups were in
danger and pursued by shadow figures.

These groups are terrorist groups with a
military-like structure, with thugs to elitists.
They called me a terrorist because this is
what government and society calls them.

They branded me in every bad way
possible, as this is how others view them.

Put your conspiracy theories aside. This
is not what this is about, though it may look
like it.

I became an unintended victim of
domestic terrorism and violence and sadistic
and ritualistic madness. If I was not smart
and had professional experiences where I
identified certain covert patterns and
practices, I would have had a similar fate as
Sandra Bland.

Stories like mine are movies like *The
Matrix*, mixed with *Jumper*, *Eagle Eye*, *The
Minority Report* and *Next*. I wish this was a

dream and not real, then maybe I could make sense of it and know I was truly crazy and paranoid? But, it is a real story.

In fact, when people ask me how I am, I state "great" because no one really wants to hear I am endangered every day, everywhere I go and my father and his family had something to do with it, while he and his family act like they are holier than thou.

I have learned the art of hiding my feelings for the sake of others.

Today, my life is still in danger. I moved many times, changed my habits (so these groups cannot easily predict activities and places I go), even lived low key, again, the stalking, harassment and threats continued. While doctors and government say I am delusional, I know otherwise. These groups physically and verbally threatened Jaime and I life.

Through coercion, intimidation and the fear of reprisal, they made me and others believe my father, my ex-husband and others were not involved and that I wasn't being harassed and that I was mentally ill to cover up these groups and rogue agents' involvement.

Remember these terrorist groups have the backing of the government. It is all about something my father participated in or done in his past and to me at birth, which has possibly affected my life. This is one of many reasons why I am going through this stuff.

And if I am anointed as I suspect and others suspect, this means that my father, those who helped them and those bad elements in society and government are royally f^&ked!

Once the right person gets a hold of this information…, that is all I have to say.

I don't know the extent of what my father, others and this suspected experimentation has done to me (from birth) or the effects on my life (and my daughter's life, since I had a child).

I have yet to get any compensation for the acts committed against me. I was told I am entitled to major (and I mean major) compensation under the law (as much of this committed against me amounts to terrorism and other things hint to governmental abuse, illegal and non-consensual experimentation committed on me and other things I wish not to mention).

This doesn't include damages owed to me by XJ #100 district, CPS and others who participated and endangered my life. I doubt

BERNICE RATHE

I will receive this (and all of it), as these groups and my father don't want me to get it, as this major compensation means possibly resources, opportunities, status and the ability to help others.

Also, while witness protection programs have a good rate in protecting people, it is not an option (as it was told). You see these groups operate and are connected within the government, like terrorist or spy cells working in certain places and gaining access to information or systems or use national security reasons to illegally access information on others and use against others.

Look at the U.S. Marshal who tracked me down and harassed me. Enough said?

In some ways, my experiences are like a celebrity or wealthy person without the status or fortune. Celebrities, the wealthy and their children are often targets too.

The difference is most people recognize celebrities and the wealthy, so people are watching out for them and can recognize their names, faces and know who they are, making it difficult to spread lies or deception to others or to harm the celebrity and their children.

The government may take their concerns more seriously than the average person's concerns. Not to say celebrities have it better, but celebrities and the wealthy have wealth to protect themselves with use of security, secured homes, the best life insurance and lifestyles to avoid certain activities and people who could enter their lives to harm them (for whatever reason).

Years ago, I heard Angela Davis was speaking at a local college, so, I went. Prior, I researched her story and found my story similar (we were both accused of gun crimes and being a terrorist).

I felt her struggle. I am living proof it is still alive and well, by chance I am living it in my journey.

There were clear differences, however. I neither belonged to a radical or militant group and nor do I want to be.

Her father and his family didn't almost kill her because of hate and envy.

Her father didn't have help to endanger her life, then hospitalize her to discredit her.

She most likely didn't have a child who also witnessed and experienced similar things.

Plus, awareness was higher during those years, having little technology, people sought out information to make themselves knowledgeable.

BERNICE RATHE

Today, I can't say this is the case. How so?

It didn't stop these groups from trying to kill Ms. Davis and myself. Don't believe me? What do you think falsely pegging someone as a terrorist does?

That's a big target on someone's chest! And I mean big.

Oh, let's not forget falsely pegging someone as a crazy, gun-toting terrorist who would shoot up a school. This places a bigger target on the chest!

I am pretty sure whoever ordered (sorry, sold me to) these hate and terrorist groups didn't do so because they were helping me or that the person(s) wanted to have tea and crumpets with me in the future. I am sure of this.

This doesn't include the state-created harm done to me from birth and whatever my father and others did to me at birth and now too. If you add that, the target on my chest would be huge. Essentially, these groups made a sport of endangering my life.

Other stories stood out to me too, like the histories and deaths of Dr. King and U.S. President John F. Kennedy. Ironically, sadistic individuals connected to extremist and hate groups killed these iconic and dynamic men.

Despite the conspiracy theories, these groups also stalked Dr. King and President Kennedy before their unfortunate deaths, despite the notoriety and huge security detail.

If these groups did it to me (and I am anointed), imagine what they can do to you and others and are doing now, especially if they didn't do certain things to me but could do it to others. Everyone, harassing me and endangering my life, worked together and against themselves, the government and humanity.

These activities are "secret" or "public" management systems (pay to play and for hire revenge systems, i.e., like paid protesters). If you take everything into consideration, including the sophisticated methods, tools, groups and people involved in this harassment, this amounts to torture, terrorism and espionage.

Bad, corruptive people and systems use every tactic to silence victims and make them invisible (or more invisible than before) so things aren't brought to light.

The best thing a person can do for victims like myself is to provide support, a voice and visibility to victims like myself and even well-paying, protected jobs, since many of these groups try to dismantle victims economically.

This is a large part as to why the nation's economy is not on track. Imagine hundreds of thousands of victims like myself who have been targeted and limited to opportunities.

I am sure there are individuals who can validate what I am saying. However, their silence neither helps nor protects no one.

When you cannot discern between good and bad people and systems, then it is time for a change.

Terrorists are essentially activists but terrorists use their activism for evil. They need victims. Without them, terrorists can't survive and have no purpose.

To defeat terrorism, we must not fall victim to it. To prevent and combat terrorism, people must become aware of the tactics and methods and how terrorists use every tool, person, and system to achieve their goals such as hiding in black budgets, state secrets or in other ways. This also helps to identify, detect and prevent it from occurring to one's self and others.

Bea Giovanni

Terrorists never stop, so why should government and society stop in investigating, prosecuting and protecting the public?

I am sure this isn't the best articulated story. I have nothing to prove here.

This is my truth. It is a part of my healing and my daughter's healing, so any negative critics are irrelevant. If you think I am thinking negatively, I am not.

What would you do in my situation? Right?

If I am right on any of this, the joke, ridicule and hatred is on everyone else who ridiculed, harassed, stalked and hated on me and not myself. If you didn't get it by now from what happened with my daughter and me, certain public entities and systems are no longer secure but compromised and resources are being wasted.

These groups thought they outsmarted the government and others and that these groups were the highest or the only ones and no one was greater. If I am correct, these groups will soon find out they never outsmarted anyone.

They were never the highest or the only ones. Someone and something is always

BERNICE RATHE

higher and there are things none of us will know and understand.

Further, it isn't what is written that one should be afraid of but what is unwritten.

Chapter 20: Revenge Was Served Very Cold

Life settled in for me. I eventually found suitable work as an executive of a technology company. It was rewarding, fun and paid well. Plus, I got to travel to some awesome places.

Life seemed relatively okay. I gained back my retirement, benefits and was back in a good place. I was not complaining …

Shortly thereafter, I had a WTF moment. WTF is all I have to say.

Umi's predictions came true. One day, I played the lottery, like usual, and checked my numbers. I could not believe it, I had won several hundreds of millions of dollars (and that was after taxes, so you could imagine how much I won, which was one of the biggest jackpots). Not bad for buying a $2 ticket, right?

I kept playing the lottery but different games. And guess what? I won again and it was, again, several millions of dollars (after taxes). God is good! All the time.

Many people don't believe that people win the lottery or that it is a scam, but it is not. It may be one of the best things to happen to humans.

See, you put in $1 or so and get back lots more (if the amount is large like it was for me). Yes, taxes may eat up the winnings, but it is far more than what you started with or even put into the lottery. Plus, it helps education.

After winning the lottery, I paid off my student loans and our home and got my credit to an even better level than before. Jaime, me and Natalie traveled and set up shop in two other locations: a vacation home (or getaway home) on an island in the continental U.S., and another home elsewhere in the continental U.S. (all of which we found on a bargain). With my winnings, we were able to afford privacy, safety (for the most part) and convenience.

As a family, we also started a foundation. We also started several businesses, one of which was a natural and organic food line that proved to be highly successful and a brand that had staying power and was very competitive. All of our businesses were successful.

Individually, we were able to start our own projects and also become successful in our individual ventures. I started a real estate

investment company, which became one of
the premier real estate development
companies in the nation serving a varieties
of communities and needs while some
properties combined sustainability and green
living initiatives.

I also started other businesses, which
also proved very successful (to the point
where others wanted to buy into a
franchise).

But, what really was my pride and joy
was my innovation business. All of the ideas
and inventions that I imagined would be
fueled into my innovation business.

It cutting edge. I had several patents. I
was able to also help others with their
business and innovation ideas. I became
something like a female "Stark Enterprises"
like in Ironman the movie.

I was also so proud of Jaime. We
endured so much and we both came out of it
miraculously stronger. After she graduated
college and matured into a young woman, I
bought Jaime her first home of her choosing.

As a mother, this helped me with one
less worry, since Jaime would have a stable
and safe place to call home. This is
especially if something ever happened to
me.

BERNICE RATHE

Jaime also took up my creative arts idea we once created together. Jaime and I were co-founders and I help to run the fiscal operations, while she ran the creative operations.

After experiencing everything we did, Jaime and I added a component of the creative arts business that offered therapy. So, it was no longer about arts education but it offered therapy for domestic violence, abuse and trauma survivors and victims as well.

Natalie started a holistic wellness business, in which she always envisioned. Being that she was a natural at counseling, this fit well for her. This also meshed well for the therapy component in Jamie and I arts-based business.

Again, all of our businesses were successful, where others wanted to buy into a franchise.

Unfortunately, the story does not end here.

As I stated before, Umi's other predictions came true, which I hoped did not. After winning the lottery, I knew that Umi was the 'real deal' though she joined into the madness towards the end of her life. I am not sure if she did it to protect me from these groups (as to gain inside information) or because she gave up.

Whatever the case, her prediction meant that these groups would be killed. This was not a happily ever after story. In fact, it was the direct opposite, and one in which none of these groups and the government seen coming.

If Umi's predictions and the other psychics predictions were true, then I was anointed (i.e., I was God-like or God possibly reincarnated). This also meant that the messages I received, which I thought were delusional, were warnings and I held the key to the world's fate. Yet, no one believed me and I was forced to deny these things.

While these groups were so focused on this 'illuminati' crap, it was actually evil and not some New World Order who was causing confusion and chaos.

These groups were so idiotic and silly to think that I was a part of any of this. I am not a part of any of this stuff.

Besides, if anyone wanted to entertain the notion of this "conspiracy of the illuminati," from what I read online, the 'illuminati' does not accept women into their group. If anything, it would be possible that my father and others and these groups were all a part of this illuminati conspiracy. But, who knows?

Like I was saying, it was not the so-called 'illuminati' behind this, it was an ancient evil. This evil was here before humankind (and it is unclear whether this evil has a compact with God to touch not the anointed, but who cares, it is still evil). It is similar to the snake in the story of Adam and Eve.

There have been many theories on this like the 13th angel or apostle, similar to the 12 star animals, apostle and astrology. Every civilization drew of these things in the caves and left messages for us or even transcribed this into biblical stories but we ignored it.

Whatever the case, no government and no militia group or secret society seen this coming, as they were too occupied with evil's distraction in believing other agendas.

Evil had already attacked numerous times and used these groups before. Evil used Hitler, the KKK, and others to effectuate this agenda by killing numerous people in the belief that they would live, have power or rule for 1000 years.

This was all lies, as it only made evil more powerful by getting massive consent and recruiting more people to enter the ranks of government and to get behind these systems to access public systems at large and strike a balance of trust and deception.

This is why there are so many first responders, EMS, police, military, fire, service contractors (like HVAC, fire equipment service companies, electricians, cable installers, security, etc.) and Masonic members in these places. These individuals will be used as slaves and later extinguished or killed to serve evil's cause.

These individuals were essentially lied to and it was too late to undo what has been done. Evil had access and the machinery that could infiltrate and confuse systems and technology.

BERNICE RATHE

Chapter 21: No One Believed

C urrent day: Music is playing, Bernice, wearing sporty shades, is driving. She stops at a stop light waiting for the light to change and looked over to the other car's driver and passenger, while she mimicked the lyrics to Beyoncé's 6 inch song.

Bernice smiles, nods, and drives off after the light changes. The other driver looked in amazement and excitement, happy that Bernice engaged them. They recognized Bernice from her celebrity status, being a notable business professional and having a well-respected background.

If you can recall, years prior, no one believed Bernice. But, they did believe she was crazy (and this is not to her surprise or anyone who believed her).

Bernice was a woman of color and, in a world dominated by males and racism, it seemed that God knew what it was doing. In other words, God sent a gift and to protect this gift, God wrapped it into a package where no one would ever expect to find this gift, due to their prejudices.

Despite the government's best efforts, it was not ready for what would happen, though it believed it was ready. In essence, it was like God and evil betted against human vulnerability and won.

What was apparent was that Bernice struggled with her gifts. She did not understand why others did not understand her. She also did not understand how everything she said or wrote came true, and when she did not say or write anything, these things still came true.

Bernice did not understand the full extent of her powers and that she possessed insight into future events and essentially could help stop world catastrophes (or at least lessen the damage, if not), if people believed her.

While these groups were spying on Bernice and harassing her, with every act against her, there were mysterious people in the background watching these groups. This meant that no matter if these groups stalked Bernice, harassed her, cloned her phone or spied on her online activities, snooped in her private home or vehicle, these mysterious people were already on these groups' trail.

BERNICE RATHE

How is the question. These groups thought they had the inside stuff and could do whatever they wanted.

Well, one day in D.C. while having brunch with colleagues, one of the top secret officials, Stan Clantor, an official who is known to work in the government but his position was deeper and higher than the U.S. President and anyone in government, overhears something that makes him almost choke on his food.

He hears a strange tail or rumor about a female who thinks she is Jesus and is being stalked by the government. Ironically, this tail was about Bernice.

Well, little did they know, his secret department (that no one knows about and not even the U.S. President knows about) is specifically established for this, i.e., identifying special occurrences and the coming of supernatural human beings and human intelligence and ultimately watch the "watchers" when they believe no one is watching, hence the mysterious people.

Little is known about these occurrences but it has been documented since the time of Jesus and years before in other civilizations. There comes once in a blue moon, one individual who is anointed (or has special abilities), which would help mankind on earth on this.

Clantor and his department, which spans around the world, knew the anointed person has to be protected. There is no other person like this and rarely does another anointed person come around in anyone's generation. So, protecting this individual was in the world's best interests.

In fact, evil people for centuries would hunt down these anointed individuals in hopes of starting an apocalypse or even believing they could gain special powers. This is why Hitler hunted down ancient religious artifacts and relics and even killed so many people, which amounted to a genocide.

If this tail of the female was true as Clantor heard, then evil (or Satan), as some call it, was trying to harm the individual to stop mankind's progress and harmony.

To not cause attention to his need for more information, he began laughing with his colleagues over this rumor or strange tail. Then he began asking his colleagues questions about this tail, about the identity of the female, what happened to her or where she could be found, as if he was intrigued yet in disbelief (as to not blow his cover in his secret position and department and the significance of what is occurring as few people could be trusted).

After brunch, Clantor immediately began researching Bernice's background. He searched numerous government and military databases. He also searched driver data databases and other sensitive databases detailing who accessed Bernice's driver information and any other background information.

Clantor was astounded by the number of agents and officers who accessed Bernice's files, which listed agents and officers accessing her information spanning for many years, actually since she was born. This information unknowingly to others led Clantor and his department to the numerous agents and officers who may have possibly ties or connections to these rogue groups.

He began to also research Bernice's first ever bank transactions and any and all other bank transactions. He researched bank camera footage (inside and outside the bank), along with research her credit/debit and credit card transactions and camera footage (inside and outside) if available. He even researched camera footage from other businesses and traffic cameras to identify activities around Bernice during those times. Again, he was astounded.

He found a pattern of similar individuals and these groups, dating back to the 1990s. He believed she may have been targeted since birth. But, why?

His department immediately begun cross-referencing databases and sensitive intel and top secret information on these individuals. Clantor uncovered numerous officers and agents with connections to these rogue groups.

This led Clantor to believe that many of the individuals researched were indeed connected to these rogue groups were not only embedded within government but possibly sleeper cells in the government and society for these rogue groups. Many of these individuals also had security clearances allowing them access to sensitive data, which Clantor knows that such access is critical to these rogue groups.

Clantor and his department scrambled to determine the extent of this massive breach and what information and systems were accessed or compromised by these individuals and why access was necessary.

Discussing this and comparing historical documents, governmental records on

BERNICE RATHE

Bernice, her father and others, Clantor and his department came to the conclusion Bernice was anointed and was connected to the blood line of God, and was possibly God itself. (I know right, this is crazy, but the story gets any stranger than that).

Clantor also found that Bernice's father had done something to Bernice's mother (i.e., something within her stomach) while pregnant with Bernice. This may have been military-related. Clantor did more research to make sure.

Whatever the case, Bernice's father and these groups harmed Bernice. The situation become dire for Clantor, since Bernice was anointed, which meant that the situation may transpired for so long that it may be possibly out of Clantor's hands and a catastrophe was about to occur.

Immediately after uncovering this information, Clantor met with a special panel of governmental figures who also were unknown to the U.S. President and anyone else in the government (or world, for that matter).

"I found the anomaly you searching for many decades ago and what our predecessors were searching for, now for centuries." Clantor said to the special panel.

"What do you mean?" exclaimed a person on the panel.

"Sir, the Odmos program's purpose has shown its worth. We've found what you were looking for. But, it may not be what you expect." In suspense and possibly disbelief, the panel asks, "what is it?"

Clantor states, "Not what but who. This individual somehow triggered the government's system."

The panel asks "if this is so, why didn't we know about her?" and Clantor replies "Because the government's system is corrupt. The evil element that lurked for thousands of years infiltrated into the government's system."

He goes on to say "Whatever she did, it triggered the system and helped us to identify her. The government did not offer any help since it has historically harmed and ostracized individuals like her. If she did not trigger their system, we would have not known about her."

Clantor then uses special technology that displays holographic images detailing Bernice's journey and the circumstances surrounding her life. As Clantor presents his holographic presentation to the panel, the panel are checking their systems and running various tests to verify the circumstances.

Clantor and other officials realized not only Bernice was anointed but Bernice was being targeted under a special and secret surveillance program. Also, the situation was complicated since evil hijacked several secret governmental systems, along with these groups facilitating evil's work.

This was apparent to Clantor and his department since they had been following these programs for many decades and know that the government and these groups were not helping Bernice but harming Bernice.

These groups and the government had no idea what they done. Essentially, Clantor and the panel would not be able to stop the destruction that will come about to the government and these groups as they attacked an anointed person.

The panel turns away, and in fear, summon a strange and airy figure. Clantor is in a state of shock, uncertainty (and fear as to what will happen next) and seemingly frozen as to what to say. Clantor never knew the extent of the departmental functions, but now he knew there was far more involved and at stake. In the process of Clantor's fear and shock, this figure appears out of nowhere.

The panel explains in disappointment and fear to this strange figure that its daughter has been found but she has been endangered and there are some humans who have been afflicted with the ancient evil that lurked the galaxy for many centuries.

"How do you know this is her?" the figure asks.

The panel turns to Clantor and points to him and his holographic images of Bernice's journey and the circumstances. They state "We have run the tests to confirm the circumstances and her lineage, she is your daughter."

"If this is true, where was she found, why is she not in power, why is she being harmed, my daughter is a god," angrily and loudly exclaimed by this figure.

"Universal One, we are sorry but some humans were not kind to her and they were afflicted with the evil spirit that has haunted the galaxy for centuries," the panel states.

"It does appear that her birth mother and her family did protect her and did their best. They seemed to have kept their pact with you (God). But for, her birth mother keeping her safe, she would have died in the hands of her father and his family. We've found they are a part of this evil. He seems to have some authority in this circumstance as others follow his lead. But, it seems he will soon perish in his authority. The evil has caught up to these groups and is consuming all of them. They did not know the extent of this evil and that evil only used them and they too would be killed." various voices on the panel speak.

Checking to make sure the panel is correct, the figure states loudly, "I do not believe you, prove it."

"Universal One, she passed all the tests, she is the only one to defeat evil at its own game. No one but your daughter can do this. She also resembles you," the panel explains.

The figure turns into a human body and walks towards the holographic image, while Clantor looks in amazement and trips on himself, trying to move out of the human figure's way. The human figure (or the Universal One) resembles Bernice and Bernice looks like the Universal One. The Universal One looks delighted and excited and wants its daughter now.

The Universal One states "I am thankful for my daughter's birth mother and her family, where are they? Please provide them with my gratitude and flourish them with resources."

Clantor and the panel sadly explains "Bernice's birth mother died, she could not hold on any longer and Bernice's mother's family has been suffering since Bernice's birth father and his family used evil to undermine your authority."

The One states with angry and loudly, "Well, their suffering stops today! Please kill Bernice's birth father and his family and anyone else helping them or who has harmed Bernice and Bernice's mother and her family. Let those know who are working with evil, their fate has come and that harm done will be repaid with their lives. Make them know what they have done to their world and who Bernice is. This system ends with Bernice. If anyone shall oppose this, kill them. If not, your world will perish as evil will continue to terrorize and destroy your world's existence."

The Universal One explains that there was only one rule: Clantor and his civilization were told, when given this secret function, to not harm the anointed individual but protect this individual as all of civilization depended on the individual. It was similar to a 'matrix' and everyone's life depended upon this person being able to live freely in peace while exploring the world, helping or fixing issues as the individual seen fit.

Sadly, this did not happened but the opposite happened. Clantor learned these groups and the government sabotaged Bernice's life, which was connected to the source, the Universal One. This meant careers like becoming a licensed attorney or even working in government were either blocked, sabotaged or set up for Bernice to fail.

The panel and Clantor studied the information for some time and concluded from the acts of these groups and the government blocking Bernice's path has created a ripple effect in the world's dynamic and economy.

This was why things occurred that should have not occurred such as Bernice's daughter and niece being sexually assaulted, as it was the fault of Bernice's father who brought this evil into everyone's lives.

Also, these groups created ripple effects in the world's economy and relations. This was why the economy was hurting and society about to collapse.

Despite the nation's best efforts and tight budgets, the nation's economy would never recover. Other countries would not trust the nation and began protecting its own citizens within the nation's borders. In essence, these countries also refused to renegotiate with the nation or do business with it.

Clantor hoped that this could be reversed. But, after speaking with the panel and the Universal One, he found there was no way in reversing what these groups and what the government blocked. The only way was for the Universal One to destroy the world and start anew, which Clantor and the panel knew would not be the best solution for anyone.

The best that could happen was for these groups and government to compensate Bernice and provide whatever opportunities to make up for what was lost. This task was ordered by the panel and the Universal One to keep Bernice happy, since she held the fate of the world.

Bernice was the direct connection to the One and she held the prophecy of the world.

In the meantime, what Clantor and the panel were more concerned about was Bernice's safety and if she was still alive, since the Universal One did not want any

BERNICE RATHE

harm brought to her and for any harm to stop or else the Universal One would destroy earth. If something happened to Bernice, then the world would definitely be on its way to doom's day sooner rather than later.

The next thing Clantor and his department had to do was find Bernice, which became a task in itself, without letting the government know of its existence. Recalling in the tail he heard, he remembered another female who was involved, who apparently had a wealthy family and was believed to have facilitated much of this harassment via her family's money and government connections.

Remember this female was not the only one stalking and harassing and endangering Bernice's life. Clantor actually could have found all of these groups and investigated them to catch them in the act, which was not out of the question for Clantor. However, the female was the easiest to surveil since the government and the shadow government would not catch onto either Clantor's operations, their identities, their roles in society or even resources (or the specialized technology they only possessed).

Bea Giovanni

Clantor knew in order to find Bernice, he had to find and surveil (and investigate) this female to catch her in the act, which would essentially open several cans of worms. Yet, Clantor knew it was worth the risk.

Clantor and his department were ready to make themselves known to the government, these groups, and the shadow government. The government, these groups and the shadow government operated for many centuries thinking they ruled the world alone, unchallenged and all their secrets were safe.

However, Clantor's plan required governmental collaboration, which Clantor and his department could not trust, being that these groups were embedded in government and facilitating these secret surveillance programs for pay to play purpose. The same system in which Bernice was used as pawn in these groups' pay to play stalking and life endangerment games. Therefore, Clantor and his department crafted a careful and deliberate plan that would not expose their department's secret.

BERNICE RATHE

Chapter 22: Caught in the Act

C lantor and his secret department devised a plan to catch this female in the act. But, he knew it was risky since these surveillance activities and these groups were state secrets, not including the fact that Clantor and his secret department was simply non-existent (and not just a state secret but "the secret").

He was less concerned with the state secrets of the surveillance activities and groups, since it was a matter of time when these state secrets would be exposed. Clantor knew (like Bernice also knew) that these groups were operating under an illusion. Evil had created this illusion of power, privilege and control, and these groups did not understand this.

In fact, if someone challenged these groups and their authority, they would see their authority or power was not what it was. It was merely because everyone in the world tended to go along with this illusion of power, privilege and control and provided them with this privilege and access. But, in reality, no one had any more authority or privilege than anyone else.

Because of this illusion, this is why there was discrimination and other harmful acts against each other in the world. These groups and their symbols and ritualistic acts symbolized evil. These things were their "trademarks" (or what some call the mark of the beast).

Police, military and fire affiliations were all a part of evil's army. Some, like the fire professionals, even represented the brimstone of hell.

These groups and individuals did not know that they sold their souls and were forever lost through their consent or oaths. Not even Jesus could help them now.

Interestingly, Bernice had been the only brave soul to challenge these groups. This was arguably because most people were afraid of them.

But, like Bernice knew, Clantor knew that not everyone would fall for this illusion of power and would eventually challenge them, especially if they knew that Bernice was not crazy and was anointed.

It was a matter of time when someone else challenged these groups. When this person did, these groups would have a rude awakening to the reality of this illusion. But, Clantor could not wait for this to happen.

It goes without saying that Clantor was more concerned with the potential exposure of his ultra-super role and the secret department. Because the plan could not be carried out any other way and time was of the essence, Clantor needed the plan to be done now. Plus, after the plan goes into effect, he knew that people would start asking questions about who, what, where, and how.

Yet, he knew this had to be done and that the secret department could not be traced as its operations were mobile, in transit (via air, road, waterways, etc., similar to Agents of Shield operations).

Plus, the secret department did not function on revenue or funding from any source as the department had unlimited natural and human resource to achieve its goals. Even so, Clantor and his department had to be super careful in devising and carrying out this plan.

Unknown to the world, Clantor and the secret department had special technology that no one else had in the world. Some would say it was alien technology. Whatever the case, its technology could not be replicated, duplicated or stolen, since the technology operated per the genetic composition controlled and designed for each secret official.

Receiving official orders (per a process only those who were authorized knew), the government acted on this plan. Fusion centers, secret agents, reserve forces, secret domestic cells, and others all coordinated their efforts in this plan. All not knowing that the secret department was the one behind this plan.

With secret, soundless helicopters from above (like drones) and secret armored vehicles and both invisible and visible military style outfits in the cut from all angles and for several blocks and tracts of the city area were strategically positions, the plan was in place.

"Hands up, get on the ground!" several agents, armed, shouted at this female.

This female was operating military and government technology, as well as facilitating and working with terrorist groups (i.e., extremist groups and hate groups throughout the U.S.).

Her family had money and had ties to a world of crime, so she connected to it and essentially got caught.

BERNICE RATHE

She was caught in the act of terrorism and in the act of harassing and stalking (and endangering) Bernice.

This plan would also catch numerous other groups involved. Groups and individuals would begin to turn on each other and disclose other information that would lead to other people and entity involvement.

It was like whatever oaths or rules against "snitching" went out the door. These groups saw themselves and their families in danger and not merely in criminal trouble.

Entities and groups that thought they would never get caught were caught. People and entities began to look back and realized that the information given to them or acts they were told to perform relative to Bernice were in fact terrorism and against Bernice as well as against the government.

They also realized that none of these entities or individuals ever thought to tell Bernice or anyone else at any point in time of the suspected terrorist acts against her or against the government, despite Bernice's insistence she was being targeted.

At that point, it did not matter to tell Bernice, as she obviously knew she was in danger and targeted and that there were groups acting against the government. Informing Bernice was unnecessary at that point. She did what she had to do to protect herself and she did so very well.

It was not that they did not understand. They simply did not care about Bernice or what would happen. Remember these were individuals who were either racist, petty, jealous, sexist or phobic.

These individuals and entities either rejected or denied Bernice of employment, an attorney licensure, basic service anyone would receive or invaded her privacy by disclosing private information (though the information was nothing sensitive or of importance).

These groups and individuals would create something out of nothing. They were petty.

If Bernice sneezed, they were trying to get someone to corroborate whether they were offended by Bernice's sneeze. But, with all seriousness, these groups did things against Bernice that were never done to others.

It was a pattern of these groups and individuals. These people were in rage. It did not matter if it was race rage, gender rage, religious rage, envy rage, or just plain rage, Bernice was the reason for the season in their mind.

If someone complained about Bernice, it was apparent that the complainer was a part of this harassment. How so?

Well, Bernice, before all of this harassment, never had a single enemy or person who disliked her. She was well-liked and popular.

She also kept to herself, helped others and stayed out of other people's business. Actually, she still does today.

The point is that they did these things and people were talking about the evil of these groups. Word spread very quickly about these groups, to the point that others in society began to identify these activities and groups as well.

These individuals and entities now wished they would have believed Bernice, as their lives were in danger. They were trying to find Bernice to undo what they did.

But, it was too late. These individuals and entities found themselves caught in a web of a big conspiracy and their livelihood was endangered and businesses suffered.

As the public saw the madness unravel in media, many conspiracy theorists of the world were proven right. Governments around the world also went after these groups.

Additionally, large parts of society began to stop supporting these entities involved, as they did not trust these entities any longer. The world's governments began to cut off funding and support to these groups and entities, thus making it difficult for these groups to operate.

It was one of the largest busts of terrorist groups on American soil in history and the biggest global busts of terrorist groups in the world (to date).

The female, who Clantor and his team caught, tried her best to use her family's connections and wealth to get out of the trouble, including bribing officials. Some officials were actually caught in the act of accepting her bribes (including those who may have accepted political bribes in the past from this debacle concerning Bernice), since the plan also outlined this possibility.

Those caught eventually realized that Bernice was the 'real deal' and was anointed. Like in the biblical scriptures of Judas and those who persecuted Jesus, these groups and individuals killed themselves or were killed. These groups knew their days were numbered and simply did not know how their days would end.

After the plan was successfully carried out, no one knew where this plan originated from or how it was so strategically executed (with precision) since utilities, satellites, traffic cams, lights, etc. were all timely controlled (on and off) and individuals (no matter if they were civilian or a part of the plan) were all in place at the point in time where they should have been, in order to disrupt these terrorist groups.

The government contacted the other countries a part of the G8 and other world bodies and no one could confirm where this help or plan came from. It was not a military plan or a government plan. But, one that seemed to know and predict every possible scenario and an individual's origination and activities.

Later when government agents and officials questioned its own people where these official orders and plan originated, no one knew. This is when the government knew it was not alone.

The government thought it knew all it was to know about the world and universe. But, it did not.

There were many who were relieved that this major secret relative to these rogue groups were revealed as many in the government feared they too would be harmed by these groups at some point. In fact, this secret jeopardized the world's stability.

Yet, there were those who were not happy. Needless to say, some prospered from these rogue groups through black budgets and additional income.

They were those who wanted to know why Bernice was so special and why these things happened. They would eventually know what made Bernice so special.

Clantor and his ultra-super department, via its cryptic technology and coordinated ultra-super agents' efforts, will make them know and understand what all of them done. This would be something they will never forget.

Let's just say that s**t got real (very real).

Because of this unknown help and the capabilities that no government possessed (and the fact that the government was exposed, no matter how they tried to persuade others or misinform others), the government had to go on the defense as well on the offense and now make public the state secret of the surveillance programs and groups that have been in the shadows for many decades. This included the connections to the military, police, fire, Masonic, utilities, etc. [In fact, the government will later see, if it did not do this, more lives and destruction would most likely have occurred.]

Not to many people's surprise, the government's attempt at public disclosure would be initially foiled by these groups (since these groups were afraid for their lives if this secret was made known). But, somehow, again, the unknown help assisted the government in publicly disclosing these state secrets.

People and leaders of the world would later connect Bernice was never crazy and was silenced and threatened as to what she knew. Yet, Bernice, unknown as to what was occurring, did not know her predictions and so-called paranoid delusions came true.

People now began to help Bernice. In collaboration with the government, many people also watched and helped to catch others, who were a part of this madness, around her and Jaime in their daily life.

These groups would scatter, change behaviors or even pretend as if they were helping me (or anything that would create misinformation). But, none of this would work.

Everyone around Bernice and Jaime would see the truth and catch these groups. This is where people then began to find many others around the world were being targeted in the same way.

This would trigger activists around the world to activate to help in identifying and catching these individuals and groups, in preventing harm to other victims who were targeted like Bernice.

This began a ripple effect of a chain of help and events for people all around the world. People began to realize that these groups were operating in secret and harming and terrorizing everyone's lives. This was basic, pure evil.

As one could imagine, Bernice was even more popular and sought after, now for good and noble reasons. There were communities and thousands of people looking for Bernice as they wanted her in their communities.

They realized that wherever she went and whoever accepted her would be blessed and take benefit from Bernice's anointing.

BERNICE RATHE

They also realized that those who rejected, harassed, harmed or otherwise got in Bernice's way did not benefit but things got worse for them, no matter if it was a community, state, group or person that wronged Bernice as they eventually suffered. No amount of money pumped into these entities or areas would help those who rejected, harassed, harmed or got in Bernice's way.

In the meantime, the plan did not stop there. In fact, these groups and many others including Bernice's father and his family and her ex-husband and his family found themselves endangered.

Due to Bernice's anointing and the consequences that followed, these groups would be scorned for this madness. These hate and extremist groups were like kids playing dungeons and dragons or cops and robbers (they played into this illusion).

Sadly, these groups would be also tortured in secret chambers and killed (scenes of interrogation of these groups and intimidation and threats towards these groups as to what they did to Bernice, with eventual scenes of screams from these groups, begging for mercy, forgiveness and to be left free and stating that they will not do it again).

Bernice's family would be protected but not Bernice's father and his family and Bernice's ex-husband and his family.

This would be one of the first signs in the ending of these secret societies, as The Universal One did not appreciate that they treated his daughter, Bernice, in this manner.

BERNICE RATHE

Chapter 23: The Next Terrorist Attacks

So, now that it is clear God did not make a mistake and Bernice was anointed, the next steps were the hardest since time was not on Bernice's side or the world's side. Bernice had to help stop this evil from destroying the U.S. and human civilization as we know it.

Getting a group of racist, sexist, phobic, ungodly and sadistic individuals to believe Bernice of the urgency and the prophecies that could either make or break society, was not the hardest part, since they would have no other choice after seeing what all of them done to cause this destruction. This is especially since they made Bernice a part of this madness and bringing their issues into Bernice's life, via harassing her and endangering her life, i.e.

These groups would be begging for help to prevent their lives and their families from being extinguished.

What was difficult was to help those who tried harming and killing Bernice as well as helping those who stood by and watched, while Bernice was harmed.

Plus, the government's efforts or intentions did not help, since it pushed her away from her desire to protect and serve or work in the government.

Bernice was not anti-government. She actually believes there is a place for government. But after her experience, she was not sure what role the government plays in this.

Bernice could only do what she could, since no one could stop the destruction since they attacked Bernice (an anointed person) and God had one simple rule: touch not my anointed.

This was all because evil tricked them into believing Bernice was not anointed but crazy and Bernice was later labeled and forced to accept this label.

Clantor realized that neither the government nor his secret department will be able to protect everyone (when and not if the global terrorist attacks occurred).

Clantor went to the secret panel to discuss the potential risk assessment. They decided, though tricky, that they would be only able to protect a fraction of the world's population, and that the evil elements of the

BERNICE RATHE

world would be eventually eradicated through the universal karmic shift (or clap back, for lack of a better word).

This clap back was due to the evil elements targeting Bernice, which had unfortunate ripples in the world. Bernice was not supposed to be stopped, blocked, harmed or otherwise rejected in society. Because of this, the universe had to make right what was wrong, or else the world would be destroyed.

Knowing this, Clantor and his team were on the hunt to locate Bernice. Fortunately, Bernice was found and secreted away to Clantor, though the government thought it had secured Bernice's location (and had "eyes on her") after the huge terrorist bust.

Bernice met with Clantor and his panel. In amazement and fearful as to what would happen next, Bernice sat listening to Clantor and his panel.

No scorn or anger was directed or told to Bernice since they knew whatever she experienced was very evil. No one could judge her, since she experienced something not many people in the world ever experience and live to tell.

Also, Bernice was key to stopping their destruction. They knew if any harm was directed to Bernice or at Bernice, this could stop their progress in securing society. Instead, they were focused on stopping the terrorist attacks that was organized by this evil.

As Clantor explained what they knew, Bernice said "What are you talking about?"

Clantor said "cut the crap, we know you are not crazy." Bernice replied, "I am sure you know I am not crazy but this is my reality."

"We know you are not crazy because of this. While these groups think you are seeking the truth. You already know the truth. We gather you are seeking justice." states Clantor as he shows Bernice a holographic presentation of her life journey and all the circumstances.

Clantor also explained (or at least tries to explain) that Bernice is anointed. The panel stops Clantor and explains to Clantor that this would come later and to protect Bernice while trying to stop these groups and evil in these global epidemic of terrorist attacks.

Clantor and the panel explained that they need Bernice's help with stopping the future attacks. They also explained they have technology that would help in capturing these terrorists or lessening the attacks but it works with rare people like Bernice.

We need to know what will happen, as our technology is limited (even with time technology). Hesitant, Bernice was not convinced of whatever Clantor and the panel stated.

However, Bernice was unaware of the major developments of Bernice's tormentors in that many of them were caught and were facing the wrath of God or karma (in so many words), since she was anointed and the universe had to make the situation back whole. Clantor and the panel decided to disclose this information to Bernice, which was critical in getting Bernice's cooperation.

Bernice was somewhat surprised and startled as she was not certain if she was anointed until this confirmed it for her. But, how and why did this happen to her, Bernice thinks to herself.

She explained she does not have some inside knowledge to this kind of information in stopping any attacks and that messages come to her from afar randomly (most of the time) and that she was not good at timing. But, she could still communicate when she focused and had good clarity.

Clantor asked her to try to see what she can find as the world is at stake. Bernice, under pressure, thinks very hard but nothing comes about.

After hours of contemplation and relaxation, Clantor and his team come back to this request. Bernice has more clarity than before.

She stated she is picking up that the terrorist attacks would most likely occur while these groups are using these systems or practices. "What do you mean?" Clantor asks.

"I mean evil will attack these police stations, military bases, fire stations, fusion centers, and other secret locations while these groups are monitoring and surveilling and stalking people." Bernice states.

She further states that "Because no one is expecting a crisis or emergency at the places of responders, since they are prepared, no one would think to secure the locations; even if they secure these locations, evil will creep into the locations or areas via secret and undetectable devices in the water and air systems (like smart bombs and smart technology). It is like the world will be in self-destruct mode. I am getting messages that these groups committed a very big wrong and it has caused the world dysfunction. "

As Bernice looks in silence and listens for messages, she says "Major and minor transportation routes and air spaces will be blocked. This could be blockage due to construction, road hazards and even intentional signal device changes or road closures.

Smaller areas will be overwhelmed and entry and exit to these areas would be blocked. There will be no one to help anyone in need, since these groups would be preoccupied in surveillance operations and reserves and secret operatives will have no access to anything that could help."

"Communities, big, small, minority or not, will participate in the destruction. They will help in destroying the public utilities and in harming and killing first responders. These first responders and other groups will try and hide their affiliation but because these groups are exposed, the communities under surveillance and those oppressed will seek retribution.

Evil will not care and evil's promises to these groups would be broken. Evil used these groups and their affiliations and secret access and clearances as a means to an end." exclaimed Bernice.

"The communities will also not care since these communities already depend on each other for help. These communities know they were under surveillance by these public employees, entities such as fire, police and military for years but no one could articulate it and some were scared to say anything out of fear of losing everything," stated Bernice.

"But, they now realized they already lost everything since these surveillance groups damaged their lives and used their authority wrongfully, including with having supremacist groups participating in this stuff and harming not just these communities but everyone. Basically, people will be pissed and angry that the government allowed it and kept it silent, while thousands of lives were lost, killed or destroyed in the process," Bernice stated.

She also stated, "These secret alliances and societies will be killed individually and some collectively during their secret meetings or gatherings where these groups will be killed in explosions. These various groups and their guns and their god will not help them."

BERNICE RATHE

"Take it back. Say it will not happen," angrily stated Clantor. He was fearful of what Bernice said. He led a super-secret department and did not want anything to happen on his watch.

He will later learn that no matter if Bernice said it or not, the events would happen. As it would be explained to Clantor by the panel, Bernice cannot control what messages the universe sends to her.

Bernice continues to tap into the universe's messages and states to Clantor, "You will not be able to control them, no matter the weaponry, since these acts will be random, spontaneous and no one will be easily identified and smart technology and ancient technology will be used," further states Bernice.

"This is why the groups and individuals (like military, Masonic, cable, phone, HVAC, fire equipment service companies and other service contractors and those who have "public" and "secret" access and top secret clearance to systems), and those who are deemed automatically trustworthy without question, were recruited. They would have access to these systems and other major utility services and most likely already installed snooping and other surveillance and secret devices into certain systems.

Many people got into these positions very easily through their veterans' job preference and benefits given to veterans. Plus, many of these groups had either a secret oath or immunity in their positions. So wherever acts committed would be protected, no matter the situation.

But, what these groups thought they were doing was not actually the real purpose, and these groups and individuals were used. In an ironic twist, the same technology and access to these systems will be used against these same groups and individuals.

You will not be able to stop it. Maybe lessen the damage? But, you cannot stop it," she states.

Bernice also said "Once these groups are uncovered, these groups will be starved in funding and these programs will be cut. The world will not want these programs or groups anymore. So, technology will replace these groups and their purpose.

Despite arguments and manufactured acts created by these groups to justify why they are needed and their subsequent technology hacking into the new technology, systems and processes, these groups will be unsuccessful in their attempts.

It will be the end but these groups will continue this madness yet will get no way. Actually, the entire DoD will be abolished and the programs will be dispersed among existing programming.

The DoD will never had this kind of power ever again. I believe your secret department has technology that will make sure that this imbalance does not happen again."

Bernice also picked up in her messages that there was some ways to lessen the damage. Some ways would be to institute state of the art technology to physically monitor and record all workers and their activities on and off the job and to establish protocols and chain of command approval on accessing records, databases and when responding and investigating cases.

Bernice also conveyed that naturally, there may be backlash over privacy concerns. But, after these activities are revealed to the public and world, few would object as they do not wish for this to occur again.

She also stated that another way was to start anew in government, which would essentially make it more difficult for the groups to operate. This would include scrapping the security clearance systems and access and establish a new one that uses a special technology that identifies these potential groups and individuals and rid governments of immunity.

Essentially, the public worker's role is a contract with the public anyway. This meant that public workers like police, fire, military, officials, judges, etc. would all be required to purchase liability insurance.

Like doctors and other professionals with liability insurance, when questionable or illegal acts occurred, immunity was not an option, an investigation will occur, and open disclosure will be a mandate. Plus, if too many violations occur, liability insurance is not obtainable, which also means the worker is not employable if they cannot secure liability insurance. This would incentivize workers to disclose what they know and not participate in blue walls or secrecy.

Clantor anxiously asks Bernice, "How do we catch these groups?" Bernice mimics Clantor in a comedic voice, "How do we catch these groups?" and laughs. He does not find it funny, but his staff does find it funny as they chuckled quietly in the back of the room.

Bernice did not understand that Clantor and the panel were limited and uses the specialized technology granted to them that no other person or government in the world has. They were not anointed like Bernice. This was explained to Bernice,

So, Bernice settles herself and says, "So you want to know how to catch them. Well, everything you need to know is simple and right in front of you. You do not need me to tell you."

Clantor and his staff are still confused. So, Bernice assists them and begins to tell them how to catch these groups. "Here's how you can catch them …" (Bernice details how these groups can be caught and what to expect).

Clantor and his secret department knew some methods, explained by Bernice to lessen the damage, would be far-reaching for the general population, while other methods were extremely simple and actually was a major flaw in these groups' operations. But, Clantor thought eventually it may work and this would be needed for the future.

In the meantime, Clantor and his secret department rush to coordinate efforts to devise a plan that would help lessen the impact on the world. Bernice is temporarily left to her own device, while Clantor and his secret department depart into another room.

Clantor seeks counsel from the panel, who firmly state that there is no other way out of this destruction.

The panel stated, "What has happened has caused a galactic shift in the universe since the universal rule was broken. Breaking this rule causes everything to misalign and the only other way to realign the universe is to let it run its course."

The panel did suggest that the Universal One can, however, offer support. Clantor makes a formal request for the Universal One's assistance.

Hesitantly, the panel, who are the only ones to authority to summon the Universal One, asks the Universal One for additional support.

Upon hearing Clantor's request and plan, the Universal One sends his best support, Michelangelo and his army of angels. With this help, Clantor and his secret department operate in the background, assisting earth and the various governments from self-destruction, though these governments still did not know where the help originated.

During these times, a universal cryptic message is sent to world's powers: "You may have thought you have saved your world. However, evil still lurks. If you do continue to use this system or any system, evil will masquerade and penetrate it and it will destroy your existence. It is your benefit that you help in ridding your world of this evil. If not, the universe will be force to swallow Earth and start anew. Godspeed."

Chapter 24: The Answers

After the evil and damaged these groups and government caused, Clantor did not care for them anymore. Further, he did not trust them, especially with secrets that he held. This is when he decided that the government would no longer have access to this technology or information.

After saving many lives and stopping as much damage and catastrophe as possible, Bernice is invited by Clantor and the panel into a special training school, where only Bernice is trained and no one else. This was the only way to do so.

He feared that if they knew her powers, they would want her for their own evil purposes. Clantor made sure that these individuals and groups had no access to Bernice, from that point on.

It goes without saying that Clantor also saw that Bernice was not merely anointed but a perfect fit for the secret department's special training school, which virtually no one had attended in several centuries.

BERNICE RATHE

Bernice was adaptive and could dress and manipulate her body and image to resemble either male or female. In fact, as Clantor researched, there were times where Bernice was mistaken as a male and other times she was mistaken as a child.

There was no doubt that Bernice was intelligent. She was able to learn multiple areas of knowledge as well as understand the complexities of what happened in her situation, which no one else could understand. It was rather interesting, since Bernice understood the universe at its core and that certain lessons are repeated (similar to what was conveyed in the religious texts), which, again, no one knew or failed to understand.

Finally, Bernice was fit in every way. She built her body and mind to be strong. The years that her tormentors took to harass Bernice, she took that time to fine-tune her physical fitness and mind. Knowing these things, Clantor and his secret department would be stupid not to recruit Bernice into this program.

It was a matter of convincing Bernice, since she did not want to do so, especially after all she experienced.

But, Bernice has no choice in the matter, as she would later find.

The reason why she had no choice but to enter into this ultra, secret program, similar to almost an X-Men training school, is that her lineage and connection to the source (or the Universal One) mandates so, per the universal rule and balance of the galaxy.

In essence, Bernice has an obligation to the galaxy to use her gifts for the galaxy.

Clantor and his secret department visits Bernice at her home to secret location to prepare her for her special training school experience.

At that time, Bernice would be elevated into the air and a machine scans her entire body, healing her, with a scene showing simultaneous miraculous healing of Bernice's daughter, Bernice's wife and Bernice's family from any evil that tried harming them. Bernice is then elevated down to the ground, confused where she eventually shakes this confusion off.

The panel and Clantor leave the room (with the panel summoning the Universal One). Bernice is left to her own devices in a room. As she waits for the next steps for the training school, the Universal One enters in a strange airy figure like being.

BERNICE RATHE

Bernice is not frightened but is more amazed and drawn to it.

The Universal One says "Thank you, my child, for not being afraid of me. You and I are both the same, which is why you are not afraid. I am your mother, I am your father, I am what you have been feeling all of your life. When we believed your family was not your family or that you somehow different from everyone around you in the world, this is why. You were never of this world but my child, of me."

At first, Bernice tests out whether this figure is real or a test by Clantor and the panel. But, she realizes it was a real encounter as the figure transformed into a human figure, resembling Bernice.

She asks the Universal One a series of deliberate questions, "How did I come here, why was my mother my mother and my father my father? Why do bad things happen to good people? Why? Why do some people act evil and others act good? Why me?"

The Universal One replies (as both of them walk and converse), "Yes, you have many questions. I have the answers. But, right now, let's focus on one thing at a time." An eerie sound and darkness came about with Bernice Giovana Rathe, the

Universal One and shadowy, clandestine
figures walking away with an unnerving
chuckle from everyone, including Bernice.

Giovana. God.

The beginning of the end of evil begins ...

[A scene opens with images of Bernice
being trained at a super, ultra-secret facility
that enhanced and improved your
supernatural abilities.

Another scene shows Bernice covertly
saving innocent people from the evil while
living a lavish life with her wife, daughter
and loved ones.

Scenes showing that no matter where
Bernice went, she was constantly
surrounded by an ultra-secret, unknown
clandestine group (connected to Clantor's
secret department) and a special protection
unit of different group of men and women,
masking as everyday common individuals.

This was like no other protection unit in
the world and far more advanced than the
secret service protection or witness
protection units anyone has ever seen.

A final scene shows Bernice becoming
second in command under new

BERNICE RATHE

constitutional and presidential rules and a new government (as Vice President of the U.S.A., as there were no other trusted individuals to serve as VP in case evil struck again, which it will).

Bernice's adversaries would now wished they never hated on her, as she, Clantor and his secret department held the key to the world's survival....]